Charles Taber Congdon

Tribune Essays

Leading articles contributed to the New York tribune from 1857 to 1863

Charles Taber Congdon

Tribune Essays
Leading articles contributed to the New York tribune from 1857 to 1863

ISBN/EAN: 9783337418434

Printed in Europe, USA, Canada, Australia, Japan

Cover: Foto ©Andreas Hilbeck / pixelio.de

More available books at **www.hansebooks.com**

TRIBUNE ESSAYS

LEADING ARTICLES

CONTRIBUTED TO

THE NEW YORK TRIBUNE

FROM 1857 TO 1863

By CHARLES T. CONGDON

WITH AN INTRODUCTION

By HORACE GREELEY

" The shop of war hath not more anvils and hammers working to fashion out
the plates and instruments of armed justice in defence of beleaguered truth,
than there be pens and heads there, sitting by their studious lamps musing,
searching, revolving new notions and ideas wherewith to present, as with
homage and fealty, the approaching reformation."—JOHN MILTON's *Speech for
the Liberty of Unlicensed Printing.*

NEW YORK
J. S. REDFIELD, PUBLISHER
140 FULTON STREET
1869.

E. O. JENKINS,
STEREOTYPER AND PRINTER
20 N. WILLIAM ST., N. Y.

CONTENTS.

	PAGE
Prefatory Notice.	xi
Introduction	xix
Perils and Besetting Snares.	1
Inaugural Glories.	6
Mr. Benjamin Screws.	8
Mr. Mason's Manners.	13
The Great Rogersville Flogging.	16
Mr. Mitchell's Desires.	20
Mr. Mason's Manners Once More	24
Presidential Politeness.	29
William the Conqueror.	33
Benjamin's Second Notice	38
The Reveries of Reverdy	42
The Foresight of Mr. Fielder.	46
Mr. Mitchel's Commercial Views	50
Father Ludovico's Fancy	54
Mr. Choate on Dr. Adams's Sermons.	58
University Wanted.	61
Mr. Pollard's "Mammy"	63
A Church Going into Business	68
A New Laughing-Stock.	73
A Cumberland Presbyterian Newspaper.	79
Nil Nisi Bonum.	84
Two Tombstones.	88
The Perils of Pedagogy.	92
Josiah's Jaunt.	97
A Biographical Battle.	102
Mr. Bancroft on the Declaration of Independence.	106

CONTENTS.

Modern Chivalry — A Manifesto............................ 110
Mr. Fillmore takes a View................................ 116
A Banner with a Strange Device...................... 121
A Southern Diarist....................................... 124
Dr. Tyler's Diagnosis.................................... 128
The Montgomery Muddle — A Specimen Day.............. 131
Ready made Unity and the Society for its Promotion....... 136
A Private Battery................................ 141
Southern Notions of the North........................... 144
Alexander the Bouncer............................. 148
Roundheads and Cavaliers............................ .. 151
Wise Convalescent 155
Slaveholder's Honor..................................... 158
No Question before the House........................... 163
Bella Mollita — Soft War..................... 168
The Humanities South... 172
The Charge of Precipitancy.............................. 177
The Assassination 181
Striking an Average..................................... 183
The Coming Despotism........................ 187
Abolition and Secession.................................. 192
A Bacchanal of Beaufort................................. 197
Concerning Shirts....................................... 201
Fair but Fierce......... 204
Bobbing Around 208
Niobe and Latona....................................... 213
Secession Squabbles........................ 219
" Biblius "... 224
Cold Comfort.. 226
Extemporizing Production.................... 230
Very Particular... 234
Prudent Fugacity..................... 238
Extemporizing Parties........... 243
Platform Novelties...................................... 247
Prophecies and Probabilities............................. 251
" Drawing it Mild " in Memphis.......................... 256
Loyalty and Light........................ 260
Hedging 265

The Trial of Toombs.................................... 269
The Council of Thirty-Five............................ 273
Davis a Despot... 279
All Means to Crush !................................... 284
Northern Independence................................. 288
The Constitution — Not Conquest 292
Train's Troubles...................................... 297
The Slaveholding Utopia............................... 300
Twelve Little Dirty Questions......................... 304
Democracy in London................................... 308
Laughter in New Hampshire............................. 312
Slaveholding Virtues.................................. 316
Roland for an Oliver 321
Historical Scarecrows................................. 325
The Other Way... 329
Saulsbury's Sentiments................................ 334
Jefferson the Gentleman............................... 338
The Contagion of Secession............................ 341
Davis to Mankind...................................... 346
Union for the Union................................... 351
The Necessity of Servility............................ 355
What shall we do with Them ?.......................... 360
Pocket Morality 366
Waiting for a Partner................................. 370
At Home and Abroad.................................... 374
Mr. Davis Proposes to Fast 377
Mr. B. Wood's Utopia.................................. 379
Mr. Buxton Scared..................................... 384
Charleston Cozy 387
The Twin Abominations. 391
Victory and Victuals.................................. 395
Sus. Per Coll... 399

PREFATORY NOTICE.

In making this compilation, I have trusted that the memory of the reader would be sufficient for the explanation of most allusions; and commentary would not only have cumbered these pages, but would hardly have been fair. Nor have I ventured upon any corrections or alterations of importance. These articles are precisely what they profess to be; they were, from day to day, hastily written to serve an immediate purpose; and they are, therefore, entitled, I hope, to a lenient and charitable judgment.

A book like this would be of little value if it did not, in some respects, illustrate one of the most extraordinary changes in the opinions of a great people which history records. The election of Mr. Buchanan seemed definitely to indicate not merely the perpetuity of Human Slavery in this Republic, but the acquiescence of the people of the Free States, or of a majority of them, in the extension of that unhappy institution. Its opponents, if not silenced, were decidedly defeated, and the Democratic Party, after a hundred previous audacities, continued to hold the Government with something of a feeling of invincibility. There remained, it is true, throughout the North and West, an Anti-Slavery sentiment which no misfortunes could overcome; but a considerable measure of its activity was to be found among those who abstained from political methods; while two classes of men, the one religious, and the other political, still vehemently insisted that agitation of the Slavery Question was in itself an immorality deserving rebuke, and requiring vigorous suppression. Of these remarkable apostles of an untimely conservatism, I may be permitted briefly to speak.

One who is outside the pale of ecclesiastical organizations, and who is not an assistant in the manœuvering of their machinery, finds it difficult to comprehend how any confessor, in the possession of his natural mental faculties, should ever have thought it possible to reconcile Slavery with the precepts of Christianity; yet many unquestionably were left to believe that the Institution was Divine in its origin, and that it was still authorized by the Divine sanction. The hearts of men we may not be permitted to judge, but surely there is no law which forbids us to make a conscientious estimate of their heads;

and he who, upon the strength of two or three little texts—upon the fact of the existence of Slavery among the Jews and in the Roman Empire—upon that small portion of history which records the curse upon Canaan, could assert, and in pulpit, newspaper, review, and volume, persist in the assertion that the Slavery of Four Millions of Men, in the Republic of the United States, in the year of Christianity One Thousand Eight Hundred and Fifty, — that such Slavery, utterly modern in its theory and practice, was a thing to be not merely justified, but applauded and defended in the pulpit—he, I say, who could make this large demand upon the faith of his neighbors, must have had one of those narrow and monkish natures which may be capable of a certain degree of usefulness in drilling battalions of neophytes, but which are equally incapable of lofty views or elevated aims. If such an one happened to mix a little ethnology with his theology, he gave to the world an irresistible amalgam, which in his opinion precluded argument and paralyzed retort. I suspect if all the literature of this kind, printed in defence of Slavery, could be gathered together, that against all natural rules, a peculiar and disagreeable smell would be noticed in the atmosphere, and that it would even be perceptible in Heaven.

I do not know that the Pro-Slavery Politician was a whit less absurd; but he had the advantage of confining his argumentation to matters of earth and sense, and of uttering low things from a lower standpoint. He did not "pass the flaming bounds of time and space;" but restricting himself to the somewhat different atmosphere of Washington, he was content to limit human progress by existing enactments, and to plead precedent against the piteous appeals of those who sued for redress *in forma pauperis.* He had more than the respect of the proverb for "whatever *is.*" He not only believed it to be "right," but he proclaimed it, at the top of his voice, to be immutable. Whatever the Slaveholder asked for, he was ready to accord; and naturally the Slaveholder soon learned that he could not ask for too much.

The position of the Pro-Slavery Politician was, although the Institution might be hard, cruel, a breaker of hearts, a bender of bodies, and a destroyer of souls, that all this wretchedness must be carried to a sort of political profit and loss; and although Slavery had its evils, yet that it was better to endure them than to fly to others—the endurance being unfortunately the pious and patriotic perquisite of the Slave! The matter finally settled itself down into one hard, unflinching formula—The Union must be preserved.

This was the end of controversy. This was the limit of discussion. This was the Alpha and Omega of our political gospel. This was the touchstone of legislation.

Of course, political science being thus reduced to its simplest elements, the Slaveholder having any measure at heart, needed only to cry out that, if denied, he intended to secede, to carry his point with marvelous and triumphant celerity. Mr. Buchanan was a Northern man, but although he is dead, the sad and mortifying truth must be spoken: he had so disciplined himself in this school of what may be called "unconditional surrender," that he no more dreamed of resistance than he dreamed of resigning. He was no better and no worse perhaps than his friends; but he had the misfortune to be their representative. To the last moment of his administration, Mr. Buchanan was faithful to the traditions of his party; and while the bugle call of sedition was sounding through half the Republic—while its flag was defended by a handful of beleaguered and starving men—while the country stood aghast at the unchecked rapidity with which Treason was stalking over the land, this last, it may be hoped, of all such Democratic Presidents, surrendered a Government which he had done nothing to save into the

hands of a Republican successor.   The times of trial
and endurance, of the waste and the glory of war, of
painful vicissitude and final victory followed.   As the
result of that extraordinary struggle, we have now, for
the first time in our history, a Government which,
being consistent with its avowed principles, may truly
be designated as "Democratic."   As I write these
pages, I cannot sufficiently express the gratification
which I feel at the enormous mass of nonsense which
events have eliminated from our future political discussions.   When I began to write for *The Tribune*,
there was hardly a political virtue, hardly a fundamental social truth, hardly a time-honored maxim of
humanity, hardly an elementary principle of justice,
which we did not have to fight for as if they had been
discoveries.   There was the ethnologist proving four
millions of men to be monkeys.   There was the
"statesman" demonstrating that the Constitution
was framed expressly to sustain Slavery.   There was
the clergyman showing Human Bondage to be as
necessary as Original Sin.   There was the simpering
novelist depicting the pastoral pleasures of the plantation, and the patriarchal felicities of the Blacks.
There was the lawyer pleading that, in certain
cases, the Habeas Corpus is good for nothing.   And
under all there were crowds of prejudiced and un-

reasoning men of every social grade, from the highest
to the lowest, who denounced every objector to this
condition of affairs as a destructive and a radical,
and who thought a flourishing trade with the South
worth all the morality ever propounded, from Plu-
tarch to Dr. Paley.

It would, doubtless, have been easier—I know it
would often have been thought in better taste—to
have taken a low and despairing view of public
affairs, and sadly to have predicted the second coming of chaos. But, partly perhaps from a constitutional habit, I was led to consider serious subjects
cheerfully; although I hardly ever made a jest upon
the subject of Slavery without a feeling of self-rebuke.
But it must be remembered that the gentlemen upon
the other side were already in the field as mourners,
and had pretty much monopolized the business of
groaning. Nestor was with them, and so was Herac-
litus; and if the country was to be saved by crying,
they were clearly designed to be the saviours. They
were angry often enough at finding serious subjects
lightly treated, and they did not relish a style which
sometimes made havoc of their dignity; but, upon
the other hand, it may be said that there were those
who did not at all relish their mournful methods, and
who could not see that they were taking any very

promising way to avert the calamities which they predicted. But I am sure that there was not a morsel of ill-nature in the criticisms to which they were subjected.

With these considerations, this little volume is presented to the reader, with a hope also, which may be justly expressed, that he will remember the original and temporary purpose of its contents.

INTRODUCTION.

WHENEVER the history of Journalism shall be truly written, one of its most interesting chapters will be that which traces the infancy and growth of that potent creation of our century, the LEADER—that is, of the most important and conspicuous Editorial or Editorials, printed in the largest type, and occupying the most prominent position. I say occupying, though the axiom that "Where Macdonald sits is the head of the table," applies here as well as elsewhere. Since the Electric Telegraph obtained its full development, the more prominent and interesting dispatches, or the Editorial summary thereof, will probably attract the first glance of a majority of readers; but the Leader soon commands and fixes the attention of all.

The Editor is he whose fiat decides what shall and what shall not appear, and in what garb, with what sanction, complete or qualified, that which does appear shall be presented: he, in many cases, writes but sparingly—in some, it is said, not at all. Probably, no person likely to be intrusted with the conduct of an influential journal ever supposed himself qualified, even if he had time, to discuss *all* the topics which require elucidation in its columns; hence, the engagement of able, intelligent writers to treat of the various themes which, from time to time, invite discussion, aside from those who, in the various departments—Literary, Commercial, Legal, Dramatic, Musical, etc., etc.—hold a more responsible and semi-independent position. The writer of a leading article is often a statesman of wide experience, or a scholar of ripe culture, who volunteers, or, on solicitation, consents, to elucidate a subject of which he is master; sometimes accepting, at others declining, compensation therefor. More commonly, however, leading Editorials are written by those who have given their youth to study and their earlier prime to service in the humbler walks of the profession, in which they have developed and perfected the capacities which they now exemplify. They are scarcely a tithe of the number who aspired to the position they have achieved—the vast majority having failed in the attempt. Liberally compensated and accorded a just

and wide consideration, they are raised above servility or unworthy complaisance by the consciousness
that their widely-recognized talents ensure them employment elsewhere, if that now accorded them
should ever be withdrawn. The Republic of Letters
has few citizens more eligibly placed or more honorably regarded than they.

Some members of this class are men of all work—
ready, at the word of command, to review the most
ponderous tome that embodies the latest and least
intelligible speculations in German theology or
Scotch metaphysics—to report a masquerade-ball, or
to chronicle the latest Paris fashions; but the better,
if not more numerous, class do that work only (or
mainly) for which they are specially qualified, and
to which they are attracted by their studies, or their
tastes—often by both.

In the protracted, arduous struggle which resulted
in the overthrow and extinction of American Slavery,
many were honorably conspicuous: some by eloquence; more by diligence; others by fearless, absorbing, single-eyed devotion to the great end; but
he who most skillfully, effectively, persistently wielded
the trenchant blade of Satire was the writer of the following essays. Lowell's "Hosea Biglow" and "Bird-

ofredum Sawin," were admirable in their way, and did good service to the anti-Slavery cause; but the essays herewith presented, appearing at intervals throughout the later acts of the great drama, and holding up to scorn and ridicule the current phases of pro-Slavery unreason and absurdity, being widely circulated and eagerly read, exerted a vast, resistless influence on the side of Freedom and Humanity. There are reprobates so hardened in iniquity as to defy exposure, scout reproof, and meet malediction with contempt; but there was never yet a wrong-doer so callous as to feel indifferent to being laughed at. No tyranny, no outrage, was ever yet panoplied in mail so strong or so close, that the shafts of Satire would not pierce it, and leave their barbs fixed in the quivering flesh beneath.

The papers which follow are a part of the political and social history of the last twelve eventful years which ought to be preserved in a convenient, accessible form—a part which will be found livelier reading than most History, and hardly less instructive and profitable. It has been widely asserted that the Editorials of *The Tribune* were among the chief incitements to the late Civil War. It is well, therefore, that many of the most pungent and exasperating of those Editorials should be collected and published in this volume, so that our children may judge of the provocation they afforded to Secession, and the consequent desperate, bloody struggle for the lasting dismemberment of our Union.

Wit has oftener sped its arrows in the service of Despotism and Oppression than in that of Liberty and Humanity. The Negro has long been its favorite target; his repulsive color, his uncouth features, his shambling gait, his idiotic merriment, and his grotesque politeness, have all been portrayed and exaggerated in defense of his enslavement, or in ridicule of any attempt to excite sympathy for his sufferings and invoke effort for his deliverance. "How can you feel, or even affect, interest in such a caricature of the human form?" was the burden of pro-Slavery logic throughout the last generation.

Our author met the traducers of the Black race on their own ground, and vanquished them with their own chosen weapon. Never compromising a principle nor truckling to a prejudice, he turned the laugh on the jesters and set the public to mocking the mockers. While others demonstrated the injustice of man-selling, he portrayed its intense meanness, its unspeakable baseness, its monstrous unreason, in colors that even the blind must perceive. He drew two figures which no one could help abhorring, and, when

all had evinced their irrepressible loathing, he showed the less repulsive to be the Slaveholder, and the
other his Northern ally, apologist and champion.

Such was the work to which he devoted his time
and talents; to what purpose the following pages will
attest.

H. G.

New York, Feb. 1, 1869.

TRIBUNE ESSAYS.

PERILS AND BESETTING SNARES.

An institution morally bad seldom deludes the world
into the belief that it is practically a good one.
Wrong and injustice are not only insufferable, theoretically, but they have a hard way of rendering
nations, societies and individuals exceedingly uncomfortable. By the indulgence of petty vices, we may
sometimes lapse into a dreamy slumber, and thence
into decided decomposition; but a continuous and
absorbing mistake, like that of Slavery, gives us no
peace, and makes our mornings and our evenings
full of disquietude and contention.

The Slaveholder, so far from securing for himself
and his family that soft and lassitudinous enjoyment,
the desire for which is his moving principle, is surrounded by unseen perils, and is the constant victim
of nameless apprehensions. His retainers cannot
meet for prayer or for pleasure, without alarming
him; a poor half-fed, half-clothed, half-sheltered and
hard-worked toiler cannot look sulky but his master

1   (1)

sees in that black face a general insurrection; a Northern newspaper arriving at the post-office is savagely squinted at as if it were an infernal machine; and the very chit-chat of the market and the tavern is scrupulously sifted in search of abolition sentiments. The great house is tremulous with alarms, and stands always in dread of the humbler quarter-houses. There is a revolution on foot in the garret. There is a gunpowder plot in the cellar. Betty is putting arsenic into the soup in the kitchen, and Sam is secreting a rusty musket in the stable. All this reconciles us to blundering Irish servants, to half-cooked breakfasts, and to half-blackened boots, to the innumerable inconveniences attending free service on which our Southern friends are perpetually descanting. There is a pleasure in feeling comparatively safe. There is rapture in the conviction that your throat is decently assured from the knife of the assassin.

How easily the slaveholder is frightened, and how thoroughly, helplessly and hopelessly he is frightened, is proved by the astonishing willingness which he exhibits to hang his two-legged chattels. His public spirit in this regard is remarkable; and the recent alarms of insurrection have furnished us with many notable instances of such magnanimity. To kill a dog that has worried sheep is not uncommon; but then no dog is worth one thousand hard federal dollars, nor has Governor Wise made any enraptured prophecy of a rise in the canine market. The truth is that all the fuss and flurry, the public palpitation and panic, the excitement and executions which we have witnessed, prove with a rigidity of logic of which statistics would be incapable, the pitiable weakness of the Slave System. Such events as those which we have been obliged to record, render all apologies, excuses, extenuations and sophistries of no avail. They knock our twaddling friend, Mr. Richard Yeadon, as flat as his own style; they make ludicrous the elegant simplicities of Mr. Simms, and they demolish the card-castle theories of Mr. Calhoun, reared with so much patience, and at such an expense of ↑ ne, of thought, and of ingenuity. And most espf ally do they dissipate the Abrahamic fancies of good President Lord, who, with a great deal of theology and an infinitesimal infusion of Christianity, has proved black to be white, to the satisfaction of himself, of six other doctors of divinity, and of *The Journal of Commerce.* In the multitude of his bondmen the patriarch found strength, but the bigger the gangs of the plantation, the greater the weakness of the whole establishment. In South Carolina, this species of property has reached a point beyond which accumulation seems to be impossible; yet the State is in the last stages of constructive pauperism, and would not have a doit to cross itself withal, did it not keep watch and ward with blade and blunderbuss. Abraham walking through his fields with a revolver in one hand, a cowhide in the other, and a bowie-knife between his reverend teeth — who can imagine such a preposterous figure?

We have said that these insurrections as they are called, or rather the fears of them, demonstrate the weakness of the whole system of Slavery—a weakness that ramifies in every direction, and is felt in finance and in faith ; in personal character and in the public character; in manners, habits, and all the phenomena of social life.   This is true of it in a time of peace, when there is no pressure from without, and no extraordinary demand upon the resources of the State. Comparatively, at such a time, an indulgence in cowardly stupidities may be harmless.   But a war is by no means impossible.   We have vapored and swaggered and played Pistol; we have indulged in the pleasing luxury of Ostend manifestoes; and, in theory at least, we have demolished most of the reigning dynasties of Europe, just as effectually as we have demolished Greytown.

But suppose the dogs of war should become too strong for the Marcy of the future, or should grow restive in their leashes, with no Palmerston to restrain them.   In the event of war, have our readers considered how frightful would be the results of an invasion of the Southern country?   That there would be invasion nobody can doubt; nor can any one suppose that a sagacious enemy would strike at us in the strongest places.   Then, indeed, the noblest natural resources of the country would only prove its bitterest curse.   It would be better to be without great gulfs, if they only invited the menacing fleets of the enemy; without mighty rivers, if they merely served for the transportation of hostile flotillas ; and, with the threatened country in no better situation socially for defence than the South would be, the invitation would be inevitable, and the chances eagerly improved.

With a sparse white population extending over an immense territory, a repulsion of military and naval forces would be, under any circumstances, difficult; but how would those difficulties be increased and complicated by the presence of masses of irritated and despairing men, hopeless of happiness save from the ruin of a country which had proved to them only a stony-hearted stepmother! The imagination shrinks from the contemplation of scenes in which the customary horrors of war are aggravated by those of a servile insurrection — conflagration, massacre, and wide-spread ruin! It is not enough to say that in such a contest we should be victorious, for victory would be obtained at a cost frightful to estimate — at the expense of a depleted treasury and a diminished population. Those who sneeringly ask us what the North has to do with Slavery, had better devote a few moments of leisure to a contemplation of those contingencies; and should they have any difficulty in coming to a conclusion, we have only to refer them to the condition of South Carolina during the War of the Revolution.

January 8, 1857.

INAUGURAL GLORIES.

THE gentlemen who do the didactic and the reflective for the picture-newspapers, have enlarged in sentences, more or less leaden, upon the moral grandeur of the inauguration spectacle; and have with patriotic pride speculated upon the wonder, not to say envy, with which the bedizened Embassadors must have gazed upon the fire-companies and the Pennsylvania militia. Admitting that we had a fine melodrama on the fourth instant, we have now come naturally to the farce. We certainly do not think that the Diplomatic Corps ever witnessed at home anything like this scramble for place, this contest for collectorships and clerkships, this pother about post-offices: in short, if we may use a coarse word, this grand grab for provender. The Malakoff was not more closely invested than the White House is now; and we verily believe that no Russian soldier in that stronghold was ever in half so much danger of his life as Mr. Buchanan is at the present time. We can easily imagine, without personal observation, (for we have only asked for the appointment of our friend Cass,) how the poor President is baited and bullied and beset; how the hungry beggars do invade the privacy of bed-chamber, of library and of parlor; how the perpetual knocking at the portals sounds in his ears like the unmentionable gentleman's tattoo—a *reveillé* of continually-recurring wretchedness. We all know what a chronic bother are the little boys and girls who come into our areas for broken victuals; but what are they to swarms of adult mendicants, swarming from all quarters and bawling for more cold pieces of patronage than any President ever had or ever will have to bestow ? We never before fully appreciated the nursery line which bade our childhood " Pity the sorrows of a poor old man."

We do not know that the quadrennial mania is any higher now than upon previous outbursts ; but as the republic expands, there are more offices to bestow, and, of course, a great many more people to fill them. We only refer to the matter now, to ask these tormenters of the President if it be really their desire to kill him ?—if they are bent upon moral murder ?—upon an assassination by worrying ? Is Mr. Buchanan to be drawn like a badger ?—to be hunted like a fox ? to be pestered, perplexed, harassed into his sepulchre ? Are they in league with Mr. Breckinridge to take off the President ? If not, let them raise the siege and withdraw their eager forces ? His Excellency is an old man. He may bear his years bravely, but we should remember the proverbial ounce which breaks the camel's spine at last. We hear from Washington that the President is showing marks of senility, and that his friends are really uneasy about his health. If this be so, it should require no Hippocrates to inform them that the best treatment of the illustrious patient will be found in their immediate departure for the rural districts. They can leave behind them their petitions—the certificates of their virtues, the affidavits of their capacities, the evidence of the gross incompetency of their rivals ; and Mr. Buchanan with such aid can make up his mind without a personal in-spection of their lean and hungry faces. The double distilled extract of rats which they gave to the Presi-dent at the National Hotel, was sanative in compari-son with this procession of spectres around his official chair!

The nation has twice felt the death of a president to be an extraordinary misfortune. In both instances it lost a good executive officer, and in both found the Constitutional compensation for the loss to be but a dubious solace. The two Vices have turned out badly, and we do not want a Third Accidency.

March 17, 1857.

MR. BENJAMIN SCREWS.

A FRIEND has sent us the business card of a gentle-man in New Orleans. It is not the custom of this newspaper to advertise gratuitously, but in this case we so far depart from our rule as to give this pleas-ing announcement without expense to Mr. Benjamin Screws. It is as follows:

Now we do not intend to speak harshly of the enterprising Screws, as some of our more ardent brethren might do. We know it to be the custom of negro-owners to snub and to cut the negro-broker; but for our own part, if human beings must be purchased, and if this two-legged locomotive merchandize be absolutely necessary in social economy, and if without it this blessed Union cannot possibly be preserved, we do not see but that somebody must deal in it, and why should not that somebody be Mr. Benjamin Screws as well as another?

Our Southern friends are really too hard upon the Slatters and the Screws. As well might we at the North turn up our noses at our butchers and sneer at our bakers. As well might a Wall street gentleman, in a tight place, flout the accommodating philanthropist who lets him have money to pay his note withal. You are in New Orleans and you want to buy a carpenter. Screws has first-rate ones constantly on hand. Your wife tells you that Venus, the cook, is really getting too old, and you take this superannuated piece of goods to Screws and exchange her for a more youthful article, paying such boot as Screws and equity may demand. Who will say that Screws is not a public benefactor?—a most useful and worthy member of society? We shall defend Screws. We see him in his office constantly striving to keep up a full assortment; we see him endeavoring to strengthen himself in the department of "house servants;" we see him laying in a fresh stock of blacksmiths, or adding to his already large and well-selected

1*

collection of field-hands; we see him inditing an advertisement of large and late importations from Virginia, calculated, he trusts, to please the most fastidious taste, both as to quality and price. This can be
no light labor.

Screws does not get his little profits for nothing.
He has to keep his eye out when the coffle-gang comes
in; he must watch the market; he must buy to please
the preferences of his customers; he must select
healthy parcels; he must be artistic in picking out
the pretty packages. In addition to this, Screws, being naturally a man of tender feelings, is exceedingly
harrowed and rasped in the gentler departments of
his soul by witnessing painful partings between the
goods—the shrieks of the prime mother; the sobs of
the warranted housemaid; the agonies of the A1
carpenters and the griefs of the superior blacksmiths.
This renders the business of Screws peculiar; for
nobody ever saw two cotton-bales distressed at the
idea of parting, and the emotion of separated sugar-
boxes is yet to be observed.

Screws is in precisely the condition of the soft-
hearted fish-wife, who is obliged to flay the eels alive,
or in that of the good-natured butcher, whose customers must have lamb in the season. But Screws has
a public duty to perform, and he performs it. It is a
discredit to human nature that, after all these services,
Screws should be so shamefully treated. He receives
no vote of thanks, no service of ponderous plate, no
canes with inscribed heads, no pistols with the gratitude of the donors. The customers of Screws pay him

his money, and then instead of asking him to dinner, or to partake of the friendly drink, instead of tenderly squeezing his hand upon parting, they shun him as if he were fever-stricken. A hard time of it has Screws; and if we could do anything to alleviate his woe, and bring negro-brokerage into good repute, perhaps we would. Unfortunately for Screws, we can not. Society has prejudices which are impregnable.

We must, however, try to correct a notion which is totally unfounded. The prevailing impression is that Screws deals altogether in black goods; and these being considered of a low and degraded, although useful kind, the reputation of the business among the genteel has suffered accordingly. This is all very unjust. A gentleman in New Orleans, in writing to his correspondent in New York, says: "If you have any prejudices against buying black carpenters or smiths, Screws can furnish you with white ones, or those who are nearly so." Our readers will see that Screws deals in white folks. He is no mere "nigger"-broker, although with commendable modesty he so writes himself upon his business card.

In still another department, Screws might be useful. The New Orleans gentleman to whom we have referred, wants a wife. He had commissioned his New York friend to find him one, but Screws almost tempted him to withdraw the order. "From some samples," he writes, "which Screws showed me this morning, I am half inclined to recall my commission to your firm to furnish me with a wife, as I saw one or two almost agreeable enough to satisfy even my fastidious taste. Price, $2,000 each. But I will not withdraw my commission, as you may supply me without the outlay of so much ready money. Besides, the two ladies I saw were from Virginia, and I do not much like the F. F. V." Here now is an opening for Screws. He can go into the wife-selling business. But, alas! upon further reflection, we remember that he is in it already; nor has it enhanced his respectability a morsel.

Well, Screws must struggle on as well as he can; and since he cannot be respectable, must content himself with getting rich, which, no doubt, he will do, unless several of his most valuable parcels should abscond, or a few of his choice samples die of grief or fever. Meanwhile, we have endeavored to give him a hoist in the world, for which we have no doubt he will be duly grateful. But he need not trouble himself to write us a letter of thanks. It always gives us pleasure to assist the meritorious. We believe that very few of our subscribers deal in the staple commodity of Screws, but if any of them want to buy a man or a woman, we advise them to call at "No. 159 Gravier street, New Orleans," before purchasing elsewhere.

April 14, 1857.

MR. MASON'S MANNERS.

WHAT are good manners? What is politeness as distinguished from rusticity? Miss Leslie has written a little elementary book intended to teach our Yankee girls how to behave themselves everywhere —in the church, in the drawing-room, in the railway-car, and at the *table d'hôte*. Mons. de Meilhauval has also compiled a *Manuel du Scavoir*, which is said to be a great polisher, but we have never seen it, and therefore, for all the good Monsieur might have done for us, we remain in our original ursine condition.

But if we have books for brides and bridegrooms, with treatises upon every manner of incoming and outgoing, incident to human life; if we have complete letter-writers and *vade-mecums* for all kinds of persons, why should not our ministers plenipotentiary and our embassadors extraordinary have a manual of as much authority as that of General Scott is with infantry? Why should they not be taught to go through their paces, their genuflexions, their advances and their retreats? How must we have suffered in the estimation of polite Europe for the want of such a work, to the compilation of which we do respectfully entreat Mr. Peter Parley to devote his declining years! Might not such a volume, however elementary in its inculcations, have shown to John Randolph, of Roanoke, (*clarum et venerabile nomen!*) the impropriety of approaching in a pair of buckskin breeches the enthroned Majesty of Muscovy? or of falling before Royalty upon his knees?

For performing these two feats, the Lord of Roanoke drew eighteen thousand dollars from the treasury of his country, and did that country no conceivable service whatever. Might not a little previous study have saved Minister Hannegan from devoting himself more to Bacchus than to Vatel, Puffendorf and Wheaton, and from being kicked out of the principal taverns near the court to which he was accredited ? Might not such a volume have saved James Buchanan (with due reverence his name is here mentioned) from the gross impropriety of the Ostend Conference ? Might not such a volume have persuaded a certain Secretary of Legation not to desecrate the sacred seal of Columbia ? Might it not have wheedled and coaxed another Secretary of Legation into paying his debts before leaving Paris, so that shopmen would not then have inquired of every American purchaser, when the American Diplomatist intended to return ? Pray let us have " The Diplomatist's Own Book !"

We have been betrayed into these suggestions by seeing mentioned in the newspapers a painful error, into which the Honorable John Y. Mason, the august representative of this country near the Court of Louis Bonaparte, recently fell. We wish to speak with tenderness of Mr. Mason, because, notwithstanding his innocence of the vernacular of Gaul, he has shown a great desire to acquit himself creditably, by arraying himself upon court-days in the small-clothes and cocked-hat proscribed by the late Mr. Marcy. It is also understood that he would rather stay in Paris than come home, for a reason that he has; that he is not personally a devoteè of the principle of rotation, and that as for resigning he will see Mr. Buchanan —— first.

But this is a weakness, if it be a weakness, with the whole diplomatic body. In fact, we think we can hear Mr. Buchanan chanting to our friend Cass:

Why do n't the men resign, my Cass—
  Why do n't the men resign?
Each one seems coming to the point,
  But never sends a line.

Mr. Buchanan ought not to be so impatient. Suppose that he were abroad, and did not want to come home; how would he like to be pricked in the tender parts of his constitution?

But the reader may fancy that *we* are never coming to the point. It is not a point at all. It is the back of a chair. Of a chair, we believe, at the Tuileries. And of a chair with an empress in it—an empress descended from a Scotch merchant and an Hidalgo of the bluest blood of Spain. Near that chair thus imperially occupied, sits the Representative of the United States of America. Perhaps he is standing; but that makes no difference, for the back of the chair might have been a high one. He might also have been masticating the weed of his beloved Virginia; but details, however important, are denied us. Suddenly he throws his arm about the back of the chair of H. S. M.! Oh, heavens! what next? Will not that arm descend upon that snowy and

swan-like neck, which we have all so much admired
in engravings? Goodness gracious! what might have
followed? From the chair-back to that other back,
and so on! Depend upon it we were only saved by
good luck from a war which all the cunning of diplomacy could not have averted!

"Oh, Diamond! Diamond! thou little knowest the
mischief thou hast done!" cried Newton when an ill-
conditioned cur overthrew a candle, and burned all
the crooked mathematical computations of years.
"Oh, John Y. Mason!" say we, "thou little knowest
what mischief thou wert in danger of doing!" The
venerable Benton once said of Embassador John:
"If the man has a belly-full of oysters and a handful of trumps, he will thank God for nothing more!"
If that hand had been "going it better" or "nary
pair" on that fatal night, we should have been saved
from this national discredit.

August 13, 1857.

·

THE GREAT ROGERSVILLE FLOGGING.

WE gave the other day the First Chapter in the
History of the Great Flogging behind the Second
Presbyterian Church in the town of Rogersville,
Tenn.— a ,flagellatory event which will hereafter secure for that edifice, heretofore humble and unknown,
honorable mention in ecclesiastical annals. We
showed how the "boy" of Netherland—Deacon of
the church aforesaid, and colonel of some regiment,

the number and arms of which are to us unknown—
was properly chastised beneath the shadow of the
sacred caves. The object of this whipping was to
produce in the "boy" a penitent frame of mind; to
extract from him a confession of the name of the evil-
minded and Bad Samaritan who had helped him to
run away.

Now we propose—this being one of those cases
which demand profuse details—to give the Second
Chapter. The tongue of the "boy" remained dumb.
He groaned and bellowed in the most pusillanimous
manner at his stripes, in such a sonorous way, in
fact, that the soft-hearted neighbors had serious
thoughts of interfering, and of rescuing the weak-
minded floggee from the strong-armed flogger. But
there was a certain other "boy"—venerable and sil-
ver-haired this "boy" was—and it occurred to the
Deacon-Colonel that this ancient juvenile knew something of the running away and hiding of the first-
named "boy." "Boy" Anthony bore peculiar relations to Deacon Netherland. In by-gone days, when
that present stern champion of the Presbyterian
Church was in his swaddling-clothes, the "boy"
Anthony had helped to nurse him, had played with
him, had carried the sucking Colonel upon his shoulders a hundred times.

Certainly poor old "boy" Anthony, under circumstances less pressing and less dangerous to the Presbyterian Church, might have hoped for a little mercy
—a little mollifying recollection of the old times—a
little yielding to gentle reminiscences. But the spirit

of Netherland was up. Here was the Second Presbyterian Church in Rogersville rocking to its foundations, to say nothing of the blessed structure of our
political institutions, which was vibrating in the most
alarming manner. So Netherland smothered his emotions and sternly subdued the promptings of pity, and
determined to extract the secret from the breast of
Old Anthony. He gave him up to be coaxed by the
seductive "cat" into a confession. Anthony was
taken by a negro-trader into an adjoining county.
It was the blessed Sunday—but the better the day
the better the deed. They conducted Anthony into
a stable. He had not the honor to be flogged behind
the Second Church, but he did have the honor to be
flogged in a stable—an edifice similar to that in
which, about nineteen centuries ago, our Saviour
was cradled. He was carried, the poor "boy" Anthony, into a loft, and the ceremonies commenced.
This holy and acceptable living sacrifice was stripped
to nakedness, stretched on a plank, his arms tied together under a plank, his feet to a post, his head to a
brace, so that the old "boy" could not move at all.

Now for the instrument of flogging. It was no
common utensil. It was no vulgar cat-o'-nine-tails.
It was a carpenter's saw. Carpenters are scripturally
classical. Joseph was a carpenter. Hence the theological propriety of using a saw. 'Tis a Mississippi
invention, and all honor to the gallant State which
introduced it! Well, they were rather hard on the
"boy!" The neighbors closed their windows that
they might not hear his cries. The women whim-

pered—as the women will—till the owner of the stable stopped the proceedings, probably being ashamed
to have them noticed by his horses. The trader was
disgusted, and carried Anthony off to have his polishing completed in Rutledge. The slave went into fits,
but for all these, he was taken to a jail and the whip-
pings were renewed. The sheriff interfered. The
stony-hearted jailer interfered. So the whipper was
compelled to break off, and Anthony after waiting a
week to be healed, returned — by a singular coin-
cidence—upon a Sabbath evening to his home.

Now it is quite a remarkable fact, that in the opinion of the neighbors, all this labor of the trader was
ill-expended, and that Boy No. 2 knew nothing of
Boy No. 1, his fugacities and hidings. Hence, all
this perspiration, this exertion, and even this Sab-
bath-breaking, was labor lost. Because if Boy No. 2
had nothing to tell—and it is certain that, in spite
of his tortures, he did tell nothing—what was the
use of whipping him? It was a sheer squandering
of saws, blood, muscle and whips, to say nothing
of the needless harrowing of Colonel Netherland's
feelings.

However, the Colonel showed himself to be a regular Roman. He did not wince when poor Anthony
dragged his mangled body home on that Sunday
evening. He snapped his fingers at the Rev. Samuel Sawyer when that weak-minded priest censured
him. He defended the deed. He called upon the
church to dismiss the Rev. Samuel, and the church
obeyed.

Thus ends the Second Chapter in the History of the Great Rogersville Flogging. We have written it in no lightness of spirit, if with some lightness of speech. There are certain human inconsistencies and foibles, so terrible and degrading, that we greet them with a laughter which is akin to tears.

September 5, 1857.

MR. MITCHEL'S DESIRES.

A MYSTERIOUS philosopher of Massachusetts somewhere has remarked, that " consistency is the vice of little minds." If this aphorism is to be accepted, then we may suppose Mr. John Mitchel's intellect to be of gigantic proportions, and his brain by several ounces heavier than that of Webster or of Cuvier was found to be. For of all the erratic men of a race notoriously erratic, Patriot Mitchel has turned the most bewildering flip-flaps. As a political artist, he may be said, like some celebrated painters, to have changed his manner: and his last manner is precisely the opposite of his first.

The denouncer of English tyranny; the champion of Irish liberty; the persecuted for freedom's sake; the man who nearly thrust his neck into a hempen cravat in his eagerness to emancipate Ireland; this man is about to start a newspaper somewhere at the South, solely devoted to apologies for oppression, to vindications of absolutism, to eulogiums of Slavery.

New light has broken upon the soul of John. He has been permitted, by a benignant Providence, to behold the errors of his early career, and to recognize the exceeding beauty of broad plantations well-stocked with broad-backed " niggers." Since his conversion, John has grown in Pro-Slavery grace with a rapidity really marvelous. Since he made his first startling confession of his yearning for *one* plantation and *one* gang of fat field hands, John has advanced his pretensions, and now expresses a desire for *two* plantations and *two* gangs of adipose chattels.

This is all very well. While one is wishing, it is just as cheap, and a great deal more fascinating, to wish largely, and moderation in this atmospheric architecture has never been a Milesian characteristic. At the same time, we advise the neighbors of this aspiring patriot to be on the alert. One of George the First's Dutch mistresses, being hustled by a London mob, called out from her carriage : " Do n't hurt us, good peoples ; we come for all your *goots !*" " Yes, d—n you, and for all our chattels, too," was the reply. Mr. Mitchel may succeed in convincing the Slaveholders, who are sadly in need of smart champions, that he has come for their good ; but if he continues to exhibit such an overweening propensity for " all their chattels, too," they may not only consider him too expensive to be indulged in, but they may also harbor a suspicion of his disinterestedness which would be painful. They may insist upon the rule that " half 's fair."

Mr. Mitchel, if we may judge by his prospectus,

has entered upon his new duties with commendable spirit. It is always pleasant to witness the fresh zeal of these novices. It is seldom that they stick at anything. They do not simply go the whole hog, but a whole herd of whole hogs. Slaveholders, born and bred in the midst of Slavery, and who have heretofore suffered themselves to be pretty enthusiastic advocates of the institution, stand aghast at their own moderation when they listen to men who come among them, and who volunteer to assist them. When the visual orbs of such are purged of any remaining film of free notions, and the John Mitchels see Slavery (as they say) for themselves, they always discover more beautiful things in it than were ever dreamed of by the Slaveholder. To tell the truth, they generally overdo the matter, and are more rapturous than is absolutely necessary. When they say, as John does, that Slavery is the finest institution in the world; that it is vastly more promotive, than Freedom, of the prosperity of a State; that it is the best thing for the master and the best thing for the slave, why they talk hyperbolical nonsense, and are regarded by Southern men who hear them with profound contempt.

Those who have had the best and most extended opportunities of studying the institution know that such talk is mere babble. The man who is listened to with the greatest respect is he who, while he sees no remedy for the evil, admits that an evil it is. Therefore, we conjure Patriot John, by all his hopes of a seat in Congress, by his love of many plantations, by his peculiar passion for corpulent negroes — by all these we conjure him, to moderate his raptures. Otherwise, people will be apt to call him an old humbug.

In pursuance of our advice, we think that Mr. Mitchel had better say nothing more of the reopening of the African Slave-Trade. If one people are to go to Africa for slaves, why may not another people go to Ireland for the same commodity? We hope we shall not offend Mr. Mitchel's Hibernian sensibilities by the question, but how would he like it if a French ship should carry off from the coast of Ireland, and into Slavery, a select assortment of his aunts, uncles and cousins; in fact, the cream of the Mitchel family? But the Africans are black, and the Irishmen are white—when they are not *very* dirty. True enough; but color has not heretofore saved the Irish people from the most terrible oppression.

We suppose that a certain town-major Sirr—John may have heard of him—flogged white backs with as much gusto as John will flog black ones, should he come to own them. But the Africans are shiftless and degraded. Well, we have heard it just intimated that some Irishmen are not, after all, models of smartness and prudence. But then, Africans cannot help themselves. We should like to know how well the Irishmen have helped themselves for many centuries. We have no desire to speak with the slightest disrespect of the many noble efforts of that people to throw off the yoke; but when an

Irish patriot, as Mitchel professes to have been, argues
that the black man is not fit for freedom because he
is not free, it is perfectly proper for us to ask this
Irishman why the rule is not applicable to the condition of his own countrymen. But, out of our respect
for an unhappy land, we will not pursue the subject.
Many and grievous have been the burthens of Ireland; she has now another to bear in the apostasy
of a man whom she once delighted to honor.

September 9, 1857.

MR. MASON'S MANNERS ONCE MORE.

ANATOMISTS have been much bothered to determine the uses of the pineal gland and the spleen;
and what these mysterious organs are in the body
physical, embassadors, ordinary and extraordinary,
are in the body politic. When a respectable Boston
merchant, more remarkable for his knowledge of
"domestics" than of diplomacy, was appointed by
our Government to St. James (where he cut a sumptuous figure and spent double his salary for the honor
of his country), he had a painful recollection of having somewhere read, or at some time heard, that an
embassador is " a person sent abroad to tell lies for his
country;" a service which he did not care to undertake. To solve his doubts, he went to Mr. Edward
Everett, who is authority in Boston for every point,
from a disputed passage in Euripides to the config-

uration of the great toe of a statue, and asked him simply if he should be obliged to tell the lies aforesaid. Mr. Everett promptly responded in the negative. So Mr. Lawrence went to London, and gave those excellent dinners which to this day are recalled with grateful salivary glands by those who partook of them.

Thus we have excellent authority for rejecting as a scandalous old libel, the mendacity theory. But there is yet another, the mendicity theory, which has lately been received with some favor. An embassador is sent abroad in order that he may make money enough to pay his debts; and it is understood that the present august representative of this country at the Court of Napoleon III., is retained in office expressly that he may "realize" to that pleasing extent. Our readers, particularly in these times of monetary pressure, will agree with us that no more commendable motive could actuate a man to do duty in short breeches upon gala-days at court; and at any rate, we are certain that the creditors of the gentleman alluded to will coincide with us in the opinion.

As there is very little for an American minister to do in Paris, save to disport himself upon proper occasions before the imperial eyes, we do not see why Mr. Mason should not have the pay as well as another, provided there be no worthy Democrat who owes more and has less to pay it with. In such case, the shortest and hardest-up man should be allowed the privilege of procuring for American travelers, tickets of admission to see the Beast of the Tuileries.

2

But Mr. Mason's claim must be considered as paramount until some Democrat entitled to write *pau-
perrimus* after his name shall dispute it.

Under these circumstances, what cruelty is it to
Mr. Mason, and what injustice to his creditors, to
circulate false tales about his demeanor before royalty, thus touching him upon a most tender point,
and, as it were, sticking pins through his court-stock-
ings directly into the embassadorial calves ! And to
impeach his conduct, too, at that Court of all others ;
a Court where everything is conducted upon principles of the very pinkiest propriety ; a Court which
maintains a grave Chamberlain expressly to teach people how to behave themselves, which official has written a hand-book of manners, to which Mr. Mason no
doubt gives his nights and days, just as young persons desiring a good style of writing English, " must
give their nights and days to Addison !" And to
charge him, too, with hugging the Empress of that virtuous realm — an offense which, constructively, might
be considered capital, and which might have obliged
the offender to part with his head — a portion of the
body necessary to the man if not to the embassador !
And to impute to Mr. Mason this offence, when his
fate was in the hands of James Buchanan — that
mirror of continency, that more than Joseph, that
Pamela of Presidents ! -

But the story, incredible as it first appeared, came
to us so well authenticated that, careful as we are,
we published it with comments appropriate to the
terrible disclosure. But let us not be lightly blamed

when it is considered that *The Richmond Enquirer*, a journal usually so careful of the honor of the F. F. V., also gave the narration publicity. We both relied upon the alleged authority of *The London Court Journal*, which is your very Sir Oracle on scandals connected with palaces. As we were deceived into doing injustice to Mr. Mason, we accord him the amplest reparation in our power.

Know all men, women and children by these presents, that Embassador Mason did not hug the Empress. Two Virginians residing in Paris—whether creditors or not does not appear—have written, the one to *The National Intelligencer*, the other to *The Richmond Enquirer*, indignantly denying the truth of the scurvy story; while the editor of *The London Court Journal* has solemnly declared over his (or her) own hand, that the hugging paragraph never appeared in that newspaper. "The matter being beneath the notice of His Excellency," these two friends in need and friends indeed, have rushed to the rescue, and Mr. Mason's character is upon the courtliest of legs again.

Indeed, out of this furnace of affliction (his friends say that the story has " saddened him ") Mr. Mason has come burnished and refulgent and brighter (a great deal) than our new cent. He ought to thank the enemy who devised this scandal, for it has procured him several of the strongest puffs which he ever received in his life, and that, too, just in the nick of time. It seems that of all the diplomatic body he is the pet of the Emperor, and also (in a strictly Platonic way) of the Empress. Whether, like Mary of Argyle, he is "loved for his beauty, but not for that alone," we cannot say; but of the affection there can be no doubt. Here is the certificate :

"I know that on the 1st of January last, when the Emperor received all the foreign dignitaries, he greeted the American minister in the most cordial manner; and after expressing his best wishes for the continuance of good feeling between the two governments, concluded by hoping that he (Mr. Mason) would remain at his court for the coming four years. These words were heard by the Russian Embassador, who told our Minister that it was his duty to repeat the words thus addressed to him in his official capacity, to his Government, but Mr. Mason, with the modesty of true merit, has, I am sure, remained silent upon the subject."

We rejoice that Mr. Mason's "modesty" has not kept this valuable information from the Cabinet at Washington, where it will produce an excitement. Mr. Buchanan will, of course, act upon the recommendation of Napoleon, as the preference of that monarch ought to be conclusive. So much for Mr. Mason as a diplomatist. But it is as a man of manners, of polish, of civility, of the best breeding, that he gets the cleanest certificate. So far from being a big bear, he is Chesterfieldian, and as punctilious as a professor of etiquette or a Chinese mandarin. Instead of needing instruction himself, he is just the man to teach others. Here is his "character" as given in *The Richmond Enquirer:*

" In any question of manners, he possesses the kind sensibility to prompt, and, unimpaired, the just faculty to discriminate what, as regards the occasion, it seems most proper and befitting to do or to avoid."

There is no name given, but we know the writer of this to be a gentleman by the fine language which he uses. It reminds us of a reply sent by a courtly negro to an invitation, in which he regretted that "circumstances repugnant to the acquiesce would prevent his acceptance to the invite." Now we know why they want Mr. Mason to stay at the Court of France. They want him there " to show them how to do it." Like Mr. Turveydrop's, his deportment is beautiful. Should stern policy demand his recall, let him be made Master of Ceremonies at the White House, and with a happy blending of " foreign airs and native graces," show the ruler of this realm to his people.

October 2, 1857.

PRESIDENTIAL POLITENESS.

WHEN we parted, in by no means a heart-broken state, with Mr. Pierce, and settled ourselves to bear as best we might the reign of Mr. Buchanan, the general opinion was that we had made a change for the better. There was a notion that Mr. B. was a more respectable man than his predecessor; or, at any rate, that he would be more forbearing in his treatment of his antagonists, and less likely to do hard, ungenerous and ungracious things. In fact, despite the little Ostend escapade, Mr. Buchanan ran very much upon the merits of his respectability and figured in the multitudinous speeches of his champions as a venerable pacificator. It must be confessed that he has done very little in that way thus far. He seems to exhibit rather the querulousness than the placidity of old age. On the contrary, Mr. Pierce was particularly polite, and often advanced the most indefensible opinions in language of more than sophomorical elegance. When at his worst in public policy, he was most dulcet in his demeanor; and he vetoed necessary measures with commendable suavity. Mr. Buchanan, we regret to observe, is rather snappish, and too much inclined to snub the humble petitioners who approach the throne. The different characters of the last and of the present President may receive illustration from the following facts:

Last January, when Mr. Pierce was about to retire from the presidential glees and glooms, he received from the American Bible Society a copy of the Holy Scriptures, " as a token of their high regard for the office which he held." We do not know to whom the Society could more appropriately have made the donation than to one who, during his administration of public affairs, was singularly unmindful of many of the teachings of The Book. Uncharitable people might say that Mr. Pierce's case was like that of the man who, upon being asked by a distributor if he had a copy of the Bible, produced two leaves, with the apologetical remark, that "he had no idea that he was so 'near out.'"

But in all respects the gift was creditable to the Society, and we hope that it will prove profitable to Mr. Pierce. A suspicious and touchy man, however, upon receiving it might have resented the presentation as implying a suspicion of his sore need of the instructions of the volume, and of his lack of a copy of it. But Mr. Pierce behaved in no such ungracious way. On the contrary, he sat down at once and wrote a charming letter of acknowledgment to the Society, paying the handsomest compliments to the book in particular and to the Christian religion in general. To be sure, he said some things in it which rather puzzle us; albeit we suppose that they are perfectly plain to *The Journal of Commerce* and other sheets less benighted than our own. After putting in, as became a sound Constitutional Democrat, a reminder "that in our political institutions there is no union of Church and State," Mr. Pierce informs us that "Christianity animates our nation; it is the true spirit of good government; it is the characteristic and peculiar quality of modern civilization—the all-pervading principle of our laws, the sentiment and the moral and social existence of the people of the United States."

This is well expressed; and we are not surprised that it gives our friend Forney's newspaper, from which we copy it, much calm satisfaction. But the ease and accuracy with which it is to be interpreted will depend upon what kind of Christianity Mr. Pierce refers to. The truth is that there are several varieties now in vogue; and when presidents write upon theological subjects, they should be careful to let us know to which particular kind they are alluding. If Mr. Pierce in the above elegant extract referred to the new Christianity invented by the Dr. Rosses, expounded by the Rev. Brownlows, and practically exemplified sometimes behind the Presbyterian meeting-house in Rogersville, Tenn., why then the meaning of the sentence is as plain as a pike-staff. That *is* the Christianity which "animates our nationality," and is too much "the all-pervading principle of our laws"—a Christianity which does *not* let the oppressed go free; but which chases them with blood-hounds, or with the hardly milder myrmidons of the law; a Christianity which, if it does not sanction, fails to rebuke, adultery, cruelty, and one great continuous theft of the earnings of the poor. But if Mr. Pierce refers to that other Christianity of older date, which inculcates good-will to man, then we confess that his words are as mysterious to us as if they were written in Egyptian hieroglyphics. Still this has nothing to do with the manner of the letter which all will admit to be remarkably civil.

How different the style in which Mr. Buchanan received his present! Certain gentlemen in Connecticut remarking with pain that he seemed to be ignorant of the principles of the Constitution, as well as of his official duties, prepared and sent to him a little memorial, in which some of the simplest of these principles and duties were pointed out in plain language. The donation was not a magnificent one, it must be confessed, and not worth half so much as those big cheeses which it used to be the fashion to present to presidents. But the donors " gave all; they could no more; though poor the offering was." That Mr. Buchanan would have found a study of the paper profitable, we confidently aver. But instead of devoting himself to it like a good scholar, he ungratefully wrote to the Connecticut gentlemen a letter, the burthen of which was, " Thank you for nothing !"—a letter the very opposite of what may be called genial, and as puckery as a persimmon before the frost.

Some writer (French, of course) says that he prefers bad morals to bad manners; and without going to that extreme, we must say that suavity in a public officer is by no means to be despised. The mistress of the White House is said to be a well-bred young woman ; and we advise Mr. Buchanan to entrust his more delicate correspondence to her. Female tact will amply atone for any lack of political knowledge.

October 10, 1857.

WILLIAM THE CONQUEROR.

In these days of general and wide-spread modesty, we dote upon impudence. We are pleased to see or to hear from a man who, in disregard of all the decencies of public life, approaches the administration

2*

with a front of brass, and with lingual abilities of the curliest serpentine order. We have said many things sharp and severe of Mr. William Walker, the distinguished pirate. If our memory serves us, we have held him up to the public as one who, by all right and law, should be suspended from that plant so different from all other trees, and which bears a fruit not yet classed by the horticulturists. Not to put too fine a point upon it, we have thought that if it were right to hang anybody, it would be eminently fit and proper to hang William Walker.

We beg pardon of our readers for this mistake. We have not understood William. We have not, we confess, made proper allowance for that sublimity of insolence which amounts to a virtue; for that panoply of "niggerism" which enables any pro-slavery adventurer to place himself at once in confidential relations with the Government; for that catholic principle which permits any discontented Yankee to transmogrify himself into a Spaniard, a Hottentot, or a Nicaraguan. Our political estimate was too narrow. We should have understood that the reigning monarch of that empire—so extensive and powerful—was by no means required to keep himself permanently squatted upon his august throne; but that he might give himself leave of absence from the Imperial domain whenever pleasant or convenient; that he might run away, and so live to fight another battle; that his departures from the realm, albeit sometimes compelled by the ingratitude of his subjects, and an occasional bayonet probe *a posteriori*, urged nothing against his legitimacy. Be it known to all people, then, that the present and perpetual Executive of the Republic of Nicaragua is now a wanderer and an exile; but, whether with or without the pomps of power and the modes, forms and shows of authority, that he is still Governor, and is not, by reason of his truancy from his dominion lessened in his authority by the ninth part of a hair. Are we not right in admiring the stern persistence which can maintain itself under such circumstances? The king is dead—long live the king!

Sweet William has written to the Hon. Lewis Cass —at this moment, unless dead, our Secretary of State—upon terms of equality, and as one great functionary should write to another. William appears to consider himself a modern Themistocles, quite entitled to what he calls "the *rights* of hospitality." He does not happen to have a Secretary of State near him just about this time, and thus he is compelled to discard etiquette and to communicate *in propria persona*. He is quite pained to learn that Mr. Cass intends to prevent his return, with his "companions," to his own Principality of Nicaragua. He is still more hurt to learn that there is a rumor that he designs to violate the Neutrality Laws—popularly supposed in the least well-informed parts of the United States to be still in existence.

Now, in spite of his palaver, it is necessary to bring this marauding William up with a round turn; to tell him that, politically, he is a humbug, and that, practically, he is a felon. Any disreputable corsair

can write to Mr. Cass. Gentlemen of a burglarious
turn of mind, sent to a seclusion from this wicked
world, may open a correspondence with Mr. Secretary. Pens, ink, paper, three-penny stamps are;
among the commonest and cheapest of conveniences.
William may write and so may we. It is in our
power to send word to the Secretary that we have
subjugated Orange county, in the State of New York,
and that hereafter in that bailiwick the jurisdiction
of the United States will not be acknowledged. Perhaps our letter, however, would not be telegraphed
to the morning papers. Therein William has the
advantage of us. Beaten, expelled, exiled, ruined,
dethroned, he can still write to the Government of
the United States. So much for having re-estab-
lished Slavery where it had been abolished.

The "Republic of Nicaragua," according to William, is "the Republic of Walker." Although the
last vestige of his authority has disappeared in that
State—although he is neither sent for nor wished for
—he still assumes to be the Governor of that ilk.
How shall we with ordinary patience treat this bit of
brazen assumption? If the people of Nicaragua are
his admirers, and passionately desire to have him
once more ruling over them, why, in the name of all
that is reasonable, does not William at once rush into
the arms of his affectionate subjects? Why does he
need "companions?" And why, if he cannot give
up the delights of friendship, should the "companions" carry rifles, knapsacks, bayonets and cartridge-
boxes? Why should they not sail in peaceful galleys

to Realejo? Why should not these "jolly companions" march into Leon waving olive-branches or white flags? Your country calls you, William, and you should not disregard her entreaties. Go and win! But why write to the Secretary of State?

Nothing strikes us more forcibly than the eminent consideration with which Walker regards the Neutrality Laws of this country. He, the exiled Nicaraguan, is the guest of the United States; and can he possibly disregard its statutes? We do not know. We are afraid he will, if he can. Before he became a Nicaraguan, he was, if our memory serves us, a Lower Californian and a Sonorian. He repels with "scorn," and also with "indignation," the idea that he intends any violation of our laws. But how does he propose to go to Nicaragua? Solitary and alone? Unarmed? We fancy not. He can only depart for that country from these shores with an armed retinue; and we do not place much confidence in the assertions of thieves that they intend to purloin upon quite legal and Christian principles. The crime of which Walker professes such an abhorrence, he committed, as all the world knows, in 1853. And he will commit it again, if he is allowed the opportunity. Let us have no more nonsense!

BENJAMIN'S SECOND NOTICE.

SCREWS again — B. Screws, Esq. The well-known B. Screws. Not to go into untimely refinements, Benjamin Scréws. The individual doing business in Gravier Street, New Orleans. The only trader heretofore puffed in these columns without being distinctly ranked as an advertiser. The man who deals in the cerebrums and the cerebellums, the skulls, the wind-pipes, the chests, the abdominal regions, the legs, the heels, the great toes, and the little toes of his fellow-creatures. The man who sends out a card, announcing his large and well-assorted stock of human goods, who has the warranted cook-maids, and the blacksmiths, and the carpenters, and the pretty, wasp-waisted, bright-eyed little yellow women, for that matter, if you will but please to call for them. Everything choice, solid, muscular, fascinating, and even voluptuous, upon the premises of Benjamin Screws. Twice we have given Mr. Screws a notice, and our readers may well be weary of him. But we feel it to be our duty to stand by Screws as a well-marked biographic phenomenon of the century. The great flesh-broker is in trouble, and at such an hour it is not for us to desert him. He is at present in a sore state of litigation, brought on by his efforts to furnish the inhabitants of Louisiana with A1 house-maids and field-hands, and to make everything pleasant in the homes of New Orleans.

Screws is now in the noble attitude of a plaintiff. Heretofore we have considered him as a defendant.

When last we had occasion to speak well of him, Screws was in that receptacle popularly and in common parlance known as "the jug." Screws, in his intense and unwavering exertions to supply everybody with "field-hands, house-servants, carpenters and blacksmiths," had sold the boy Toby to Colonel Hardy. Toby, instead of being a good, patient, hardworking and generally useful boy, had the audacity to die of the measles. Toby, before the measles, and before passing into the broking hands of our friend Screws, was owned by one Whitfield, of Mississippi. Whitfield sent Toby to Screws to be sold. And Screws sold him. And Colonel Hardy (of what regiment is not stated) bought him. And Toby suffered himself to catch the measles and died, notwithstanding his benefactor, B. Screws, Esq., had warranted him sound in limb, wind and muscle. Actually popped off with the measles! Imagine the anguish of B. Screws, Esq.! Imagine the greater anguish of Colonel Hardy, who had nothing but a cadaver, when he fancied he had paid $1,350 for a tip-top nigger! Imagine the still greater anguish of Mr. Whitfield when he heard that Toby was dead and Benjamin Screws would not, except upon legal compulsion, pay him over the $1,350 — Toby's price. There seems to have been a great deal of distress all around. Whitfield was distressed for the $1,350; Colonel Hardy was distressed at having only the fatal measles, when he expected a fine field-hand; and dear Benjamin Screws was distressed, because he had, in a thoughtless moment, compromised his character as a negro-broker by disposing of a measly African.

"Send me my $1,350," wrote Whitfield. "I can't do it," wrote Benjamin in reply. "Toby," he continued, "is dead — of the measles. I warranted him against the measles and all other cutaneous disorders. He had one of them, however, and his life has paid the penalty of his audacity. Hardy says I must pay him and not you." Whether or not friend Screws ended with "d —— Toby," we cannot say. Very likely he has, in the most unnecessary manner, consigned Toby to that fate before this.

Well, to make a long story short, Whitfield, having an eager appetite for his money (as who has not in these days?), walked B. Screws, Esq., to the calaboose, upon a charge of embezzling. The benevolent Screws was actually locked up. And all because nigger Toby had the measles. The report from which we copy, that of a New Orleans newspaper, states that Mr. Screws was "paraded before the public under no very pleasant relations." Whitfield wanted the $1,350; Hardy wanted the $1,350; and, of course, Benjamin Screws did not passionately desire to pay $2,700, to say nothing of the loss of his lawful commissions. It was a dead lock. But we think we have the key to unlock it.

It is evident that all this trouble comes of Toby's willfulness in dying of the measles. He had a grudge against Whitfield for selling him; against Screws for broking him; against the Colonel for buying him; so he died! It served him rightly, the ungrateful black person ! What would be thought of an ordinary servant, who, in the height of the season, should have the meanness to go away and catch the measles, and die just to avoid working ?

When Screws was haled before the court, the judge said : " Go, Benjamin ! thou art innocent." And he did go, and stirred up his stock, we suppose, in a lively manner, by way of venting his feelings. But he did not stop with the floggings, the paddlings and the picklings which the law allows. He had been hurt in his good name. The tenderest portions of his constitution had suffered an abrasion. So he brought Whitfield to account "for falsely and maliciously charging him with embezzlement." This civil action for incivility is still pending in New Orleans ; and we hope to report that Benjamin Screws has recovered enormous damages.

Many persons have supposed Benjamin Screws to be a myth — a fabulous personage — a creation of this newspaper. But it becomes more and more certain that Screws is a veritable being. We append his card, with an apology for not reproducing it in its original elegance — an act of justice which our typical resources will not permit. Here it is, as well as we can give it :

" BENJ. SCREWS, NEGRO BROKER, will keep constantly on hand, Field-Hands, House Servants, Carpenters, Blacksmiths. Office, No. 159 Gravier St., New Orleans. References: Shade F. Slatter, Thompson, Allen & Co., Maccaboy & Bradford, New Orleans."

November 26, 1857.

THE REVERIES OF REVERDY.

WE have made a discovery — a literary discovery. One of the sweetest and prettiest writers in this land of Hail Columbia, is the Hon. Reverdy Johnson, of Lyndhurst, near Baltimore, in the Commonwealth of Maryland. When, as became watchful journalists, we underwent the perusal of the proceedings of the Palace Garden Democracy, we found Judge Parker not fascinating, his only joke being green with the moss of several centuries, and his serious, alarming and hortatory passages, so intolerably, consummately and miraculously dull, that we were nearly in as much danger of coma as the Union — Heaven bless the dear old venerable concern ! — is of dissolution.

Judge Parker does not appear to be one of your brilliant men, the sort of person to hang up in a dark alley. He is solid, we suppose, and sensible, and practical, perhaps, and able. But not a shiner — at least not in a report. Then there was the Hon. Jefferson Davis, who intimated that we Republicans are men of low "instinct," Mr. Davis being, we suppose, a man of instinct high, lofty, elevated, sublime, towering, soaring and tall. This disrespectful language did so discompose, disarrange and irritate our minds, that we incontinently vowed to read no more of Jefferson Davis, so that we missed all his serene gems and blushing flowers, and were compelled to fall back upon Reverdy. He was, as the young ladies lisp, "be-you-tiful." A kind of frisky Dr. Johnson, we should say, stately, but smiling; sesquipedalian, but fascinating; plethoric, but pretty.

The epistle of Reverdy to the New Yorkers is good. As we perused his well-padded sentences, we were so solaced by sound that we ceased to look for sense, but suffered ourselves to be borne upon the tide of his eloquence, quiescent and unresisting. When Reverdy described the wreck and ruin of Dissolution, we could hardly go on, and yet, some strange fascinating power fixed our right orb on the page, while the left organ of vision performed a series of vibrating winks at a curiously rapid rate. These phenomena were accompanied by an almost irresistible desire to place the thumb to the nose. Dissolve the Union, says Reverdy, and you are physically, morally, socially and economically "done for." He uses no such vulgar language, but that is what he means. He says to us: "Dissolve, and your downfall commences, and rapid will be its *progress*." A *progressive* downfall, Heaven save us! must be something perfectly awful, and suggests the dire catastrophe of Jack and Gill and the well-known pail of water.

But hearken to the Baltimore Jeremiah! Having smashed the Union, he paints the cruel consequence of the division to the Northern half, or, to speak more accurately, two-thirds. Our "magnificent commercial marine will be one no longer." Minus the Stars and Stripes, it will go at once to the celebrated locker of D. Jones. We shall "dwindle to the feebleness of a German principality." We

can only " traverse the deep by permission of the
great nations of the world." " The charm of your
enterprise," says Jeremiah Johnson, " will be broken,
the foundation of your strength destroyed, and you
remitted to worse than infantile imbecility."   A
pretty prospect, indeed !

Mr. Johnson concludes with " total ruin," and thus
finishes the most melancholy epistle which we have
read for many a day.   We will do him the justice
to say that in the water-cart style he is easily first.
Choate is lurid, but Johnson is moist.   The only
encouraging thing which he says is, that the Kansas
excitement is permanently closed ; and he exults
thereat.   If he really thought so, he might have
made his letter somewhat shorter and a trifle gayer.
Why doleful dumps should now the Johnsonian mind
oppress ; why he should continue to sigh, and sob,
and groan, and grunt, and cry, and choke ; why he
should persist in shouting fire, now that the fire is
extinguished ; why he should not, the danger past,
come out of the tombs, shave himself, and put on a
clean shirt and a smiling face, he may know, but we
certainly do not.

Does he like the luxury of woe ? Does he find
tears sweet ? and sighs pleasant ? and apprehension
comforting ?   We advise him to bid farewell to idle
fears, and to wipe his eyes with a star-spangled pocket
handkerchief.   Let him profit by the example of
John Van Buren, who wrote to the Palace Garden
to say that he could not come to the meeting, but
sent his best love and encouragement.   John may

sometimes swear and sometimes laugh, but he knows altogether too much to cry. So, upon this occasion, he comes bravely up to the scratch, and does not doubt at all. He is in the most altitudinous spirits. He sees victory in the distance preparing wreaths for the inevitable and triumphant Democracy into a particularly large chaplet for himself. Now, we like pluck, and we must say that the Prince presents a contrast very much in his own favor to the dyspeptic Mr. Reverdy, who must watch over that sensitive nature of his carefully, or he will be doing himself an injury in the next dangerous month of November.

We thought that the fashion of lugubriosity had gone out, and that our public men of the Democratic party were about to show a little valor, and affect a confidence in the stability of the Union, even if they possessed it not. But they get worse and worse. The Hon. Rufus Choate, as we understand, now wears a hair shirt, fasts for seven days together, and spends all his leisure hours in offering prayers for the preservation of the Union. The Hon. Edward Everett has been a stranger to happiness for several years, and here turns up the Hon. Reverdy Johnson, by not a little the most frightened man in the Confederacy. Now, we are for a modicum of fun, and cannot possibly see the use of fingering our eyes, snuffling and trembling, like boys seeing, or expecting to see, a ghost. Care, too, which remorselessly killed the cat, will kill these sensitive patriots, unless they better control themselves. We, therefore, recommend to Mr. Reverdy Johnson some light purgative medicine, regular hours, cheerful society, and a reasonable effort to rely, just the least in the world, upon Divine Providence.

October 21, 1858.

THE FORESIGHT OF MR. FIELDER.

A VOCALIST of the last generation, celebrated in his day, and called Incledon, while listening to the performances of Braham, was accustomed to wish that his old music-master could come down from heaven to Exeter and take the mail-coach up to London, "to hear that d—d Jew sing." Mr. Herbert Fielder, of Georgia, who is the latest champion of disunion, and who appears to have muddled himself into something like sincerity by too much reading of Mr. Calhoun, in a pamphlet which he has put out, and for which he charges the incredibly small sum of fifty cents, utters a similar wish.

Mr. Herbert Fielder admits that Gen. Washington, in a certain document usually called "The Farewell Address," strongly deprecated the dissolution of the Union. In the course of his disquisition, Mr. Fielder supposes Washington to descend from heaven, with or without the aid of a parachute, but still, we suppose, in full regimentals, with what Mr. Fielder calls "important dispatches." So changed are we, according to Mr. F., that the angel Washington would not know at first where to alight. But Mr. F. is certain that after hovering over the land for a while and taking sights at us, we suppose with a telescope, Washington would drop upon the Slave side of the line and immediately call a Disunion meeting. "Should the experiment ever be made," says Mr. Fielder, "that would be the result."

Unfortunately it is not violently probable that the experiment will ever be made. The second advent of Washington, in spite of Mr. Fielder's invocation, is not an event which will occur this week or next. We shall wait some time, if we wait for Washington to come down to help us; and Washington himself might object to such a mission. However, in the absence of this illustrious ghost, Mr. Fielder undertakes the patriotic duty of enlightening this great nation. He proves to a demonstration that the Southern States are down-trodden, bleeding and bound—completely under the thumbs or toes of the North—slaves, vassals, serfs of the commercial States! "There she sits"—"she" meaning the North—"levying tribute on the Southern agriculturist, to clothe in costly purple and feed on sumptuous repast the lordly manufacturer." Quite touching! But those who are taking out their handkerchiefs may put them up again, for Mr. Fielder immediately goes on to prove that the Southern States are the most prosperous, enterprising, intelligent and the happiest communities in the world. The benevolent and sympathetic reader is thus placed in a most uncomfortable position, and does not know whether to grin or to groan. But as he has paid his half dollar, he has, we suppose, the right to choose.

Mr. H. Fielder, we will do him the justice to say,

is a first-rate hater. He throws down his glove in the preface with an unmistakable sincerity. "I hate the North," says Mr. H. Fielder, ferociously. "I love the South," says Mr. H. Fielder, tenderly, not to say amorously. Having thus proclaimed his freedom from all possible unworthy prejudices, he advances with zeal, demonstrating the prosperity and prostration of the South with a sort of ambidextrous logic, which would have astonished Archbishop Whately. He opens, indeed, with a burst of amiability, and a sort of grim politeness, soothing to consider. "It is optional," says Mr. Fielder, "with the public to read the title-page, and to throw it (the book) down without a perusal, or to read it."

Herein it will be seen that Mr. Fielder's pamphlet differs from all other pamphlets heretofore ushered, or hereafter to be ushered, into this reading world. We cannot sufficiently appreciate Mr. Fielder's obliging condescension. We will, however, do him the justice to say, that he is occasionally entertaining and sometimes remarkably pretty. For instance, when he speaks of the doughfaces, who, poor fellows! are doing their best, he forcibly and eloquently says: "The voice of our friends at the North, *if we have* any there, (ungrateful doubt!) is as feeble, compared with that of the enemy, as would be the force and power of a cooing turtle-dove upon a solitary oak in the forests, when a thousand hungry eagles with whetted beaks and distended claws were already on the wing for the assault." One turtle-dove with a thousand eagles—a thousand hungry eagles, a thousand eagles with whetted beaks, a thousand eagles with distended claws—one turtle-dove assailed by such a winged host would be, we admit, in a condition of considerable peril. We introduced the passage to show Mr. Fielder's mastery of style, which is a most convenient accomplishment when one has very little to say and a desire to say a great deal. But we pity the doughfaces. The whole body of them thus compared to one miserable, little lonesome pigeon !

We will do Mr. Fielder the further justice to say, that he really does seem to consider Human Slavery to be altogether beautiful. It is evident that if he were not Fielder he would be a field-hand—if he were not a slave-owner he would be a slave. He does not seem to think that there is any material difference between the rapture of owning and the rapture of being owned. Slavery is sweet alike to his mental and his religious constitution. He duly lugs in the Holy Scriptures. He quotes, " Cursed be Canaan !" as if it had never been quoted before. We have short, biographical notices of Noah, Ham, Shem, Japheth, Abraham, Hagar, Jacob, our old friend Onesimus, and our old friend Philemon. One of his pages bristles with Biblical references : Gen. ix. ; Lev. xix., etc., etc. The dear old *"doulos"* is again trotted out. The creature-comforts of Southern chattels are duly and admiringly dwelt upon. The blankets of the Black, his raiment, his pork and his pone when he is well, and his potions and pills when he is sick. Then his condition is contrasted with that of white workmen

3

at the North, who are, as usual, described as ragged and ruined, as paupers or prisoners, as starving or stealing.

We fancy that we have met with something like this line of argumentation before. Mr. Fielder takes it up with an enthusiasm which leads us to suppose that he considers it to be a novelty. If he does, he is very much mistaken.

We think we may say, in conclusion, that so far as Mr. Fielder is concerned, the Union is already dissolved. The case now stands thus: Thirty-two sovereign States *versus* Herbert Fielder, Esq., of Georgia. Mr. Fielder has not, at the latest dates, proceeded so far as to seize the public arsenals, post-offices, revenue cutters, etc., but we presume that he will do so at his earliest convenience—that he will elect himself to all necessary offices, and so found a Republic which will knock the ideal of Plato to splinters, and afford to an admiring world a revival of the glories of Sparta, Athens, Assyria, Carthage and Rome.

November 18, 1859.

MR. MITCHEL'S COMMERCIAL VIEWS.

AMONG the most consistent philosophers at present engaged in the support and defence of Human Slavery, we must certainly rank that illustrious patriot, John Mitchel, the Irishman, who is at present grinding in the slaveholder's mill, and who will be transferred, when his owners are ready, to the mill at Washington, in which the grinding will be worse and the pay proportionately better. Those who are not over-nice in their moral notions, who like to behold perversion perfect, and who find a fascination in the utter wreck of humanity, will be enraptured to learn that Mr. John Mitchel has reached the lowest depths of mental degradation, and is now about the most beautifully unpleasant person connected with the American press.

In his way—which is not a very fragrant way—he is now positively accomplished. We do not think that any future offenses of his can be ranker or smell higher than that which has now been committed. He is laudably ambitious to sink; but we believe that his ambition should, and in the nature of things must, now rest satisfied. When a man honestly believes—and, of course, Mr. John Mitchel is honest—in man-stealing and man-selling, it is exceedingly creditable to him to have the moral courage to avow his belief promptly, plumply and plainly, without circumlocution or extenuation. "I am a villain," said an Irish actor in a barn, with knit brow and general truculent physiognomy. "That's a fact!" exclaimed some admiring critic in the gallery. "You lie!" responded the indignant histrion.

But Mr. John Mitchel does not so answer, when his frank avowal meets with a similar response. He puts on his sweetest smile, makes his best bow, and blandly acknowledges that he is a villain—a traitor, and proud of his treason—a kidnapper, and proud of

his kidnapping. His brazen boldness is the most delicious thing of its kind which has ever come to our
knowledge; except through the pages of Jonathan
Wild the Great. He makes us think of the old
Border Ruffian of Scotland, who "sae rantingly, sae
dauntingly" danced round the gallows-tree. We are
indebted to him in this prosaic time for a new sensation. A champion of Irish Emancipation transmogrified into "a nigger-driving Yankee," and still yearning
for new gangs and fresh niggers, is an object for any
traveling menagerie, and cannot be gazed upon without awe, and other sensations too numerous and too
peculiar to be mentioned.

We do not know that our readers will be at all
surprised when they learn that this Irish patriot has
plainly avowed himself the champion of the African
Slave-trade. He is more Southern than the extremest
Southern soldier of Slavery; and like most converts
of the kind, he makes an ass of himself in avowing
his conversion. Southern gentlemen who have heretofore deluded themselves into the belief that they
were tolerably faithful to the Institution, are lectured
with tremendous severity by this Irish brave, and are
reminded by him, with more vigor than modesty, of
their duties. They are told, in fact, that they lack
"pluck," which is, we suppose, the most mortal insult
which can be offered to your genuine Southron; that
until they come out boldly for piracy—that is for
what the civilized world has agreed to consider as
piracy—they are a set of wooden spoons, talking
much, it is true, about chivalry, but without one par-

ticle of chivalry in their composition. Such frank-
ness is delightful to us; but the slave-mongers of the
South, who have done their best to be bad, and have
honorably struggled to be models of inhumanity, may
think it a little unkind and altogether undeserved.

For our part, although South Carolina has small
love for us, we will not stand calmly by and hear her
thus slandered, without saying a good word in her
defense. We say plainly to John Mitchel, that he
does the slave-holder gross injustice. We do not believe that they lack a relish for piracy. On the contrary, we believe that they would engage in it with
commendable alacrity, if they thought that it would
pay expenses. They probably understand their own
business quite as well as Mr. John Mitchel understands it; and if they are satisfied that a given course
of action will not be profitable, they cannot be expected to engage in it simply to gratify him.

Mr. Mitchel propounds a theory of negro-importa-
tion in a gay, rollicking, humorous spirit, in which
the blood-thirstiness of the thug is agreeably dashed
with the overflowing humor of the Hibernian. He is
especially funny about the king of Ashantee, who has
a lot of " fine cheap fellows for sale," and Mr. Mitchel
proposes, in his light way, " to patronize the king of
Ashantee." He plants himself upon what he calls
" the human-flesh platform," and gloats and giggles
over his horrible theories, as we may imagine the
king of Dahomey dilating with rapture as he puts
the last skull upon one of his amiable pyramids. Well
is it to be merry and wise, but we suppose that we

must not blame this poor Exile of Erin for being merry, and otherwise. If a man must eat the bread of dependence, we will not grudge him the marmalade of merriment.

December 1, 1858.

FATHER LUDOVICO'S FANCY.

The Popes of Rome have accomplished some very tough and apparently hopeless work in their day; and this historical fact, we suppose, emboldened the present papal chairman, to lend his sanction—possibly without due consideration—to an enterprise apparently Utopian, which has been initiated in Naples. For there is in that charming city a certain Father Ludovico, a monk, who is highly zealous and particularly interested in the conversion of Ethiopia—it never having been the luck of the weak-minded Ludovico, to peruse those overwhelming ethnologico-theological exercitations manufactured by our divine Southrons, in which it is distinctly proved that, although " a nigger," whether he be or be not a human being, can " get religion," yet that it must be an inferior religion, not founded upon the intelligence of the professor, but something of the nitrous-oxyde description, inhaled by the sable convert, and making him " feel good," he knows not how or why. This process has, indeed, been found wonderfully effective; and we are not, therefore, startled to find our religious contemporary, *The North Carolina Presby-terian*, asking the masters of that State why, in the name of common sense and the very cheapest econ-omy, they do not stir up a revival; because, as *The Presbyterian* justly observes, "The market-value of a pious slave is greater than that of an impious one, while a lively faith improves his personal appear-ance"—plerophory being followed by pinguiosity, and solemnity by sleekness.

But the species of religion admired and cultivated in North Carolina, and especially in Rogersville, Tenn.,—where the sweet-souled Colonel Netherland gave his negro that beautiful basting behind the church, which, through these columns, has passed into history—this species is one which Father Ludovico does not appear to fancy. He clearly has not em-braced the American notion that a black body who cannot read his Testament, and to whom the hymn-book is a jumble of hieroglyphics—who has a good opinion of the Deity, but a much clearer one of his driver—who works out his salvation by spading and digging faster and more steadily than his profane fellows—who grows safely stupid as he grows sweetly saint-like—is as fit for heaven as circumstances will admit. On the contrary, the good Ludovico begins with the head, and so ingeniously works his way down to the heart. Nor does he shrink from solv-ing the problem under the most adverse circum-stances. He does not select negroes who have by contact caught a color of civilization, and who have been morally if not physically bleached.

Padre Ludovico sends for his negro-neophytes directly to Africa, and brings them, burned black by Equatorial suns, with skins of ebony, and blubber-lips, and frizzled-hair, and the Ebo shin so enlarged upon by General Wise—brings them to Naples ! He knows that the heads are rather hard, but he feels perfectly satisfied that if he can get anything into them, it will have small chance of getting out again. So Father Ludovico goes cheerfully to work with his black possibilities. He teaches them Latin, Italian, French and Arabic, adding to this polyglot process, instruction in geography, arithmetic, physics, chemistry and elementary geometry. Having thus trained these animals in secular accomplishments, he adds to their stock of knowledge "the doctrine of the Catholic Church," and sends them home to Christianize Africa. And very successful is the Father Ludovico with his animals, in spite of their facial angles and bone-bound brains. At a recent exhibition of the cultivated beasts, everybody was charmed ; the Cardinal-Archbishop of Naples was delighted ; the Prime Minister was in raptures, and "several other distinguished personages" were filled with admiration, as the achievements of Padre Ludovico quite overshadowed Mr. Rarey's equine triumphs, and plunged all previous monkey-trainers into oblivion and human contempt. And what Father Ludovico is doing, the Abbe Olivieri is also doing at Naples, for the negresses, so that when Africa is christianized, it seems highly probable that it will be done rather after the fashion of Rome, than the fashion of Rogersville, in the State of Tennessee.

We know that it is exceedingly wrong, although not quite so unpopular as it was two or three years ago, to say one word in praise of the Roman Church, or in extenuation of its alleged errors. But, whatever may be urged against it, nobody can dispute its boldness, and activity, and far-reaching sagacity. In the enterprise under consideration, we have another added to innumerable previous instances of its faith in human culture; a faith transcending the most recondite speculations of the ethnologist; the daintiest exegesis of our Doctors of Divinity; the most stalwart prejudices of the white race; a faith in the human soul and not a faith in this or that tint of epidermis.

To draw the conclusion of the congenital, hereditary and hopeless imbecility of a race, from that portion of it which, for more than a century, has been so busy in helping others that it has had no time to help itself—which has been systematically and perseveringly brutalized—which has been surrounded by the light of human civilization, and yet continually and cautiously blindfolded, is to blunder in the beginning, middle and end of the whole matter.

We hope the Presbyterian Church South, and all other Southern churches, will duly consider the example offered by the "Babylonian Dame." *Fas est ab hoste doceri*—it is just the thing to be taught by an opponent. We can imagine the surprise, and even the consternation, which would ensue, if the

3*

population of the quarter-houses should be summoned by the overseer—this one to receive a French grammar, and that, Lindley Murray, and the other, Malte-Brun. We would not plunge into the middle of things in such a reckless way, but would set out with due simplicity, with primers and pictures, and good serviceable horn-books. "But," interpose the Patriarchs, "teach them their letters, and they will all run away!" Well, if fit to run away, able to run away, and desirous of running away, why should they not run away?

February 2, 1859.

MR. CHOATE ON DR. ADAMS'S SERMONS.

THE Essex Street Church, in the city of Boston, enjoys the pastoral supervision of the Rev. Nehemiah Adams, D. D., and the distinguished confraternization of the Honorable Rufus Choate—a combination of felicities which hardly any ecclesiastical body of this age or of any country can boast. The twenty-fifth anniversary of the settlement of Dr. Adams was held last Monday evening, and Mr. Choate made a beautiful speech upon the occasion, in which he principally advised the congregation to study the Greek and Roman languages, and by no means to abstain from the perusal of Shakespeare. Passing to a consideration of the ministry of Dr. Adams, Mr. Choate declared that its chief charm for him had been, that the Doctor had never preached anything but pure and undefiled religion, and had never hurt the feelings of the Honorable Mr. Choate, who said :

"Never in an introductory prayer, never in a hymn, occasionally, or in the ordinary course of public worship, never by an illustration in any sermon, by any train of association, right or wrong, have I been carried back into the world that I had left."

From this it will be seen how exceedingly Mr. Choate has enjoyed his religion, and how much the church must have enjoyed him, and how perfectly serene everything must have been in Essex Street. This is why the Rev. Nehemiah Adams has been presented by his congregation with a piano-forte, valued at $400 ; and with $2,000 in hard. cash, and "other valuable articles." In truth, Mr. Choate argues the matter with great profundity. Hear him !

"The great concrete of practical politics, the workings of our special confederated system, the laws and conditions of our very artificial nationality, will he— the clergyman—permit me to enquire whether or not his deep studies, *aliunde et diverso intuitu*, have enabled him to know anything of them ?" That is to say, a clergyman may understand Shakespeare and should understand Greek and Latin, but politics he cannot understand. "He will," said Mr. Choate, "have learned from his Bible that the race of man is of kindred blood ; but he cannot know how far these glorious generalities are modified by civil society."

Mr. Choate is clearly advancing. Some years ago he discovered that the "generalities" of the Declara-

tion of Independence were glittering. And now he
has discovered that the generalities of the Holy Bible
are glorious. In fact, if we understand him at all,
he would cut off the clergyman from all interest in
human affairs, from all observation of a government,
without which there could be no churches and no religion, from a judicious direction of the political sym-
pathies and emotions of his parishioners, from all attempt to save them from passion and selfishness in
their politics, and from a bad conscience in their political relations. Now Mr. Choate has read more than
most men in history, as is evident enough from the
countless historical allusions which crowd his ora-
tions; and he knows that in no age at all remarkable
for spiritual progress and the development of religious liberty, have piety and politics submitted to the
divorce which he proposes. If we would have our
religion worth anything—if we would secure for it a
practical influence and a computable value—we can
no more separate it from our politics than we can
separate it from our domestic relations. If there be
in this question of Slavery no moral element—if it
be perfectly indifferent in the sight of God, whether
we are humane and brotherly and benevolent, or the
opposite, so we do but join the church of the Rev.
Dr. Adams—then Mr. Choate is right and his pastor
is right. But this is substantially suggesting that in
politics a man cannot go morally wrong. We have
hardly reached that point; but we cannot, of course,
keep pace with Mr. Choate. For it seems to us, that
if politics have invaded the pulpits of New England,

the invasion has been strictly limited to matters of common morals. By the discussion of these, we should be very sorry to have Mr. Choate disturbed.

April 2, 1859.

UNIVERSITY WANTED.

THE foundation of a seat of learning, in which for many successive generations the youth of a nation may learn the Greek and Latin languages, with a sprinkling of Conic Sections, and a mild flavor of Campbell's Rhetoric, is a matter which occupied the minds of our fathers, and not seldom appeals to the pockets of us, their degenerate descendants, inasmuch as it is the fashion, upon all possible occasions, in all proper and improper spots, to found what is called a University, and to invite juvenile aspirants to enter for the purpose of induction, deduction and seduction, within its thrice-consecrated walls. We are, therefore, not at all astonished to find *The Louisiana Democrat* declaring that the subject of " A Southern University" is now " engrossing the master-minds of the South," which means, of course, what it modestly declines to express, that it is universally engrossing the attention of the whole Southern intellect; for all Southern minds are well known to be master minds. Harvard is to be rivaled, and Yale is to be knocked into a common hedge-school. " The South," says *The Democrat*, " must establish a University where our sons can drink deeply." We believe that they have not drunk sparingly in those institutions of learning already established; but *The Democrat* does not allude to cock-tails and punches; for when it speaks of "drinking deeply," it refers to "the pure streams of learning." In favor of that particular tipple *The Democrat* is arguing.

"Where our sons," it goes on to say, "may drink deeply from the pure streams of learning, without imbibing the poisonous waters of bigotry and fanaticism—where the high-toned, chivalrous youth of this sunny land can receive the highest collegiate degrees without submitting to the galling restraints forced upon them in Northern institutions, by men who are at variance with their principles, and envious of their beautiful, luxurious and wealthy home."

Of course, it is necessary to have a college where there shall be no sunrise prayers and subsequent recitations; where the Commons table shall be adorned by early turtle and late lamb; where it is the prescribed privilege of Freshman and of Sophomore to pull the presidential nose, or to assault an offending tutor. It is a college in which every Freshman may be called to recitation by his private and personal Sambo, and may even employ a learned "nigger," if he can find one, to "coach" him through Euripides and Cicero. This is the college which is to knock into a sort of classical and mathematical Carthage, dear old Harvard and always respectable Yale, Dartmouth, which produced Rufus Choate, and all other Northern seminaries whatever. No wonder *The*

Louisiana Democrat looks forward to such a foundation "with pleasant emotions," and anticipates "a
new impetus to the science, learning and literature of
a great country."

A Southern University! What a pleasing notion!
How suggestive of exegesis, cumulative and conclusive, concerning Joseph, Abraham and Moses, Paul
and Onesimus, illustrating the true significance of
"*doulos*," and historically, critically and classically
proving that "a nigger" is not a white man—a position which, considering that nobody has disputed it,
our Southern philosophers seem to be over eager to
establish—bursting upon us with rekindling ethnological light, and sweetly and sagely conducting us to
a serene acquiescence in the sanctity of slaveholding!
This is what a Southern University would do; this
is why a Southern University should be established;
this is why our contribution to the scheme—one brass
cent—may be had by any person bringing the proper
certificate, upon call, at the counting-room of this
Journal.

April 22, 1859.

MR. POLLARD'S "MAMMY."

There are many instances of filial piety recorded,
and very properly recorded, in history. The reader
will please recall that which has most warmly touched
his sensibilities, or most closely captivated his memory
—of some Athenian son or Roman daughter, illustri-

ous for obedience or devotion—and when contemplation has warmed him into an admiration of the Ancients and an inclination to depreciate the Moderns,
we shall triumphantly bring forward Edward Pollard,
of Washington, in the District of Columbia, Esq., as
the champion, in this behalf, of the present day. Mr.
Pollard has printed a pamphlet in defence of the
proposition to re-open what may be most properly
called the African Man-trade. Of Mr. Pollard's arguments in this production we cannot speak, for
many reasons, the chief of which is that we have not
seen them. But what Mr. Pollard may think of the
slave-trade is of small consequence when compared
with his filial devotion; and the expression of that
feeling we have seen, for it has been disintegrated, if
we may say so, from the main work, and, in the highly
respectable character of an Elegant Extract, is now
making a fashionable tour through the newspapers.

We trust that the Reverend Doctor Adams has
seen this wandering small paragraph; that it has
rendered moist his venerable eyes, and warmed the
cockles of his ancient heart. For it appears that
when Mr. Edward Pollard was a boy, his father had
not merely the happiness to possess such a son, but in
addition to this blessing in tunics, Mr. Edward Pollard's father—not to put too fine a point upon it—
owned niggers. As Mr. Edward Pollard lives in
Washington, and is therefore, *prima facie*, an impoverished office-holder, the presumption is that the black
diamonds are no longer retained as heir-looms in the
Pollard family, but have been sold by papa Pollard,

and sent to enjoy themselves upon the sugar-planta-
tions, or to paddle and plash in the rice-swamps.
Edward Pollard, Esq., has therefore the inestimable
privilege of indulging in the Pleasures of Memory,
and the way in which he does it is creditable to his
heart. He sighs not for the stalwart field-hands,
worth one thousand dollars apiece; he mourns not
for the yellow hand-maidens with taper waists and
languishing eyes; he weeps not for the coachman
who guided his father's chariot; the laundress who
got up his infant linen; the cook who prepared the
domestic hominy; or the scullion who scrubbed the
ancestral floor.

From these treasures, worth, in the aggregate, a
very handsome sum of money, Edward Pollard, Esq.,
turns to drop a tear upon the grave of his " mammy."
" Mammy" was Edward Pollard's nurse. From the
sable heart of " mammy" he first drew his snowy sus-
tenance. In the dark arms of " mammy" he tasted
the titillation of his first dandle. From the black
hand of " mammy" he received his initial corn-cake.
Her voice chanted his vesper lullaby and summoned
him to his matin ablutions. Mr. Pollard " confesses "
—although, under the circumstances, we do not see
the necessity of the qualification—that he is not
ashamed of his affection for his " mammy." She died;
for all " mammies"—even the " mammy" of Mr. Pollard—were or are mortal. Then came her sepulchral
honors. Wiping the copious tears from his eyes, Mr.
Pollard informs us that " in his younger days" he
made " little monuments over the grave of his mam

my." How many he made he does not inform us. What material he used, we are not told; but we know that infant architects have a partiality for mud.

And now Mr. Pollard, discarding the sentimental, waxes savage. Standing over the grave of his "mammy," and suddenly getting angry without any apparent occasion, he cries: "Do you think I could ever have borne to see her consigned to the demon abolitionists?" There is really no need of all this vehemence. We perfectly understand the case. We appreciate Mr. Pollard's feelings. We know that he could not have borne it. For who then would have ministered to his necessities? Who would have darned his juvenile hose? Who would have rocked his cradle? Who would have "run to catch him when he fell, and kissed the place to make it well?" And, moreover, had "the demon abolitionists" caught Mr. Pollard's "mammy," he is perfectly certain that they would have "consigned her lean, starved corpse to a pauper grave." From which we infer that in addition to the mud memorials heretofore mentioned, as erected by Mr. Pollard, in the first gush of childhood's sorrow, he has since placed over the grave of "mammy" something very splendid in the way of a mausoleum. For, as we have already noticed, "mammy" is no more; and Edward Pollard, Esq., to use his own most charming language, can "only look at her through the mist of long years." She died without the aid, assistance or cruel commerce of "the demon abolitionists," and Mr. Pollard, who appears to be an elderly gentleman, has to pay a washing-bill every Saturday, and as he d—ns the laundress in respect of buttons, remembers "mammy" and conjures up the image of "the dear old slave." He recalls how, when his "mother" scolded him, his "mammy" protected and humored him; and seems, in his desolation to have come to the conclusion that this is rather a weary world. There appears to be nothing to do but to put Edward Pollard, Esq., out to nurse—dry-nurse or wet-nurse, according to circumstances—and to strive by every tender art to divert his mind from the distracting memory of the original "mammy." Of all the poor white people in Washington, he seems to be in the lowest spirits—if we except Mr. James Buchanan.

Whether the result of Mr. Edward Pollard's grief for his "mammy" will re-open the African Man-trade, is more than we can determine. The connection between his bereavement and that branch of commerce we have been somewhat at a loss to discover. We have been able to conclude only that there now exists at the South a dearth of "mammies," and that Mr. Pollard, having felt through long years the want of that most useful article, seeks to replenish the market by the importation of what we may call the raw material. Left himself an orphan in respect of "mammy," at a tender age, with his locks unkempt, with his face dirty, with his mouth pitifully gaping for gruel, and with his trousers torn, he looks forward to future Pollards—still, if we may use the figure, mere shrubs—in a like condition of emptiness and squalor. He seeks, like a true philanthropist, to provide for

their great want; and when the importation commences, "mammies" will, we suppose, be regularly
quoted in the Prices Current. Meanwhile, Mr. Pollard's case must be attended to by the charitable. A
pair of "mammies"—one for him and one for the
White House—should be purchased at once by a
subscription.

May 18, 1859.

A CHURCH GOING INTO BUSINESS.

YES, and such a business! None of your vulgar
huckstering! your piddler-pedlery! your small barter of such insignificant commodities as rice, cotton,
corn or tobacco! Had the General Assembly of the
Cumberland Presbyterian Church, which met at
Evansville, Indiana, on the 28th of May, A.D. 1859,
speculated in steamboats, or sold plantations, or
played bull or bear with dubious stocks, somebody
might have protested against making God's house a
house of merchandise; but the Assembly, jealous of
its dignity and emulous of ecclesiastical decorum,
traded in nothing meaner than men, and thus preserved from the scandal of a censorious world the
respectability of Cumberland Christianity. This is
more pleasing to the fastidious mind, because, as we
perceive, a decent demeanor before the world is rigidly
inculcated by the Cumberland creed, the professors
of which were warned by the Moderator, just before

the adjournment, " to walk circumspectly before the
community in which they were sojourning." This
Mentor might, indeed, have used the spirited words
of General Bombastes Furioso: "Adieu, brave army!
don't kick up a row." He did, indeed, with charming modesty, remind the General Assemblers, that
they were " the light of the world," and he, we presume, may be regarded in some sort, as a pair of
snuffers, charged with the responsible duty of keeping the wicks clean from death's-heads and climbers.
We suppose that his advice was heeded, and that the
reverend members smoked their cigars and took their
toddies discreetly; for we do not hear of any of them
in the calaboose — and now for the mercantile speculation of the Cumberland Church!

It seems that Brother Davis, late the Treasurer of
the Assembly, is no more, he having yielded to the
Great Extinguisher sometime ago. The Cumberland
Christians could have borne their bereavement with
tolerable equanimity, if Brother Davis, in the hurry
of his departure, had not forgotten to settle his
accounts, and had remembered to leave money
enough behind him to discharge a balance against
him. To speak plainly, although it is painful so to
speak, Brother Davis died a defaulter; and the Trus-
tees, as became faithful stewards, forthwith took out
that carnal weapon called a writ; secured that
worldly result, a judgment; and, finally, obtained
against Brother Davis's Administrator that persuasive document styled an execution. But an execution against a dead Treasurer, even of the Cumber-

land Presbyterian Church, is of small value, unless
the sheriff can find something satisfactory whereupon to levy. So that officer, casting about, discovered a small lot of "niggers" formerly the property
of Brother Davis, which the Administrator had put
out of his possession by some kind of hugger-mugger,
but which he disgorged, so to speak, upon receiving
a bond of indemnity. Then the General Assembly
of the Cumberland Presbyterian Church went into
market overt, with its little flock of niggers, and
did, with many invocations, we suppose, of God's
blessing on the transaction, dispose of the same at
public vendue, and receive the consecrated cash
therefor.

The affair, however, is not yet comfortably settled.
The Administrator threatens an action. The Widow
Davis threatens another action. So that the pur-
chase-money remains in the ark of the tabernacle,
nor will it be safe for the Assembly to spend a dime
of it until all manner of courts of common law and
eke of equity, have passed a great variety of decrees,
issued a large assortment of injunctions, received
various verdicts, listened to many a long-drawn pleading and prosy argument, and increased the sheaf of
rebutters and rejoinders, sur-rebutters and sur-rejoin-
ders, to gigantic proportions ; and as these luxuries
of the law are expensive, it is not improbable — we
say it dolorously — that every individual "nigger"
will be used up in fees, retainers and other costs,
before the affair is terminated.

And what then will become of the missionary work

of the Cumberland Presbyterian Assembly? For, be it known to the reader, that, when the Assembly had completed this small transaction, and run off its stock of human beings at tolerably high rates, it solemnly dedicated the net proceeds to the missionary cause. We do not know in what particular part of the world it is proposed to oblige Heaven and favor Christianity, by the noble expenditure of this money; but for once, we hope that the obdurate King of the Cannibal Islands will be left to his fate, and that the Cumberlander will remember that charity begins at home. As these fortunate " niggers " have been permitted, by the wisdom of the Cumberland Church, to devote themselves to the work of extending the arena of the faith, they should at least have the chance of reaping some benefit, personally, from the transaction; so that, when Kentucky has been thoroughly Christianized and converted, at their personal expense, they may receive, as the result of their devotion, fewer floggings and fuller fare.

But, we ask with great deference, must it not be to each of these favored bondsmen a source of pure and proud satisfaction to know that, in the providence of God, they, the lowly, the oppressed, and the degraded, have been permitted to become living sacrifices upon the altar of the Cumberland faith? When one of them shall see a new pine steeple glittering with fresh and radiant paint, as it shoots into the air, he may take off his hat, if he have one, and exclaim : " That is my leg !" When a precious pentecostal season arrives, and the crop of Cumberland

Christians is fast ripening for a glorious harvest, how pleasing it will be for one of the Presbytery's negroes to cry: "Behold the work of these ten stubbed fingers and of these brawny arms! I am Paul and Apollos—behold the glorious increase which God has given!"

Here, then, is another evidence of the unnumbered blessings of Slavery! Which one of all of us, fervid as may be our devotion, and tender as may be our sympathy with the benighted and gall-embittered world, will do for the Great Cause what these Kentucky negroes will do? When the clinking boxes are going up and down the aisles, and with much fervor and noise we deposit our sixpences and shillings, we undoubtedly experience a thrill of satisfaction at our own generosity, and are much soothed by the calm approbation of our own consciences. But who of us would be willing to mount the auction block, and to listen to the "going, going," until we finally heard that we were "gone?" Where is the pious and portly pillar of some prosperous Cumberland church who, as the doxology ended, would not feel uncomfortable upon being told that the missionary cause required his sale, incontinently, and that he must, instead of going home to the piping-hot joint and subsequent pudding, be disposed of to the highest bidder? Would he not protest? And if he should swear a little, do you think the Recording Angel would use indelible ink? So selfish, so shrinking from self-devotion, so mindful of our own ease, so careless of the souls of our brethren, does this

pernicious freedom make us ! Whereas, we suppose
that these poor negroes submitted to their fate without a murmur, and blessed the pious hands which
felt their muscles and saw the light of Christian love
in the eyes which examined their teeth. Some natural tears, perhaps, they shed as they marched from
home, or from all of home which they had possessed;
but a couple of prayers, or a hymn or two, made
everything serene, and they submitted to their destiny
with all the sweetness of religious resignation.

But, as we have said, the final disposition of the
sacred funds is yet uncertain. The Cumberland General Assembly is holding on with faithful tenacity;
but the heirs of the defaulting Treasurer are still
active. If, then, holy negroes should by and by learn
that they have not so much benefited the church as
the lawyers, the information may cost them a pang.
We are afraid that they will be apt to consider themselves wasted and squandered. If we ever hear of
the end of this matter, we shall take the liberty of
informing our readers.

June 13, 1859.

A NEW LAUGHING-STOCK.

REALLY, the gods are good. If Pan is sometimes,
as during the present season, a little niggardly, or
red-eyed Mars unusually rampant, have we not always
Momus with us, and reason to bless the sensitive divin-

4

ities that banished him from Olympus? What an intolerable world this would be, if all the fools were out of it! But we need not fear for the succession, while the sunny sections of this confederacy continue to produce such a crop of choice ones, born to the motley. The last and finest fool who has wandered here, is an ancient gentlemen from New Orleans — a certain General Palfrey — who left Massachusetts half a century ago, and who came to Boston to celebrate the last Fourth of July. Had he but made his festive and anniversary visit sooner, he might have eaten dinner at the Revere House with the Hon. Benjamin F. Hallet, and filled himself at that peripatetic and perennial fountain of dish-water. Had he even given notice of his intention of visiting Boston, different arrangements might have been made. Unfortunately, his guide took him to the Music Hall. Unfortunately, Mr. George Sumner was the Orator of the Day. Unfortunately, Mr. George Sumner did not know that the New Orleans gentleman was in the house, and so missed the opportunity of gratifying an illustrious personage. Unfortunately, Mr. Sumner, instead of spouting in a safe and general way, after the old fashion, discussed freely and earnestly the Dred Scott decision, and did not speak in very affectionate terms of Mr. Chief Justice Taney. To this, General Palfrey was obliged to listen. His too officious friends had probably conducted him to a front seat, so that egress would have been difficult; and pleased or displeased, he was compelled to stay.

If Mr. George Sumner had been speaking in New

Orleans, or even in Washington, the General might
have silenced him by knocking him down ; but such
an experiment, however sweet, safe and effectual elsewhere, would have been a perilous one in Boston.
So the martial veteran was forced to keep quiet.
We do not understand why he did not go into convulsions. His escape from apoplexy appears to us
little short of miraculous. But he did escape, and
the oration delivered, went down to Faneuil Hall,
with a sour stomach and a feeble appetite for his
dinner. Here he masticated in grim wrath until
somebody gave, as a toast, " Cotton Cloth," or " Cotton Culture," or " Cotton Gins," or " Cotton Hats,"
or " Cotton Something," and the company called
upon General Palfrey to respond. He arose. He
pulled out the plug—if we may use the expression
—and deluged the company with molten lava. He
relieved himself. " He thought," says the report,
" that it was rather hard to be invited to a celebra-
tion for the purpose of *hearing* the laws of the United
States trampled under foot." He considered Mr.
Sumner's oration ill-timed, and " he was not afraid
to say so." Of course he was not afraid. He knew
how perfectly safe he was in Boston. He knew that
no tar-pot was bubbling in the neighborhood. He
knew that the company would keep their feathers to
sleep upon. He knew that no bludgeon would drum
a retaliating tattoo upon his reverberating cranium.
He knew that no committee would wait upon him
and warn him to leave Boston within twelve hours.
Of course he was not afraid.

But suppose that at a Fourth of July dinner in New Orleans, some ardent New Englander, having listened to a spicy and spasmodic attack upon his opinions, or to some concentrated sneer at the home of his love and honor, should dare to rise and to retort. Imagine the riot! Picture the excitement! Think of the glassy shower thickening around those fated brows! What meetings would there be! What ardent and active committees! What thunderous resolutions! With what rapidity would the imprudent Norman be hurried from the dinner-table to the jail, and from the jail to the railway station! Nay, the unfortunate offender might fare worse. His house might be ransacked and his shop plundered; his family might be insulted, or might read in the morning papers that its head had been hung from a lamp-post, or that the pistol or the knife had done the work of the halter.

Oh, it is all very well for some wandering patriarch, the owner of a score or two of black men, when he comes within our borders, to assert and to exercise freedom of speech in a way which makes us very sick, if it does not make us very savage. We must sit and quietly listen while some inane babbler blasphemes our religion, sneers at our policy, questions our patriotism, distorts our motives, and insults our common-sense. It has not occurred, thus far, to these tindery folks, that their blundering nonsense is as disagreeable to us, especially upon the Fourth of July, as the plainest Anti-Slavery discourse could possibly be to them. That is because we do not employ their own practical and unscrupulous method of protest. That is because, when we are insulted, we keep our tempers, and too often hold our tongues.

We suppose that this singular lack of common courtesy, this disinclination to take what they are so willing to give, exhibited by Southern men frequently upon occasions in themselves insignificant, may be attributed to a certain brutality of intellect, to be observed also in some of the lower forms of animal life. The old gentleman who made such a distressing show of himself in Faneuil Hall is not to be despised, for he is a human being. Foolish and weak as he is, he is still " a man and a brother." If Providence has not bestowed upon him the ordinary intelligence of humanity, or if his opportunities have been so limited that he cannot deport himself decorously at a civilized dinner-party, we should regard this Thracian as we do the inmates of a lunatic asylum, or of a school for feeble-minded youth. No moral law commands us, however, not to laugh at him in our sleeves ; and if such law existed, it would not be respected. But we will be contented with a quiet giggle. When a bull-dog has lost all his teeth, he may growl as deeply as he pleases. When he has not lost his teeth ; when he can bite as well as snarl, and proposes to exercise the biting faculty upon our calves, it may not be amiss to brain him. But an ancient Tray, like General Palfrey, should be privileged to go through the whole gamut of growls, and, to vary the performance, if he pleases, by a solfeggio of snarls.

This view of the matter seems to have been that of the Fancuil Hall committee. General Palfrey was, after all, not angry enough to run away without finishing his dinner — he was too old a dog for that — so that after the repast was over, and people were deserting the banquet-hall, a small sort of a lawyer got upon his legs and "proposed a toast complimentary to the General." Then somebody called for the inevitable three cheers. Then others shook the General by the hand, so that he went back to his tavern quite mollified, and reassured that there was still a little dough left in Boston. We think that herein the more sagacious spirits of the company pursued a judicious course. Had General Palfrey ambled away in his wrath, nobody can tell how the trade of Boston might have suffered. And if there was policy in these little attentions, there was also humanity. This native of Boston was spared the pain of feeling that flunkeyism had altogether died out in the city of his nativity; and he will return to his crescent home to tell his neighbors that while the public men of New England are hopeless traitors, the gentlemen who eat the public dinners are not bad fellows to break bread with after all.

July 11, 1859.

A CUMBERLAND PRESBYTERIAN NEWSPAPER.

WE have recently printed in these columns several articles upon the newspaper press of the South and West, and have amused ourselves, if not our readers, by a little off-hand dissection of what may be properly termed the morbid anatomy of journalism. We have observed in these sheets almost incredible ignorance, and certain radical vices, which are more to be deplored than an innocent disregard of the rules of taste and of grammar. In the course of our researches, we are sorry to say that we have found the secular papers, in the cheap qualities of good nature, good sense and veracity, far in advance of those which are printed avowedly for the promotion of the Christian religion ; and of all the sacred emissions which we have had the misfortune to notice, we think *The St. Louis Observer* to be the most curiously unenlightened and the most miraculously illiterate.

The Observer is the organ of the Cumberland Presbyterian Church—a considerable society, numbering many professors in Kentucky, Indiana and Missouri. It was this Cumberland Presbyterian Church which, when its treasurer died a defaulter, sold his negroes upon an execution, and then voted the money to the cause of missions ! Upon this pious vendue *The Tribune* made a few comments which have not met with the approbation of *The St. Louis Observer*, we are sorry to say ; which have, in fact, excited the choler of that meek and lowly publication to a degree quite incompatible with coherence.

We find, indeed, in the rantipole observations of *The Observer*, no attempt at a denial, but an extenuation of the facts upon which our remarks were based. The "niggers" were sold: the church took the money: the church voted the cash to the missionary cause. We should have been glad of a plain refutation of the whole tale, and should unquestionably have been gratified in this regard, if the facts had not been too patent to be concealed by the utmost prodigality of falsehood; if the Rev. Milton Bird, (O musical name!) who is the editor of *The Observer*, had not known that mendacity would only make matters worse, by giving the children of sin and unrighteousness an opportunity of showing to an uncharitable world, that some Cumberland Presbyterians to the solace of man-selling join the luxury of lying.

The Observer, leaving the matter of the man-vendue as it was, we are at liberty and leisure to luxuriate to fatness—if laughing will make one fat—upon the extraordinary literary performance of the Reverend Milton Bird, who is jealous of other birds, and declares, that our article was manufactured at the suggestion "of some buzzard about Evansville." The actual expression of the Rev. M. B. is coarser than this, but as we only print a secular newspaper, we cannot afford to be as free in our speech as a Cumberland Presbyterian when he denounces what he calls "the intermeddling of ungodly men."

The Reverend Bird, *imprimis*, remarks that this journal is "like an irritable hedge-hog rolled up the wrong way, and pierced by its own prickles." Good

— metaphorically and zoologically good! It is then emphatically stated by the gentle Bird that "we deserve to be skinned with a hackle, and smeared with aqua-fortis." Probably. And yet it would be painful. We are thankful, therefore, when *The Observer* of St. Louis — we were at first fearful that Brother Bird would be here immediately with the necessary implement and fluid—we are thankful, we say, when *The Observer* had the goodness to observe: "But we forbear!" Only he does n't forbear. He immediately calls somebody in Evansville, Ind., "a pole-cat." Also "a buzzard." Likewise "a cynic." And to conclude, "yellow-eyed." "A cynical pole-cat" crossed upon "a yellow-eyed buzzard," would produce a treasure indeed for a meandering menagerie.

The Reverend Milton Bird, after these trifling indulgences in epithet, grows " 'umble" after the manner of Mr. Uriah Heep; for, crooking the hinges of his knees, he expresses himself piously, as follows: "We trust in God to keep us humble, and give us a spirit of forbearance and kindness towards those who injure us." We say "Amen!" The Rev. Bird has evidently a very high idea, if not of the goodness, at least of the omnipotence of the Creator. Meanwhile, the humility not having arrived, the Bird continues to be slightly abusive and boldly figurative in its song. We are told that *The Indiana American* and and *The Tribune* have "to the utmost of their bilious capacity, discharged the pent-up contents of their gorged livers." Excellent again! We are get-

4*

ting stronger and stronger ! All who do not see the propriety of supporting missions by selling "niggers," are declared to be "violent, bitter, selfish, and in a morbid, unbalanced, disordered state of mind," "pouring out slime, gall and vinegar " "But let us pray for our traducers and persecutors," says *The Observer*, suddenly changing its tone, "that they may repent of their sin and find forgiveness, and escape the doom of all liars (here the ferocity breaks out again), "who have their part in the lake that burneth with fire and brimstone." We do not object to being made the theme of good men's prayers, but if the Reverend Milton Bird will be kind enough not to pray for us, and if he will mention our wish to the other members of the Cumberland Presbyterian Church, we shall not only feel much obliged, but more comfortable.

The Reverend Milton Bird then proceeds to communicate to us the following information : "The Gospel wages no war on the external organism of society." Ah, indeed ! The Gospel wages no war then against crime in its manifold forms—no war against covetousness and greed—no war against the selfish policy of tyrants, whether crowned or mere whip-crackers and "nigger"-drivers—no war against brothels and gambling hells and grog-shops—no war against infidelity to marriage vows or the theft of woman's chastity—no war against that man who though cased in a legal panoply, treads under foot the widow and the orphan—no war against the world —no war against the flesh—only war against the ridiculous unwillingness of sundry reprobate human beings to join the Cumberland Presbyterian Church! And the Rev. Milton Bird thinks that in this view of the duty of a church, he is sustained by the Apostle Paul! We know that it is a vain wish, but would that we could see the Great Missionary to the Gentiles and the Reverend Milton Bird face to face for a few moments! We can fancy the Saint of St. Louis opening his pocket-testament and airing a little text from Ephesians, another small scrap from Romans, another small scrap from Colossians, a fourth bit from Timothy and a morsel from Peter: but no mortal mind can conceive the terror of the rebuke which would cause the Reverend Milton Bird to howl with repentant anguish, and to request the favor of a small mountain to cover him.

The audacity of such men as he is, must be an apology for the introduction of such an illustration. Poor praters, they know not of what—coarse, unenlightened gabblers of sublime teachings, very dear to the heart of humanity—polluting with the unsavory messes of social shame and sin the golden vessels of the altar—making the Father's house a house of merchandize and a den of thieves — encouraging mockery, exciting skepticism and confirming unbelief —narrow, without pity, and zealous, without brains; there is nothing for it, but to leave them to the bitter laughter of the satirist and the unspeakable commiseration of the wise. Grace may indeed supply the deficiencies of the mere intellect, while the heart remains tender; but what grace can rescue him whose heart grows hard as his head grows soft, and who increases in selfishness as he decreases in intelligence ?

July 25, 1859.

NIL NISI BONUM.

THE old and amiable rule of speaking only with kindness of the dead, is one which, in this world of small comity, we have no wish to disregard ; although it is one the final violation of which is simply a question of time and the natural result of historic doubts. All character is dubious. There may be those who with perfect honesty do not admire Fenelon, and do admire Diderot or Voltaire. Indeed, it is only when a human career is closed that we are in a position to estimate its value, purport and upshot. The public life of a public man is public property. We may not indecently hasten to draw his frailties from their drear abode ; but the mere fact that he has gone to that account to which indeed the meanest and most magnificent natures must go, certainly affords no authority for slandering the living. If the late Mr. Rufus Choate, while he succeeded as *nisi prius* lawyer, failed as a statesman, we do not know that this gives Mr. Edward Everett, who has also failed as a statesman, the right to stand in Faneuil Hall and to censure to the best of his not inconsiderable ability, those who have been more fortunate. Mr. Choate may "have had little fondness for political life, and no aptitude whatever for the out-door management, for

the electioneering legerdemain, for the wearisome
correspondence with the local great men, and the
heart-breaking drudgery of franking cart-loads of
speeches and public documents to the four winds,
which are necessary at the present day to great success in a political career." "Still less," Mr. Everett
went on to say, "was he adroit in turning to some
personal advantage whatever topic happens to attract
public attention — fishing with ever freshly-baited
hook in the turbid waters of ephemeral popularity."

If such language as this should fall from a young
man just entering upon public life—from a young
man hoping to be representative, or senator, or president—we might consider such an expression of opinion to be at once candid and courageous ; but coming from an old man—from one well versed in the
arts which he denounces—the " electioneering legerdemain," " the wearisome correspondence with local
great men," " the heart-breaking drudgery of franking cart-loads of speeches and public documents "—
from one who if he has not been " adroit in turning
to personal advantage topics happening to attract
public attention," has not been averse to the attempt
—coming from such a man may not these opinions
and their somewhat querulous expression be rather
the result of disappointment than of any peculiar
public purity. We do not know anybody who has
written more " letters to local great men " than Mr.
Everett, and some of these which we have seen were
so full of feeble complaint that they would ill bear
publication. We do not know anybody who in his

day was more willing to improve topics "happening to attract public attention."

Everybody will remember that when fillibustering "happened" to be in fashion, Mr. Everett was a fine fillibuster. Everybody who heard it will remember the Plymouth speech, in which Mr. Everett declared that "the work must go on," by which he meant, that the "manifest destiny" of the United States was to conquer and annex the kingdoms and republics of South America. Everybody who ever heard of it, will remember how Mr. Everett subscribed for the Sumner testimonial, and how he afterwards attributed the indiscretion to illness. Surely no gentleman whose personal history is crowded with incidents like these, is in a position to sneer at "the distinguished active statesmen of the day." Nor did the memory of Mr. Choate require any such apology. A lawyer in great practice, exceedingly devoted to his profession, and relying upon its emoluments to meet a personal expenditure which was always large and frequently improvident, he preferred to give his time snatched from the duties of the bar to liberal studies, or to the preparation of "discourses on academic occasions." And because he did so, and trusted to the wise instincts of his nature—because he knew himself, as others knew him, to be in place rather in the court-room, than in the senate-chamber—it does not follow that other men with a more positive taste and talent for public employment, were either his moral or his intellectual inferiors.

Moreover, if his political aspirations had been never

so ardent, he entertained fatal opinions, which in the heat and hurry of his speech he continually betrayed. If he cared for any democracy, it was the old democracy of Athens. If he believed in any constitution, it was in the unwritten constitution of Great Britain. He sneered at the Declaration of Independence. He girded and jibed at the most limited alliance between humanity and politics. Slavery is the surest touchstone of political character at the present time, and the test was fatal to Mr. Choate. He thought to be enslaved was the best for the blacks, and that to enslave them was the best for the whites. The people of Massachusetts were not of his mind; but we will do him the justice to say, that for the opinion of the people of Massachusetts he cared very little. There was an inherent love of paradox in his nature, which a long practice in the courts did not, of course, diminish. Clear-headed men were not deceived by the fulmination or the fulgidities of his rhetoric. He was careless of personal consequences, and would at any time risk success for the sake of startling. In avoiding political duties or in unfitting himself to discharge them—in suffering himself to drift into the turbid and alien waters of sham-democracy — in seeking with scoffs and sneers to silence the discussion of great questions — in timidly avoiding the conflict when danger was at its height, Mr. Choate did nothing worthy of imitation or eulogy.

We are not permitted to avoid the duty of saying all this thus plainly, but the responsibility of any pain which we may give to any honest admirer of

Mr. Choate, must be borne by his Faneuil Hall Eulogist. It is better that we and those who are of our mind should be thought harsh or unfeeling, than that the young men of America should be made to believe that this life which has now closed affords them the best example—that the syren sentences of Mr. Everett should mislead them from the path of public duty— that his example and his words should beguile them into an avoidance of their political responsibilities, into a contempt for the theories, or an admiration for the general practice of our government; into lives secluded, sybaritical, and proudly, boastingly shallow and useless. The times are full of great occasions, and suggest great duties to the sinewy and courageous nature. We can spare something of scholarship, something of intellectual elegance, something of fastidious taste; but too many noble minds have already been smitten, too many lives once full of promise have been wasted; our short history already records too many tragedies for the sensitive, and too many comedies even for the most inveterate satirist.

July 29, 1859.

TWO TOMB-STONES.

As a general rule, human beings in selecting the rewards of their own labor prefer cash to tomb-stones —a fact which Mr. Thomas Moore noticed in his monody on the death of Sheridan. If a master mechanic should assemble his journeymen-carpenters, and should say to them : " My dear fellows and devoted friends ! I have noticed the extreme vigor with which you plane and the splendor of your sawing, and how charmingly you hit the nails on their heads. I shall not insult you by offering you money, which you would only foolishly squander if I should give it to you ; but I have determined, if you will only work for me during your natural lives, and work well and not grumble, to give to each of you the prettiest grave-stone in the world, with the most flattering inscriptions setting forth your many virtues, and particularly how you cheerfully worked for me without making any charge therefor. All of which, I doubt not, will be satisfactory to your ingenuous minds." Our own impression is that the famous hammerers and dexterous sawyers would decline the offer as one unsuited to their modest taste.

At the South, however, and under the beautiful influences of the institution, it seems to be different —a grave-stone being the great object of life with the faithful African. At least such appears to be the opinion of *The Fayetteville* (N. C.) *Observer.* The editor of that newspaper recently had occasion to go into a grave-yard, doubtless for purposes of moral reflection and philosophical study, and while there he actually discovered in the corner allotted to slaves, "two marble tomb-stones." What proportion these "two" monumental wonders bore to the undistinguished resting-places of less fortunate chattels, we are not told ; but they so attracted the attention of this able editor, that he immediately went home and wrote a leading-article on the subject, headed, "What is African Slavery?" He seems to have come to the sage conclusion, that whereas the system allows an occasional grave-stone to a departed slave, it is altogether a beautiful system, to be sustained by the united intellectual, moral and political energies of the Republic. He writes, evidently, upon the presumption that free negroes never have their mortal lives cheered by the prospect of monuments after death, and that they must therefore be unhappy—a grave-stone being the one thing worth living for, or rather worth dying for. His dilations upon these points are charmingly humane and sympathetic.

Tomb-stone No. 1 was erected "by the mistress of the family over the remains of a most valuable servant and friend, and it bore the inscription, "MY OWN GOOD LUCY." There is consideration, there is loving requital for you! Twenty, perhaps thirty, it may have been fifty years of chamber-work or of kitchen-work, of dress-making or of hair-dressing, of daily obedience and of hourly devotion; and when the wearisome toil is over, and the faithful feet can no longer come at call, and the loyal hands can no longer minister, all this service is repaid by a place in the back settlements of the cemetery, and an epitaph of the Lydia Languish description! Ample reward! Who would not have been "My Own Good Lucy," "most valuable" (say $1,000) before death, and so sincerely (we have no doubt) lamented afterwards. There has been nothing like it since Byron gave his dog a monument at Newstead. No wonder the Fayetteville man did write his touching article to let a weeping world know all about "My Own Good Lucy."

Tomb-stone No. 2 was inscribed: "UNCLE HARRY. MARK THE PERFECT MAN!" Now, we are at a loss to decide what this inscription means. Does it refer to "Uncle Harry" physically? Was he what a dealer would pronounce "sound" and A1 for the New Orleans market? We suppose not, for he is spoken of by *The Observer* as "an old man." He was a Baptist. He could read his Bible, and he did read it. It is also mentioned that his wife was "an excellent cook"—a remarkable combination of merits in "one lot!" Whether "the excellent cook," if dead, has a grave-stone, or, if living, a fair prospect of that ornamental remembrance to solace her stewing and boiling labors, we are not informed.

Such stuff as this *The Fayetteville* (N. C.) *Observer* prints is always caught up by the dough press, and especially by the dough-religious press, and is paraded ostentatiously as if it really meant something. So far as it goes towards proving anything touching the slave system, its good influence upon the master, its justice to the slave, its information is worse than useless, for it deludes some honest, well-meaning and weak people out of the common sense with which the institution should be considered. Nobody says that there are not benevolent masters. Nobody says that there are not contented slaves. Nobody says that there are not individual cases in which the relation is a happy one.　But nobody upon the authority of these isolated instances, appealing to sensibility rather than sense, should judge of a system which must be theoretically bad, and is known to be bad in practice.

September 1, 1859.

THE PERILS OF PEDAGOGY.

MR. CROAKER, in a chronic condition of alarm, lends to one of Goldsmith's comedies much of its vivacity and mirth; and the dreadful fright of a certain Mr. Matthews, member of the Virginia Legislature, is comic enough to temper the austerities of the recent tragedy.　We knew that John Brown would be a name wherewithal to conjure several generations of undutiful infants into obedience at bed-time, just as it has jostled children of larger growth into unwinking watchfulness, and scared the Commander of the Crustacea into unoyster-like volubility.　The fearful forebodings of our Virginian friends do not surprise us. It is perfectly natural for them to dread the spontaneous combustion of *The Tribune* in their post-offices —the explosion of infernal machines in their cellars —poison in the kitchen, or rifle-balls flying through the drawing-room windows.　Sir Boyle Roche regarded it as one of the principal perils of the Irish Rebellion that gentlemen might any morning awake with their throats cut; and the apprehensions of the

Virginian chevaliers — not to mention particularly those of their wives,—must be inconsistent with balmy and restorative slumber. Under such perilous circumstances, no vigilance, however suspicious, can be thought untimely; nor is it strange, while others are fearful of death in the pot, that the Hon. Mr. Matthews should fear death in the primer. Such, it appears, is precisely the nature of his apprehension. He dreads not only New Englanders, but the gifts they bring with them; he distrusts alike their reading-books and their rifles; their spelling-books and their swords; their penmanship and their pistols. The Hon. Mr. Matthews, having directed his mind to the philosophy of education, has discovered that there is a constitutional as well as an unconstitutional way of teaching the mystery of " a, b, ab ;" that rebellion may be fomented by the words which signify to be, to do, or to suffer; and that fire and slaughter may lurk in the Rule of Three. So the Hon. Mr. Matthews, no doubt after profound and unutterable pondering, has offered in the Virginia Legislature a Resolution—a startling Resolution—a very remarkable Resolution. Here it is :

" *Resolved,* That the Committee of Schools and Colleges inquire into the expediency of reporting a bill, prohibiting School Commissioners throughout the Commonwealth from subscribing to any teacher, male or female, who hails from the North of Mason and Dixon's line, unless they shall have resided in the State of Virginia for at least ten successive years previous."

The fact that Mr. Matthews should consider such a motion as this necessary to the salvation of the State, would seem to show that Northern teachers, whether male or female of sex, are rather a formidable body in Virginia. May we be permitted, without violating any moral, political or religious law, to ask, humbly, of course, and only honestly seeking information, how it has happened that Virginia, having children to teach, has fallen into the egregious error of sending abroad for teachers? Why have not native acquirements been respected? Why have native talents been left unemployed? Why has the infant population of that enlightened State been committed to the tender mercies of Yankee school-marms? Why has she permitted the unholy hands of "servile" New England pedagogues to box the ears of her children, or to apply the tingling birch to the tenderer portions of their constitutions? While protecting bivalves, why has the Governor of that State neglected her boys? What is a steam-packet running to France in comparison with well-educated girls? Was ever such fatuity? Where were the native, well-born, orthodox teachers "hailing from *south* of Mason and Dixon's line"—good, safe, responsible guides in petticoats or pantaloons, with sound Constitutional principles and proper views of the Christian religion?

We have heretofore thought that a demand in the market indicated a dearth. But Gov. Wise knows better the resources of his State than we do. He knows that it is needless for Virginia to send to the North for gifted persons to teach the steps of a quad-

rille, the value of a semi-breve, the art of embroider-
ing, or the mysteries of water-colors. He is a miraculous arithmetician, but he has fellow-citizens who
can cipher as well as he. Does he absorb all the
grammatical knowledge of the State? And if he can
so bravely brandish that celebrated weapon, known
as the Sword of Virginia, has he not fellow-citizens
capable of flourishing the instrument of flagellation,
and of long experience in the art of chastisement?
But perhaps we do not do justice to the Honorable
Matthews and the Honorable Wise. We ought certainly to take into consideration the recorded opinion
of the philosopher last named. He has made innumerable discoveries; and one of them, we believe, is
the vanity of all human knowledge. He is dubious
in respect of reading, and he regards writing with
distrust. In that Public School System which others
have weakly respected as the safe-guard of society, he
sees only danger to the Republic. He despises books.
He loathes newspapers. He believes in good, safe,
sound, substantial ignorance, with the same fervor
with which less enlightened men have regarded human knowledge. He sees in human culture only
human misery. He is the legitimate successor of
Mr. John Cade.

Now there may be those who look upon these opinions of Gov. Wise with horror or contempt; but he
shall not lack in these columns defense, or at least
extenuation. He is, we confess, our model slaveholder. If Slavery is to be perpetuated—if God, the
Bible, the laws, public policy, political economy, all

demand its continuance—then ignorance, no matter how dark or how deep it may be, is bliss, and wisdom is folly. Why should a man-owner be well-educated? Will mental cultivation make him a better driver, a better breeder, a better bargainer when he has occasion to sell women or to buy men? Why should he industriously acquire a refinement which will unfit him for the sterner duties of his daily life?

A man may be a capital task-master—an adept in flogging, and a connoisseur in pickling, without being a Bachelor of Arts. A mistress in Virginia, although she may be incapable of mental exertion, may thank fortune for her imbecility, for she can bear with patience wrongs and falsehood which would drive a cultivated woman to insanity. There is a certain redeeming fascination even in a consistency of crimes. If we were in Virginia, compelled to witness every hour the crowding evidences of human folly—the legalized negation of all that rescues our common nature from contempt—the ambition to win all things without the resolution to win them by earnest effort—the folly which supposes that violent passions have power to repeal the laws of nature—we would ask of Providence if by no miracle wrong could be remedied and right established, that we might partake of the besotted destiny of our neighbors, and might forget forever that we were not made like the beasts that perish. To this condition Gov. Wise would reduce his fellow-creatures, black and white, in Virginia. He is right. If black men are to remain beasts, it must be upon the condition that white men shall share the bestiality.

January 10, 1860.

JOSIAH'S JAUNT.

VARIOUS forms of polite invitation are upon record, such as, " Will you come to the bower I have shaded for you ?" " Will you walk into my parlor ?" as the spider said to the fly. " Will you come and take tea in the arbor ?" etc., etc. Another matter of momentous importance, to be discussed and decided only in full family Sanhedrim, is whether the Smiths shall be asked and the Browns shut mercilessly out. But it is a still more solemn affair when a Sovereign State wishes to give a party, to determine upon the choicest and most enticing formulas of bidding, as well as the particular guests to be bidden ; and we cannot, therefore, pretend to estimate the gratitude which Massachusetts should feel for Mr. Josiah Perham, who may be called the Brown of International Visiting, and whose exploits in the department of public festivity are worthy of this particular mention. Three ideas, it would appear, have entered the brain of Josiah, viz. :

1. Massachusetts and Virginia are not upon thee-and-thou terms ; 2. If Virginia would but pay Massachusetts a visit, partake of her comestibles and her potables, and listen to the chief orators and brass bands of Boston, a return of ancient good feeling

5

might be reasonably anticipated; 3. I, Josiah Perham, am just the gentleman to engineer this exceedingly delicate business. Whereupon, Josiah kindly
desiring to save all possible trouble, resolved himself
to be, *pro hac vice*, the Commonwealth of Massachusetts, and accordingly wrote a polite billet to the
Hon. John Letcher, Governor of Virginia, inviting
the principal inhabitants of that State, the Representatives, the Hangmen and other public servants,
to come immediately to Boston, to join in a grand
Constitutional Jubilee. Nothing could exceed in
delicacy the terms of this missive. Knowing the
depleted condition of the general Virginia purse —
not as yet distended by the much-desired-but-not-as-
yet-built European-and-Old-Dominion steamers — Josiah, in his note to Governor Letcher, considerately
promised to send " free tickets for all, or nearly all,
the journey from Richmond to Boston," leaving the
gratuitous cock-tails and juleps to the care of the
Mayor of Boston, after the arrival of the way-worn
and thirsty pilgrims. In this amiable letter, the enterprising Josiah dwelt in an eloquent way upon a
variety of topics, and notably upon the warm friendship of the " sage of Monticello " (meaning Thomas
Jefferson) for the " sage of Quincy " (meaning John
Adams). Wherefore, in order that " common friendship may be made strong and mutual confidence
greatly increased," Josiah mentions the fact of the
" free tickets," and reiterates seductively his request :
" Will you come and take tea in the arbor ?"

Now, when this polite summons, so festively differ-

ent from the subpœnas which Virginia is wont to
send to Massachusetts, was received by the Hon.
John Letcher, he seems to have been either frightened or delighted; for he instantly sent a special
message to the Legislature, communicating to them
the communication of Josiah, which was treated with
due respect, being first laid upon the table and then
ordered to be printed. The private note of Perham
thus rose at once to the dignity of a full-fledged Public Document, and as such will occupy a prominent
place in all future histories of Virginia. The ages
will know that there was a Josiah—that he was
hospitable—that he asked Virginia to take tea in
Boston, and, alas! that Virginia would not come,
and did not even send her decent regrets. At this
moment, to speak metaphorically, Josiah's great
Union tea-pot is remarkably cold and his arbor dis-
mantled.

Before concluding to come to tea, the sages of Virginia waited for the opinion of that arbiter of all
elegant things, the Editor of *The Petersburg* (Va.)
Express, who, after due pondering, has decided that
until Massachusetts shall have repealed sundry laws
"hostile to the South," Virginia will not drink a
Massachusetts cock-tail, will not eat a Massachusetts
dinner, will not sleep between Massachusetts sheets.
Undoubtedly a stunner for Perham! Virginia is not
to be " honey-fuggled " even by free tickets. For the
present, the benevolent Josiah is floored; but, full as
we are of sympathy for Perham, in a condition of
languishing disconsolation, with his lights fled, and

his garlands dead, and his banquet-hall deserted, we advise him to proceed, as fast as his emotions will permit, to the Massachusetts State House, then and there to request of Senators and Representatives the immediate repeal of all " legislation hostile to the South," in order that his tea-party may " come off." In this way more than one bird will be slain by Josiah's missile. The Union will be cemented; agitation will cease; Governor Letcher will fold to his manly bosom Governor Banks; the brass-bands will blow; the flags will flutter; the gifted talkers of either State will be relieved of their verbal drop-sies, and all will go considerably more merry than any number of marriage bells, while brethren united, like birds in their little nests, with many tears of joy, will bless the name of Josiah, surnamed Per-ham, the Dispenser of Free Tickets and Peace-Maker-General to the States of Massachusetts and Virginia!

And yet will Josiah permit us to whisper to him a word of caution? He is, no doubt, a veteran show-man, and may in his day have domesticated in a single cage a Happy Family of cats, rats, owls and rabbits. He may rely upon his long experience, but has he seriously considered the consequences of his proposed re-union? We will imagine Virginia ar-rived, washed, dressed, cock-tailed, and breakfasted. We will imagine Mr. Perham marching the illus-trious consignment of Free Ticketers to the Com-mon. Can he then be sure of his animals? Suppose Governor Banks, in saluting the Perham pilgrims, should say something unpleasing to the Southern ear ? Is Josiah sure that his jolly visitors would not lapse into their orginal savagery ? Would not snap their revolvers, flourish their bowie-knives, and swing stalwartly their sticks ? Josiah would not certainly feel good if a battle-royal should ensue. What would he do with the dead bodies of his Virginians, particularly if the Directors of the Railways should raise technical objections to Free Corpses ? Of course the State of Virginia would not permit her gallant dead to be quietly interred in Yankee soil. Of course the remains would be sent for ; and, of course, Josiah, as the instigator of the fatal fray, would be called upon to foot the bill. What a doleful termination of the Josiah-Jubilee !

We notice that last week the Massachusetts House of Representatives considered Mr. Perham's gratuitous public services, and did not very highly approve the same, being undoubtedly of the opinion that it could do its own inviting without outside assistance. Josiah, like most public benefactors, was scurvily treated. One Haskell thought Perham " a fool." One Shaw insisted that he was a " nuisance." Upon this a lively debate ensued, but the question of " fool " or " nuisance " was not put to the House. It seemed to be agreed that he was either the one or the other ; and, whether brainless or a bore, we can easily understand why the Virginia Legislature — not the Massachusetts — treated his invitation with a certain degree of respect.

February 21, 1860.

A BIOGRAPHICAL BATTLE.

If poor Mr. Choate could rise this morning from the dead—and many of his admirers believe that he is restrained from returning rather by lack of inclination than lack of power—he would find an exceedingly inky battle raging over what would have been his remains if he had not arisen. But Mr. Choate undoubtedly expected to have his life taken after he left it; for it is the fate of all great men to be picked up at last by hungry biographers, who pacify their appetites as soon after the lamented demise as possible, and then provide for themselves annuities by the exhibition of the skeleton. That there should be jealousies in the distribution of the net proceeds of anybody's death, is as natural as it would be to find a company of hyenas making a division of their game without regard to Christian principles or Chesterfieldian good manners. When Dr. Johnson had given his valedictory roar, how many rushed forward to earmark the body—Hawkins, Mrs. Reynolds, Boswell, Mrs. Piozzi! What a scrambling there was, what a scene of anecdote-snatching! How everybody claimed to have been robbed by everybody else of priceless stories and of invaluable reminiscences! It rained pamphlets, and the air was thick with recriminations. That Dr. Johnson did not walk upon such provocatives, goes far to invalidate his own doctrine of ghosts; for, with his good will, we do not believe that Boswell would have been permitted upon a single occasion again to get comfortably drunk, or the

Thrale to forget her departed brewer in the arms of
her Italian fiddler. Still, there were reasonable extenuations of the biographical mania then, and such
are not wanting in the case to be presently considered.

In these matters of life and death, the biographer
who is active enough to be the first in the market,
will dispose of a dozen editions before those of less
alacrity have printed their initial chapters. The
Reminiscences of Choate, put out by Colonel Edward
G. Parker, have, among other merits, that of novelty; and although they have not escaped censure in
critical circles, they are entertaining. But Colonel
Parker is in trouble. He is censured by *The Atlantic Monthly;* he is cut up by *The* (London) *Saturday Review;* he is rebuked by Mr. Joseph Bell, who
has Mr. Choate's memory in his special keeping; and
he is treated by *The Boston Courier* very much as
Captain Lemuel Gulliver was by the first Yahoos
whose acquaintance he had the pain of making. Unless Colonel Parker — who is not of the Regular
Army, but in the Militia Service of Massachusetts—
shall make a great deal of money by the sale of his
publication, he will wish that he had fallen upon his
own sword, before venturing into the battle of print.
The "family" is dreadfully angry. To speak indi-
vidually, Mr. Joseph Bell is disgusted, and has written a special epistle to *The Courier* informing the
world of that fact. Colonel Parker's poor little book
is declared to be "an outrage on the living and the
dead." Colonel Parker has already retorted upon

"the family" and *The Courier*, and, in time, if they have not done so already, "the family" and *The Courier* will retort upon Colonel Parker. With a reasonable economy of ample materials, we see no ground for believing that this controversy will be terminated during the lives of the parties, and it may, being a family matter, as well as a matter of money, be continued by their heirs, executors and administrators.

Meanwhile, the Life of Mr. Choate appears to be of proprietorship as doubtful as that of vulcanized rubber, out of the harassing uncertainties of which Mr. Choate, when alive, made a snug sum enough in the courts. Only one thing is certain. We are exhorted "to wait and get the best;" to reserve our money and minds for the genuine Family Biography which is now in course of preparation; and to exert as much shrewdness and caution in possessing ourselves of the real article, as if we were purchasing the Macassar Oil or the Aromatic Scheidam Schnapps. We have had a tolerable experience of advertising expedients in our day, but we confess that we have observed nothing neater than this. The Duello of the Dictionaries is child's play compared with it.

In the meantime, while suffering ourselves to be entertained by Colonel Parker's "Reminiscences," we await with impatience the Family Biography. Everybody knows what a capital character a man receives when his relatives write his life. We anticipate nothing less than the portliest of folios, unspeakably dignified from title-page to colophon—a grave and stately narrative—a story heroical, of which the central figure will be Mr. Choate, more like Jupiter Ammon than a member of the Suffolk Bar. The family is right. Pray what does the world want of Mr. Choate in his shirt-sleeves? Of Mr. Choate laughing, chatting, cracking jokes? of Mr. Choate careless of money, of appearances, and of his chirography? of Mr. Choate in his character of human being, fond of the same food and drink which nourish and cheer ordinary creatures? The real Family Choate will be of incomputable altitude, with a voice like Olympian thunder, and an eye of flame divine. The eloquence of the real Family Choate will be more than Demosthenean, Ciceronian, Burkean. The law learning of the real Family Choate will surpass that of Pothier, Eldon, Story and Shaw, C. J. The classical learning of the real Family Choate will rival that of Porson and Dacier, of Bentley and Parr. The piety of the real Family Choate will be something approximating to the apostolic. With every virtue, and without a fault, he will be placed in the Biographic Pantheon which is so inexpressibly dignified and so portentously dull.

Now, speaking simply for ourselves, and with no wish to interfere with the family arrangements, we must say that we have never found such biographics too edifying. We like Clio well enough, in a homespun gown, writing with a plain, honest goose-quill, of human lives and of earthly achievements. In our estimate of a public man, we do not deem it advisable to begin by taking it for granted that he was of

5*

perfect character. The world thinks as we think, and has always thought so. It does not care to have its heroes always in full dress. Writers of biography have too often befooled mankind—have too often given us some sublime creation of their own fancies, something painfully virtuous, something

> —— " Too bright and good
> For human nature's daily food."

Mr. Choate's biography may not be worth writing at all, for his life was not an important one to mankind ; but if we were to elect his biographer in view of our own entertainment and instruction, we should vote not for the family, but for Colonel Parker.

March 17, 1860.

MR. BANCROFT ON THE DECLARATION OF INDEPENDENCE.

Mr. Rufus Choate, deceased, has left upon record his opinion, that the ethics of the Declaration of Independence are merely "glittering generalities." Mr. Caleb Cushing, muzzy and mazy as he is, in thought and expression, has contrived to assert, with tolerable clearness, that in his opinion " all men are *not* born free and equal." Mr. Charles O'Connor is of the same mind. So in his day was Mr. John C. Calhoun. Of course there is nothing to be astonished at in this resort to arrogant paradox. These gentlemen, living or dead, having determined beforehand to defend a bad system, could begin the work in no other way than by ignoring the axioms of the Revolution. Not until the broad humanity of the Declaration had been explained, philosophized and sophisticated to mere nothingness, or to something sadder, were these traitors to universal humanity able to repeat, without blushing, sentiments too revolting to be suddenly and nakedly promulgated. Their dismal conclusions, which dogmatically forbid all hope of the equality of man, in view of any human government, will hereafter be read with wonder, and are too signal a departure from the traditions of the Republic to be presently or speedily forgotten. Their most natural refutation is to be found in the steady, the intuitive convictions of the American mind.

The doctrines of the Declaration of Independence are not to be comprehended in all their beauty and sublimity by the closest study, any more than they are to be wasted away by the shrewdest verbal criticism of the letter of the instrument. Great as were the abilities of those who framed it, they were—and any men would have been—unequal to the task of condensing into words, of confining within sentences, the great idea of political equality which informed the general American reason and heart. They left us a letter, noble only because it was the exponent of a noble spirit. The letter might be perverted and controverted—might be faithful to the ear of the world, but altogether false to its hope—but the spirit would remain, incapable of a double sense, and useless to palterers.

We did not need it, but we are happy to have the opinion of Mr. George Bancroft, the best known of our historians, that the Declaration was not "a tissue of glittering generalities." Mr. Bancroft contradicts the late Mr. Rufus Choate point blank, and in words which are curiously responsive to those of that advocate; for Mr. Bancroft says distinctly that the Declaration "avoided specious and vague generalities." Again, those who have been misled by the indignant or contemptuous repetition of the phrase "higher law," will have ampler opportunities of exhibiting their virtuous horror when they read what Mr. George Bancroft has written. "The bill of rights which it (i. e. the Declaration) promulgated, is of rights that are older than human institutions, and spring from the eternal justice that is anterior to the State." He must possess very rare powers of distinction who can find any substantial difference between "the higher law" and the "rights that are older than human institutions"—rights that "spring from the eternal justice that is anterior to the State."

But Mr. Bancroft goes still further; nor can we forbear the pleasure of quoting his own admirable words: "Two political theories," says he, "divided the world; one founded the Commonwealth on the reasons of State, the policy of expediency; the other on the immutable principles of morals. The new Republic, as it took its place among the powers of the world, proclaimed its faith in the truth and reality and unchangeableness of freedom, virtue and right. The heart of Jefferson in writing the Declaration, and of Congress in adopting it, beat for all humanity; the assertion of right was made for the entire world of mankind, and all coming generations, without any exception whatever; for the proposition which admits of exception can never be self-evident." Moreover, and in illustration of the glad tidings and their universal application, Mr. Bancroft says: "The astonished nations as they read that all men are created equal, started out of their lethargy, like those who have been exiles from childhood, when they suddenly hear the dimly-remembered accents of their mother tongue."

Mr. Bancroft, it will be seen, does not speak with the fashionable timidity of dyspeptic students. He does not maunder about races, nor take refuge within the cheap defenses of ethnological sciolism. His political philosophy "makes the circuit of the world"— his political morality is applied to "the entire world of mankind, and all coming generations, without any exceptions whatever." After Mr. Cushing's pilferings from encyclopedias and stereotyped nonsense about white and black and yellow races—after the intolerable conceit, ignorance and inhumanity of his imitators—after the inconclusive conclusions of text-twisting and text-splitting doctors of divinity—after the ignoble efforts of fools and of knaves to extenuate a moral wrong by appeals to physical distinctions—it is pleasant to find a man like Mr. Bancroft adhering to a sensible and simple construction of the axioms and adages of honest and fearless Republicanism. These trimmers—these torturers of plain words, of

plain morality into tenth century sophistications have
now their answer, and they have it from a very high,
if not from the highest quarter.

June 27, 1860.

MODERN CHIVALRY—A MANIFESTO.

WE read in one of the noblest of English poems that
" a gentle knight came pricking o'er the plain;" but
we do not read, in whatever other way he made an
ass of himself, that he published three close columns
of nonsense in any newspaper of the period. He dab-
bled in blood, and not in ink; he brandished a sword,
and not a goose-quill; he murdered infidels, and not
his vernacular; he was invincible in respect of dragons, but he recoiled from the perils of authorship;
and as he was much more expert at riding than reading, he never seems to have thought it necessary to
quote, by way of justification, from any of Doctor
Caleb Cushing's Cyclopedias whenever he slaughtered
Paynims and ravished their wives. Our modern chevaliers are vastly more accomplished; and whatever
prowess they may hereafter exhibit upon the gory
field, it must be admitted that they make war by
proclamation with irresistible, or perhaps we may say
with irrefragable vigor.

We do not remember in the history of Chivalry
anything like " An Open Letter to the Knights of the
Golden Circle," which has just been printed in *The*

Richmond Whig, by Sir George Bickley, President of the American Legion and K. G. C. Since Sir Walter Raleigh, there has been no fillibuster so accomplished as Knight George. In urging his men-at-arms to rush to the rendezvous, he strengthens his appeal by quoting from history in the most miscellaneous manner, and by using terms the most recondite and scientific. He speaks of the days of Nimrod, Ashur, Fohi, Mizraim, Athotes, Memnon, Solomon, Hiram, Uleg-Beg, Gengis Khan and Psammeticus, as if they were only of yesterday, or the day before. He makes an off-hand allusion to Pyramids and Sphynxes with an ease which is perfectly tremendous. We do not know any Doctor of Divinity who has exhibited such perfect familiarity with the intentions of the Almighty. He uses all the hard philosophical terms with as much ease as if he had been born under the Portico, swaddled in the Lyceum, educated in a German University, and subsequently adopted and nurtured in sesquipedality by Jeremy Bentham. He evidently means to invade Mexico according to all the laws of Logic and Mental Philosophy. Thus we are told that Asia and Africa "have long since passed from fetichism to analyticism, and finally to syntheticism"—in consequence of which interesting transmogrification the Knights of the Golden Circle are invited to meet, on the 15th of September proximo, on the beautiful banks of the Rio Nucces. All difficulties are to vanish before "the energetic analyses of the Americans;" and in the opinion of Sir George Bickley, K. G. C., the entire Mexican army will fly

like cravens from the very first round of "pure syn-
theticisms" to which he proposes to subject it; nor do
we blame him if, as he admits, at such a prospect,
"his heart swells." We should think it would. We
do not wonder, when thus he meditates the easy glories
of charge, with Webster in one hand and Worcester
in the other, that he also declares that unless his gallant knights do their duty, "future ages may well
reprobate our dereliction." Our own opinion is that
future ages will by no means let them off so easily;
and will be satisfied with nothing less than penalties
only to be expressed in words of ten syllables.

Sir George touches upon one exceedingly interest
ing point. All adventurers who leave the scenes of
their nativity to grapple with fortune in foreign lands
have a pet grievance. Æneas was fairly smoked out
of house and home, or the world would have had no
Rome. Sir George Bickley, K. G. C., is also mounted
upon his injuries. As "a Christian," as "a consistent
man," as "an energetic Anglo-American," he is much
displeased with the difficulty of enforcing the Fugitive Slave Law in Boston. "The conflicts between
the State and Federal authorities" have rasped the
more delicate parts of his nature. Although not a
medical man, he volunteers the opinion that, "as a
nation we have been poisoned." The Republican
party has "grown to colossal proportions." The F.
S. L. cannot be executed—not Botts, nor Yancey,
nor Wise could, as President, execute it. The crimes
of the North are manifold. It is guilty of a population of twenty millions, while the South has but

twelve. In respect of land, it is equally reprehensible—seventy-five acres to a man, while the South has
but forty-five. " Be we men," Sir George would have
said, if he had thought of it; " Be we men and suffer
this dishonor ?" Alas! the poor South, oppressed by
all the rules of arithmetic, the victim of a pitiless nu-
meration—what can she do better than to throw herself for safety and for succor into the amorous arms
of Sir George Bickley, K. G. C., President of the
American Legion ? He is the Moses for her money.
He will show her the green pastures and the still
waters—a Canaan of coffee, of corn, and of cotton;
a Paradise of tea and tobacco, of sugar and rice—
where there will be " work for all," and more especially for " niggers "—where there will be " free
religion," (Doctors of Divinity growing, as we are
told, spontaneously in the poorest soil)—where there
will be " free education"—two Universities, we suppose, in every shire-town, each with a full *corps* of
presidents, stewards, tutors, bell-ringers, bed-makers
and professors of Greek.

Then, too, there is unhappy Mexico—the heart of
Sir George is undergoing a horrible hemorrhage on
her account; and the ears of Sir George are filled
with her cries for " help." He proposes, his Knights
of the Golden Circle assisting, to give her " a rank
among nations"—to rescue her from " the brigand
and barbarous brutes who now burn, pillage, murder
and destroy her"—and a very handsome thing it is
in him to offer to do it. Therefore, let Bickley's
Braves all be " on the south bank of the Rio Nueces by

the 15th of September—there to organize and await the action of our friends in Mexico." There will be a pleasant march—there will be just fighting enough to sustain the interest of the expedition—and then for a revel in the Halls of Montezuma, with no end of liquor and ladies! We can see Sir George now, in our mind's eye, with a monopoly of two señoritas and a private bottle of *aguardiente,* surrounded by the chiefs of his army, and martially and melodiously whistling Yankee Doodle. If this will not give Mexico "rank among nations," we do not know what will. What the rank will be we leave the reader to determine.

But Sir George, like a prudent commander, directs his Golden Knights not to come to the south bank of the Rio Nueces empty-handed. They are requested to bring with them "wagons, mules, oxen, horses, cattle, spades and blankets." Nothing is said of "two towels and a spoon." Perhaps the last is at least included under the general head of "instruments," which the knights are also requested to provide. But we are afraid that the word has no such pacific signification. "Instruments," we fear, mean revolvers and rifles, bayonets and blunderbusses and bowie-knives, powder-flasks and bullets. If not, why does Sir George inform us that in good time his "emigrants" will beat the sword and the rifle, the cannon and the lance, into agricultural implements? This will, after peace, be, of course, the proper and poetical thing to do; but how can it be done without, if we may say so, the raw material? How can you make a cannon into

" an agricultural implement," if you have no cannon
to begin with ? We defy Sir George Bickley, K. G.
C., to do it.

It must not be supposed that any body who pleases
can join this gallant " emigration." In the first place,
every knight must bring to the Rio Nueces not less
than " twenty dollars" in hard cash. O discouraging regulation ! A man may be bold—a man may
be brave—but unless he can by begging, borrowing
or stealing raise twenty dollars, his room will be
better than his company on the banks of that shining
river. But we have still more discouraging intelligence. Sir George gives timely notice that none but
respectable men can march under his colors. He will
have no "rowdies." We are not sure that he will
not confine his enlistment to church-members in good
standing. Those gallant men, therefore, in this city
and elsewhere, who propose to consecrate themselves to
this knightly work, will see the necessity of instantly
commencing their purgation, and of looking about to
see which of their friends has twenty dollars in cash
to spare. For cash, after all, is what Sir George will
stand most in need of. To slaveholders he makes a
most piteous appeal, calling upon them in the name
of all that is good and great to draw their pocket-
books instantly, and to send to Col. N. J. Scott, of
Auburn, Ala., the neat sum of one million five hundred thousand dollars. We are afraid that it is just
possible that Col. Scott will be obliged to wait awhile
for that money ; and our advice to Sir George, if he
really desires to be the Alexander of Mexico, is to

courageously make up his mind to defray all the expenses out of his private resources, which are undoubtedly unlimited.

We beg leave, most respectfully, to call the attention of our friend, Mr. Buchanan, to this Proclamation. It may divert his mind from a too constant contemplation of his recent misfortunes; and he may pleasantly employ himself during the brief remainder of his official existence, either in assisting or arresting this expedition—it really makes no difference which. Should he determine to try a new sensation, and for once insist upon a rigid execution of the laws, we beseech him not to begin with a Proclamation, for in that particular line of warfare he cannot for a moment compete with Sir George Bickley, K. G. C.

July 26, 1860.

MR. FILLMORE TAKES A VIEW.

Ex-Presidents are undoubtedly beings vouchsafed to us by way of confirming the truth of that Scripture which declares that though one should rise from the dead, yet would not men believe. Ex-Presidents, to be sure, are not always exactly dead; and even Mr. John Tyler, who never during his official days had a superfluity of vitality, has recently shown the usual sign of life in a decayed politician, and has written a letter. The Ex-President, therefore, may be considered not so much dead as "done for." He is like an

old coat, past service when skies are clear, but pretty
sure to be brought out in rainy weather—a garment
shabby, but passable in a fog; split here and there,
but in all its looped and windowed raggedness better
than total nakedness; or to pursue the figure, fit
enough to be straw-stuffed and hoisted upon a pole to
terrify the croaking crows. Of these relics, it may be
said, that while there is life in them, there is a letter.

We learn accordingly that Mr. Fillmore, from that
very library, we suppose, which witnessed his Know-
Nothing adjurations, wrote upon the 19th of December, 1860, an epistle to Somebody, which only now
do we find emerging from Somebody's pocket and
creeping into the public journals. It appears that
Somebody requested Mr. Fillmore to go to the South
as a Grand Plenipotential Pacificator. For that high
office by Somebody was Mr. Fillmore nominated, and
by Somebody was he unanimously confirmed at a
Union meeting held by Somebody expressly for the
purpose. Mr. Fillmore is urged to undertake this
"patriotic mission." He may smell tar and see pros-
pective feathers. He may have a fearful dream of
being ordered "to leave within four-and-twenty
hours." He may feel an uncomfortable rail between
his august legs, or a still more uncomfortable cravat
of the hempen variety around his highly respectable
neck. So he has issued in his own behalf and has
served upon himself a writ of *ne exeat*. If the Union
can be saved by letter-writing he has sheafs of pens
and quarts of ink and reams of paper at its service;
but if the Union can only be saved by a danger-

ous journey in mid-winter, why the Union may be damned. This is what Mr. Fillmore with much verbal gentility and chaste circumlocution, says; and it is the most sensible thing he ever said in his life. Ex-Presidents can be better employed than in going upon tom-fool errands for anybody.

But while declining to travel for the benefit of the public health, Mr. Fillmore is willing to talk in that behalf, and to talk, as we think, in a discreditably loose way. Here is what Mr. Fillmore "wants." "What I want," says he, "is some assurance from the Republican party, now dominant in the North, that they, or at least the conservative portion of them, are ready and willing to come forward and repeal all unconstitutional slave laws, live up to the compromises of the Constitution, execute the laws of Congress honestly and faithfully, and treat our Southern brethren as friends. When I can have any such reliable assurance as this to give, I will go most cheerfully and urge our Southern brethren to follow our example, and restore·harmony and fraternal affection between the North and the South."

In order fully to estimate the unspeakably amiable and redundantly fraternal spirit of this tid-bit, from which it appears that Mr. Fillmore is anxious to preserve the peace by quarrelling with his neighbors, we must bear in mind the posture of public affairs. The strongholds of the Government in the hands of the rebels; the American flag dishonored by the hostile artillery of thieves and pirates; the country assailed by land-rats in the Treasury and by water-rats in

Pensacola Bay; the Constitution defied by delegates in convention, and by mad and drunken rioters with arms on their shoulders; Senators false to their oaths, and eaten up by undignified passion striding from that chamber which has been the scene alike of their promises given and of their promises broken; the country wantonly alarmed, and its great interests gratuitously threatened because law-abiding men will not submit to law-breaking men; at this moment, when we are to be bullied out of the right of suffrage, and scared into an abandonment of our dearest franchise, Mr. Fillmore, who breathes the same air and treads the same soil with us, lectures us upon our short-comings and our sins, and drawls out his stale reproaches as if he were our keeper or our king. He is out of date. He learned the fossil formula, which for the hundredth time he reiterates, long ago, when he was in a public place, if not in the public service. When he was in fashion, it was also the fashion to talk as he talks now. He assumes that the Republican party is not ready to repeal unconstitutional laws; is not ready to live up to the compromises of the Constitution; is not ready to execute the laws of Congress honestly and faithfully; is not ready to treat our Southern fellow-citizens as such. This, we upon our part rejoin, is something worse than mere gratuitous assertion. It is the vulgar and uncharitable gossip of the pot-house; it is the small change of political sneaks; it is the weak and artless subterfuge of creatures with an irresistible propensity to crawl, and with just sense enough to be ashamed of the degradation;

of men whose souls are in the stocks, and who have the prices-current written upon their hearts.

But if Mr. Fillmore be really in earnest, we should like to ask him why we are to be driven at the bayonets' point to the stools of repentance which he has been kind enough to arrange for us? Were the lamps so nearly burned out, and were we such incorrigible sinners that nothing could bring us to a sense of our perilous state but the traitorous pranks and headlong perjuries of South Carolina? Does Mr. Fillmore believe that the North, intelligent and honest as he knows it to be, will refuse one jot or tittle of what it honestly owes to its unfortunate fellow-citizens of the South? For ourselves, we think that demands thus far have been made upon us altogether too loosely, and even inexplicitly. We are to humble ourselves as sovereign States have rarely been humbled by the cruelest misfortunes of war; and with the hot haste of recent converts in the political church, we are to repeal laws, already old upon our rolls, at the demand of volunteer advisers, and in deference to the ex-parte dictum of ex-Justices and the theoretical decisions of amateur commentators. If these laws, of which Southern grumblers and their Northern allies complain, were presently oppressive and intolerably grievous, we might extemporise extraordinary legislation, and make hot haste to redress the injuries which we have heedlessly inflicted. What sharp agony, what recent insult, what shame new and impossible to be suffered has forced South Carolina into an attitude of crime? How many slaves has she lost by the operation of Personal Liberty Laws? Which of her citizens have they impoverished by a penny?

Mr. Fillmore in declining to go to the South will never have the smallest cause to regret a decision which has saved from fresh mortification the evening of his life. No eloquence of his could have quieted the insane rage of the Charleston oligarchy. No astute compromises, though he had *carte blanche* upon which to write them, would have satisfied the ambitious politicians of South Carolina. He might have gone upon his mild mission with his portfolio full of pretty bills and possible amendments; but he would have returned, if at all, leaving behind him the same madness, with a new element of mockery.

January 26, 1861.

"A BANNER WITH A STRANGE DEVICE."

Our obligations to the Anarchy of South Carolina are too enormous to be expressed. Bolted she has; quite a large amount of our personal property has she taken with her, but she has left our dear old bird. She has spoiled the gridiron, but she has spared the goose. We have him still, beak, talons and feathers! For us, dis-United States though we may be, he will continue to soar and scream and spread his wings. From our banner a star or two may madly shoot, and a stripe or so may fade; but we keep our bird—creature called by our name—our pet fowl, so admired and respected in the principal Courts of Europe. He

G

has not nullified. Without him we had been bankrupt in our blazonry, hard up in our heraldry, a colorless, flagless, standardless, buntingless, pennonless
people. With him we may indulge in dreams of future glory to some extent gratifying. Let us indulge!

The Southern Confederacy, it would seem, is sick
of ornithological devices. In cropping the eagle, it
crops the whole feathered race. There were birds to
be had for the catching—buzzards, vultures, condors,
adjutants, flamingoes, parrots, daws—but it will have
nothing to do with them. In its present melancholy
condition of political chlorosis, it has a stomach only
for snakes. At Montgomery the other day, after the
Convention had concluded its pleasing labors of disintegration, the lovely ladies presented a banner to
the delegates, whereupon was embroidered, probably
by their own delicate digits, a huge rattle-snake, so
done to the life, that by the mere force of the imagination, he was distinctly heard to rattle. "*In hoc
signo vinces*, Mr. President!" said the ladies, or rather
they would have said so, if they had understood Latin.
"To be sure!" the President responded. The whole
scene must have been a pretty one.

Snakes and ladies! The conjunction may not appear to the fastidious a particularly felicitous one.
There is an old, a very old story of a snake and a
lady, and of a short but important conversation between them respecting the edibility of a certain apple,
in the course of which the slimy creature observed:
"For God doth know that in the day ye eat thereof,
then your eyes shall be opened; and ye shall be as

gods, knowing good and evil." We have all read of
what happened after the. fatal bite. We all understand what that little pippin has cost us. Adam seceded, under a strong pressure, from the garden, and
none of his descendants have been so fortunate as to
return to its enchanting scenes. The snake has not,
it appears, in spite of all his bruises, amended his old
habit of oily lying. He whispers still to the ambitious
and the discontented and the restless: "Bite and be
brave! Bite and be presidents, generals, dukes or
kings! Bite and be happy! Bite and be as gods!"

Under the combined influence of ambition and
whiskey, the Confederated Adams are yielding to the
blandishments of the serpent. In the wreck of social
happiness, in the destruction of a free government, in
the chaotic dissolution of all political institutions, in
the shame and sorrow and alarm of intestine broils,
in the rule of madness, under the heavy hands of irresponsible dictators, or tossed about at the caprice
of insurgent mobs, the amateur revolutionists of the
South may find that bitter in the belly which was so
sweet in the mouth, and may learn that it is easier to
rouse than to quiet the father of lies. Have they forgotten that other text: "Because thou hast done this,
thou art cursed above all cattle, and above every beast
of the field; upon thy belly shalt thou go, and dust
shalt thou eat all the days of thy life?" Whatever may
be the temptation of cotton, it is hardly probable that
foreign nations will fall violently in love with the
rattle-snake. They will fear to meet him in every
bale; they will find him printed on every shirt; and

they will rank the flag upon which he is painted with the black banner of pirates or the threatening devices of Asiatic barbarians.

Let the Southern Confederates, then, revise their blazon ! They have a large variety from which to select — lions, leopards, pelicans, unicorns, bears, griffins, dragons—the whole menagerie of heraldry. Why will they endeavor to introduce such a disagreeable creature as the rattle-snake into the society of Christian nations ? If they must have one on their flag, the King of Dahomey is the foreign potentate for their diplomacy.

January 31, 1861.

A SOUTHERN DIARIST.

Who would not, if he could, read history in perpetual diaries, and so have done forever with philosophic historians and historic philosophers? Who will not join with us in the regret that Noah kept no log? Who does not prefer Pepys to Clarendon or Hume ? Who can assure us that Walter Scott's Journal will not be read long after his romances in prose and verse have been forgotten? Who would barter Byron's memoranda, smirched and hasty, for a dozen Childe Harolds, and a regiment of Laras, and who would not buy back from the ashes to which mistaken friendship consigned them, those Memoirs burned by Tommy Moore, which would have been cheaply saved to English literature by the destruction of all the peer's poetry? And who will not be enchanted to learn, that amidst the war of revolution, the din of disunion and the noise of nullification, an ingenious gentleman of Columbia, S. C., is keeping a "Journal" and printing it by bits in *The Yorkville Enquirer*, thus—to use his own noble language—"attempting to sketch the rapidly-changing features of the times as they vary under the influence of events whirling into notice so telegraphically." Better writing than this we have never read, and if the gentleman goes on at this rate, we know well enough who will be the Xenophon of the war.

The business at Columbia, as we gather from this journal, is principally campanological. They have a new bell in that city, and they ring it continually. On Tuesday, 8th ult., they rang it for the secession of Florida. On Thursday, 10th ult., they rang it for the secession of Mississippi. On Friday, 11th ult., they rang it for the secession of Alabama. On Sunday, the 13th ult., they do not appear to have troubled the bell-rope at all. Upon the 9th ult., having heard of the flight of the Star of the West, the diarist exclaims: "This intelligence did not surprise us. We were already looking the reality of war in the face." Were they? And did they relish the prospect? Smoking cities, blockaded ports, famished wives, starving children, insurgent negroes—did they like the picture? Like it? How can any one be so simple as to put the question? Like it! We tell you that they pine and pant to be persecuted; they prefer to be wounded; they will be much obliged to the gentleman who may shoot them; wounds will be welcome; gore will be glorious; houselessness sweeter than hospitality. "A long and bloody war" looms before the rolling eye of the editor of *The Yorkville* (S. C.) *Enquirer* as the sun-rise of the millennium. An ounce of lead in his clavicle would, we fancy, materially mitigate his ardor.

It was upon Saturday, Jan. 12, while "hundreds were engaged in training with pistol and rifle," the afternoon being, as we are told, "vocal with the music of preparation," that the diarist made the following entry: "If it were conceivable that all our men could be killed, South Carolina need not despair; her women can defend her!" The imagination is thus carried back to the Amazonian regiments, to the petticoated squadrons of the King of Dahomey, to Boadicea and Joan of Arc. It is rather a drawback to find that the Lady Lancers, the Amazonian Artillery, the Female Fusileers, the Sweet Sappers, the Modern Miners, the Pretty Pioneers, the Side-saddle Cavalry, will not be wanted until "*all* our men are killed." Not being a woman, and still less a she-soldier, we cannot undertake to speak with absolute accuracy; but we should be a little dubious about the female fighting after the quietus of all the men. How will Mrs. Col. Cotton be able to lead the Heavy Mothers to the charge, when her dear departed no longer animates her by his martial smile? How will Arabella, of the Light Artillery, deport herself at the guns, when Augustus sleeps in a soldier's grave? Who believes that the Maid of Saragossa would have rammed the great cannon with such astonishing virulence, if there had been no gallant gentlemen looking on ?

To return to our Diary. On Monday, 14th ult., we find the following discouraging entry : " The war does not progress." As the hart panteth after the water-brooks, and as the thirsty soul panteth after the whiskey barrel, so does this man of memoranda pant for blood. Monday the fourteenth was a "blue Monday" indeed. Nothing to ring the bells for; no excuse for extra libations ; even the small-pox subsiding —how monotonous in Columbia must that day have been. Something of the solitary sensations of Robinson Crusoe must have come over our jotting gentleman, for his diary comes to a dead stop. He ceases suddenly to chronicle " the rapidly changing features of the times in Columbia," and begins to abuse Mr. Buchanan as " a poor old man." This we cannot but regard as a gratuitous insult. Poor, Mr. Buchanan is not. Old, he may be ; but we are ready to wager dollars against dimes that the President is not half so old as he appears to be. The mistake is a natural one. Good guessers, familiar with his proclamations and messages, and computing his years from his drivel, would undoubtedly think him somewhat older than Old Parr ; but we have good reason for believing that he is very little, if at all, past one hundred. At any rate, he is old enough to be spared the insults of those whom he has served well, if not wisely ; whereas he seems to be rather worse off than Shylock was on the Rialto. Southern gentlemen must swear, we know, but why call poor old Mr. Buchanan

a liar and a dog? 'T is inexpressibly shameful. If
we were Mr. Buchanan, we would turn anchorite;
we would retire to some secluded cave, and there,
over a moderate allowance of the choicest wheat
whiskey, would we strictly meditate the thankless-
ness of mankind. What more, we beg leave to ask,
in behalf of an injured old gentleman, and outraged
O. P. F., would the Seceders have of the President?
Has he not been theirs—*corpus*, unmentionables and
all? Do they know a friend when they have one?
For them a Fond Functionary has given up reputation, self-approval and a respectable place in history,
a re-election, sound sleep and a good appetite. What
more would they have? Do they want their servant,
just sinking into the gaping grave, to close his cheq-
uered existence by committing a great number of
enormous perjuries? Will they not be fond of him
unless he will forswear himself? Will they keep no
faith with this too confiding ally? He has loved
them to doting. And what is his reward? Poor
old man!

February 4, 1861.

DR. TYLER'S DIAGNOSIS.

WE are happy to perceive that in these days of excitement, one moderate man—one exceedingly moderate man—the most moderate man of modern times
—a man without the slightest pretension to ability of
any sort, is still in full possession of his inkstand and

pen, if not his tongue. We need hardly say that we allude to John Tyler, of Virginia, whose recent visit to Washington, if it has not saved the Union, has at least produced a correspondence enlivened by the united abilities of Mr. Tyler and Mr. James Buchanan. That correspondence, too precious not to print, is now before us. Seven elegant epistles have been added to the literature of our language, and of these we beg leave to offer to the eager reader the following compendious abstract:

No. I. Mr. Tyler informs Mr. Buchanan that he has taken lodgings at Brown's Hotel, in order to preserve the peace of the country; and wishes to know when he can be "received" at the White House.

No. II. "This evening at eight o'clock, or to-morrow morning as early as you please," responds the hospitable B.

No. III. Mr. Tyler represents to Mr. Buchanan that "his health is too delicate to make it prudent for him to encounter the night air." He will therefore call in the bright, rosy morning.

No. IV. "Why is the 'Brooklyn' frigate sent South, Mr. Buchanan?" fiercely asks Mr. J. Tyler.

No. V. "An errand of mercy and relief," responds our beloved B.

No. VI. "Why are you planting cannon at Fort Monroe?" interrogates J. T.

No. VII. "I will inquire and let you know," replies J. B.

Here the thing breaks off. We have no words in which to express our sense of the exceeding astuteness,

6*

courtesy, vigor, elegance, profundity, conciseness and general anti-sesquipedality of these letters. We are only troubled to think that so dignified a beginning should have had so lame and impotent a conclusion. If Mr. Tyler had only followed up the struggle with Number Eight—if our President had but sent off Number Nine—if Mr. Tyler had then countered with his Ten—if Mr. Buchanan had immediately got in his Eleven, to be followed by a smart delivery of Mr. Tyler's Twelve, who knows what these champions might have accomplished after a mutual polishing, we will say up to Round CXL? As it was, Mr. Tyler could only write to the Governor of Virginia, to say that he had nothing to say—to report that he had nothing to report—to inform his Excellency that there was nothing of which to inform him. " I have great confidence," observes Dr. Tyler, " in the action of my pill called the ' status quo.' Mr. Buchanan promised to take the ' status quo,' but no ' status quo' would he after all take; in consequence of which Executive disinclination, the President is in a state of ' status quo,' I am in a state of ' status quo,' Virginia is ditto, and the country is ditto." Thus terminated Dr. Tyler's visit, and to Virginia did he return with his despised and ill-treated bolus. We are sorry to notice that he was not " admitted into the inner vestibule of the Cabinet." To be sure we do not exactly understand what an " inner vestibule" may be; but we are satisfied that it is such a *sanctum sanctorum*, such a place of places, and such a closet of closets that if Mr. Tyler had therein met Mr. Buchanan, and had

suddenly presented the "status quo" in a mild medium of Monongahela to the President, what with the
surprise and the spirits, the "status quo" would have
glided down the Executive œsophagus into the Executive stomach, and so in a state of chyme through the
Presidential pylorus into the next proper place in the
Presidential person—and all with the happiest possible effects. But it is useless to speculate. What is
the value of a doctor, when the patient pitches his
medicines out of the window? What could Dr. Tyler
do when Mr. Buchanan steadily refused to take his
physic? "What could he do," says the reader, "but
write another letter to somebody else?" Sir, or Mad-
am, that is precisely what he did.

February 8, 1861.

THE MONTGOMERY MUDDLE—A SPECIMEN DAY.

Mr. Thomas Carlyle has given somewhere a droll
and piquantly cynical description of a new-born baby,
with its pink skin, its irrelevant motions, and its many
and meaningless wants. A new Government, when
extemporized, not because it is needed, when rather
it starts from a stercoraceous bed of corruption and
venality, is always the object of laughter to settled
States and solid statesmen. In its assumption of
regal airs, in its strut and swagger, in its monkeyfied
politics, it reminds us of nothing more forcibly than

of "The Two Right Kings of Brentford" in "The Rehearsal:"

> *1st King.* Hasten, brother King, we are sent from above.
> *2d King.* Let us move, let us move—
> Move to remove the fate
> Of Brentford's long united state.
> *1st King.* Tarra, ran tarra, full east by south.
> *2d King.* We sail with thunder in our mouth;
> Busy, busy, busy, we bustle along.

Or if we may be permitted to make another quotation from the same pregnant play, it shall be this:

> *King's Phys.* What man is this that dares disturb our feast.
> *Drawcansir.* He that dares drink, and for that drink dares die;
> And knowing this dares yet drink on, am I!

We suspect that there are a sufficient number of Drawcansirs in the Southern armies who not only dare drink, and dare die for drink, but who would be very apt to die without drink; yet we take it for granted that the men of Montgomery are all solid philosophers, who leave liquor to the poets and the common soldiers, and whose sole and sublime amusements are the construction of paper Constitutions, the begetting of bodies politic, the evocation of cash out of chaos, and the general transmogrification of a small slice of the late Union into a Confederacy. The millinery department of Mr. Jefferson Davis's new political concern seems, however, to make the weightiest drafts upon the Southern Congressional intellect. A nation without a flag is no nation at all—that sublime truth, at least, has dawned upon the Southern Confederated mind. Confederate Curry, of Alabama, the other day brought a bushel of flags, of striped and of starry flags, of white, red and blue flags before the Congress, and exhibited them to the delegates just as that abhorred creature, a Yankee peddler, shows his rainbow merchandize to the old ladies. One he dwelt upon affectionately, as it was " designed by a gentleman of rare intellectual endowments;" and upon its ample and variegated folds the eagle was preserved in all his plumed and pugnacious perfection. The name of the rare and intellectual gentleman is not given ; but with all the rarity of his intellectual powers, his pipe was soon put out, so to speak, by a lady, who sent a piece of patch-work which was exceedingly admired—a remarkable fact, since it is said to " preserve much of the resemblance of the dear old flag," which we should not think would make it exceedingly beautiful in the eyes of thieves and traitors. The Congress, being much dazzled by all this display of bunting, referred the whole subject to the Flag Committee, which, without delay, has created and reported the necessary banner. Thus the Confederacy is provided for in that respect at least, and what more can it desire ?

Cash, clearly ; for even a Southern Confederacy cannot live upon loquacity alone. Cash, therefore, the Congress has proceeded to raise, or rather, not to speak with frightful inaccuracy, has resolved to raise, to the extent of fifteen millions, whenever anybody with more bullion than brains will lend that trifling sum for eight per cent. One cannot but notice the exceeding modesty of this proposition, and particularly the high rate of interest which the Confederates promise to pay. The Rothschilds will be upon their knees for that loan, and, with tears in their eyes, the Barings will beg for it. But what we exceedingly wonder at, is the moderation of Congress. Why limit the "raise" to $15,000,000? Why not resolve to borrow $150,000,000? It will be just as easy to obtain the larger sum as the lesser, and it hardly appears respectable for the new nation to set itself up in business upon a petty fifteen million capital. What will the pickings and stealings, so necessary for the development of patriotism, be worth with such a trifling stock as that to filch from? Why it will hardly keep some men, heads- and fronts of the Confederacy, too, in pocket money for a quarter! Do you suppose that peculators who only stood by the United States while there was a dollar in the treasury, which they could "convey," will render their inestimable services for any such petty plunder?

Then, too, we are sorry to say that the Congress, on this same specimen day, wasted its precious time in hearing petitions for patents, and in referring them. Now when we consider that discovery and invention are shown by the facts and the figures to be quite out of the Southern line, we cannot but regret to see the energy of the Congress wasted in raising a Patent Committee at all. In 1856—and other years will show a like proportion—South Carolina took out *seven* letters patent; Georgia, *nine;* Florida, *one;* Alabama, *eleven;* Louisiana, *twenty-four;* all the Slave States, *two hundred and ninety-one* against *one thousand nine hundred and eighty-two* taken out by the Free States. There would seem to be several things making more imperative demands upon the Confederate Congress than a Patent Office.

A poor but honest State, struggling with financial difficulties, and striving in good faith to secure a position in the family of nations, is worthy of the respect of all mankind; but a State seeking existence at the cost of a cruel and unnecessary rebellion; a State false to its traditions, and traitorous out of mere petulance, must be very strong indeed in money, men, and all other material resources, in order to maintain itself. The South cannot complain that it has been slandered by its foes. It stands to-day self-accused and self-convicted. From its own newspapers, and from the speeches of its leading men, and by their own passionate confession, we can prove it behindhand in commerce, in intelligent agriculture, in letters and in popular enlightenment. Governor Wise has said this over and over again, in numberless letters, of his own State of Virginia; and what is true of Virginia is true of her Southern sisters. Do the really intelligent men of these unfortunate States, imagine that acts of Congress, whether in Montgomery or in Washington, will bring wealth, industry, prudence, energy —lines of steamers, miles of railway, great commercial centres? Secede, and secede again, but the curse and blight of Slavery will still remain! It will be a lesson to the world; it will fill a sad but priceless chap-

ter in history ; but we may well ask that our erring
brethren may be spared the sorrow and mortification
of teaching it.

March 11, 1861.

READY-MADE UNITY AND THE SOCIETY FOR ITS PROMOTION.

It is a pleasant thing for brethren to dwell together
in unity. There can be no mistake about it. The
Scriptures say so, and "The American Society for
Promoting National Unity" backs up the Scripture;
so that the thing may be considered as good as settled.
Especially when we consider that Samuel and Sidney
Morse, Hubbard Winslow and Seth Bliss indorse the
Society, and that in so doing they approve the Scriptures. Gentlemen amorous of unity could not certainly have done a more sensible thing than to begin
by uniting themselves. It is all very proper. The
Patent Soap has its Company, and so has the celebrated Paste Blacking—and why not Unity?—not a
Unitary Home, for that the gods forbid!—not a Unitarian Unity, for that would hardly suit those members whose names are as yet published—but what we
may call a Religious-and-Political Unity—designed,
as we are informed, to make everybody of one mind
with everybody else upon the subject of Slavery—that
mind being also *The Journal-of-Commerce* mind, the
bias of which is, we presume, not uncertain.

We are inclined to think that The American Unity

Society has cut out rather more work for itself than it will be able to accomplish during the remainder of the present century. It is morally impossible for men to be united upon this topic. The man who owns a man will never agree with the man who is owned. Here is the first fatal split; and nine hundred Morse Societies, working for nine thousand years, could not alter that primal, elementary and discouraging fact. Even though men who do not own slaves may now and then agree with slave owners, yet the number even of these must always be small, compared with the number of those who do not so agree. People who cannot read Greek, and who have not been enlightened upon the signification of a certain little Greek word of six letters, will not unite upon this point with gentlemen whose consciences are in their lexicons.

The Society of National Unity intends to go to work upon what in medicine would be called a counter-irritant plan. According to *The Journal of Commerce*, the Society is "to employ a small army of talented lecturers to follow in the wake of or to precede Abolition lecturers, to pluck up the Abolition tares, and destroy them." Well, this is *one* way of promoting Unity, we must confess. We should very much like to see Mr. Morse's "small army of talented lecturers" wrestling with Mr. Parker Pillsbury, and holding high debate with Mrs. Lucy Stone. How the "talented lecturers" would fare in the scrimmage, or in what woeful plight they would come out of it, we can easily imagine; but how these mighty debaters, stirring up villages, distracting societies, and making the squabble chronic, would promote Unity is more than we can see.

The American Unity Society has "briefly indicated its views" in what it calls a "Programme." It begins with an attempt, cold-blooded, specious and deliberate, to falsify history—not a very good way of promoting Unity, we would suggest. We quote from the "Programme:"

"The popular declaration that all men are created equal and entitled to liberty, intended to embody the sentiment of our ancestors respecting the doctrine of divine right of kings and nobles, and perhaps also the more doubtful sentiment of the French school, may be understood to indicate both a sublime truth and a pernicious error. Men *are* created equally free to do the will of God, and will be equally rewarded by him according to their deeds. But they are *not* created equal in personal endowments, nor in their relations to providential arrangements."

There are so many falsehoods in these few lines, that we hardly know where to begin their exposure. But, in the first place, we say that no honest construction of the text warrants the assertion that our fathers referred, in these great sentences, to the divine right of kings and nobles alone. They do not say anything about "government" in the beginning. They start with a pure, bold, naked abstraction, independent of governmental forms altogether. Read the words: "We hold these truths to be self-evident, that all men are created equal; that they are endowed by their

Creator with certain inalienable rights; that among these are life, liberty and the pursuit of happiness." There is the proposition. What follows? "That *to secure these rights*, GOVERNMENTS are instituted." Not rights for government, but government for rights, higher, holier than the government itself. Government is secondary to right—that is what Thomas Jefferson meant to say, and did say, with a clearness which no guess nor gloss can obscure.

Then see how these new "Unitarians" dishonestly —yes, that is the word; we shall not change it—dishonestly muddle the great charter! "Men *are* created *free* to do the will of God, and will be equally rewarded by him." That is: a man is *free* to go to a prayer-meeting, to toil without wages, to live wretchedly, and to have no hope but in death—that is doing the will of God; but he is not free to better his condition; he is not free to run away, he is not free to keep his own wife from concubinage, nor his own children from vendue. He will be "*equally* rewarded by God"—was there one man in the American Congress who understood "equal" in that sense? We do not believe that there was; and we do not believe that Morse & Co. believe so. What is that ugly word "LIBERTY" doing in the Declaration? Liberty applies only to political status. Except in purely theological discussions, what has "a free and equal slave" to do with Liberty? Ah! say Morse & Co., the Fathers meant by using that word to refer to "the more doubtful sentiment of the French school." What is this "doubtful sentiment?" Why are not

Messrs. Morse, Winslow and Bliss a little more explicit? Why do they undertake to slander, not Thomas Jefferson who had Gallic proclivities, but such a man as John Adams, who hated French politics and French reforms? It would not have been altogether safe for Mr. Samuel J. B. Morse to have told John Adams that the Declaration to which he had deliberately set his hand, incorporated any "doubtful sentiment of the French school." We can imagine the old man kindling into sublime wrath, and with fiery energy pouring out hot words of scorn and of refutation. We can imagine him exclaiming: "No, sir! I did not mean any *doubtful* sentiment of the French school—I meant the *undoubted* sentiment of the old Saxon school; and I yet stand by my faith, sir!"

We presume that our readers have already had enough of the "Programme." We promise not to detain them much longer, but here is a gem of a sentence: "It is," so say the Programmarians, "by confounding the providential with the moral, instead of regarding the former as means wisely employed by the latter, that men become infidel and radical in their schemes of reformation." What are the men who say this? Are they Platonists or Christians? Do they hold to the *divinæ providentiæ fatalis dispositio?* Do they literally interpret the maxim, "Whatever is, is right?" Does "providential" mean something moral sometimes, and sometimes immoral, but whatever its character, in its sense of fatal, providential? If so, then Apuleius telling dirty Platonic stories was as good a Christian as Prof. Morse is.

But there is something so hideous in this hair-splitting, in these quiddities and quodlibets with which men strive to cover the immorality and the impolicy of Slavery, that we do not care at present to pursue the subject. There is more "richness" in the "Unitary Programme;" but let these reflections suffice at least for to-day.

March 28, 1861.

A PRIVATE BATTERY.

WE find the following paragraph in the Charleston (S. C.) correspondence of a contemporary:

"A salute was fired this afternoon by Captain James W. Meridith's *private battery* in honor of the ratification of the Constitution by South Carolina, and the hoisting of the Confederate States flag."

Well, in the rapid onset of nineteenth century civilization, beautifully bewritten and philosophized as it has been, Charleston does outrun New York. There are a hundred things which are handy to have in the house. Mr. Toodles knew it; Mrs. Toodles knew it; we all know it. But do ever the most prudent of us think of providing, keeping, maintaining, casting, mounting, loading, priming and discharging a private battery? There were private fortifications, as we have been informed, in the Middle Ages. There were certain counterscarps, ravelins and moats in My Uncle Toby's garden, which might be generically classed under the head of "Private Battery." Burglars go about with their pockets full of six-shooters—real private batteries. But in these peaceful times, at least in these peaceful regions, we buy pots, pans, kettles, cooking-ranges; but we do not buy private batteries. Mrs. Younghusband does not say to the lord of her bosom: "My love, there is the nicest little Paixhan, second-hand and dirt-cheap, just round the corner—and the man throws in the balls, my dear—and I have found saltpetre going for a song, in a charming shop, and sulphur for nothing at all, and we can grind our own powder, love! and Tommy will help us to cast bullets, and, bless my soul! there is a small-arms manufacturer just below us, with the neatest swords that you ever saw—and do not forget to remind John that we are out of cartridges, and really the gardener is quite behindhand with his ditch. We may be assaulted to-morrow, Mr. Younghusband. I wish you would not be forever neglecting our defenses."

Does this sort of small talk season the South Carolina cakes and coffee? Obviously—for has not Mr. James W. Meredith put up, erected and established a private battery? Where did he get his guns? Really, we do not know! He cast them, we suppose. South Carolina has every blessing which the Creator has ever bestowed upon any State—why should she not have one more, to wit, a brass mine? She expects all the results of human ingenuity to come begging for barter at her door—why should not trampers arrive there now and then with a few seventy-sixes at a bargain? Perhaps Mr. James W. Meredith bought the guns and gave his note for the purchase money. Perhaps—

But why should we speculate? Why should the fact—that is to say, the exceedingly remote fact—that these private guns may be pointed at our private and particular business and bosoms, discompose us into querulous interrogatory? It will be a long time, we fancy, before we shall see Mr. James W. Meredith's guns gaping in this neighborhood. That battery is a fixture. It is for the protection of Capt. Meredith, Mrs. Meredith and all the little Merediths! Old Meredith maintains a battery that he may breakfast, dine, sup, sleep, sow, reap and flog at his ease. It will be an improvident procedure, and one which we hope Mrs. Captain will not consent to, for Meredith to permit the battery to go off the place. "We neither borrow nor lend batteries," should be the Meredith legend. "Buy your own batteries," should be the steady answer upon application for a loan.

It is not all of us who can afford the luxury of a "Private Battery." We have seen fearful statistics of the actual cost of discharging once a single gun. To say nothing of the expense of private gunners and swabbers and rammers and powder-monkeys. But Meredith can do it, we suppose. Meredith can keep horses and slaves and private batteries—no end of them, to be sure! Meredith's cotton is not mortgaged up to the last sprout. Meredith is flush. A whole day's bombardment would be a bagatelle to Meredith.

Of what description are Meredith's guns? Upon our life and soul, we do not know. How many? We really do not know. Long Toms, Swivels, Car-

ronades? Again, we say we do not know. How should we? We have never kept a Private Battery.
April 12, 1861.

SOUTHERN NOTIONS OF THE NORTH.

THE Southern States have heretofore known little enough of the North; from which we infer that our summer visitors from those regions have either been too intent upon their juleps, or too much engrossed in purchasing merchandize, to carry back for the enlightenment of their stay-at-home neighbors much valuable fruit of intelligent observation. We remember to have met and to have conversed with a clever Yankee woman who undertook to teach the ideas of half a dozen boys and girls to shoot, upon a Virginian plantation. She told us that the general opinion of those about her was that we are so poor and so mean that we are ready to do almost anything for a shilling, and absolutely anything for two shillings and sixpence. So we find at this time the Southern newspapers roaring in a fussy and fiery way about "hordes" of Northern "mercenaries" sent to cut the general Southern throat. Upon these two words innumerable changes are rung, and of them two comments will dispose.

"A horde," according to our idea, is a gang of men intent upon plunder; and "hordes" usually go where there is something beside "niggers" to steal. Rome was a fair prize for the Goths; but all the Confederate States together would hardly furnish "loot" enough for a pair of rapacious regiments—certainly not enough to tempt men from the comforts of home to the discomforts of the field. Nine-tenths of the wealth of the South is in fancy human stock; of no particular value to the soldier of fortune—of no value at all to the patriotic Northern volunteer. Mercenary, indeed! These noble soldiers who have just left home and comfort and their loved ones to fight the battle of the Constitution, asking no recompense but the consciousness of rectitude—mercenaries! If so, then Warren and Washington, then Hamilton and Schuyler were mercenaries! If so, who would not be a mercenary?

The men of the North know indeed the value of money. They know what it will do; and they know, as Southern rebels will find out to their cost, just the right time to spend it. History hardly records such a profuse, yet enlightened liberality as that which the Northern States have exhibited. It is hardly an exaggeration to say, that the entire wealth of cities and towns, of private corporations and of individuals, has been tendered to the Government upon its own terms. We do not believe there are ten thousand persons in Massachusetts who have given nothing or done nothing for the cause. And that which is true of Massachusetts is true of every other free State. Mercenaries, indeed! We do not have to put the screws upon our bank directors here to obtain a public loan. There is a race of giving and a competition of munificence.

This in time will, we hope, satisfy our quondam

7

brethren in Virginia, South Carolina and other territories of the United States, that we are not so miserably poor as they have been kind enough to suppose.
After all we have given to the sacred cause of Law
and Order, we have still a dollar or so left; and can
even borrow a little should our present stock fail us.
But we have hardly touched the popular pocket yet.
So the sooner the subjects of Jefferson Davis stop laying that particularly flattering unction to their souls
—that silly notion that we are exceedingly poor—the
less they will by-and-by be disappointed. Our property is n't fugacious—has n't two legs—does n't run
away or get sick and die.

Another Southern notion is that the moment we
begin to be pinched and bread to grow dear, we shall
all be under the domination of King Mob and his
army of starving artisans. They do not seem to take
into account the fact which they will be sternly compelled to take into account ere long, that war will
make employment for our able-bodied men. If there
should be mobs the law will put them down, just as
at the South mobs put down the law.

Still another Southern mistake is that the rebellion
has a powerful party at the North. Slavery once had
such a party; but men, whatever may be their Pro-
Slavery views, do not care to be themselves slaves.
The North is pretty well united now by a common
danger. Here and there a grumbler pursues his avo-
cation, but he is careful not to be loud in the indulgence of his favorite pastime. Thus far, there is really
no difference of opinion worth mentioning.

One Southern newspaper now before us says : " The North is mad." In one sense, it certainly is—somewhat angry it certainly is; but we have all around us at all hours of the day and night, cumulative evidence that there is a method in this Northern madness. For lunatics, we are getting on remarkably well. From that eminent lunatic, Winfield Scott, down to private dotards in the ranks, there is no alarming evidence of insanity. Northern theories of liberty and of human equality seem to be hardening into pretty substantial practice.

The tone of the Southern newspapers, when speaking of the wealthy, intelligent and patriotic North as one great anarchy, and of the Northern people as " a godless mob" of " Puritans, Freelovers, Abolitionists, Mormons, Atheists and Amalgamationists," has given the gentlemen who have cast away the slave-whip for the sword quite a mistaken notion of our resources as well as of our character. Consequently, having said to us in the elegant language of Marshal Rynders, " We do n't believe a word in your d—d philanthropy," they consider that by saying so they have floored us. We beg leave to announce to them that they will find no free-love in our fire-arms, no irreligion in our revolvers, no theories in our bombardments, no Mormonism in our musketry, no cant in our commissariat, and no niggardliness in our military chests. We are not wild Indians—we are not all mulattoes—we are not all mere shop-keepers—we are not all misers—we are not all mobocrats—some of us at least are honest men, with no particular inclination to be beaten, but with a decided inclination to resist injury.

April 29, 1861.

ALEXANDER THE BOUNCER.

ALL great men have their weak side. Alexander of Macedon was given to grog. Alexander, of Georgia, V. P. C. S., is given to gammon. His weakness is "to say the thing that is not"—this being the periphrastical way in which Dean Swift's fastidious Houyhnhnms always spoke of falsehood and of falsifiers. The Hon. V. P. Alex. Ham. Stephens upon arriving at Atlanta, Ga., was "received by a large crowd;" and in return he ungratefully made a speech calculated largely to delude the "large crowd," and considerably to lower himself in the estimation of old-fashioned folk with a prejudice in favor of the truth. From a great variety of mendacities, we select the following as being, to use the words of Goldsmith, the "damnable bounce" of the occasion.

"A threatening war is upon us, made by those who have no regard for right. We fight for our homes! They for money. The hirelings and mercenaries of the North are all hand and hand against you."

Now, Stephens, what did you mean by that? Is not Washington just as much the home of the Massachusetts man as of the Georgian? You took a pretty long journey to Virginia to persuade men from the path of honor and of loyalty. Were you at home there? And if so, why are not our New York and other regiments at home in Washington? And being there, to defend what should be the home of every true American citizen, and is to all intents and purposes the home of his representatives, by what authority, upon what pretense, do you call these consistent and courageous men "mercenaries and hirelings!" What is the "hireling?" One who serves for wages. Has the Seventh Regiment gone to Washington upon a money-making excursion? Have all these brave fellows enlisted for the sake of pay, which is about as much *per annum* as some of them could at their proper avocations make in a month—to say nothing of risk to health and life—nothing of absence from their families? "Hirelings," forsooth! When you go to the Confederate treasury to draw your quarter's salary, O Alexander—mind, we do not say that you will get it—pray will you then be a hireling?

Mercenaries are those who are "retained as serving for pay"—as, for example, Jefferson Davis, Alexander H. Stephens and other Confederate notabilities—for pay of some kind they certainly intend to get, either in praise or power or pence. The soldiers of the United States may receive a pittance; but if this sweet squad of Confederate officials are not mercenary, why are our brave militia-men mercenary?— our soldiers extemporised from the field, the factory and every haunt of industry? Answer that question, Alexander!

The rapidity with which an Italian buffo-singer can

deliver the words of his song is tediously slow in comparison with Mr. Stephens's volubility of untruths.
If we might speak a little coarsely, being somewhat
provoked, we would say that he lies like lightning.
He told the Atalantese a succession of Munchausen
stories—how Maryland had resolved "to a man to
stand by the South"—how "all the public buildings
in Washington have been mined for the purpose of
destroying them"—how an attempt had been made
"to burn the whole city of Norfolk"—how only the
interposition of Providence prevented a second "conflagration of Moscow." All these agreeable and ingenious fictions and Fernando-Mendez-Pinto-ish rec-
reations were strangely diversified by strong threads
of piety and patronizing allusions to the Deity, complimentary observations on Providence, with little
prayers here and there interpolated. In fine, a more
curious *olla* of a speech we, who have read many
speeches, do not remember. So having finished—
that is, having exhausted his invention—the Vice-
President went to bed to dream in a good, improving,
orthodox way of Ananias and Sapphira.

Mercenaries of the North!—hirelings of New England, of New York, of Pennsylvania! "Goths and
Vandals" though, according to Gov. Pickens, you be,
pray, whatever may happen, try to tell the truth.
See what a mean figure V. P. Alexander cuts, standing in a tavern balcony, retailing silly gossip to his
gaping dupes!

A lie is like a tumbler of soda-water. It foams
and frizzes, and is palatable at first, but in a moment

is only fit to be thrown out at the window. Thus far the Southern Confederacy has been mainly maintained by public fibs, by private fibs, by the fib telegraphic, the fib editorial, the fib diplomatic, the fib epistolary and the fib oratorical. We think that there must have been many Gascons among the original founders of South Carolina, and if so, how have they improved upon their ancestors!—upon those worthy people who *did* now and then tell the truth by accident!

May 11, 1861.

ROUNDHEADS AND CAVALIERS.

WHAT is chivalry? What is a chevalier? Why, because a person is a man-owner should he be styled a horseman? Or why call him a chevalier, if you come to that, simply because he is an ass? What is there in the fact that a man is tolerably white and lives in Virginia, by the toil of others, which should induce *The London Spectator*, for instance, to liken him to Prince Rupert or to Peveril of the Peak? Or to go further back, if you look into the charming pages of Froissart, you do not find that Sir Robert de Namur tarred and feathered anybody; that John of Gaunt owned " niggers ;" that Sir Charles de Montmorency was addicted to cock-tails before breakfast, or that Lord Robert d'Artois was a tavern-brawler. The fascinating chronicle tells you of " honorable enterprises, noble adventures and deeds of arms;" but such really do not remind you of anything done by

Preston Brooks, or Henry A. Wise or John Tyler. Even if the English "Cavaliers" did "plant Maryland and Virginia," which is not true, although so often and so confidently asserted, the condition of very considerable portions of both of those States would seem to indicate a sad deterioration of the blood, through the admixture of that of several Royal African houses and overthrown black Stuarts. With all their faults, neither few nor small, the English cavaliers were gentlemen, and did neither mean things nor cruel ones, as the Virginia cavaliers continually do. The English cavalier would have been ashamed to get into a tempest, torrent and whirlwind of wrath with a woman—some small school-mistress, perchance, who had offended him by going to conventicle; the English cavalier would have thought it a work below his condition to arrest pedlars or to confiscate their packs; the English cavalier would have scorned captious and unreasonable disloyalty to a long-established government; and the English cavalier, with as many peculations on his shoulders as now weigh down those of Floyd, would hardly have attended at any court except a Court of Justice. In short, the English cavalier was generally a gentleman, and the Virginian cavalier is generally not a gentleman—a pretty broad distinction. This Virginian gentleman, as the vulgar error paints him—frank and generous to a fault, of speckless honor, and even of a religious turn, quick to resent a vile action, no matter where or by whom committed—this Sir Roger de Coverley, of the New World, does not now exist, even if he ever existed;

and figure as he may in those dreadful novels which only Virginians can write, his form and embodiment could not be found in the Old Dominion, although, for his production, a considerable premium were offered to the exhausted treasury of that province. He is a myth now, perhaps he always was.

Then, again, it is a great mistake to suppose that the opposition to slavery-extension, which the Northern States exhibit, is purely a Puritan feeling; for a deal of it is of old Dutch origin; and more of it has grown up in spite of Puritan predilection for a literal interpretation of, and a strong respect for, the Hebrew Scripture. The truth is, so far as the Scriptural argument is concerned, that the Puritanical spirits are at the South, and holding slaves there by virtue of perverted texts out of Genesis and Deuteronomy, and fine-spun theories about the curse of Canaan. The Puritan error, if such existed, happened to be precisely the error into which the philosophical and religious slaveholder always tumbles. He is the fanatic. He it is who, honestly perhaps, opposes his crude and interested convictions to the decision of the rest of the world. He it is who repeats a spectacle—too often, alas! exhibited — a spectacle of the fondness with which human nature clings to a delusion all the more fondly *because* it is a delusion. All the world knows that the moral and economical argument is upon our side. Nobody supposes it to be right to enslave men, except those who have either a direct or indirect temptation to enslave men. Which is nearest to that dark side of the Puritan character which Southern news-

7*

papers sneer at—Dr. Fuller or Dr. Wayland? How much of a Hebrew was Dr. Channing? On which side is the Rabbi Raphall himself?

Men seem inclined to take it for granted that the hostility to slavery is simply a religious one, and that every Abolitionist has become so through his moral convictions alone; as if economy had had nothing to do with the matter; as if it had been left undemonstrated that Slavery is bad policy; as if there had not been a strong appeal to the Anti-Slavery pocket as well as the Anti-Slavery heart; as if such books as "The Impending Crisis" had never been written or never read. But now all arguments against the institution have been left behind by the fatuity of slaveholders themselves, who by their rude violence to the Constitution, and their intolerable disregard of the popular verdict, have shown that Slavery makes them the enemies of peace, of law and of order, and is therefore, through its influence in this way, the enemy of, and inconsistent with, social happiness. This result, no matter from what point it may be viewed, is utterly unnecessary. This Rebellion has come to demonstrate how terribly damaging Slavery is to social character. The best friends, not merely of human, but especially of Southern happiness, are those who seek to stay the hands of this madman, bent so resolutely upon self-destruction.

June 6, 1861.

WISE CONVALESCENT.

WHEN, a few days since, we heard from Gov. Wise, he was in the hands of his medical man, taking his pills and potions with a perseverance and a punctuality which seems to have been rewarded; for his Excellency is now clothed at least, if not in his right mind, and is making speeches with all that lunatic force which has always, in the day of his bodily health and strength, characterized his frenzied eloquence. He took the field in his finest fulgurant style, at Richmond, Va., on the 1st inst., though it is only lately through *The Charleston* (S. C.) *Courier* that he reaches us in red-hot report. He followed Jefferson Davis, and in the matter of fuss and fire, he floored that official completely. In pure, unmitigated and sublimely inventive mendacity, we are inclined to think that Mr. Davis can give the Virginian any odds, and then vanquish him; but in the beautiful art of saying nothing and of seeming to say a great deal, Wise is still unsurpassed, nay, unapproached by any mortal. In this speech, he is especially sanguinary; for he spouts a campaign through the whole of it, and puts us to the stand in a peroration. It is all "fire," "blood," "the Lord of Hosts," "fiery baptism," "rivers of blood," and at the end of this, our inconsistent though brilliant orator, adds: "Be in no haste—no hurry and flurry." No flurry, quoth he!—that from a man who lives, moves' and has his being in a flurry—who is, so to speak, an embodied flurry! No hurry—that *to* men who have precipitated this wicked war, because they knew that the least delay would be fatal to their criminal hopes! because they were afraid to give the Southern people an opportunity of thinking! because time would surely show their injuries to be imaginary! No hurry and flurry! Why, without these there would have been no secession of Virginia at all. Flurry was the beginning of it, and hurry was its consummation!

Both orators upon this occasion—both Davis and Wise—seem to take it for granted that Virginia has been dreadfully injured by the military movements of the Government in that State. They graciously permit us to fight, but insist upon themselves selecting the field, planning our campaigns, and directing all our movements. For example, Davis, who has made Virginia the battle-field quite as truly as we have accepted it as such, says: "Upon every hill which now overlooks Richmond, you have had and will continue to have, camps containing soldiers from every State of the Confederacy; and to its remotest limits every proud heart beats high with indignation at the thought that the foot of the invader has been set upon the soil of Old Virginia." That is to say: this General Davis has transported his forces—horses, foot-soldiers and artillery, to Virginia, to menace, and, if he can, to capture the Federal Capital, and when we meet him nothing daunted, he tells the Virginians that *we* have invaded their State! There is an incoherence about this which can hardly be referred to the utmost possible saturation in whisky. We should have permitted the unmolested concentration of one or two hundred thousand men upon this sacred soil of Virginia—we should have allowed Washington to fall an easy prey to the Confederate Army—we should have gone on considering a hostile State as neutral, while she was forging weapons for our destruction; but as we did not do this, as we saw fit to meet the enemy upon his own soil before he could by his presence pollute ours, we are invaders, we are mercenaries, we are assassins, we are incendiaries. Why do not the fire-eaters of Virginia, instead of complaining, thank us for giving them so large a provision of their favorite diet? What would they have said of us if we had kept quietly at home?

It is a blunder for a military man to boast. War is to a considerable extent a matter of fortune and mere chance—something at least which military historians admit, although they may not be able to define it—must always be taken into account. Governor Wise says that he is "a civil soldier"—he is not, certainly, a soldier military enough to avoid saying: "Your true-blooded Yankee will never stand still in the presence of cold steel." To this we can make no retort without falling into the same error; but we may safely suggest that men are not likely to run from an enemy whom, of their own free will and mere motion, they have traveled several thousand miles to meet. And when our armies have "extended their folds"—we quote the Wise words—"around Virginia as does the anaconda around his victim," we beg leave to suggest that the State has quite as good a chance of remaining a victim as of becoming a victor. "The tools to him who can use them;" but when a man or State or army has none, what then is to be done? Governor Wise tells his soldiers to "get a spear—a lance! Manufacture your blades from old iron, even though it be the tires of your cart-wheels. Get a bit of carriage-spring and grind and burnish it in the shape of a bowie-knife, and put it to any sort of a handle, so that it be strong —ash, hickory or oak." This looks desperate. When Gov. Wise says, "Take a lesson from John Brown!" when he condescends to say this, we think that a slightly milder style of boasting would be safer and more becoming.

June 19, 1861.

SLAVE-HOLDER'S HONOR.

DR. WILLIAM H. RUSSELL, the peripatetic philosopher and friend of *The London Times*, complains, if we may credit a telegram from Cairo "that his correspondence has been tampered with by the Rebels, his letters being altered, and in some cases not sent at all." Had this fact come sooner to the knowledge of Mr. Russell, it would, we fear, have diminished his relish for that celebrated bottle of Old Madeira which he drank near Charleston, and his appetite for the excellent official dinners eaten by him in Montgomery. If anything could diminish the self-satisfaction of The Thunderer, we should think it would be the publication of the fact that, for so many weeks, and

upon such a subject, its sacred columns have been
controlled by Davis, Cobb, and Benjamin. If anything could change to something like an inclination
that stern neutrality which has puzzled us all, we
should think it would be the discovery that in its
august person, *The Times* has been made the victim
of petty larceny by the descendants of Prince Rupert
and other cavaliers. It may be an extenuation when
a man intends to pick your pocket, that in pursuit of
his purpose, he asks you to dinner, and accomplishes
his nefarious project while you are cutting his mutton and sipping his champagne. We wish *The
Times* joy of its high-toned thieves, of its larcenous
cavaliers, of its cut-purses all of ancient families, of
its sneaks all with unexceptionable pedigrees! Mr.
Russell is already at the West, and will soon be again
at the North. We can promise that in neither quarter will his letters be in danger. He may write them
with the perfect assurance that they will go forward
to their destination unopened, and of course unalter-
ed. We may be fanatics, but we do not steal; we
may be mere shop-keepers, but we do not tamper
with the mails ; we may be bigots, but no letters are
opened in our Post-Offices as they are in those of
England and Russia.

The stercoraceous power of Slavery to develop all
the cardinal virtues, has received another illustration.
Seedy patriots of Alabama, very much in debt to the
North, where distance from home lent an enchant-
ment to their persons, and a power as of triple brass
to their faces, feeling, when the miseries of maturity

came upon them, at once a disinclination and a disability to meet their bills, have counseled with the Lord High Chancellor Dargan of their State as to the propriety and legality of repudiating. There never was such a Chancellor for sagacity and profundity and erudition as Dargan is. Dargan says at once: "Don't pay a red cent. These Northern creditors are public enemies. In the name of Justinian, I charge you to withhold the cash ! The Law of Nations forbids payment and so do I ! If you pay so much as a sixpence to your Northern creditors, I will have you indicted !" Pleasing opinion ! Every debtor refuses at once to pay, every bank to collect and every public notary to protest.

Now, as between distinct and independent nations, actual belligerents, Dargan is right in his law, although it is a very barbarous law at the best. The hardships of war have been in many ways mollified, yet this vestige of ancient and savage hostilities still remains. But under the circumstances of the present conflict, there are two considerations—one moral and the other legal—which will suggest themselves to every intelligent and just man, even in the Confederate States. How far, in the first place, have these hostilities been precipitated merely for the sake of avoiding just pecuniary obligations? How many men have become big-voiced Secessionists, because their pockets were empty and their promises to pay imminent ? Whatever hoar and antiquated Law, in the person of a perjured Chancellor, may say, the man who rebels in order that he may repudiate, is

both a traitor and a swindler, and worthy of the
jail should he escape the gibbet. In spite of Law,
he is still a liar, and no possible number of precedents can give him a sweet character. In a time
of peace, as in a time of war, he would find some
specious and sneaking excuse for avoiding his promises to pay.

In a war like the present there is no reason why
obligations as between man and man should not remain in full force. It is true that Alabama has asserted herself to be an independent State, but so, for
most of the essential wants of trade, she has always
been. Our merchants could only sue her citizens in
her own courts, except under accidental circumstances. She does not pretend, no seceding State can
philosophically claim, to have so altered her political
relations that foreign creditors cannot collect demands in her own courts. It is claimed that the State
of New York is a belligerent, and as a component
part of the American Union, she undoubtedly is;
but it is not claimed, and it cannot be with truth, that
hostilities exist between the States of New York and
Alabama. The very tenacity with which Southern
men cling to their doctrine of State Rights, is against
them in this matter. Why should the merchants of
the separate States suffer by the acts of the General
Government?

No: we believe that every honest Southern merchant—and there must be such—will pay his debts
if he can, and as soon as he can hereafter if he cannot
pay them now. This will, indeed, be the only safe

course for a business man in these parts to pursue.
Whenever peace is restored—it does not matter for
the purposes of the argument in the least upon what
terms—the Southern trader must come to New York
to buy, or to Philadelphia, or Boston. He must come
either with cash or clean hands, and something better
than a thief's record, if he would be sure of obtaining
merchandize. Every repudiator will be known at
the counters of trade, and instead of being wined, and
dined, and smiled upon, and trusted, he will be met
coldly, and as frigidly informed that the " terms are
cash." Repudiation will then be found to have been
a most costly luxury, and it is pretty certain that a
man who cannot command credit in New York would
be as badly off in Richmond or Charleston, although
these cities should become flourishing marts. The
taint of the swindler will stick to him, and those who
now applaud will be the last to trust him. Trade is
based upon private honor, and there is not a market
in the world which will not be shut against the merchants of Alabama for fifty years to come. This is
the stubborn fact which no amount of bluster can
alter.

John B. Floyd, for instance, Brigadier-General,
Confederate Army, is there a single man doing business in this city, no matter what may be his politics,
is there a single man who would trust John B. Floyd
to keep his cash ? who would give him any responsible situation in his counting room ? who would even
allow him to be in the counting-room without somebody to watch him ? And really after this decision,

is there a tailor in New York who would trust Chancellor Dargan for a pair of breeches? States repudiating their obligations must in the long run pay for the little luxury.

June 23, 1861.

NO QUESTION BEFORE THE HOUSE.

WE live in an age of extraordinary political exhibitions; and he whose appetite for novelty is the nearest insatiate, will have no cause to complain of the variety of the entertainment. As human nature forbids a perpetual torture and tension of anxiety, we must sometimes laugh though matters may be at the worst; and the satirists of England have already taught us to laugh at the British House of Commons —a body with wonderful talent for impaling itself upon the horns of a dilemma, and for wriggling itself out of the difficulty with no marked regard either for dignity or decent consistency. There is a farce called " The Two Gregories ;" but we do not believe that off the stage there were ever two Gregories so absolutely Gregorian as the Gregory of the Imperial Parliament — the honorable member for Galway. Gregory of Galway fell an early victim to the charms of the Southern Confederacy, and loving, however well, not in the least wisely, he was for its instant recognition and admission into the community of independent powers. He put his passion into a motion, and he put his motion before the House; but when the time came for putting the unhappy motion *to* the House, Mr. Gregory discovered that the House desired to have nothing to do with the motion aforesaid. The demand for its withdrawal though civil was peremptory. Mr. Gregory made an affecting speech, complaining that the Southern Confederacy was "accused of unwarrantable secession, and its members were called traitors and perjurers." "Withdraw!" cried the House. "I will," said Mr. Gregory. *"Sine die!"* cried the House. "I will," said Mr. Gregory. And the subject dropped.

Now, for our own part, although the manipulation of this red-hot resolution might have been a delicate and difficult business, we are sorry that it was not kept in hand just a little while longer. Mr. Gregory should have made another speech. He should have informed the House and the world what, in his opinion, treason is. He should have given his private notion of perjury. He should have shown what there is in the great American roguery which elevates it to virtue—what there is in the forswearing of States which differs from the perjury of individuals—in what way our Government has provoked a civil war; or, if he failed to show that, how the Southern secession is to be taken out of the category of wicked and noisome revolt. But the House was too wise to permit debate. If it had done so, we should doubtless have found some champion ready to utter disagreeable truths, and to chop the invincible logic of the facts. Then nothing but the want of clear statement could have saved the make-shift management of a

few shop-keeping men from the contempt which it
deserved, and from the indignation of the British
people.   It would have been shown how many sacrifices—some of them, indeed, inconsistent with political probity—have been made by the Northern people, that, if possible, this conflict might be averted.
Tersely, but triumphantly, Congressional history
might have been adduced—Gag-Resolutions, Compromise Tariffs, Fugitive Slave Laws, Kansas-Ne-
braska bills and all !   It might have been shown, for
the truth is of record, that the Republican Party,
though exasperated as never political party was before, by gratuitous calumnies and unprecedented
wrongs, protested with its whole force against the
apprehension of slaveholders, as the excess of injustice and of idle fear.   An untried Administration
could do but little, except protest; yet, by all fair
laws of political warfare, it was entitled to the benefit of its protest, and to an opportunity of proving its
ability to carry on the government, and of its desire
to carry it on in a just and wise spirit.   Certainly
a slow and cautious House of Commons would have
rated at its proper value the precipitancy of this
spasmodic uprising—would have weighed and found
wanting in all elements of integrity and honor, men
who commenced debate on civil affairs by drawing
the sword.   After such an exposition, however bald
and defective, Mr. Gregory would hardly have talked
again of the cruelty and injustice of branding the
Confederate Catilines as perjurers and traitors.   They
are both.   No amount, no ingenuity of special plead-

ing, can alter the patent and indelible fact. When the history of these distracted times shall be written, as it will be by those who are already gathering materials for the labor, the petty contemporary interests which now becloud men's judgments, will have passed away. Should that history disclose the Confederate Slave States as proper objects of Anglo-Saxon esteem and sympathy, and our own Government as inhuman and unchristian, then the whole world is all wrong as to right, and public morality is the most pitiable of mistakes. If it shall be decided that a civil war waged in the name of Freedom for the extension of Slavery was holy, necessary and just, we hope for consistency's sake, when civilized Europe no longer calls itself Christian, and when the Anglican Church has embraced the faith of Mohammed, that such a decision will be made, 'and not before.

Then, indeed, should a House of Commons yet remain in Great Britain, it will be perfectly proper if any member is old-fashioned enough to speak of international honor, for the Speaker to call him peremptorily to order, and to remind him that there is "no question before the House." But now when we consider the historical, the commercial, the literary, and even the political ties which bind the best part of the British with the best part of the American people; when we remember too, that the English Government has not thus far kept silence upon American affairs, and has announced a policy, or the puzzling similitude of a policy ; when we reflect that all the diplomacy of Downing Street cannot in this contest keep England in an affected posture of cold and unsympathizing neutrality forever; we confess that this shrinking from a sore subject assumes in our eyes an unpleasantly craven aspect, and argues a very un-English faith in hand-to-mouth expedients. But while we feel thus, we feel, too, that if the American Republic cannot maintain itself without the encouragement, and we may say the patronage of foreign nations, the sooner it falls into final and hopeless and undistinguished ruin, the better. God is said to help those who help themselves; and most nations are respected in proportion to their ability to sustain themselves without external leagues and amities. If we can fight this battle at all, we can fight it alone. Subsidies, arms, armies, the offerings of foreign States, we have not asked for, and have neither wish nor right to ask for; but that moral countenance, the best gift that one great nation can bestow upon another, we have a right to expect from England; nor do we think it will be refused us by that portion of the nation the good will of which is best worth having.

June 24, 1861.

BELLA MOLLITA—SOFT WAR.

WHEN Osric, the water-fly, called upon Hamlet to arrange the tilt with Laertes, he did not forget to speak in high terms of the latter as " an absolute gentleman, full of most excellent differences, of very soft society and great showing—the card or calendar of gentry." There are some men, and some of them are journalists, who, having all their lives been accustomed to speak of slaveholders and slaveholding in their mealy-mouthed way, cannot now, in the very tempest of the national danger, change to something like a masculine tone. The Northern corpses upon the fields of Virginia appeal to them in vain. Men and women driven from their Southern homes because of their Northern birth and blood, appeal to them in vain. They shut their eyes to things vulgarly dishonest—to ignoble repudiations and gratuitous bankruptcies, and to an official treachery almost without a precedent in history. " Fight!" they say to our noble volunteers—" but fight with foils! Fire ! but fire with blank cartridges! Lay on, Macduff! but lay on softly!" How many times already have we been reminded that the rebel Southerners are our brethren! This may be, according to certain codes, a reason for not fighting with them at all; but a contest once undertaken, we respectfully submit that they have ceased to be brethren, and have become simply enemies. Brothers who dispatch the wounded and mutilate the slain are not of that intensely fraternal pattern which is worthy of the highest reverence.

They are entitled to whatever consideration the laws of war permit—not one jot or tittle more.

But there is one particular of tender solicitude which we confess we do not well understand; and that is the hot haste in which some of our generals return fugitive slaves. Why is this species of property to be given up more than munitions of war? A black man who can dig, cook and assist in general camp-work, is certainly quite as valuable to keep *for* one's self and *from* one's enemy as a gun, a cask of powder or a horse. Slaves in all ages have always been among the spoils of war; and if we can obtain them without fighting for them, in fact, by their running to us, so much the better. If, by the fortune of war, a Virginian rebel has his house burned, is it the intention of Congress to soothe his grief by building him another domicil? Why not, if you are also bound to restore to him his runaway negroes? There may be a difference, but we do not see it.

The truth is, the flippant gentlemen who undertake to assure the South that this war at its honorable conclusion will leave slave property *in statu quo*, exceed their commissions. They are promising utter impossibilities. Under any circumstances—the Southern Confederacy established or overthrown—the strength of the institution of Slavery can never be what it has been. The South is utterly bankrupt now; but in what a condition will it be when it has lost the advantage of perhaps half-a-dozen crops; and is crushed under an enormous public debt, which must be paid by taxes on negroes or not paid at all! On the other

8

hand, admitting the States which have seceded to
have been reduced to wholesome obedience to the
Constitution, Slavery can never again be an auto-
cratic, domineering and impudent power. On the
contrary, it will understand—for this is the lesson
which reverses will teach—it will understand, that it
holds its very existence by the tenure of good behavior. In one of these ways or the other, Slavery may
be affected by the war.

And why not? Why should a war about Slavery
be begun, continued and ended, leaving Slavery just
where it was? If the free States are to have no protection in the future from the aggressions of Slavery
—if all the weary work of the last thirty years is to
be done over again, with its agitations, excitements,
mobs and lynchings—with its corruption of the souls
of public men — with its quadrennial struggle and
with its Congressional conflicts, peace will be no peace,
and treaties misnomers. The Republican party in a
great majority in all the States in which it has an existence at all, has always claimed that slaveholders
were unreasonable in their demands. Will peace
bring no change? If so, peace will bring either disunion or dishonor.

At any rate it does not seem to us that this is a time
in which to crook the hinges of the knee. For the
present the seceding States must be regarded exactly
as they are—as forsworn and mutinous members of
the Union, and as such entitled to no more consideration than it may be politic to show them. A considerable portion of the white population of these States

has forfeited its life. The returning supremacy of the laws in any other land would be followed by wholesale judicial executions, which by law written and by law common would be justified here. We are not aware that these criminals, after causing an amount of suffering which the agonized mind refuses to compute, are entitled to a sort of Jack Sheppard sympathy, though it come from no higher source than *The Day Book* newspaper. You may be reasonably sure, when you hear a man bewailing the wrongs of South Carolina, that he has no particular affection for New York, though it may, by courtesy, call him a citizen.

The time for soothing promises and carminative compromises was when such negotiation was possible. The patchers-up of peace had full swing—and what did they do? They talked morning and evening, in season and out of season, well and badly—but what did they accomplish? They filled an immense number of pages in *The Congressional Globe*, but they "took nothing." It was then proposed to fight—and fight away! say we, in God's name, and may He help the right. Whatever may be the distresses and inconveniences of fighting, we should have thought of them before beginning.

> "How uncertain
> The fortune of a war is, children know."

But about the cause in which we are engaged, there is no uncertainty. The Government of the country is pitted against the government of the plantation

—Freedom against Slavery—Simple Right against Complex Wrong; and it is better to perish with the Government, with Freedom and with Right, than to yield for a single day to a coarse and arrogant domination.

July 31, 1861.

THE HUMANITIES SOUTH.

ARMS have it all their own way in the regions of renegade revolt, throughout which the toga is unceremoniously discarded. Even the Rt. Rev. Father in God, Polk, of Louisiana, as our readers already know, has discarded godly lawn for golden lace and the Lives of the Saints for Scott's Tactics. But now sadder news comes to us. The Southern colleges and universities are giving up their erudite ghosts in every direction. Upon the authority of *The New Orleans True Witness*, a religious sheet, we have to state with pain that Oakland College, a celebrated Haunt of the Muses, is no more—that La Grange College, a renowned Seat of Learning in Tennessee, is also defunct—that Stewart College, an Academic Grove in Tennessee, has also been cut down in the full foliage of its usefulness—that the University of Mississippi, at Oxford, is sitting like a bereaved mother, with nobody at her generous bosom; and that the Centenary College, at Jackson, La., no longer dispenses crumbs of culture in that part of the world.

These venerable piles are all deserted; no more their ancient rafters ring to the song of

"*Propria quæ maribus* had a little dog;
Quid esse was his name."

Sucking Southerners have ceased with tottering steps there solemnly and studiously to pass over the *Pons Asinorum.* The ardent youths have all gone to the wars; and the no less ardent Faculties have thrown away their spectacles and followed suit. This, it must be allowed, is a classical collapse and a mathematical mischance, and a sad stroke to Sacred Theology; and especially to that branch of the latter upon which the Divine Institution of Slavery is builded. Heretofore, it must be confessed, the Patriarchs have leaned upon learning to the extent of their acquirements. They have flogged and begotten yellow bastards, and then sold them not with caution covert, but in market overt, without a misgiving; and they have done this upon strict Abrahamic principles partly, and partly because the Greeks and Romans did so, to say nothing of the Barbarians.

But now ethnology, chronology, philology and archæology have all come to grief in these demesnes which they once did so illustrate; and Dr. Fuller, if he really does want to serve the cause, should at once convert his useless lexicons and chrestomathies into cartridges, and give his whole stack of ancient sermons to the same sacred service. What is a classical point to a Colt's pistol? a text to a trumpet? the Sa-

cred Canon to a rifled-cannon ? Philemon to fighting ?
why bother about Ham when you have a chance to
hammer the heads of the confoundedly illiterate Yankee Doodles ?

To be sure, it may be urged, that whereas the
Southern neophytes and other students have heretofore mainly resorted for polish and illumination to
Northern seminaries, it is not wise, since they can
no longer do-so, to permit the Southern rills of learning, however thread-like, to be choked. We take a
different ground. The South is fighting for the sweet
satisfaction of continuing in a semi-barbaric condition. It is attempting to found a republic, not upon
knowledge, but knavery. It means to ignore the
Law of God, sometimes called the Higher Law, and
why should it study theology ? It intends to tram-
ple upon the rights of man, and what has it to do
with law natural, civil or common ? It has surrendered itself to a coarse and bestial inhumanity, and
why should it crave the sweet influences of philosophy and of poetry ? It has need to study but one
science—the science of oppression—and the hard human heart, in that branch of learning, has in all ages
been its own best teacher. It scoffs at all which has
made the Nineteenth Century the cultured child of
the past and the hopeful mother of the ages to come ;
and of what value to such a nation will be the record
of human triumphs or of human reverses ? Why
should it waste its time and treasure in the erection
of stately colleges and academic cloisters, when to the
brutal eye of its wealthiest citizens, the finest archi-

tecture is to be found in slave-huts and barracoons?
Why should it gather together libraries when there
is not one printed book of value in this world, which
is not an uncompromising reproach of that hideous
social system, and an irrefragable argument against
its possible perpetuity?

No: in a slaveholding Republic ignorance is bliss,
and enlightenment must bring the torture of remorse
and the trembling of fear. The prototype of the
Southern slaveholder is the African King, who,
gleaming with palm-oil and glorious in a painted
skin, drives down to the shore his squalid files of
shivering captives, and sells them to the missionary
of civilization, whose pirate bark is anchored in the
offing. The Monarch of Dahomey is the real founder
of the Confederate States of America. Their enlightenment, their theology, their civilization, their
political economy, have all been learned of that hideous and howling savage; and all they are, and all
they pretend to be, and all they care to be, the
barbarians of the Slave Coast have been before
them.

Yes: they do well to give up their colleges; they
will give up their churches next—and then—who
knows?—perhaps their clothes! Given the independence of the Southern Confederacy, and who can
assure us that within a century the governor of
South Carolina will not kneel upon his naked knees,
in all the splendor of a tattooed skin to adore some
dirty little fetish idol? Nations that have been civilized, and have lapsed into semi-civilization, are quite

as likely to fall still farther backward as to go forward; and there is a Power presiding over the
world's affairs which can blight as well as build up,
and which has declared that they who causelessly
take up the sword, by the sword shall perish.

Southern statesmen and soldiers, unless the downfall which we have indicated shall be utterly precipitate, will learn in time that one idea of genuine political equity is worth all the armies of Xerxes or Napoleon. The faith of the slaveholder is force, and so
is his philosophy. Hence his notion of a well-armed
soldier is of one who carries " one sword, two five-
shooters, and a carbine." This is actually the equip-
ment proposed in *The Richmond Whig* for 10,000
men who are " to carry fire and sword into the Free
States." Why not add a full suit of chain-mail, a
bow with arrows, a tomahawk, a scalping-knife, a
lance, a dagger and a sword-cane! This idea of
making a traveling arsenal of a soldier, is like a
stage-manager's notion of a pirate, who is invariably sent before the audience bending beneath weapons, offensive and defensive. It is an old-fashioned,
barbarous conceit quite worthy of a people which has
given up its universities and colleges. It is not by
any means certain that we shall not have war-paint
next; or, perhaps, imitations of those terrific paste-
board dragoons, wherewithal the unfortunate Chinese did not scare away the forces of the British
Empire. The number of weapons which the stoutest
and most alert soldier can effectively use, even in
carrying fire and sword, is limited; and we advise

the Ten Thousand to restrict themselves to single blades and a box of friction-matches for each.

August 9, 1862.

THE CHARGE OF PRECIPITANCY.

The *London Times* says : " Though civil war is the most frightful of all wars, the Americans plunged into it with less concern than would have been shown by any European State in adopting a diplomatic quarrel." In this little gem of malicious generalization, there is a lurking fallacy which divests the thunder of all its terrors; and which proves that a newspaper may be sufficiently pompous and at the same time insufficiently philosophical. "The Americans"—one would like to inquire civilly what this newspaper means by "Americans." Who "plunged" first—the United States or the Confederacy? Or did both plunge simultaneously? Can a man who finds a thief in his chamber, and who jumps quickly from his bed, be charged with immoral "plunging?" Were the measures of the Buchanan dynasty justly answerable to the censure of over-velocity? Did we not diplomatize? debate? hold conventions and propose compromises? Was not this continued long after the Charleston batteries rendered the reinforcement of Gen. Anderson impossible? · It is shameful to libel us in this way. No people ever shrunk from a war as we have shrunk from this. The seceding States, by the very act of secession, closed the door of adjust-

8*

ment in our face. The Convention of South Carolina
passed the Ordinance of Secession on the 20th of December, 1860, at fifteen minutes past one o'clock in
the afternoon; and since that day and hour there has
not been a moment when that State would, nay,
when she consistently *could*, diplomatize. It is true
that she sent her commissioners to Washington after-
ward; but she sent them as the representatives of an
independent State. Then, indeed, we were not precipitate enough. We contented ourselves with declining to receive this absurd commission, but we did
not send its members instantly to prison, as we should
have done, and as any other government would have
done. Imagine three Irishmen arriving at St. James's
with information that an Irish Republic had been
established, of which they were the accredited representatives, charged with proposals for the dismemberment of the British Empire! They would be locked
up as lunatics, or worse; while we permitted men
whose errand was a studied insult to our sovereignty,
to depart in peace. Was there any "plunge" here?
If so, it was a very mild one.

The attitude of South Carolina from the first was
a declaration of war. The act which consummated
her treason afforded no basis of reconciliation. It
contained just eighty-two words. It was a naked defiance of the United States; and could no more be
explained away than a blow can be explained away
among men of honor. It was a conclusion of the
pleadings, and an offer of the ordeal of battle. Northern men who had squandered their political fortunes

in the service of the South wept, persuaded, dissuaded and exhorted. There was flux of fine speech—an avalanche of propositions! At all this South Carolina laughed, as, to be candid, she had a right to laugh. Of the wisdom or good taste of these appeals, we say nothing; but we do say that they were made; and that the public mind of the North was at one time in a condition which caused those who while they loved peace well, loved honor better, to tremble. Who, then, can fairly say that we "plunged" into this contest with unconcern?

But we committed, it seems, another offense. South Carolina merely indulged in treason—our crime was leze-majesty against taste. Our newspapers "heaped every conceivable opprobrium upon Southerners." We did not sufficiently bate our breath. We did not softly enough whisper our humbleness. It was found that, Shylocks as we were, there was a lower depth of concession into which money could not tempt us. To tell the truth, we were a little afraid of the sarcasms of our European critics, and we shrunk from the insolent leading-articles wherewithal, if we had been false to truth and honor, *The Times* would have regaled us. We thought that in the presence of such crimes, indignation was a virtue. Our catalogue of past grievances was a long one, and when the culmination of them came, a people accustomed to no censorship of speech, uttered its convictions with a rude energy which offended none but trimmers. To our credit be it said, we were a little out of patience. It was South Carolina that half murdered our Senators in the Capitol; it was South Carolina that rifled mail-bags, impressed our sailors, banished our citizens, and always stood ready to defy the general Government. We only lost our equanimity when a State which for nearly a century had been receiving our bounty with one hand and smiting us with the other, abandoned even the forms and shows of loyalty, and placed herself in an attitude of unmistakable high treason. We were called upon to taste the bitter fruit of our latitudinarian policy—of our compromises and concessions —of patched-up peace and hollow truces. Then, we admit, we did not measure our words. We were in a condition too perilous for politeness of parlance. We became plain and. downright, and called a spade a spade. It may have been wrong, but for all that it was very human.

But this ready Jesuit of the London press having done the North all the mischief of which insinuated censure is capable, smilingly adds: "We consider that the course of events in the United States has been perfectly natural, and that Americans have only done what Englishmen or any other people, under the same conditions, would have done also." The world is wide; intelligence crowds; the size of newspapers is limited; and one is at a loss to consider, why a leading metropolitan journal should waste so much space in proving that Americans have acted as any other people under the same conditions would have acted. If in the management of our affairs we have not fallen below the standard of human intelligence, but on the other hand have done the precise thing which we were compelled to do, then we are at liberty to fall back upon the merits of the original question, and to demand of foreign nations a rigid and unswerving neutrality. Governments are not to be conducted by any infallible laws of success and failure; it is enough for all the purposes of international comity if we, in the midst of our many distractions, approximate to what is just and prudent. The right intention and the resolute endeavor should secure the respect if not the alliance of every Christian nation.

September 8, 1861.

THE ASSASSINATION.

Mr. Edward Everett, in his eloquent and patriotic address before the Mercantile Library Association in Boston last Wednesday evening, admitted that in his opinion there was a plot to assassinate Mr. Lincoln before his inauguration, but with characteristic amiability, Mr. Everett added : " wholly without the privity, I cheerfully believe, of the leaders of the Secession movement." One is loth, in these days of mental depression, to interfere with the " cheerful belief" of any man ; but is there a person of clear perceptions who does not also, if not cheerfully, at least certainly, believe that intelligence of the taking-off of the President would to-day be received with rapture by " the leaders of the Secession movement" in Richmond ? We must estimate men as they are. Would there be anything more shocking to the moral sensibilities in the assassination of a President than in the assassination of a Senator? Does Mr. Everett, or any other gentleman, remember to have read in any Southern newspaper, or to have heard from any Southern statesman, a disavowal of the championship of Preston Brooks? If so, he has been more fortunate than we have been. We know, from our own observation, that the perpetration of that crime, concerning which Mr. Everett improved many occasions to speak eloquently and properly, gave sincere pleasure to more than one Southern "leader." That Brooks meant murder, we have never doubted—the manner and the persistency of the assault would have proved so much in any police court this side of the Potomac. That Brooks, if he had accomplished murder, would have been indicted, tried, convicted and executed, he may think who pleases. The judicial record shows that the penalty imposed upon the culprit was shamefully disproportionate to the crime of which he was found guilty. Many a man has gone to prison for life for precisely the same offense, and many, we suspect, for a lesser one. Mr. Brooks died in his bed, and outside the jail; and his mourning friends have erected to his green and fragrant memory a sky-pointing pyramid. For what? Why, for attempting an assassination. Would they have done less for its accomplishment?

There is hardly "a leader"—that is, a man who plays at being a leader of this crazy Confederacy—who has not fought duels, or engaged in bar-room brawls, or headed a lynching of some luckless Abolitionist. Does Mr. Everett find it in *his* kindly nature even to believe, if these notable guides had been informed of the projected murder of the President, that they would have lifted a finger for its prevention? If not, then they were at any rate morally assassins, and did in theory aid and abet. Would lewd and unknown fellows have undertaken such a momentous enterprise without the sanction, tacit or implied, of their superiors in social position? This is a question which the thinking reader can answer for himself.

October 21, 1861.

STRIKING AN AVERAGE.

A CERTAIN newspaper emits the following gem of well-informed charity: "The people of the Southern States, if no better, are no worse, and certainly no more foolish than the average of mankind." Considering that the Average of Mankind eats its guests and even its grandfather; worships idols; goes in its own skin; cannot comprehend that two and two make four; is brutish, ignorant, sensual, thievish, gluttonous, improvident and superstitious, our polished friends in Richmond will pant with pleasure at this comprehensive compliment. To us it seems about as foolish as the average folly of mankind. But if this writer, as we suppose, meant to say that the people of the seceding States, are no lower in the scale of civilization than the people of the other

States—the people of the State of Massachusetts, for instance—then we take issue, and deny the truth of his assertion. In support of this denial, we refer to the Census Report, *passim*. If it shall be asserted that a people without schools can be as well educated, or a people without churches as religious, as a people with many schools and churches, why, he who asserts it must be foolisher than that great fool, the Average of Mankind!

Without repeating here the Statistics of Mr. Olmsted, who is a keen observer, we beg leave to refer the reader to the travels of "Porte-Crayon" in the Southern States, illustrated by his own clever pencil, and published in *Harper's Monthly Magazine*. The author is a Southern man, and so far an interested witness; and we are sure that nobody would have believed, but for his decisive testimony, in the barbarism to be found in North Carolina.

But it is most convenient to argue directly from the point of Secession. The fact that it is a great crime without provocation, and a blunder almost idiotic, knocks both nails on the head and clinches them. Secession is Wickedness and Ignorance. On the one hand, it is Passion, Pride, Ambition and Greed. On the other, it is Folly and Stupidity. The Seceders may not be any worse than the Hottentots, but in a certain sense they are no better.

It will be said that Massachusetts has talked of seceding. This is not true. Certain men, some of them of tolerable culture, but none of them of much political account, may now and then have spouted nonsense ; but the popular mind of Massachusetts has never even approximately assented to the doctrine. Her leading statesmen have always ardently disavowed it, and the Union has been a cherished sentiment of her people.

But it will be said that the people of the Southern States have been deluded by the Southern aristocrats. So much the worse for their wisdom ! Nobody ever thought a flock of sheep to be a flock of philosophers, because with multitudinous bleat they followed a silly bell-wether to destruction. Besides, what are the seceding States doing in this age and domain of Democracy, with Aristocrats ? Jefferson's Virginia, the pet daughter of Democracy, gone to the deuce to please her Aristocrats !

But no : again it will be said, you do not understand. The Virginian kind is a Democratic-Aristocratical Democracy—a Despotism tempered by mint-juleps, plug tobacco and "niggers." You must not suppose for a moment that the man with one nigger is *obliged* to obey the man with one thousand niggers —he only obeys because he delights to do so. Only he knows, this forlorn man with one nigger, if he offends the man with one thousand, that a dozen scamps with no niggers at all will be hired by the well-supplied Aristocrat to tar-and-feather, shoot, stab or hang, the poor man with one nigger. That's all ! That is Virginia Democracy ! As for South Carolina, why, we confess that she is our pet State. She never babbles of Democracy. *Quoad* niggers and poor whites, her refined, learned, rich, polished, nice, noble Aristocrats believe in a Despotism, beside which that of the Metternich school ripens into a kind of genial liberalism. Let her alone, and in five years we shall have the Court Guide of her Emperor illustrated by the names of Prince Pod, the Count of Cotton-Plant, Sir Robert Rice, and of many esquired gentry. What will become of the Average of Mankind, poor fellow! then, and in those swampy regions, we can only guess; but we are disposed to think that there will be a rise in the whip-market of the Empire.

It has been one of the chiefest causes of negro slavery in this country that it has demanded of the North, as well as the South, a general muddle of the human intellect, as the only safe, proper, constitutional cure of our complaint. This was natural, but none the less disgraceful. Thank God that at this end of the land at least, we shall hear no more, or not much more, of this dismal sophistry—this never-ending, still-recurring jangle of Inferior Races—of the Curse of Canaan—of the Compromises of the Constitution, of which nobody can give us the name and nature. The swift besom of war has swept away much of this rubbish. We stand more nearly upon the ground of solid truth than we have for half a century past. This is at least encouraging.

October 22, 1861.

THE COMING DESPOTISM.

THE roving prophet of the great London newspaper, in a late letter, foretells remorselessly the downfall of the liberty of the Press in America. He has had conversations with some Army-officer who told him that presently the army would come to New York, and suppress, by violence, all criticism of military movements. After the accomplishment of this enterprise, we are told, the Army will proceed to establish a Despotism and exalt a Dictator. After this—but here the prophet stops, most provokingly, we think; for while the fit was on him, it would have been obliging if he had treated us to a couple of columns more of the mysterious future. It is merely tantalizing to have a Bickerstaff at all, if we are to be put off with less than ten hundred Olympiads. And yet, for our own humble part, we must confess to a tolerable degree of quietude. The newspaper press is its own champion and watchful sentry; and it will take care for that liberty by the tenure of which it exists. The task is not, indeed, so hard a one as it was in England not many years ago, when Lord Eldon was accustomed to send to Newgate every editor who thought Bonaparte a better general than the Duke of York. In the advance of civilization, certain facts become philosophically settled; and among these is the fact that when one newspaper is tyrannically suppressed, ten, still more obnoxious, are sure to take its place. It may happen, indeed, as a matter of mere military policy, that the Government may feel

compelled, during the existence of actual war, to control the circulation of journals openly in the interest
of the enemy; but the right to do this, by no means
implies the right to prevent the discussion, in good
faith, of any public policy. No Government can be
expected to become the common carrier, in a time of
extreme danger, of libels aimed at its very life. But
there is an easily perceptible distinction between an
attack upon the existence of a Government, and a
criticism of its measures. Every Administration expects and tolerates opposition. It is the mischievous
hostility which is not content with less than a blow
at the whole political fabric, which must be restrained. This distinction the American people, ever jealous of their civil rights, well enough comprehend.

It is easy, certain things being conceded, to suppose
plausibly enough certain other things. Given an
army itself so servile, and its leaders so corrupt as to
attempt the destruction of newspapers, and we have
an army likely, in some mad moment, to attempt the
overthrow of the Constitution. If we are in peril of
this we cannot avoid it; for it is a danger incident
to our position. But on the other hand, it seems to
us that now, when we are asking so much of our
citizen-soldiers, it would be the extreme of discourtesy,
childishly to suspect them. We have called them
from domestic happiness and the ease and safety of
peace; we have asked of them the utmost of sacrifices
in the greatest of causes; and, luring them only by
the gathering cry of loyalty to liberty, we have placed
in their hands the ark of the Constitution. It is

no time for distrust. It is no time for foreboding. It is no time, Heaven knows, in a sneaking spirit of cynical suspicion, to doubt the honor and worthiness of human nature. When soldiers like ours, Freemen all of them in blood and bone, who never knew a master before, are submitting with hardly a solitary murmur, to the extreme rigor of military discipline, it is but fair to presume, that only an indelible and paramount affection for free institutions could have called them to the field, or kept them there.

It is easy to hint and to insinuate. But where is the general officer who has given in the past, any sign or token that he contemplates any such usurpation? And by what right is it assumed that well-educated and intelligent soldiers can be seduced into becoming the mere instruments of a single ambitious and unscrupulous man? We have not undertaken war for the sake of war, nor would fifty years of fighting make it palatable to the national mind. The genius of our people is no more military than that of the people of England. We can fight but we prefer peace. Moreover, those who speculate in this loose way upon the future of the Republic, leave out one essential element of fair calculation. The loyal States are not in arms because they are eager for political novelties and bent upon political experiment. They are in a position of the most thorough and absolute conservatism. They are contending under the sway of no insane fancies, and they are the dupes of no brilliant dreams. The Revolted States, it is true, are entering upon untried fields, and engaging in the pursuit of phantoms; but we know just where we are, and just what we are seeking.

There is the Constitution as the Fathers of the Republic framed it. There are the laws which they enacted, and the laws which we have enacted. Before us are our political duties not complicated and dubious, but simple and easy to be understood. We bring to this great trial a sober sense of the value of human liberty, and we strike no blow without a thought of the blessings of freedom. It is not in such a school as this that we are to unlearn all the lessons of our history; it is not under such influences, that we are to surrender our most creditable prejudices; it is not while we are desperately clinging to the traditions of the Republic, that we are to fling ourselves at the feet of a despot. When foreign nations judge us, we claim something on the score of character. It is grossly unfair, and no better than sheer trifling with historic examples, to predicate our future upon the fate of less enlightened and more turbulent states. We claim that our social problem is not perplexed by the presence of large masses of hungry and ignorant men, to whom any change may prove, or may seem, a blessing. Is it then for nothing that our populations are, as a rule, well educated? Is it for nothing that we have a more general diffusion of intelligence than can be found in any other land? Are all our multiplied institutions of learning and religion impotent for good influence upon the popular mind and morality? If so, let us hear no more of the blessings of knowledge! Let us do our best to bring back the old mediæval midnight! let us burn our school-houses and our libraries! let us, with what stomach we may, own that man is a fool, from head to foot, and make the best of a bad matter by having at least a hollow laugh at our own ridiculous destiny!

For ourselves, whatever of good-hap or sorrow the future may hold, we do not yet bate one jot of heart or of hope. Why should we, at a moment like this, when the people are proving that patriotism and self-devotion are not empty words? And why should we insult honest men, who are giving their lives and fortunes to the cause of human freedom, by speculating upon the chances of their all becoming slaves? If they were fighting for plunder, if any unhallowed dream of personal aggrandizement called them to the field, we might suspect their integrity. Moreover, while the General Government is thus assailed, we find every loyal State calmly carrying on its political administration, preserving the peace within its borders, and levying large taxes which are cheerfully met by the citizens. As the parts are, so will the whole be. The political stability of the States will insure that of the Union; and when that fails us, it will be time to fear a Dictator, and not till then.

November, 7, 1861.

ABOLITION AND SECESSION.

THE war has put some over-nice gentlemen in a pretty pickle. These are hard times for Mr. Facing-Both-Ways. For several years he has been blandly repeating : " Our Southern Brethren ! Our poor, injured, forbearing Southern Brethren !" But the Southern Brethren having so unmistakably gone to the bad—having surrendered themselves to the most unfraternal antics—having fallen feloniously upon that Constitution which has been Mr. Both-Ways' private and public and particular pet—he is forced to look about him for something to admire, and, as ill-luck will have it, he finds his ancient enemies, " the Abolitionists " (as he calls them), working devotedly for his poor Constitution, while he—where is he ? Not merely outside the caucus, but pretty nearly outside all creation !

In this hot struggle there seems to be nothing in particular for him to do, except to utter warnings which nobody heeds, and to give advice which everybody laughs at. He falls into a rage, and begins an indiscriminate damnation. To the pit he consigns the North, and to the same torrid place he sends the South. He calls loudly for " Union," but he cannot find it in his heart to unite with anybody, and so he goes on day after day blowing hot and cold, and telling his neighbor for the five-hundredth time that he is no " Secessionist," but egad ! he is no " Abolitionist." He fancies that this is conservative, and so it is, of brains ; for in such boys' play, there will be but a scanty expenditure of that article. He calls a meeting, and resolves that he is a patriot, but that he is not an "Abolitionist." He issues an Address expressly to let the world know that he is not an "Abolitionist." He nominates a candidate who is "No Secessionist" and "No Abolitionist," and he solemnly votes for that candidate as the representative of what he is pleased to call his "Principles ;" when the lamentable truth is, that what he thinks to be "Principles" is merely a hodge-podge of Notions, Prejudices, Traditions and other lumbering Nonsense. Having done this, he is satisfied. Things may go from bad to worse, but he is as complacent as an old lady who, having foretold a rainy day, wakes up to find the windows of heaven wide open.

We are led to these reflections by the solemn fact that in the Fifth Ward of the city of Boston, a little meeting of Constitutional-Union-Democrats voted the other evening, that they were for "the vigorous prosecution of the war," but that they were not "Abolitionists." A more unnecessary disclaimer we can hardly conceive of. It requires a modicum of brains to be anything of the kind. But we cannot blame these timid gentlemen ; nor will anybody blame them who considers that an "Abolitionist" is also an Infidel, an Agrarian, a Foe of Human Government, a Dupe of his Conscience, a Woman's-Rights-Man, an Anti-Sabbatarian, a "Spiritualist," a Phrenologist, a Water-Curer, a Vegetarian, a Fourierite and an Opponent of Tobacco and Capital Punishment. All Male Abolitionists wear Beards. All Female Abolitionists

9

are " Bloomers." All of them being tainted by
"Peace Principles" are avowedly in favor of Insurrection, with Fire, Bloodshed, Rape, Anarchy, and
a general whiz of everything. No wonder that a
smug-faced Constitutional-Union man, just as highly
respectable as it is possible for one of our fallen race
to be, takes all possible pains before he so much as
lifts a little finger for his country, to have it distinctly understood, though he may be in little danger, that he is not an "Abolitionist." His dudgeon
at the accusation is a portion of his respectability.

Now, it is no part of our business either to attack
or defend the American Anti-Slavery Society. It is
a distinct organization, and it is abundantly able to
take care of itself. But, before we consign to the
limbo of the wicked this poor word " Abolition," we
would like to ask, if there be in this whole State of
New York, for instance, one well-informed and conscientious person who is not an "Abolitionist ?" This
is the way to put it :

Here is this Negro Slavery ; it has been our tor-
ment and our curse, our daily and our nightly danger ; it has brought us to this shame before the nations ; it has attempted to overthrow the institutions
which we love, and which our fathers founded; it
has changed peace to war, plenty to want, confidence
to doubt, and ease to discomfort ; it has wasted our
material wealth, and it has hardened the hearts of
our brethren against us ; it has enfeebled the mind,
contaminated the pulpit, made dim the distinctions
between right and wrong, and discredited our demo-

cratic professions which, but for this curse, would have been the hope of the world! God favoring, circumstances permitting, the way opened by a Providence which will indeed be Divine, shall we not rid ourselves of it and forever? Where is the intelligent Northern man, we care not how he may politically style himself, who will not say from the bottom of his heart, to such a question, "Yes!" If this is to be an "Abolitionist," we should like to look in the face of the poor creature who will say that he is not one.

This is no longer a question of morals. It has rather become a question of common sense and of common safety; of ordinary prudence and the least possible foresight. We are arguing for no particular scheme; we are demanding no hasty action; we feel as much as any the need of a circumspect policy; but upon the naked question of "Abolition" or "No Abolition," we believe that every honest, thinking man will be ready to own himself an "Abolitionist." Shall we send down this inheritance of division and distraction to our children? Are we such cowards as to impose upon them a burthen which our fears and weakness shrink from? Shall the Union be restored only again to be jeoparded? Shall we have done our whole duty well and wisely, if we transmit to the next generation this frightful bequest of civil quarrel? And has our day been so full of glory and of historical achievement, that we can well afford to throw away this golden opportunity of redressing the injuries of an unfortunate race? And yet men shun the subject and shrink from the problem, because its solution is difficult, and strive, by a senseless babble of Constitutional obligations, to be rid forever of the matter. Is this brave, manly, or becoming?

We say "No!" And, if saying so puts us into the "Abolition" category, we accept the place as a place of honor. Many a good, brave, loyal man shares our opinion; many a citizen who has given his blood as if it were water, and his money as if it were dross, to the Republic, thinks as we do. And by what right is such a patriot to be classed with traitors in arms against the Republic? By what law, even of the cheapest personal civility, do these libelers couple the names of the sound and the rotten, of law-abiders and law-breakers, of footpads and freebooters, with the honest names of Christian gentlemen? And who are these new Mentors who assume to direct, advise, censure, persuade and exhort an immense majority of the voters of the Union—arraigning their intelligence, questioning their motives, imputing to them selfishness or silliness, venality or incapacity? Where is the record of their political successes? Where were they when this storm was gathering, that they did not by notable pilotage save us from the cruel shore of death which threatens us?

Abolition and Secession! Light and Darkness, Truth and Falsehood, Right and Wrong, Fact and Fallacy, are as nearly alike. Heaven help us if, in these dark days, which are weighing down our very souls, we shun truth because it is not pleasant, and strive to exorcise this devil of Slavery, by the gibberish nine times worn out and ninety times weaker than water, which sham-conservatives so glibly utter. Better fling at once every musket into the Potomac and recall our gallant men, than to prate follies at home, which will make their doughtiest deeds of none effect! If we must have the disgrace of a substantial defeat, let us meet it at once, and before we have murdered — yes, that is the word — any more men! If we must yield at last to the slaveholders, and think their thoughts and do their dirty work, let us at least save our money, for that will be a consolation in the lower deep of our degradation!

November 9, 1861.

A BACCHANAL OF BEAUFORT.

THE good news from the Naval Expedition has already, as to its more momentous details, been discussed and digested; but a distinguished person, deserving of historical fame, who figured, or rather who fell at Beaufort, will miss his immortality unless we amiably give him a hoist. When Capt. Ammon, with three gun-boats, visited Beaufort on the day after the action, "but a single white man was found in the village, and he was drunk." Such is the laconism of the telegraph, than which nothing can be more teasing; for we are left utterly in the dark as to the name of this cool reveler, who refused to intermit his libations to the god of whisky, even in the sulphurous presence of the god of war. In a poem like Campbell's "Last Man," namelessness might be artfully adopted to heighten the impression; but in matter-of-fact annals the hiatus is to be censured and deplored.   If some gentleman of a curious turn had been intrusted with the dispatches, he would have told us the title of this tipsy chevalier, who when all else was lost, resorted to his bottle for consolation; and who was found with that glass weapon lying empty by his manly side.   These vinous views of military duty are not novel, as the " cannikin-clink" in Othello sufficiently attests.   And does not the old recruiting song say that

> " A soldier's life, if taken smooth and rough,"

is, surely,

> " A very merry, hey down derry sort of life enough ?"

When care came with our cruisers, corn-whisky remained—not long, we fancy; but still long enough for a triumphant wooing of oblivion.   Others might run, but this brave man could not—it was not in his devoted legs to do it; others might be craven but he showed no lack of spirit; and while the fugitives left him to his fate, he slumbered as sweetly as ever Anacreon did upon the thymy ground of Teos, and was perfectly comfortable though twice a captive. This singular circumstance is to us suggestive.

Sir Paul Rycaut relates of a certain vizier—name given by Sir Paul, but by us forgotten—that after taking Candia he discarded his good Mohammedan temperance principles, and getting into a habit of intoxication, was soon so stupid of brain and so benumbed as to his senses, that his superiors reformed

him by a judicious application of the bow-string.
Now we have never favored letting cotton out of the
rebel ports; but would it not be politic so far to relax
the vigilance of the blockade as to let the "cratur"
in? If the rebels will but promise to drink them—
and of that we need no assurance—why not let them
have all the strong waters they pant for? Why not
send them brandy in bombs, and "old wheat" under
a flag of truce? why not drop bottles of tipple into
their camps from our balloons? Who does not see
that we might have one of their Major-Generals in a
mania à potu in a week! Then, of course, he would
fancy himself to be Alexander the Great, and in his
jollity he would kill some Col. Clitus, whose kinsman
would kill the General, and his cousins, in turn, Clitus's cousins; and so with a merry go-rounder of
murder, we should have half the commissioned officers of the Confederacy dead speedily. But this is
digression. We must return to the cup-captured
citizen of Beaufort.

We are apprehensive that Mr. Barnum has been a
little rash in offering a reward of $1,000 for the catch-
ing and caging and delivery at his Broadway establishment of this "last man" at Beaufort. If the Great
Showman was not in earnest, he should have remembered how easily this curiosity may be caught, and
how soon a bold Gordon Cumming may make prize
of such a lion in his liquor. It will be a pretty piece
of business if some fair morning a van should arrive
at the Museum door with the trenchant tippler of
Beaufort inside! What would Barnum do? His

constructive genius may extemporize tanks for whales, or a sufficient tub for the hippopotamus; but is he prepared to maintain a creature who will require puncheons upon puncheons of the choicest brands of the best Bourbon? The enterprise might prove ruinous. The clever manager might be obliged to raise his prices, and that we know would break his public heart. In three weeks he would be forced to offer a reward of something more than $1,000 to anybody daring enough to take the monster off his hands.

We are upon the eve of great events. Drinks, we notice, have advanced to fifteen cents each in New Orleans. What a famine price, or rather what a drouthy price they must be held at, then, in Richmond! What would be the moral effect if the rebel army were kept absolutely sober for a month? Would they advance to our lines with repentant tears in their eyes, and their demijohns, necks down and corks out, in their hands, crying for quarter and a modest quencher? We are afraid not. Madness would probably rule the hour; and if the despairing sinners came at all, it would be to run a desperate muck for our spirit-rations. Their advance would be as impetuous as the rush of a caravan to a desert-well. They would be dangerous, indeed; fighting not for glory, but for a glass of something comfortable. We might find their raging thirst too much for our best regiments as they came at us shouting "Liberty and Liquor," "Cocktails and the Confederacy" or some other ardent slogan.

As for the Beaufort brave, as he is now a prisoner,

we hope that he will be tenderly cared for. He will
be valuable as an expert, should we be compelled to
hold any courts-martial of a particular and not pleasant kind. He is entitled to soldierly courtesy, because he certainly did show a sort of courage, albeit
of the Dutch variety. The solitary situation in which
he was found should plead for him. His noble faith
in his Spirit-Friend, preserved while guns were boom-
ing and bombs careering, and the red eye of war was
unusually fierce and wide-open, shows him to be, in
his way, an uncommon man. Take him up tenderly,
lift him with care!

November 22, 1861.

CONCERNING SHIRTS.

WE mark with wonder that a contemporary goes on
speculating and spinning, and spinning and speculating, until he involves himself in the following extraordinary cocoon : "If this mad scheme of Emancipation were carried into effect, the necessity for cotton
would reintroduce the present system of labor in less
than ten years." This is what may be termed, in vulgar parlance, "a settler." We must have cotton—we
cannot have cotton without enslaving human beings
—therefore, we must enslave human beings. Of
course, morally, there is no limit to this style of logic.
Given cotton as a *sine qua non*, and everything favorable to its culture becomes right, and equally, every-

9*

thing unfavorable becomes wrong. Before the omnipotent need indicated, all must give way. There is
a necessity that knows no law, human or divine.

A starving man may steal bread—a freezing man
may steal a coat—and man in general, that he may
not starve or freeze, may steal other men. But there
is something worse involved in this proposition, viz.,
a regenerated and disenthralled world returning to its
original sin for the sake of a shirt! It is as if our
progenitors, Adam and Eve, had suddenly discerned
the shame of nakedness while in a condition of original righteousness, and so desperately swallowed the
apple as the only way of getting themselves an outfit.
We can imagine a world without light, or a world
without heat, but a world without cotton shirts is a
cosmographical impossibility. We may make good
resolutions, reform abuses, do unto others as the golden
rule directs, provided our shirts are not taken from us
thereby; but when it comes to a matter of shirt or
no shirt, all moral considerations can only be immor-
ally regarded, and the height of virtue is to be
vicious. We do not remember anything quite so extreme as this in Machiavelli, Hobbes, or The Fable of
the Bees. The *sequitur*, of course, is, that while some
men wear shirts, other men must be slaves; or perhaps it may be put thus:

    I. Without Shirts there can be no Men.

    II. Without Cotton there can be no Shirt.

    III. Without Slaves there can be no Cotton, *Ergo*,

    IV. Without Slaves there can be no Men.

    V. Without Men there can be no World.

VI. Without a World ——

But it would be painful and it is unnecessary to go further.

Thus it will be seen that the World actually revolves not upon an Axis but upon a Pod. It progresses because something is planted. A few bad cotton crops and we are nowhere. What a cheerful prospect!

This is, of course, a change. There was a time when shirts "save their own painted skins"—as the amiable Cowper has it—"our sires had none." There was a time when man struggled through his dark destiny in a linen shirt. There have been great men who still cut a considerable figure in history, who knew not the blessing of a cotton shirt. It is reasonable to suppose that Solomon in all his glory never enjoyed that comfort. Alexander the Great triumphed in a steel shirt, and tippled in a silk one. Julius Cæsar—poor man!—went in wool. We have some reason for supposing that Gen. Washington himself always wore linen.

But the difficulty is that once having worn a cotton shirt, mankind must continue to wear one, or cease to exist. No more fig-leaves now! No more purple and fine linen! No more leathern conveniences! We may, indeed, fancy that ours will be the privilege, pitiable at the best, of going shirtless if we please, buttoning our coats to the chin, after a shabby genteel fashion. Not a bit of it. The eye of the Destroying Angel will pierce through broadcloth, and discover our deficiency in Cotton Shirts.

The deduction of the Eternity of Slavery from the Necessity of Shirts is not a pleasant one, but we must take it as it comes. Once, in England, they used to put the case a little differently. There it was said that Man could not live by Bread alone, but must have Rum with Sugar in it. Then the formula ran— No Slaves, No Rum and Sugar. "D— it," said honest John Bull, "in that case, I will fall back upon my Beer and Brandy." This was easy to say, but when it comes to going without a Shirt, John recalcitrates.

But, then, if Slavery cannot continue, is doomed and justly doomed by God and Man to extinction, what follows? Why, that we must resign ourselves to Shirtlessness, or at least to Cotton Shirtlessness. There is nothing more to say. The thing is fixed, and very bad it is—for the washerwomen!

December 7, 1861.

FAIR BUT FIERCE.

In the name of Zenobia, Boadicea, Moll Flanders, Jean d'Arc, and the Maid of Saragossa, we begin this article!

Now that Messrs. Mason and Slidell are "given up," just, for all the world, like a pair of fugitive "niggers," another vexatious question has arisen, viz: Did the lovely Miss Slidell, upon the deck of the Trent steamer, slap the face of the unfortunate Lieut. Fairfax?

Commander Williams, that gallant tar, who suffered

such agonies on the occasion, was the recipient of a
dinner of the public variety on his arrival in England. In his post-prandial speech, Commander Williams went at length into the above-mentioned question, and made one of those nice distinctions which
would have been appreciated in a middle-age court
of love and honor. "Some of the papers," said this
briny Bayard, "described her as having slapped Mr.
Fairfax's face. She did strike Mr. Fairfax—but she
did not do it with the vulgarity of gesture which has
been attributed to her. In her agony, she did strike
him in the face three times."

And what does Commander Williams—sly dog,
Williams is, quite a lady's man—what does he add?
Why, he says frankly: "I wish that Miss Slidell's
little knuckles had struck me in the face. I should
like to have the mark forever." There is something
more or less amorous in this frank confession; and,
if there be an old, established Mrs. Williams, we
hope, for the sake of Commander Williams, that it
will not come to her ears. Williams, it seems, likes
to be smitten by the sex; in that respect differing
from that other ancient mariner, Capt. Edward
Cuttle, who lived in continual dread of Mrs. Mc-
Stinger's "little knuckles." We wish this British
seaman good luck; and trust that he may live to
be "slapped," though without "vulgarity of gesture," by a great number of the finest women—and
that Mrs. Williams may not be one of them.

Two things in the explanation of the Commander,
our readers of a Chesterfieldian turn will notice.

Miss Slidell committed assault and battery—for which at the Tombs they would have fined her five shillings—without "vulgarity of gesture;" and she did it "in her agony." From this we infer that Miss Slidell delivered her "one-two-three" with a refinement, suavity, elegance and grace which are at least rare in the Prize Ring. O happy Fairfax, to be so struck by such little knuckles! O fortunate mariner, if you did but know it! Williams says that to be assaulted so gracefully and by such little knuckles would make him forego washing his face for the rest of a natural life passed in dreams of that delicious moment. We agree with Williams, although we are not of his marine susceptibility. If one is to be slapped as to the cheek—we beg the refined Williams's pardon—if one is to be struck, "slapped" is vulgar—if one is to be assaulted at all, one would choose to be assaulted by a fair dame, and without " vulgarity of gesture."

Young ladies who read this newspaper, and we hope profit by it, listen to our admonition! This is a world of mutation. You do not think now that you will ever be called upon "in your agony" to "hit out" at a naval officer three times; but this is a world of extraordinary changes and chances, and you may be compelled in your " agony " aforesaid, to administer castigation to a meandering husband, or impertinent lover. Take a lesson from the exquisite and scientific Miss Slidell! Dear young ladies, when you go reluctantly to your calisthenics, and when you turn a deaf ear to the teacher who begs that you will

not neglect the cultivation of the *biceps flexor cubiti*
and the *deltoid* muscles, remember that the time
may come when you will regret your negligence—
when, in fact, and not to put too fine a point upon it,
you may desire to assault somebody in pantaloons,
and may yet be afraid to do it. See what hard training—constant practice, we suppose upon Topsey and
Dinah and Phillis—has done for Miss Slidell! Why,
the moment she gets into her " agony," she proceeds
as naturally to strike somebody, as if she had been
striking somebody all her life. See her squaring off
—no, that is vulgar—see her going through the pre-
liminary gesticulations before poor Fairfax! It is a
subject for a picture. It should be put upon canvas,
and hung up in the Confederate Capitol—when there
is one. Miss Slidell, with flashing orbs and tangled
hair and crimson cheek and curling coral lips and
heaving bosom and small fist clenched—Williams says
that she did n't slap, and this proves that she did, not
to speak vulgarly, clench her fist—Miss Slidell with
her pretty feet in position, her shoulders well
thrown back, her " little hands " covering well her
" mug " and " peepers," if we may employ those coarse
words—she, the petticoated athlete, should be the
central figure of the piece. Then poor Mr. Fairfax,
looking sheepish, prepared for punishment, with "hit
me again," written upon every line of his countenance ;
while Williams, entering like a true Briton into the
spirit of the occasion, brings in the basins and the
sponges, and is ready to hold the lady's bottle! Talk
no more of a dearth of historical subjects for the

easel! Why, the death of Nelson was nothing to this!

Though we are, on the other hand, rather than else inclined to the opinion that no living painter could do justice to Miss Slidell's "agony." Sir Joshua Reynolds managed Ugolino, but we do not think that our whole National Academy, with the Sketch-Club to boot, could adequately portray this Maid of (New) Orleans in all the sublimity of hysterics. If they are up to it, all we have to say is, that they do not need plaster-heads of Medusa to paint from any longer. Williams may be within reach of a clever brush, as with ears long and erect, and admiration driving stupidity from his countenance, he stands by speechless with gratification (and a large variety of other emotions) and wondering what this charming young woman will really do next. And finally, a companion-piece might represent Mr. Fairfax reporting his dishonor to Commodore Wilkes, with this motto:

"Which when the Captain com'd for to hear it,
  He was werry much astonished at what she had done."
January, 8, 1862.

BOBBING AROUND.

THIS Civil War has unsettled other things than the political peace of the country; it has played mischief with the intellectuals of a great many people on both sides of the Atlantic Ocean, and led to a wide-spread impression that, contrary to all precedents, flax will quench fire. "Why do n't you settle your differences?" roars *The London Times.* "Why do n't you make up your quarrel?" bellows the British orator. "Let 's fix things!" observes the remainder-newspaper of the Constitutional Union Party. "Niggers have nothing to do with the war!" cries Brigadier This. "We are not fighting for the niggers!" exclaims Adjutant That. "Not at all!" responds some Congressional Orator—"very far from it!" As for the policy of the Government, so far as it is deducible from Messages, Reports, Speeches and the other usual sources of information—who knows what that policy is? For what with contradictory orders, and Laws of Congress which gentlemen in epaulets think themselves at liberty to disregard, and what with British conversion to Pro-Slavery, and the general oversetting of all past moralities appertaining to that institution, and what with the Wilkes complication, the muddle has now become so general, that it is quite time to recall, if we can, our scattered senses, and to try to understand why we are fighting these expensive battles, and enduring, with more or less fortitude, these agonizing experiences.

One curse of war is, that after it has been waged for a short time, the bustle of its management and the pressure of its exigencies push out of sight, or temporarily shoulder aside, its original causes. War creates continually new complications. Substantially, the affair of the Trent has nothing to do with the war itself; and yet, in the matter, our officer did no more than he thought himself absolutely obliged to do, and

although, so far as we were wrong, we have made
haste to offer every satisfaction, yet this wrong, ve-
nial at the worst, to a pair of slaveholders, has been
sufficient utterly to abolish the Abolition sentiment
of England. Out of sight at once goes bleeding Africa, and the poor·blacks and emancipation; and
this very England which two years ago was coddling
American fugitives from Slavery, is now threatening
so to interpose in this quarrel, that Slavery, in a fair
way to be abolished if we are not meddled with, shall
be a perpetuated nuisance and an eternal crime.
What are we to make of this odd compound of selfishness and sympathy, of this penny-wise philanthropy, of this cheap pity, which subsides into indif-
ference the moment it promises to cost a little more
than an annual subscription of a couple of guineas ?

However, fault-finding in such a case as this should
begin, like charity, at home. There is enough that
is comically curious here without going abroad in
search thereof. For instance :

Here is a newspaper—we mention no name, for it
would not be civil—but here is a newspaper sufficiently noisy in behalf of the Union and Victory and
our Flag and Eagle; which keeps rousing and rally-
ing our Brigadiers, and calling for action; which is
a perpetual fountain of pretty predictions; and is
generally as patriotic as possible; while at the same
time, if the Governor of Massachusetts in his Annual
Message alludes to Slavery as the cause and the curse,
this same amiable journal at once begins to growl
out : No such thing—" niggers " have nothing to do

with it!—let the "niggers" alone!—hold your tongue
about Slavery!—rally for the Constitution, but, as
you hope for peace, say not a word about Emancipation. It affirms that all the Abolitionists are fanatical,
enthusiastic, incendiary blackguards. If a Member
of Congress ventures to hint that to this same emancipation you must come at last, that it will not do to
leave nine-tenths of the property of the insurgents
sacredly exempt from the perils of war, the poor
Member is instantly denounced as fiercely as he would
have been two years ago, and is at once written down
as both an ass and a pyromaniac!

How long do gentlemen suppose that we can go
on in this way?

Battles are earnest matters. Men are killed, a
great many of them, in battles; and human life, at
least white human life, is worth something. War is
expensive, and dollars are dollars. There is no cause
under heaven of this quarrel but Human Slavery.
It matters not into what form of words you put it, or
whether you display or disguise it, but every child
knows that this insurrection is in, the interests of
Slavery, and of a very mean kind of Slavery at that.
If we fight well we weaken Slavery, if we gain a battle, Slavery receives a blow; our opponents are slaveholders, and they are in the field avowedly as slaveholders to redress wrongs said to be inflicted upon
them as slaveholders; while the main purport of all
their manifestoes to the world is just this—that
Slavery is in danger, and that Slavery must be preserved. What fools, idiots, dolts, knaves, or good-

natured asses are we, that we do not accept the issue which is tendered to us, when such acceptance would make us strong, not merely in the righteousness of our cause, but in material and vital assistance and alliances! Can't we afford to be strong? Are we afraid of success? Do we shrink from victory?

And what are we afraid of? Of the Constitution? What kind of love for the Constitution is that which invariably interprets it in the interests of its deadliest enemies? How are you to help the Constitution by helping those who are bent upon its final demolition? What claim to constitutional consideration have these reckless rebels, who have trampled the venerable instrument under their feet? Is it to be *all* Constitution for them and *no* Constitution for us? The worst that we wish these banded and embattled felons is that they may get just what the terms of the Constitution decree to them. We say plainly that there is no other government under the sun which would have hesitated for a moment—which would not, long ere this, under like circumstances of national peril, have published a general edict of emancipation—which would not ere this have had in its ranks tens of thousands of well-drilled and well-armed emancipated slaves—and there are very few governments, let us add, which would not have sedulously promoted an uprising of the negroes, and which would not have fought the white insurrection with a black one.

But we are nicer. The benumbing muddle is on us still. "What *shall* we do?—what shall *we* do?—what shall we *do?*" we cry with incessant and ingenious variety of inflection. " The poor blacks "—we continue—" we cannot do anything with them—poor creatures !—on account of the Constitution, you know —and the Compromise Act, you know—and they would cut all their masters' throats, you know !" So we wait quietly for the masters to come and cut our throats—which will be more agreeable to the forms of the Constitution. Which cheerful work, with a little pleasant violence to our wives and daughters, with a small robbery of our treasure, with here and there the burning of a sea-board city, we have no doubt the man-owners will soon be ready to perform— if we will only let Slavery alone !

It is right to be taught by the enemy, always pro- vided the terms of tuition are not too high. He tells us that we should let Slavery alone. And be sure he is a very sincere preceptor ! Accept the maxim— let Slavery alone—assuage its wrath—give it a kiss of toleration—and then see how long it will let you alone !

January 8, 1862.

NIOBE AND LATONA.

WE remember that when we were the reporter of a respectable country newspaper, we were sent to take notes of the doings of a Whig meeting, and of the speech of a certain Southern orator who had been sent for to come over and help us. After he had fin- ished his nonsense, he approached our humble table

with the front of Jupiter. " Sir," said he, " do you
intend to report my speech ?" " Certainly," was the
response. " Sir," he returned, " you cannot do it.
You might as well try to report red-hot balls." We
took him at his word ; wrote a respectable speech for
him and printed it, and thereby, we then did flatter
ourselves, saved for the Whigs at the election a very
pretty handful of votes. We have been reminded
of this little incident by reading " Cause and Contrast," which is a highly peppered pamphlet, the par-
turient pangs of which were borne by Mr. Thomas W.
McMahon, now of Richmond, in the United States,
Territory of Eastern Virginia, but formerly private
secretary of the Hon. Fernando Wood.

Mr. McMahon is a gentleman also whose acquaintance with that rare work, " Lempriere's Classical
Dictionary," we can vouch for, since he compares
the South to Niobe and the North to Latona, and
since he also calls plain sea-faring " sporting with the
Nereides of the deep." Now, why he should compare the South to Niobe, we do not precisely comprehend, unless it is conceded by him to be stone
dead ; and why he should liken the North to Latona
we do not any better comprehend, unless he expects
us to shoot him and the rest of Niobe's progeny.
But when Mr. McMahon is well-mounted upon his
rhetorical charger, he dashes ahead like a particularly
Headless Horseman ; and no martingale of sense is
strong enough to stop him. That which puts him
upon his most perilous paces is the prosperity of the
North. One grievous fault in the character of Latona,

is not so much that we have conspired against Niobe's babies, as that we have " banks." Also " insurance offices." Likewise " stage-coaches, railroads and steamboats." Moreover, " commercial emporiums, prosperous and magnificent."

And how have we obtained all these comfortable things ? The off-hand answer of a poor, plain man would be, that we have banks because we have capital ; and insurances offices because we have something to insure ; that we have " stage-coaches " and other criminal, though convenient, vehicularities, because we have something or somebody to carry, and that our " emporiums " are " commercial " because we have a commerce. But Mr. Thomas W. McMahon knows better than that. All these things have come to us —

1. "From the tobacco plantations of Virginia and Tennessee."
2. " From the flowery and fruitful regions of Opelousas."
3. " From the sugar lands of Attakapas."
4. " From the silver shores of the Mississippi, perfumed by groves of orange and citron."
5. " From —— "

But enough of this, though we leave a great deal of excellent fooling unquoted. The truth is that as " An ass once spoke, as learned men deliver," so he is speaking now again. What on earth has the Bank of Commerce in this city to do with " the orange and citron on the banks of the Mississippi ?" What in the name of common sense, or uncommon sense, has the Erie Railroad to do with " the flowery and fruitful regions of Opelousas ?" We are not aware that any

gentleman in this " emporium " has gone into business, and much less made money, because " the
silver shores of the Mississippi are perfumed " with
anything — orange, citron or river mud. If " the
picturesque and beautiful T. W. McMahon," as *The
Richmond Enquirer* calls him, had more of sense
and less of sonority, he would hardly have fallen into
the Hibernian blunder of enumerating the means of
wealth at the South as the causes of her poverty;
nor would he have attempted to show that Niobe is
poor because she has had a monopoly of two of the
most valuable productions of the world.

It is difficult to see why Latona is to be thus shrew-
ishly berated because she has been a good customer.
If we have bought cotton, have we not paid for it
before spinning and weaving it? If Latona has been
indebted to Niobe for tobacco, we ask in the name
of Justitia — for we also like to be classical now and
then — we ask in the name of Justitia, and Themis,
and Equitas, and other goddesses, and all the appropriate gods — we ask, if Latona has not paid for that
tobacco, short-cut, long-cut, pig-tail, plug, Cavendish,
honey-dew, before chewing or smoking it? And as
for cotton, the writer of this article has every reason
to believe that the shirt which he has on, when in its
original condition — its cottonian condition — was not
only bought upon what Thomas calls " the blessed
sea-island coasts," but was also bought at a price
fixed by the Blessed Sea-Island Coasters themselves;
that they drew for the money, and that the bills were
cashed at maturity; so that the shirt in question is

not — to be classical again — in the least a new Nessus-shirt to the wearer, but an honest garment to be received from the washerwoman without remorse and to be put on without a pang.'

Now, can McMahon lay his hand where his heart should be, and say as much of his shirt? Is he sure that the cloth of which his pantaloons are built, bought, doubtless, by an enterprising Richmond tailor in New York, has ever been paid for by the aforesaid tailor? Is he sure that he, the said McMahon, had not on at the moment of penning his splendid production, a pair of French boots bought in New York, but, alas! in New York never paid for? Niobe owes us millions upon millions, but how much do we owe Niobe, O picturesque and beautiful McMahon! If the facts could be arrived at, we should be willing to wager six cents that the pen with which this philosopher wrote, the ink which he misused, the paper which he spoiled, were all bought in New York, and remain unpaid for; and to this we will add another wager of two-pence, that the press upon which this brilliant pamphlet was printed, and the ink with which it was printed, and the virgin paper deflowered by its printing, were all bought in this or some other Northern "emporium," and remain unpaid for. Considering all these things, we are willing to confess that McMahon's blarney is about the boldest which has recently come to our notice.

Everybody has heard this McMahon's style of lamentation in private life. One man is thrifty, industrious, intelligent, and, therefore, successful;

10

while his neighbor is everything that he is not. No. 1 gets rich, builds a fine house, pays his debts, and lives in ease and contentment. No. 2 gets poor, hires a squalid house, is turned out of it for not paying his rent, lives at sixes and sevens with society, and thinking himself vastly injured, damns No. 1 as the source of all his woes. He fancies that if No. 1 had remained poor, he, No. 2, would by some fortunate bit of prestidigitation have become opulent—and he makes a fool of himself, and growls fiendishly at No. 1 accordingly. He says in the language of madness and drivel : " See that fellow—he has made his money out of me—he rides in my carriage—he drives my horses—he lives in my house, and he eats my food and he drinks my wine, and he uses my plate, and he wears my clothes."

" Two hundred and thirty one millions of dollars were," says McMahon, " the annual dowry which the South (Niobe) cast at her (Latona's) feet." He then goes on in a dreadfully low-spirited style, to say that the South is a pelican ; that we are her progeny ; that she has drained her breasts to feed us ; and he concludes by uttering other flapdoodle for the nourishment of the Richmond mind. We congratulate our provincial friends in Virginia upon the possession of such a warm writer in this cold weather ; and we are confident that a copy of his pamphlet placed near the feet upon going to bed, will be found equal to the hottest hot-water jug ever corked up to lay between the sheets.

January 22, 1862.

SECESSION SQUABBLES.

THE reckless dissensions of leaders have been the ruin of half the revolts mentioned in history. It is not impossible that Charles Stuart might have reached London, however short might have been his stay there, if he could have kept his Highland chieftains from quarreling. The operations and efficiency of our own Revolutionary Army were often seriously embarrassed by the military intrigues of ambitious leaders; and nothing but the extraordinary good sense of Washington rescued us upon such occasions from temporary discomfiture. Men who have thrown off the authority of one Government, glide with but little grace into loyalty to another; and it is when the foundations of society are broken up, that the aspiring ply with the greatest and most mischievous assiduity their schemes of personal aggrandizement.

We are not, therefore, at all astonished to find that the leaders of the Slaveholders' Rebellion are already at loggerheads; and as our sources of information are their own newspapers, we accept as a fact what we should have theoretically anticipated. The vice which proved so fatal to the fallen angels has not spared these their legitimate descendants—the little Lucifers and the great Beelzebubs of the Man-Owner's Conspiracy. Richmond, if we may credit its journals, is full of petty squabbles, and the serenity of men who profess to be the architects of new and nobler institutions is continually disturbed by the torments of an unslumbering jealousy. We have written in our time with sufficient asperity of our political antagonists; and if they have not always kept to the truth, why we, it must be owned, have not always kept our temper; and yet we never, for his sins, castigated a Pro-Slavery Democrat with a tithe of the virulent unction with which *The Richmond Whig* assaults the Davis Administration. The managers of that sheet know best whether they can afford, in their present predicament, to be hypercritical, and the pre-eminently factious of a faction; but as neither they nor those to whom they appeal have ever submitted, either in public or in private affairs, to the semblance of control, it is not probable that considerations of Confederate safety will keep one pair of duelling pistols in its case. The secession of those States was partly caused by a general passion for politics, which, in a slaveholding community, commonly afford the only avenue to distinction, and to the intelligent, the only escape from an intolerable night-mare, and life-in-death listlessness.

Secession, itself the offspring of politics, breeds in its turn a progeny of parties, each prolific of cliques, and each restive under guidance. Mr. Davis has not warmed the stool of office, before this aspirant or that newspaper seeks to push him from it; and a score of men think themselves as well entitled to the honor as he is. Are not their necks as precious as his? Why should he come in for the robes of place, and they for raggedness? Why he for eminence and they for obscurity? They made him, great as he has grown; their votes are the meat upon which he has fed.

"Why," some scion of an ancient and dilapidated Virginian house might ask, "Why is this man sovereign and I only sergeant upon (a promise of) quarter-pay?" It is in this key—a kind of mad minor—that *The Whig* pipes its disaffection. "Why has n't my advice been followed?" asks the able Editor of that paper. "Why does n't the army ravage Pennsylvania?" And then it goes on frankly to declare why. It is because the "Government"—which, of course, is not expected to even go through the motions of governing—has been "wrangling with popular generals, and piddling over petty jobs." This is acidulous as well as alliterative. *The Whig* then, really quite after the manner of Junius, says: "A child with a bauble, an old man with a young wife, are partial illustrations of our deplorable folly." The rage for fine writing has led many a Southern editor into scrapes either droll or murderous; but this man of metaphor who has contrived to compare the Confederacy to a "bauble" and "an old man's wife" has surpassed his predecessors as much in boldness as in truth.

To say that *The Whig* is discontented, exasperated, indignant and ferocious, is to say nothing adequate. Its wrath mounts to an ecstasy. Summer and winter have passed in dreary inaction. Disease and the weariness of waiting have demoralized the Confederate camps. "The finest army ever assembled" has "wasted away," and still *The Richmond Whig* has borne it with a patient shrug. But no, patience being no longer a virtue, but the most vicious of vices, *The*

Whig takes off its coat, and delivers its right and left at the culpable Cabinet, assuring its readers that certain "reputed great men" are, after all, disreputable little men, who must, unless this fine, fresh, youthful Confederacy is to go to the deuce, be reformed out of office, and give place to those who read *The Richmond Whig* regularly, and profit by its admonitions. It calls upon "Congress" to "see that other departments perform their functions," and confidently predicts that when "our side" gets inside, the vehicle will move with admirable ease and celerity. But if "Congress" should prove as incompetent as "Cabinet," nothing will remain to be done but for Mr. Jefferson Davis to go up to the House, pistol the Speaker, turn out the Members, and establish a Despotism tempered by cocktails and leading-articles.

This, then, is the Confederacy, so little compact that even the perils of war and imminent destruction cannot unite it! These are the men so little unselfish, so grossly self-seeking, that their own companions cry shame upon their low ends and disreputable aims! These are the proofs of capacity for maintaining political independence which the Rebels offer to the powers of the world! President, Cabinet, Senators, Representatives, Editors, squabble like a group of runaway boys over a bird's nest with nothing in it! Why, this would make the most brilliant victories barren; what will be its effect when thick-coming defeats, the occupation of great cities, the dispersion of the Rebel armies, the seizure of military strongholds, the complete command of coasts and rivers and gulfs, shall have brought that bitter disappointment to which only despair can succeed? Let the Rebel leaders look well to themselves then, lest the popular petard which they have been cramming with falsehoods and passions, give them a hoist more lofty than agreeable. Half the citizens of the South do not as yet know the alphabet of government. In the political ethics of the plantation they are well enough versed; they have a dim notion of governing by the aid of a long whip and a heavy-handed overseer; but of governing themselves, of permitting themselves to be governed, they have no more notion than had the Barons and Robber-Knights of the Middle Ages—the quarrelsome rag-tag and bob-tail of chivalry that followed St. Louis to Palestine. The doctrine of secession would be found in the end monstrously inconvenient, even though it should be at first triumphant; for after that, there would be "nothing but thunder." State would recede from State, County from County, Parish from Parish, Husband from Wife, and Copartner from Copartner, until, at last, we should hear from their farm in North Carolina that Chang had seceded from Eng, and that both were dead—the victims of a mania for breaking things generally!

March 6, 1862.

" BIBLIUS. "

THERE is not in this world a sadder spectacle than that which is presented by a seedy, second-hand clergyman, who has been turned out of his pulpit, writing letters to the newspapers in favor of Slavery upon Shem-Ham-and-Japheth principles. It is astonishing, considering what a poor figure such people cut, that they will persist in cutting it. But they never learn anything, and still stick to notions which were antiquated long before these choppers of cheap logic were born.

For instance, here is the Rev. "Biblius"—for so he signs himself—writing to *The Boston Courier* after the interrogative, Socratic fashion of Bishop Berkeley and President Lord, to inquire "whether Slavery, as a variety of human government, does not stand immutably in the will of God, during the present distracted and probationary state of earth and man," which seems to us very much like asking whether, while we continue to sin, we shall not remain wicked. The reverend writer is of the opinion that Congress should initiate no measure of Emancipation, because it would be an interference with "the predicted blessings of Shem, the enlargement of Japheth, and the restraint of licentious Ham, for the better conservation of the world, otherwise liable to revert to the state of Babel." The reader need n't laugh. We say that all this is before us, printed in serious black and white. Here is a man in the Nineteenth Century who is actually afraid of a new Tower of Babel!

Why does he not go farther? Why does he not predict that Emancipation will be followed, maugre the rainbow, by another flood? or by a plague of boils and blains?

This threat of polyglot confusion is alarming. We shall be found, some fine morning, talking Chinese to our neighbor who understands only Choctaw. Both the great dictionaries will become worthless. The whole world will be given to lunatic jabber, and all because of Emancipation! But worse will follow. Shem will be swindled out of his "predicted blessings." Japhet will be *ensmalled*, and not "enlarged." "The licentious Ham" will break loose, and cut all sorts of unscriptural capers. The prospect is unspeakably dreadful! The excellent "Biblius" thinks that "study would doubtless have prevented the civil war." But it is never too late to mend. Let us all beg, buy or borrow dictionaries and go at it! Congress is always purchasing this thing or that—seeds, pictures, patent plows—and why should n't it invest a million or so, in these plenteous times, in lexicons and chrestomathies! Is n't it evident that if we are to be saved, it must be, not by Major nor even by Brigadier Generals, but by sound professors of Hebrew.

At any rate, something should be done. The universe has not been in such a perilous condition since the war of the Titans. Divine Providence is in a dangerous way; and it is certainly odd that our only safeguard against "the premature catastrophe of nations" should be communications in *The Boston Courier*. Let us all go at our "Aleph-Beth-Gimmel"

10*

at once; for if we do n't, who knows what mischief may be done when Ham gets a good opportunity to break Shem's head! We do not think that we shall hereafter support any man for the Presidency who is not well up in his Hebrew, points and all. It will never do to have Providence thwarted in this loose way.

March 22, 1862

COLD COMFORT.

Do our readers remember a newspaper entitled *The Atlanta Confederacy?*—a journal which has, even in gloomy times, furnished us with matter for cheerful comment. We are grieved to announce that this once jovial sheet is now deeply "depressed at the (Rebel) reverses sustained during the winter months." According to *The Confederacy*, the thermometer is greater than the sword, and the traitors must not expect to win any more battles until hot weather is well established. At present the Southern population is "chilled, benumbed, and lifeless." At present the Southern patriot "would scarcely move from a good hickory log to dodge a cannon ball." Wait 'till the mercury bobs up to above eighty degrees in the shade! Confederate valor is of a dormouse variety. Just now, Chivalry is hybernating! Poor Tom 's a-cold! He can 't be expected to thaw into invincibility until about the middle of June. Then he will come out, like a polar bear, lean but ferocious. "Then," says

The Confederacy, he will "revel in his tropical glory." He is never irresistibly savage until he sweats. He cannot be valorous save in his shirt-sleeves. In hot weather "he pants for blood." At least, so says *The Confederacy.*

On the other hand, according to this newspaper, a Yankee is never half so valorous as when half frozen to death. He does n't begin to show himself until he shivers. He is nobody, unless the wind is north-east. He is a sweltering zany at a temperature one degree above nothing. The solar rays are more fatal to him than famine. When "the Southerner revels in his tropical glory," the Yankee "wilts, and goes under." "Mark what we say," exclaims this military meteorologist, "the first battle on a hot day, we will whip the fight." This is plucky, if not precisely grammatical. It is evident that nothing can save us but a providential succession of the nastiest North-Easters. Under these circumstances, perhaps our generals should receive instructions never to fight except when it is chilly. To be sure, a good many years ago it was not what you might have exactly called cold at Concord and Lexington; and we believe overcoats were rather than else discarded at Bunker Hill. We know something about warm weather up here, planted as we are in close proximity to the North Pole. We beg leave to assure our brother of *The Confederacy* that we do not go in bear-skins the year round. Exudation will not be a phenomenon altogether new to us. We have that rarity, "the hottest day of the season," even in these latitudes.   What says the poet, Dr. Holmes? "The folks that on the first of May, Wore winter-coats and hose, Began to say, the first of June, 'Good Lord, how hot it grows!'"   And that was in Boston, the very nursery and ague-paradise of North-Easters.

If ninety degrees above, in the shade, were necessarily fatal, we should have "a very dying time" here in New York every Summer.   One set of dog-days would leave Manhattan a desert.   Yet, somehow, by virtue of straw hats, linen coats, and ice at discretion, we do, some of us, survive surpassingly high temperatures.   We do not call ourselves absolute salamanders—nor Shadrachs, Meshachs, and Abed-negos—but we do not believe that the fiery sunbeams of Secessia will quite singe the hair off our soldiers' heads, nor that our braves will be driven to Sydney Smith's extremity, of getting out of their flesh to sit, or stand, or do battle in their bones.   Somehow, we cannot think of our gallant fellows advancing with fans in one hand and the rifle in the other.   Thus far, in more than one fight, they have shown themselves cool enough.   We hope it will not be entirely different in June.

It is curious to notice the fatuity with which the Rebels rely upon Hot Weather and the Yellow Fever. It would be still more curious to see them upon their knees praying for a pestilence—supplicating for miasma—beseeching Heaven to change the proportions of atmospheric air, and to diminish the quantity of ozone—tenderly invoking the gentle offices of the measles and fever-and-ague—sighing for the co-operation of the small-pox—begging that fate may cut us off from our quinine, and that every shell which they discharge may shiver at least one of our medicine-chests. They do not seem to remember that if death should become general, they might be called upon to die just a little. Under the most favorable circumstances, in past years, acclimation has not saved them from fatal, periodical epidemics—they have been swept off even as if they were. common mortals. How will it be with the hot skies bending over their dirty camps—with their Commissariat in confusion—with the army-uniforms and blankets in rags—with no habits among the men of self-restraint, and with but little intelligence among the officers? Will not these " children of the sun," as *The Confederacy* calls them, be in some danger of disease? The Atlanta newspaper assures us that, under these circumstances, "the current of life," in Southern arteries, "flows with accelerated speed." It may flow altogether too fast.

This acute journalist is complacent in the opinion that no Yankee will fight unless the weather be such as to make " a heavy coat and thick boots " comfortable. To be sure, some of our army-coats have not heretofore been of the heaviest, nor have our army-boots been of the thickest—but let that go! If *The Confederacy* be right, it becomes us to make haste and to do our fighting before the days of the dog-star. If the Southron " dreads cold weather," now is the time to give him a little brisk exercise.

April 30, 1862.

EXTEMPORIZING PRODUCTION.

Our statistical friend, Mr. De Bow, whose arithmetical exploits in the manufacture of Census Reports did not give the world a very lofty idea of his veracity, whatever may have been the opinion of his ingenuity, announces with some flourish that a blacking and lucifer-match-factory has been established at Lynchburg, and that North Carolina has engaged in the manufacture of pea-nut oil. Moreover, Mr. De Bow lifts up his voice jubilantly in respect of eight tan-yards in Louisa County, (State not named.) Also, many females are "spinning upon old fashioned hand-looms in South Carolina." Mr. De Bow spreads his statistics, which are dreadfully meagre, over the broadest possible surface, and brings up on bowie-knives. They are turning out these valuable weapons, it appears, with consummate alacrity, in Portsmouth, Va. And this suggests a more careful examination of Mr. De Bow's new productions, which prove to be principally bayonets, camp-stools, gunpowder, tent-poles, bowie-knives, revolving pistols, drums—and, we presume, fifes, and even flags. But Mr. De Bow, while making up the rose-colored record, and telling us that they are producing leather in Albemarle and shoes in Madison County, does not tell us how much leather nor how many shoes. There are eight tan-yards in Louisa County; but are they large or little tan-yards? and, above all, are they new or old tan-yards? and, finally, are they tan-yards in which leather *was* or *is* manufactured? We should like to have a veracious answer to the questions, because, in war, shoes are of more importance than swords, particularly in the course of a retreat. One good side of sole-leather will be worth more to the rebels than a small cargo of pea-nut oil. We are the more particular on the subject of leather, because we happen to know that there is a considerable demand even in the Rebel States for Northern shoes, about this time. Mind! we do not say that there is any supply—we only say that there is a demand.

But let us go back to De Bow! In his whole elaborate list we find only one manufactory of powder, (in Charlotte County, Va.,) which is turning out 1,000 lbs. per diem. Besides, here the fallacy of the De Bow computations is lamentably exposed in general. One hundred thousand pounds of powder, myriads of bowie-knives, mile-long and mile-wide parks of artillery, innumerable camp-stools, and millions of bushels of tent-pins, add nothing, either in times of war or of peace, to the actual wealth of the country. Nothing so adds which is manufactured simply that it may be almost simultaneously destroyed. Once more we must call attention to the fact that, physically and materially considered, war is waste. The pound of powder which is blown from a gun is gone forever, and can never by any possibility be a pound of powder again. The shell which bursts may kill a dozen of the enemy, but that is an end of it—it will never kill any more. Human industry, in many of its departments, works over and over again the same materials—such as rags,

iron, etc., etc.   But this is not true of the materials
of war, or is so only in a limited sense.   Hence any
prolonged military struggle requires both capital and
a continual reproduction of original material.   War
works with a double mischief.   It produces less and
consumes more than peace.   Mr. De Bow, who is not
the most profound of economists, mistakes a petty,
spasmodic production, liable at any time to be inter-
rupted, for a steady supply sustained by capital increased, or at least undiminished.   He is of the cat-
your-cake-and-have-it school, which is not the most
accurate in the world.   The Southern slaveholding
economists are always making this blunder.   Gov.
Wise used to say despairingly to his lazy Virginians,
"Do n't you see, that if you raise 5,000,000 bushels
of corn you will be better off, you and your niggers;
and that if you raise 500,000,000 bushels you will be
still better off."   Southern enterprise has been forever complacently contented with the discovery that
it wanted something—it has rarely gone to the labor-
ious length of supplying itself.   It has felt the want
which has palsied the production of many a people
much more deserving—the want of intelligent and
well remunerated labor.   Human beings, considered
simply as capital, with no reference to their human
rights, with no regard for the law of God's own express enactment, that the laborer is worthy of his
hire—human beings, held as horses or heifers are
held, can never be or produce permanent wealth.
Behind all apparent prosperity, there is always the
damnable fiction, which makes the most splendid

results only a show and a sham. The collapse may at any time come. There is nothing provident in Human Slavery—no saving for .a rainy season—it is all *carpe diem* in its philosophy and practice. You cannot make black men or white men real estate merely by a little loose legislation. Toward a general recognition of this truth the whole world has been struggling for eight centuries, and not without success. Feudalism went first, although it made better masters and more productive vassals than slavery, and did not imbrute the noble by ministering to his personal luxury. Slavery in the Roman Empire disappeared like a mist before the sun of the new Revelation. Men were not ashamed, even in the time of Louis X., to manumit their vassals *pro amore Dei;* while Dr. Fuller and his disciples desire to keep men in eternal bondage for the same pious reason. The one great question in Russia for half a century has been, "How shall we be rid .of serfdom?" In the United States, during their whole political existence, with a certain class, the one great question has been, "How shall we conserve Slavery?" Hence we have been, too many of us, at one endless, horrid grind of logic to prove—what all the rest of the world was practically denying—that Human Slavery is profitable; and it has all ended in Mr. De Bow's assertion, that there are "eight tan-yards in Louisa County." In sheer disgust we quit the subject. We do not believe that eighty tan-yards will save Slavery in this country, or, at last, anywhere else.

May 1, 1862.

VERY PARTICULAR.

MR. JOHN F. MUNROE is the worshipful Secession Mayor of New Orleans; and although we cannot recognize any man as a public officer who has repudiated his allegiance to the United States, yet, as somebody must do the epistolizing on the insurgent side, Munroe is perhaps as good as another for the purpose. His exceedingly cool letter of the 20th ult. to Capt. Farragut shows that he does not by any means intend to be " diddled out of the sweets of his unfortunate situation." He is quite ready to surrender the city, but he wishes to do it genteelly; like the unhappy man at the Old Bailey, who insisted upon being carried up the scaffold stairs, as he could not conscientiously in any way be a party to his own death. So Mayor, or Ex-Mayor, or Mock-Mayor Munroe is highly fastidious. As for pulling down the Secession flag, he cannot do it; for he says that his " hand would be paralyzed at the very thought of such an act." Also " his heart." This would seem to settle the matter; for, medically considered, paralysis of the heart is no joke, and is really a sort of complaint which it is not safe to indulge in oftener than three times a day, if so often. After this, Mayor Munroe begins to whimper in the following feeble style: " You have a gallant people to administrate during your occupancy of this city—a people sensitive to all that can in the least affect their dignity and self-respect. Pray, sir, do not fail to regard their susceptibilities."

Oho! Sets the wind in that quarter? Will anybody learned in the black art tell us by what necromancy, thaumaturgy, prestidigitation, or whatever you may call it, the boot has been so rapidly and miraculously transferred to the other leg? How have the "susceptibilities" of Union men fared in New Orleans, or anywhere else, for that matter, in the revolted States? How in East Tennessee, for instance? In this very city of New Orleans, the putative Mayor of which now bawls for mercy, and shivers with guilty apprehension in his official robes, how safe has it been for any man—ay! or for any woman, to question the morality of treason, or the duty of dissolution, or the exceeding beauty of Slavery, or the omniscience of Davis, or the invincibility of Beauregard? Why, it was only the other day that we quoted from what was once a respectable New Orleans newspaper, ample evidence of the existence of a reign of terror in that city. Men who refused to take up arms in defence of the "Confederacy" were threatened with the direst penalties—imprisonment, confiscation, or even death! Mechanics of Northern birth, who remained loyal to their country, have been swindled out of their wages, locked up, or forced to march in the traitor ranks. Schoolmistresses have been treated in more than one instance with excessive cruelty. Clergymen, guilty only of fidelity to their ordination vows, have been haled from their pulpits and banished. But why do we thus dwell upon special instances? Can any honest and intelligent reader deny that Secession, wickedly needless and unprovoked in its beginning, has been coarse and blood-thirsty in its progress? and now, when our victorious arms are advancing once more to the establishment of law and order, this mincing Mayor, who would not have lifted one of his pens to save any Unionist from death at a lamp-post, trusts that the "susceptibilities" of Secessionists will be regarded! We thought that we knew something of magisterial impudence up this way, but we hereby renounce all laurels in that line. We have nobody here to compete with Mayor Munroe! Pray, why did n't he go just a little further? Why did n't he make a pension for life, a bonus of $100,000, a gold snuff-box, and a gift of five hundred "niggers," the inexorable condition of his surrender? Why did n't he insist, while he was about it, upon having Capt. Farragut's sword? Why did n't he stipulate that the Secession banner should remain flung to the breeze —should not be pulled down at all—should still flaunt and flutter to soothe "the susceptibilities" of the late Mayor of New Orleans?

Then there was one other thing which stirred up "the susceptibility" of this ill-treated gentleman. "The city is yours," he writes, with indignation, "by the power of brutal force." This is shameful. To be sure, we have never heard of besieged cities taken in any other way but "by the power of brutal force;" but New Orleans, we suppose, should have been an exception. We should have captured it by some kind of human weakness. But Capt. Farragut did not see the matter exactly in that light. He went to work in the old-fashioned way, which was certainly reprehensible. The truth is, when a city is taken, it is absolutely necessary that somebody should pull the flag down—it's a way they have in war. Another truth is, that if the Secessionists are so exceeding susceptible, they should secure the comfort of their own delicate nerves by setting us a good example. There is a certain guerrilla chief, Morgan by name, who is hanging Unionists at the West in rather a free and easy, not to say reckless way; and lately he varied his murderous performances by hanging a boy! There also seems to have been a good deal of unnecessary butchery of our wounded at Pittsburg Landing, and upon other fields. If the susceptible citizens of New Orleans will form a General Susceptible Society for the Promotion of Humanity and the Prevention of Scalping, with Albert Pike for President, perhaps the next time they are called upon to apprehend—not really feel—the miseries which have been inflicted on others, they will be just a trifle manlier in their appeals. Above all, they should suppress Mayor Munroe at once. He is evidently too "susceptible" for the wear and tear of public life.

May 6, 1862.

PRUDENT FUGACITY.

IT is an unquestionable fact, that a considerable prejudice has always prevailed in military circles against
running away; and yet it must be said, upon the
other side, that when stampeding is more favorable
to health and longevity than staying, it is a man's
duty to stampede: when the ice breaks, and all the
boys fall in, who shall blame the rest for absconding?
But coming events cast but sable shadows in the
paths of Richmond editors, and they do not see
clearly why "Congress" should, just about this time,
be in such a hurry-skurry "to disperse." The pre-
eminent duty to save one's own bacon before attending
to the safety of another's will be recognized, we think,
by most persons who are in danger of cell or scaffold.
The Rebel Congress is, so to speak, the Soul of the
Confederacy; and being this, no pent-up Richmond
should contract its powers; nor is it fair to ask honorable members to continue to introduce bills, and to
conduct them with paternal kindness through the
perils of a third reading—much less to soar rhetoric-
ally and to spread oratorically—while guns are bel-
lowing outside the walls, and balls are dropping in.
It is only now and then that an Archimedes goes on
solving a problem in mathematics while Syracuse is
sacked and plundered.

The Richmond Examiner thinks "it would be
nobler and more courageous" for its Congressmen to
remain and share the fate of the city. But, really,
we do not see why *The Examiner* should have ex-

pected either "nobility" or "courage." Here is a
handful of men who, without cause or reason, have
madly misled their fellow citizens; or for no nobler
reason than selfishness, or for no worthier cause than
petty, personal ambition. What have these pretend-
ers done even for the South? Have they advanced
its prosperity, agricultural or commercial? Is Slave
property safer now than it was two years ago? Is
the Slave system stronger politically? Cogitating
these questions, and venturing to imagine ourselves,
for the moment, a patriarch, we feel that hanging at
a lamp-post is just what these sham Congressmen
should expect. No wonder they run. We do not
believe that it is altogether from the troops of the
Union that they are running. It is from deceived,
beggared, desperate men—the dupes or the victims of
the basest private ambition! When the loyalists of
the South are once more free to speak and to act, the
adventurers who led blind States into the ditch of
disunion will hardly boast stridently of their exploits.

Virginia has, indeed, little reason to love the Confederate Congress. It has brought upon her nothing
but shame and dishonor, nothing but ruined farms
and smoking villages, and wasted harvests; nothing
but blockaded ports and commerce crushed; nothing
but an inevitable and ignominious division of her
territory; nothing but a disreputable reversal of her
historical reputation; nothing but mortified pride
and lasting reminiscences of disgrace. When the
rebellion came, in spite of the threats of little, dirty
groups of Richmond politicians, the citizens of Vir-

ginia were beginning, in the recesses of their hearts,
to hope for the hour which should see them released
from the infernal incubus of Slavery. Politicians
ranted, and newspapers bullied, and Gov. Wise slav-
ered and stammered, but it was clear to disinterested
observers that the Richmond aristocracy would not
forever have things their own way; and that, when
they were trodden down into their native mud, a
speedy development of the immense internal resources
of the State would follow.

But selfish South Carolina saw fit to make Virginia
the battle-ground of disloyalty and treason, and the
Gulf States followed the example of that blustering
file-leader. It was upon the head of Virginia that
the storm of retribution broke, and is beating still.
The Rebel Congress flees to Richmond, and brings
upon that city the horrors of siege and of assault;
and when the danger becomes imminent, the Rebel
Congress takes up again the line of march and migra-
tion, and abandons those to whose hospitality it is
indebted for its feeble existence. The age is certainly decayed. The Roman Senators, we are told,
kept their seats in silent dignity, while the hands of
barbarians plucked their beards. The Confederate
Senate takes to its heels, without waiting for the first
gun. If chivalry long since died, there has been no
resurrection of it in Richmond. Orators, bill-mon-
gers, constructors of constitutions, all have "levant-
ed;" and, as *The Richmond Examiner* remarks, "have
sought for safety on their cotton-plantations," leaving the men who have housed them and fed them to

shift for themselves. Bolted! stampeded! cut! run! vanished, like so many Catilines! *Abiit, excessit, evasit, erupit!* Gone, as *The Richmond Whig* observes, "in a number of the newest and strongest canal-boats "—"drawn," as *The Whig* satirically adds, "by mules of approved sweetness of temper"— "armed with popguns of the longest range "—protected "by a regiment of ladies." Why, according to this not very mean authority, this Confederate Congress is a Congress of Cowards! Simple Cowards! No more, and no less! A cowardly cream of the cream, to be sure!

Now, we beg leave to call the attention of the reader to the fact, that these charges of poltroonery, made by Rebel editors against Rebel Congressmen, are explicit, plainly spoken, undisguised, and unmistakable in their *animus*, which is full of animosity. Virginia is to be sacrificed—to be left to the tender mercies of the Union, while the old original Southern Confederacy goes into business upon its own hook! Here is a further evidence, if it were needed, that this is a "Confederacy" without any "*Con*," where brothers in arms, associates in the foundation of a new Republic, are already at loggerheads. This beautiful Union is already disunited. This fresh, young nation is already living in a rainy season of *pronunciamentos.* It will be worse shortly. There can be no permanence in Human Slavery, for it lacks every one of the elements of stability, and there can be no permanence in a Political Government which is founded upon such a sandy fallacy.

EXTEMPORIZING PARTIES.

WHEN pestilence is raging, the manufacturers of infallible pills are always uncommonly ingenious and busy; but thus far, through our terrible political troubles, the political quack-salvers have kept remarkably quiet. The Republican party was good enough to go ahead, to take the chances of praise and blame, of success and failure, of life and death—a good party enough to grumble at, after that subdued fashion of fault-finding which was moderate enough to keep the querulous out of custody. Now that the Rebellion is in a fair way of being crushed, we predict an immense uprising of old gentlemen from their virtuous couches, an extraordinary putting off of night-caps, and an absolute hurricane of propositions. Some people naturally see no safety for the Union except in the resurrection of old-fashioned Democracy—but upon that we do not intend to waste many words. The wildest vagaries of mad Millerism are rigid common sense, when compared with this notion of the vivification of a party of which the principles are absolutely obsolete, and of which the members are mostly in the church-yard. All hope of a modern miracle being therefore absurd, it is sagaciously proposed, by one of the newspapers in this city, to reconstruct the Republican party—to purge it, to wash it, to rehabilitate it, to make it respectable, by casting out what are called its "radical" elements. The volunteer washerwoman on this occasion has kindly printed her soap-and-water programme. With eminent prudence, she condescends to allow the President of the United States to remain in the party. Also, all other persons, public or private, who will give their solemn word to refrain from "rampant radicalism"—couchant radicalism being, we suppose, permitted. Only "a conservative policy" is to be tolerated; and it is anticipated that "the radical," finding this "intolerable," will "become outrageous and bolt,"

"And leave the spoils to Crittenden and me."

Of course, after this "radical bolting, the Republican party will be the natural nucleus for all the conservative men in the country." A respectable wing of the Slaveholders will be attached, and we shall all go along again beautifully in a mild muddle of Pro-Slavery Compromises, until our sweet "Southern brethren" are quite ready for another bloody and costly insurrection.

Now, in the first place, we should like to have it specifically stated what this Radical Element in the Republican party is. It must, to begin with, be something to which not only is the President not committed, but something to which he is absolutely opposed; because, in the new arrangement, he is not to be left out in the cold, but benevolently taken in and done for. Therefore, as he is understood to favor the confiscation of the Slaves of Rebels, and is known to approve the Abolition of Slavery in the District of Columbia, and is also pledged to the doctrine of Non-Extension, we do not really see why he should not be turned out with the rest of us. We presume that he is to be kept in, only because he will not be an easy personage to expel. It is truly a most sagacious stroke of policy to seize the President in the very beginning; for the king's name is a tower of strength. But whether he will stay seized; whether he will exactly relish this summary disposition of his person and his principles, is more than we, not being a court-organ, can pretend to foretell, any more than we can foresee, what in this regeneration, transmutation, and transmogrification, will be done with the Secretary of State. We think that we have, in our time, heard him called "a radical"—of course, by his enemies; and as so many of them will be found in the same conservative boat with him, it may take all the influence of *The Journal*, which professes to serve the country, to prevent his being cast into the sea—which would be painful.

We have not ventured to say one word of the Republican party as a mass. What ordinary private people may think of such gigantic operations as these, is not of the least consequence. What is to become of the great body of the Northern voters? Will they do as they are told to do? Have they a passion for being disposed of by wholesale? chaffered for and cheapened by cliques? stuffed full of other men's opinions? completely exenterated as to their own? Ah! but we are all to be graciously allowed the Chicago Platform! We should much like to know who has asked for anything else—except, indeed, Mr. Crittenden, who, in the new arrangement, is to be allowed, we presume, a private platform of his own. And if he, why not other people who may fall into the regenerated ranks? Why not insert a polygamical plank, and rope in Brigham Young! Really, since these gentlemen are to take possession of us, of our souls, our bodies, our President, our Congress, our constituencies, our clubs, and our newspapers, it behooves us to be enquiring, with all due civility, what we are to believe after all the arrangements have been completed? Will the reconstructors leave us our name? or will they filch it from us? or will they call themselves the Reformed Republican Party? Has not that word, "Reformed," an ugly sound? to say nothing of that other word, "Republican?" Pray, how will dear Mr. Crittenden like that?

The whole scheme, it must be allowed, argues great kindness of nature in the schemers. We are not only to welcome home the Prodigal Son, but we are to have the heaviest calf all killed and dressed, and ready for him. To be sure, his highly improper conduct has cost us a great deal of money—but we must not be radical! He has well nigh ruined the nation for a whim—but we must not be radical! He has emulated the maddest red-republicanism of France—but we must not be radical! He has cost us millions of money and thousands of lives—but we must not be radical! We must leave to him the fantastic tricks, the humors, the whims, and the manias of politics—but we must not be radical! He has been all wrong, but we must not be radical in setting him right—not radical in enforcing justice, in measuring penalties, in probing swindles, in redressing injuries, in providing for the future. Oh no! When we deal with him, we must deal tenderly, maugre the dreadful trouble which he has brought upon us, and himself. We must bate our breath! We must whisper our humbleness! We must return good for evil, and in doing so we must not only be good, but goodies!

Finally, we protest once for all against the assumption that the Republican party has, in any bad sense of the word, been "radical." Considering all things, the world has reason to be astonished at the moderation which it has exhibited. The glib talk about "fanaticism" had no meaning when it was so freely indulged in during the late Presidential canvass, no more than it has now, when it is quite as freely employed by some of our professed associates. Offensive and meaningless nicknames are quite out of place in discussions so grave as these are. The Republicans do not profess to love Slavery—no, nor Slaveholders as such; they do not pretend to devise any patched-up treaties, or to seek for hollow truces; they would gladly see the cause of this wicked Rebellion vanish with the Rebellion itself; they desire not only a present triumph of the laws, but security for the future good behavior of men who have shown themselves to be reckless and desperate; yet, with all their stiffest opinions, and with all their most ardent hopes, they have never dreamed for a moment of transcending Constitutional limits, or of indulging an unworthy revenge. All speculations, therefore, which presuppose that any considerable body of the members of our Party can be drawn out of its organization by a predominance in its councils of a moderate policy, are at once absurd and insulting; and so they will be regarded, no matter by whom they may be undertaken.

May 19, 1862.

PLATFORM NOVELTIES.

There has just closed a week of "Anniversary Meetings" in Boston, under novel, not to say awful circumstances. While the struggle for Emancipation was going on in Congress; while the fate of General Banks's little army was yet in suspense; while five thousand volunteers were pouring into the city, the Men of the Platform also gathered for the yearly talk and tea; and the motley "delegates" wended their way to this church or that "temple" to the music of unusual fifes and drums. We all know what these anniversary meetings have heretofore been. In many of them there was an established routine. Somebody read a financial report; somebody then abused the "Abolitionists," and deprecated agitation; and then everybody went into the vestry for ham-sandwiches, coffee, and cut-and-dried jokes.

But the drums and fifes, with the proclamations of Gov. Andrew's proclamation, have cheerfully averted the prescriptive monotony. The Bible Society was told by Dr. Harris that "God created all men free and equal, and that we should use no man as a tool, or an inferior being to ourselves." The American Peace Society was told by Dr. Malcolm that the Rebel States should be permitted "to come in as Territories." The Young Men's Christian Association was entertained by "many merited compliments to the virtues of New England soldiers, and condoled with in the repulse of Gen. Banks's division." The Address to the American Unitarian Association was by the Rev. William Henry Channing, and urged "the unification of the various State institutions, by which we should be known as the Model Republic." Mr. Robert C. Winthrop, before the American Tract Society, managed to speak well of "that brave and gallant son of Massachusetts, Gen. Banks," which we consider to have been the most extraordinary utterance of the whole week.

At the Morning Prayer Meetings "thanks were offered for the almost uniform success of our arms." The Church Anti-Slavery Society emphatically, in a series of eloquent resolutions, endorsed Gen. Hunter's Army Order, No. 11. The Home Missionary Society was cheered by the Rev. Mr. Jenkins, who, undaunted by the fact that Dr. (Southside) Adams was in the chair, asserted that "the war will colonize the South with men who will encourage the labors of this Society." Upon the whole, we think this must have been an uncommonly trying week for Dr. Adams. It is curious to think what a sweep of cobweb sophistry, laboriously spun out of the very bowels of scholastic theology, this civil war has made. It is wonderful to note how remorselessly facts are treading down theories, and how some gentlemen, who blanched at the voice of a single agitator, are growing patriotically strong, and do not wince at the reverberations of a cannonade. The traitors now in arms against the Constitution have done it an inestimable service by silencing, we thankfully believe forever, that apologetic drivel which assumed, under every vicissitude, that Slaveholders were standing faithfully by Constitutional provisions, and honestly yielding obedience to their minutest requirements, while Anti-Slavery men, no matter what form their opinions might take, were, by the intrinsic vice of these opinions, hostile to sound politics and religious orthodoxy.

These weary years of recrimination, of slander, and of dishonorable imputations, have gone by at last; and though we are environed by a thousand difficulties, and by perils innumerable, we all breathe a purer atmosphere, and are forced to listen to fewer falsehoods. We bid our readers be of good cheer— we feel, we know, that there is health and strength in this storm, that there is union in this disunion, and a long peace awaiting the end of this sharp conflict. The platforms have been swept and garnished. Ye gods! when one remembers the rubbish which once cumbered them—limping exegesis and dusty diagnosis, split texts, ethnological puzzles, and sugar-coated pills—schemes of saving the Union by prayer, and other schemes of saving it by pugilism—reams of resolutions, rosy at once and wrathful—heaps of exenterated tracts, sleek and spliced for the Southern

11*

market—subscription papers for sending regiments of missionaries to South Carolina—when one recalls all these, how enrapturing the reflection that no more hairs are to be painfully divided, that there is to be no more mumbling and devising, no more presentment of the worse for the better reason, no more reliance upon shabby succedaneums, and that even in these awful alcoves of graduated political and moral regeneration, a spade is hereafter to be plumply called a spade, though calling it so should put the whole solar system out of joint, and make chaos come again! After such a change, going down into the very depths of our social life, who, we may ask, of all those who drank the anniversary coffee, and ate the yearly cake in Boston, did not feel a refreshing sense of reviving manhood or womanhood?

If any person fondly thinks that the Northern people are ready to go back to the deadly-lively acquiescences which created the Compromise Bill, the Kansas Bill, and the Fugitive Slave Bill, we advise him to read the proceedings of the anniversary week in Boston. They will prove to him, we think, as they have certainly proved to us, that hereafter, whatever may happen, the Slaveholders must look to some less respectable quarter than that of the Northern Churches for sympathy and succor. When this war closes, it will close upon the Northern people as thoroughly united upon the basis of a general moral principle as ever were the Slaveholders upon the lower ground of an abased self-interest. The future holds in itself good hap and evil, but whether it shall bring the sweet or the bitter, there are certain questions which will be no longer vexed in the Northern States. Very long we have been in coming to this point, and very tardy in our recognition of the simplest verities; but now there can be no footsteps backward. The Rebels have called for the previous question. Henceforth serious debate upon fundamentals is impossible, for Freedom has been vindicated by her bitterest enemies.

June 4, 1862.

PROPHECIES AND PROBABILITIES.

AMERICAN gentlemen in London have, heretofore, when invited to give a taste of their quality at Guild-hall and other civic banquets, been in the habit of uttering a speech after the following formula : "Dear old Mother England—language of Shakespeare and Milton—Magna Charta—America the child of Britannia — peace, good will, fraternization forever!" Then came cheers as hearty as Old Particular by the gallon could make them; and really, one would have thought that turtle and port-wine had usurped the place of the metaphorical milk and honey of the millennium. When our great Rebellion broke out American gentlemen, enthusiastic readers of Milton and Shakespeare, expected that, of course, England would sympathise with our Government, contending not only against treason, but against treason in behalf of human Slavery. They have been undeceived. They have been taught that with England the measure of success is the measure of morality. Very early in the contest, which is now so rapidly approaching a happy and honorable conclusion, all sensible men were forced to believe that we had nothing to hope for from English sympathy or forbearance, and that foreign criticism must be disarmed before it would become kindly. We accepted the condition which a frigid diplomatic policy imposed upon us; we have struggled alone through many reverses, and have proved the groundlessness of many apprehensions; and we have now in all sincerity to thank our British detractors for leaving us to rely, through all, upon our own energies and internal resources. We have contracted no entangling alliances in this struggle, and we shall emerge from it in debt only to ourselves. The moral effect of such a triumph is worth all the cost of the war. With victory everywhere illustrating our banners, we can afford good-naturedly to laugh at parliamentary alarmists and dogmatical newspapers. With all other experiences, we have found out the Jupiter Scapin—the Great Thunderer of the European journals; and hereafter, though he may beat his best gong never so sonorously, we shall only laugh, and say, "Well thundered! Very well thundered, indeed!" It is as fatal for a lion to go about in an ass's skin, as for John Donkey to put on the leonine hide; and a man who is in a passion every day of his life, rarely succeeds in affrighting anybody. The London newspapers told us that we could not put down the Rebellion; but that did not deter us from going bravely to work. They now tell us that we have put down the Rebellion. Gentle reader, pray do n't let the admission disturb your equanimity, for a single Union reverse would set them all to croaking at us again. The praise and the blame are of equal value. There never were such fellows as these for foretelling what has already come to pass. Having pretty well put down the Rebellion, it is certainly kind in *The Times* to admit that we *shall* probably put it down. Great reputations for sagacity have been made before in the same easy way. But we trust that we shall not painfully dishearten holders of government securities when we tell them, that in the opinion of *The Times*, though we can crush the revolt, we cannot pay our debts; because we are heartily assured that when we have paid them, the same far-sighted writers will invent a brannew bugbear. At present, Bull will have it that although victorious we are insolvent. Really, we do not remember anything cooler than this. With an immense commerce, with an unequalled agricultural production, with small foreign liabilities, with a monopoly of two great staples, and the abundant production of a third, with a people eminently skilled, by the confession of their rivals, in the art of accumulating wealth, with a territory capable of limitless production, with great fisheries and great mines, our public paper, if we may believe *The Times*, represents nothing, and will soon be good for nothing. Now, in private commercial circles, the man who studiously undermines his neighbor's credit, is usually regarded as a scoundrel; but perhaps it is more honorable to gratify a jealous spleen by predicting the insolvency of a nation. For this, as for other amiable exhibitions of disinterestedness, we must be prepared. A debt created for the defence of the Constitution, in the opinion of every intelligent citizen, is a debt created for his own benefit, relief, and prosperity; and those who have freely offered their lives in that great behalf, will hardly turn conspirators and traitors to avoid taxation. Out of the same reverence for law, which they have already so abundantly manifested, they will fulfill the pecuniary obligations which the law imposes. What right has the slip-shod speculator, to whom we have been referring, to take it for granted that the same great West, which has so generously and assiduously engaged in the suppression of one variety of treason, will itself petulantly engage in another? Is it manly, is it gentlemanly, is it even old-womanly—this persistence in the sheerest gossip of detraction?—this depreciation against which, if it were but as effective as it is malicious, the credit of no nation could stand for a year? And is it for England to assert and maintain the novel doctrine that a great national debt is tantamount to a great national bankruptcy?—for England, with a debt of her own so enormously large that no man has ever proposed any scheme for paying it without being pronounced mad? It is hardly in such a quarter that we shall seek either for advice or example.

The American people, as fully alive to the evils of

taxation as they are aware of its necessity, will hardly hug their debt as a blessing, to be sacredly preserved for generation after generation. Once, already, they have blotted out the last trace of public indebtedness with an impatience which nothing but solvency could satisfy; and they have a right to be judged, not by the speculations of an ignorant casuist, but by their own record as it is made up in history. It is hard to write upon this topic without seeming to boast; but, certainly, if a nation is to be thus gratuitously discredited, it has a right to plead previous good character.

There has been more noise made abroad about American Repudiation than the facts, disgraceful as they were, warranted; but the credit of the United States of America has always been as good, is as good to-day, and will be in the future as good as the credit of England; and we think that this is stating the case very mildly—while it is at this moment better than the credit of more than one European power, the downfall of which nobody anticipates. Until, therefore, we commit an act of insolvency, we beg foreign writers, to whom we owe nothing, to possess their souls in peace. We are not utterly deficient in prudence and economy, of the necessity of which we are every day reminded; and he who writes us down fools, before we have proved our incompetency, is himself included in his own accusation. There is an abiding compensation in all our troubles. Through successes and reverses, through doubts and distractions, not less than through encouraging good fortunes, we are making for ourselves an antiquity and a history—we are consolidating a nationality—we are storing up precious traditions—we are, in the midst of war, becoming worthy of the blessings of peace. Those who believe that there is nothing for us but a ruinous and irremediable dissolution, must be shamefully ignorant, or contemptibly besotted by spleen and prejudice. No nation could be more grateful than ours, not for foreign arms taken up in our behalf, but for foreign sympathy; yet if it cannot be ours, without a sacrifice of principle or honor, certainly there is no nation that can better afford to do without it.

June 11, 1862.

"DRAWING IT MILD" IN MEMPHIS.

WE are ready to make our solemn affidavit that there is nothing in this world like that divine philosophy which is succinctly expressed in the great command, "Grin and bear it." The conductor of the *Memphis Avalanche* has so gracefully melted into this mild mood that, Secessionist as he is, we consider him to be a credit to the craft. He owns up like a man. He admits that he is "humbled and downcast." His "pride has been wounded." What then? Does he wriggle and roar? Does he inefficiently flounder like a fish out of water? Not at all. He quietly concludes to make the best of a bad matter. Like Archimedes, at Syracuse, he involves himself in his virtue, and goes on with his studies, though the Union foot is upon the neck of Memphis. "Let us," he says, with an originality and power which are alike admirable, "let us bear with manly fortitude what we are unable to avoid." "This," he concludes, "is true philosophy—a philosophy suited to our condition." Now, this calm, godlike, serene, and unimpassioned acquiescence appears to us to be something in itself so exquisitely beautiful, and something, moreover, so much needed in Memphis, that our hope is that our editorial brother will consent to erect in that city a school for the express dissemination of his doctrine, which is much needed there—a kind of portico, lyceum, or academy—in which, like Aristotle or Plato, he may rub his true philosophy, like an emollient ointment, into the tender frames of the fevered youth of Memphis; in which he may teach them that the grace of submission is better than bowie-knives and "barkers," and a stern stoicism infinitely preferable to peach-brandy and peppermint.

There are wild ones in Secessia who clearly need this medical indoctrination and sagely sanative treatment. There are ferocious old fools, and young ones there, who talk with maniac energy of dying in the last ditch; who prattle grimly of the combustion of themselves and of their cotton; who itch to make a new Moscow of Memphis—who conceive it to be quite necessary, should worst come to worst, to blow up the universe generally, and to put an end to themselves, playing Cato of Utica with a real sword, in particular. These perturbed spirits need laying, or they will do themselves a mischief. For our part, unless the new Memphis philosophy can be brought into high fashion, we look for an unpleasant superfluity of arson and suicide in Confederate regions—squads of disgusted chevaliers popping themselves off after the high Roman fashion—piles of patriarchs, who, having first slaughtered all their niggers, cows, sows, horses, dogs, wives, sheep and daughters, will be found wrapt in the Confederate flag as in a winding sheet, as dead and as dignified as Julius Cæsar, with the remains of their former greatness gloomily heaped around them. To be sure, in the cities already "subjugated," we do n't hear of these patriotic diversions. The most rampant patriots appear to subside with a wonderful facility, and to disregard quite contemptuously the injunction to destroy themselves, in which some of their newspapers abound. We suppose, however, that they are waiting for a General Proclamation of Suicide by their mock-President Davis. They are desirous of dying according to law, and of destroying themselves constitutionally. It becomes their Davis-ian Jefferson—the best Jefferson they have, poor fellows!—himself to set the example. When all is lost, we hold that it will be his duty to blow out what brains he may have left—his remainder cerebrum, so to speak. To make the whole proceeding more sublime, he might announce that upon the 14th inst., at high noon, he intended to consummate his *felo de se,* and request his friends and admirers to hang or shoot themselves, or to take big morphine pills, at the same identical moment. Then, with simultaneous kick or quiver, or firing their own salvo over their departure for Hades, the Chiefs of Secession might secede from this wicked world, and enter upon another from which, however hot, secession will be impossible.

We throw out these hints merely from an ardent passion for seeing things done neatly. If we are to have no Confederate States, we shall need no. Confederate Statesmen. In a restored Union it will be impossible to put Mr. Jefferson Davis and his crazy cronies to any sort of use. Will they have the grace to step out? Will they have the goodness to leave an unappreciative world, and betake themselves to those places which, from the beginning, have been prepared for them?

We do not know. We confess that we are by no means assured, and the new Memphis philosophy somewhat staggers our confidence in the desiderated stampede. What if the Secessionists, as *The Ava-. lanche* would seem to indicate, should turn capital Christians—models of forgetfulness and forgiveness, after all? What if it should suddenly dawn upon the Secession mind, the smoke of battle no longer, in conjunction with extra whisky, befogging the brain, that a big plantation and a plenty of "niggers," and Slavery guaranteed by the Federal Government, will be more pleasant than the neatest and most impressive and historically correct suicide? What says *The Avalanche* man? Is he not ready to go on, letting slide innumerable and endless *Avalanches,* even under the accursed Federal banner? And if he, cream of Confederate cream—the guide, philosopher, Mentor and Palinurus of the Rebellion in those parts, is so submissive, why who can tell how many others will follow his loyal lead? What are we to do? If these great ones, when they are "humbled and downcast—their pride wounded," etc.—are to betake themselves to "a philosophy suited to their condition"—must we forgive them for the sake of science? It is a question for jurists. Such clear evidence of a penitent disposition is certainly worthy, in these wicked times, of a charitable consideration. That impulse which we all feel to spare the sick and the sorry is one of the best feelings of our common nature.

June 21, 1862.

LOYALTY AND LIGHT.

THE attentive reader will already have noticed that the Union party in Maryland is also an Emancipation party, and regards with a certain complacency the project of the President for the abolition of Slavery. Day by day we see more and more clearly that the life of a blundering and bad institution has been set upon this desperate cast, and that the hazard of the die is against it. With a fatuity which seems to us to be perfectly wonderful, and much as if the gods, determined to destroy, had first made mad, we find the admirers of the Slave-system coupling it now and forever with treason, surrounding it by degrading associations, and making it, in the mind of the whole country, responsible for the perils which environ us. It has been the architect of its own ruin. It has been very cunning in its own overthrow. Owing every moment of its existence to the coercions of positive law, and existing in spite of its numerous violations of natural right, it has been the first to demolish the bulwarks which surrounded it, and to cast contempt upon the statute-book which was its only charter. Wise men said that it was perilous to the liberties of the land, and foolish men have been kind enough to demonstrate the truth of the proposition. It has simply succeeded in achieving a bad character at home and abroad.

The Maryland Unionists, while indulging in their little harmless fling at the "Abolitionists," explicitly admit that Slavery is now "injurious to the political and material interests" of the South. We do not see how any Union Slaveholder can think otherwise; because, logically, the Rebellion has forced him into precisely this position, and will keep him there, until he disowns his fealty to the Constitution. They insist, these fighting slaveholders, with their hands at his throat and their halters dangling over his head, that if he is the friend of the Union and the Laws, he must be the foe of that institution which is the corner-stone and, for that matter, all the other stones of the Confederacy. They give him no choice. They will hear of no compromise. They declare him, if a law-abiding man, to be the bitter antagonist of Slavery, and they compel him, if he would not stultify himself, to turn Emancipationist in self-defence.

It is in this sagacious way, with a sublime scorn of all common statesmanship, that they make and keep friends. No wonder that in many of the Slave States men who see their fortunes and happiness all risked, infinitely against their inclinations, in this insane adventure, are quite willing to surrender their own slaveholding to save themselves from the slaveholding of their neighbors.

Owners of negroes, we suppose, like other human beings, may be naturally divided into fools and wise men. We remember only one really able defender of Slavery in the abstract. Mr. Calhoun brought a gigantic intellect to the service of error, and did for a patent political mistake all that great intellectual powers and an iron will could do for it. But when he died he left no successor. Puny public men babbled weak parodies of his reasoning, or more safely ensconced themselves behind his *ipse dixit*. We regard with what we believe to be a just contempt the lame and lamentable perversions of Scripture with which Pro-Slavery Doctors of Divinity have benumbed the minds and hearts of their hearers; for the inexorable logic of facts has silenced their sanctified prattle for ever.

The men who now defend Slavery are quite of another class—bloated brawlers of the bar-rooms who blaspheme and quote the Bible in one drunken breath —half-witted whites who if they could possibly have an opinion, would sell it for a pint of grog—lazy women who shrink from domestic toil as from a daily degradation—bull-dog overseers bestialized to the

low level of their vocation—wholesale and retail deal-
ers in human flesh—these are the passionate, voluble,
unreasoning and bigoted advocates of Slavery as of
something intrinsically beautiful. The day of their
ascendency in Southern society is passing away in
storm and blood. They still crawl about in the slime
and smear of their system, as hideous monsters crept
to and fro over the earth half created. They have
taken the sword, and when, in fulfillment of an eternal law, they have perished by the sword, there will
be no new hybrids to fill their places in the regenerated Republic. They will disappear, and with them
that semi-barbarous system of espionage and intimi-
dation which has made Slavery a thing exempt from
question and discussion. They have themselves taken
off the taboo, and there will be none left weak enough
to do the discredited idol reverence.

On the other hand, slaveholders of quite another
stamp, men not utterly besotted, men of homely common sense, of thought and of prudence, will begin to
speak in behalf of the simplest laws of morality and
political morality. They will say: whatever else
Slavery may be worth, it is not worth *this*—the eternal wrangle, the daily disquietude, the temptation to
political crime, the shameful disregard of political
covenants which it provokes, and the violence which
it perpetually stimulates—the uncertainty with which
it embarrasses all the operations of commerce—the
degradation of the employed and the ceaseless anxiety of the employer—the debauchery of mind, heart
and body to which it subjects our youth—the unsex-

ing of our women, the emasculation of our men, and the heathenization of our churches—no, Slavery is not worth this fearful price! To this conclusion the thoughtful and intelligent slaveholder will be forced by his interests, his conscience, his reason, his affections and his patriotism.

These are natural conclusions from the theory which we take for granted, that the Rebellion will be crushed and the Union maintained. You cannot conquer the treasonous slaveholders without conquering the cause in behalf of which they are embattled. When once the work begins there will be no going backward. Emancipate, upon principle, one thousand slaves, and you have virtually emancipated one hundred thousand. It is the first step that is costly and fearful. However small the wedge, when once it has entered it will inevitably overthrow this imposing monument of human folly, crime, outrage and suffering. Make Maryland a free state, as sooner or later it must be, or make Missouri a free State, as it speedily will be, and the criminal compact, the conspiracy against civilization, which has broken our peace, will be dissolved for ever, and even the next generation will wonder why we so long suffered ourselves to grope and stumble when the broad and bright road of righteousness invited us to walk in it.

June 23, 1862.

HEDGING.

THERE is a clever play which in spite of its wicked-ness is still read for its wit, and the coarse comedy of which is concluded as follows :

"*Flippanta.* Then all 's peace again ; but we have been more lucky than wise.

"*Araminta.* And I suppose, for us, Clarissa, we are to go on with our dears, as we used to do.

"*Clarissa.* Just in the same track."

So in the popular song of the "Cork Leg" we are told that long after the portly proportions of the Rotterdam burgher were reduced to a skeleton,

"The Leg kept on the same as before."

Slavery is the leg of the Southern Rebellion ; and we are not surprised to hear, therefore, through General Butler, of a "Southern Independence Association," which, when the Confederacy has gone to its diabolical father, is to "labor for the reconstruction of the Democratic party, or any other political organization by which the South can regain its political ascendency," nor should we be electrified to learn that the virtuous Mr. Benjamin Wood has become an Honorary Brother of this shrewd league.

"If we must go back," no doubt argue these precautious patriarchs, "let us see to it that we go back with Slavery strengthened, and with our chattels still more strongly confirmed to us ! The dear Democrats are doubtless still our friends and will help us to make this detestable Union tolerable." We must admit that this shows not only good pluck but reasonable

12

common sense. Slaveholders have found out that, Slavery preserved, they can at any time frighten the whole country—at any time bankrupt the Federal Treasury—at any time embarrass and distract the Free States—at any time, by judicious wickedness, regain lost ground—at any time sustain themselves by the might of swagger. They will be charmed if we will but forgive them. They have no objection to any number of infernal quadrilles, provided only we of the North with our soft hearts and our long purses will pay the piper.

"The Union" will still be a good word to conjure withal, while we remain forgiving and forgetful. Should Congress prove at any time intractable, or morbidly philanthropic, the Man-Owners will again take up their muskets and shoot them a few thousand Yankee Volunteers, which will afford them a sweet opening for another treaty and another kiss of reconciliation. More battles—more sieges—more hairbreadth 'scapes,—more waste of wealth; and, "we are to go on with our dears, as we used to do, just in the same track!"

So then, we are to have a truce, after all, and not a peace. Rebellion is to be like the yellow fever—it may come or it may not come, but it will be well always to be prepared for it. For our own part, after such a pacification, we are not, we confess, sharp-sighted enough to see how the slaveholding interest can upon any occasion, pending any question, fail to have its own way. Voting in Congress will be the emptiest of farces. Honorable Members for the Plantations will have little need to discuss the merits of measures. Their speeches may well be brief and somewhat after this fashion: "Do n't pass the bill! If you do, we shall revolt, you know, and really, by this time, we think that you must have had enough of that."

We do n't know what Honorable Members for New York or Massachusetts would have to say to this. They might indeed in a passion retort: "Revolt and be hanged!" but after the old emollient arrangements, Honorable Members for the Plantations would laugh at hangmen as love laughs at locksmiths. This, we take it, would be sufficient to flutter the doves from the Free States into the most amiable compliance. If not, Slavery, the cause of unnumbered crimes and of all our woes, under the operation of the three-fifths clause of the Constitution, by the aid of its resuscitated Democratic henchmen, would still vote always in its own behalf; and we should only escape civil wars by submitting to the old dictatorship.

Who can think of a return to this condition without a qualm? Not he surely whose children's bones are bleaching upon some Southern battle-field! Not he whose fortune may have been dissipated in desperate attempts to reconcile Northern enterprise with Southern sluggishness! Not he who has felt in his heart the exceeding great villainy of this war against the Union! For we believe that all persons of ordinary intelligence will look with fear and trembling, and an unspeakable grief, upon any arrangement of public affairs which shall leave us at the mercy of those miserable and unreasoning passions which Slav-

cry engenders.   Distrust is the fatal bane of all political stability.

The people of the Free States have lost for ever
that confidence in the honor of Slaveholders which
once permitted them to hope for peace however
stormy might be the portents.   The possibility of a
sanguinary revolt is settled and the probability is settled too ; and hereafter with Slavery remaining a political power in the land, there will always be a fearful looking-for of violence.   The volcano will ever
threaten.   The brightest skies will be no security
against a whirlwind.   The craziest slaveholding traitor can have no objection to such a truce, which by
leaving him without punishment, leaves him without
warning against a repetition of his crime.   The hour
he will reason, may be lost, but not the day.   The
quarrel may be for a little while adjusted, he will
say to his fellows, but we have always at hand the
means of its renewal at pleasure.   He will fervently
thank his stars for an enemy who, when victorious
over him, left all his resources unimpaired, and pre-
tending to make a peace, was content with an armis-
tice.   "Southern Independence Associations" will
flourish under the sacred noses of the Federal Courts,
and·men who have forfeited fifty lives will stalk and
strut, bully and brag, as of old, in Washington.   It is
not a pleasant picture to contemplate, but we had better know the chances now, than blunder into a Century of Anarchy.

June 24, 1862.

THE TRIAL OF TOOMBS.

It is related of the illustrious author of "Faust" that, during one of his youthful depressions—it was, we think, of the amorous variety—he determined upon suicide, and provided himself with the necessary dagger; but upon finding that the operation would be painful, he abandoned the bare bodkin business, and consented to live. Gen. Robert Toombs, of the Secession service, ought, by all the laws which regulate rebellion, to give up cotton-growing; but he finds the temptation to keep on with the cultivation too strong for him, and leaves his blacks at work in Georgia while he militates in Virginia. Randolph County, Ga., instantly lapses into a patriotic perspiration. The Randolph County Committee of Public Safety immediately communicate savagely with Toombs in Richmond. They tell him that he is a very wicked Confederate General. That he has no right to cultivate cotton. That his avarice is greater than his patriotism. That his negroes are wanted for military purposes. What follows? Ferocious reply from Toombs. Calls the Committee of Public Safety "cowardly miscreants." Also "robbers." Declines to furnish "niggers" for the Rebel service. Says he may be "robbed," but he cannot be "intimidated." Is n't it evident that Toombs's "patriotism" does n't, so to speak, come up to the scratch?— that, happen what may, he will be the last man to commit suicide?

How the Committee of Public Safety aforesaid received this most disparaging telegram, we are not informed. How they relished the new title of "cowardly miscreants," we may easily surmise. It was n't a relish at all, but a disrelish altogether. "You poor, miserable, rascally, bluffing, domineering, dirty scoundrels," says Toombs; "you vile, plundering, interloping vagabonds, you 'cannot intimidate me.'" And this to men to whom, at that identical moment, the "public safety" of Randolph County was committed. It is curious. Toombs speaks to these men as if he knew them, and knew them to be, from their heads to their heels, poor specimens of white humanity. We can imagine him talking in precisely the same way to his own private collection of blacks. That he would, if he could, truss up the august Committee, and give to each member of it a round dozen of stripes, with the accompanying pickle, we do also believe. That, after his soldiering is over, should he get back to Georgia—which is n't probable—he will shoot one or two Committee-men, is very probable. His appetite is for the *pleasures* of Secession—he has none for the *pains*—just as a man may never weary of talking of the weariness of life, but may shrink from the alleviating rope or ratsbane. And we have called attention to the precautions and cotton-limited patriotism of this Toombs, because we believe that Secession brag is altogether too successful in its demands upon Northern credulity. When a Southern orator says, with all the coarse finery of unbridled rhetoric, that he is ready to brave all—ruin, wounds and death—for the sake of the cause, those who are not blinded by his lightning language, nor intimidated by his leonine roar, may shake their heads and laugh; but the sagacious will still ask whether, when a man goes into a revolt, avowedly for the sake of negroes, he will continue in revolt when continuance will take all his negroes away from him. To put the matter in another shape, it is urged, even by members of Congress, that meddling with "the institution," by confiscation or otherwise, will so infuriate the Secessionist that he will keep on forever in his delusion, doing the most dreadful things, long after the motive for doing them has ceased to operate: *i. e.*, he will fight for Slaveholding though Slaveholding has become to him as impossible as flying. We do not believe it. It is grossly unphilosophical so to reason; and those who do reason so, whether at " Conservative " meetings or in the columns of newspapers, show more panic than pluck. Confiscation may appear to some to be as savage a remedy as cautery; but sometimes it is only cautery that will do the business. Selfishness, of which Mr. Toombs gives us such a charming specimen, is the main cause of man-owning, and that is the main cause of all our political mischiefs.

When we hear a planter talk about ethnology and the inferiority of races, and so ascending and descending the whole gamut of solemn twaddle, we always laugh, at least inwardly; because we know that he approves of Slavery, out of no sort of respect for Moses or St. Paul, but because it gives him a coat to wear, toddies to drink, tobacco to smoke, a bed to lie

upon, and a roof to cover him. When he is cornered,
out comes the truth. "Stop raising cotton!" cries
Toombs: "lend you my niggers! I will see you
hanged first!" What a dear, delightful, outspoken,
frank and candid Toombs! What a charming Pro-
Slavery Doctor of Divinity he would make, to be
sure! He isn't a man to give up all he is fighting
for, merely for the sake of winning the battle. "My
niggers! no, I tell you! Am I fighting, and bleeding,
and dying, merely that a Committee of Public Safety
may carry off my niggers? As well give 'em to Abe
Lincoln at once! Let them alone!" Well, dear
Toombs, we cannot say that we blame you for your
perfectly natural views of matters and things in general. Let us embrace!—we are speaking now as if
we were a member of the Conservative Congressional
Caucus—let us embrace, dear Toombs!

"Come to my arms, my own true-hearted."

Not a negro of the Toombs brand shall be touched!
Male and female, house-hands, field-hands, mechanics,
old, middle-aged, young, yellow or black, they are all
under the palladium of the Constitution—God bless
it!—and they shall all be taken care of—only, good
old fellow! you'll come back into the Union; that's
a dear, amiable, charming Toombs! That is, Toombs
is supposed to be such an unmitigated ass that he can
be coaxed into the Union again merely by promising
him something, which he, *vi et armis*, declares that
the Union is too weak to secure to him. On the
other hand, Toombs, having lost all his dear blacks,

having discovered that Disunion is just as powerless to keep them, and that Rebellion has depopulated his plantation, will have had sundry arguments in favor of keeping quiet actually knocked into his head, and will certainly see the necessity of making the best of a bad matter; or if he does not, Toombs Junior, who hopes to live a little longer in this pleasant world, assuredly will. To take any other course with Toombs is to put a premium upon treason, and he knows it, and chuckles over our debates. If you would crush rebellion, hit at its master passion an earnest and annihilating blow. But if you mean only to play with it for the benefit of commissioned officers and contractors—why that is quite another matter, and one which we do not care to discuss.

July 4, 1862.

THE COUNCIL OF THIRTY-FIVE.

On Saturday last, in Washington, thirty-five Conservative gentlemen solemnly resolved that "the Abolitionists will leave to the country but little hope of the restoration of the Union or peace, if schemes of Confiscation, Emancipation, and other unconstitutional measures, shall be enacted under the form of laws." The thirty-five gentlemen voted to print this rather than else thrilling opinion, for the benefit of mankind in general, and then the Thirty-five gentlemen "broke camp" and went back to their boardinghouses. There has n't been anything politically

12*

more portentous since the Three Tailors of Tooley
street issued their Proclamation, beginning, "We,
the People of England." Considering the great importance of this demonstration, it is to be regretted
that Conservators did not, by some address more enlarged than a resolution, let us know by what process
of reasoning they arrived at the conclusion that the
Abolition of Slavery would forever bar the restoration of the Union.

If we were inclined to be hypercritical, we might
ask why these Representatives allow themselves to
talk of the "*restoration* of the Union" at all? Do
they consider that by any constitutional theory the
Union is abolished? that South Carolina could abolish it? that Jefferson Davis, by any villainy, could
destroy it in any sense? Because, before a thing can
be *restored*, if we know anything of language or of
logic, it must first be *lost*. The truth is, that the
Thirty-five, in their eagerness to construct a pretty
series of resolutions, have done that which has been
esteemed impossible—they have fairly bitten off their
own noses. Right into the jaws of a solecism, as we
shall prove, tumbled the Thirty-five. If the Union
can be *restored*, then it is already *destroyed ;* and if
it be destroyed, then the right, by the simplest public
law, of the Washington Government, at war with the
Government late at Richmond, to confiscate and to
offer freedom to the Slaves, is just as clear as the
right to shoot soldiers in the field, or to bombard
cities. Nobody ever questioned the right of a belligerent in all possible ways to harrass a public enemy.

The emancipation of Slaves is a well-recognised oper-ation of war. The Thirty-five, by their most inju-dicious use of a dangerous word, have put the Rebels quite outside the pale of even "conservative" benev-olence. Whatever they may be some time hence, when restored to sanity by the grace of gunpowder, they are not now our "dear brethren," our "mis-guided fellow-citizens," our this, that, and the other, but simply, by the theory of the Thirty-five, our Mor-tal Enemies, whom it may be possible to conquer, but quite impossible to injure. When the Union is "restored," it will then be time enough for this Three-Dozen-less-One to talk of the unconstitutionality of Emancipation. A Public Enemy has no rights under the Constitution at all.

But we have n't done with the one-legged logic of the Thirty-five Conservatives quite yet. They fall into the not uncommon error of glibly grouping "Abolitionists" and "Secessionists," as if these were one in purpose and in policy. Substantially, this always means an indirect compliment to traitors, which no man of self-respect and of genuine loyalty would be guilty of. It is of a piece with that slaver-ing and anile gabble which says in circular rigma-role, "Well, the South is to blame, the North is to blame, the Slaveholders are to blame, the Anti-Slavery men are to blame—let us fix matters, and go on as we did before." Now, as it is a moral paradox to assert that he who rebukes a sin is responsible for the consequent and deeper flounderings of the sinner, so it is a political paradox to declare that the opponent of a bad policy is to be holden for the bad effects of that policy. Because Slaveholders have chosen to commit that very outrage upon the Constitution which clear-headed men have long foreseen and foretold, does it follow that the rebukers are as bad as the rebuked? Besides, it is not, as we have over and over again pointed out, it is not the *existence*, but the *extension* of Slavery, for which the Traitor States are contending; so that fear of the *abolition* of Slavery had really nothing to do with the war. Is it to be supposed that Jefferson Davis is in the field because he believed his negroes would be taken from him by the Lincoln Administration? He must be greener than green, and his mind cruder than crude, who thinks so. Even the miserable heads of muddled Secessionists did not mix up matters in that way. What Davis and other gentlemen in the man-owning business were afraid of was, that *non-extension* might prove equivalent to *non-existence*—a matter with which the North had nothing to do. Most nuisances disappear when they are cribbed and confined; and it was not certainly our fault if the " Institution " did require room and verge, which we would not grant if we could, and could hardly grant if we would. The North was resting in comparative quiet upon its vested rights and upon well-settled compromises, when the fierce and insatiable thirst of Slavery for new territory disarranged all adjustments, unsettled the National policy, and compelled us, in self-defense, to exercise our legitimate and unquestionable rights under the Constitution. It was Slavery that made up the issue of the last Presidential election; and, at present, when we are contending for Law and Order, and a Permanent Peace, the Secessionists are battling—for what? for what, but for Slavery? Now, if in hitting them we hit the pet and idol of their hot and half-crazy souls, why should these Thirty-five Congressional Conservators put us in the same dock with admitted criminals, with men who have violated so many statutes, while our only sin is that we are faithful to what we consider the fixed and fundamental law? If there had been no Slavery there would have been no Rebellion. That is, upon all hands, admitted. Then, without Slavery there can be no Rebellion. Ah! that is a *sequitur* clear enough to most men, but altogether too tough a nut for the the Thirty-five Wise Men of Washington to crack! We are profoundly sorry for their intellectual weakness; but instead of asking us to stultify ourselves, they should, for their own part, try to think with a little more accuracy.

We hope that we are as willing to pardon injuries as our neighbors are; but at the risk of being regarded as revengeful, we must admit our inability to keep pace with that eminent Professor of Forgiveness and Forgetfulness, Mr. Richardson of Illinois, who said in the Conserved Caucus, that peace can only be restored by saying to the masses at the South, "You have done wrong! Lay down your arms and you shall not be touched." But should Congress decide upon this emollient course, let Richardson be the United States Embassador to the camps of the Rebels!

Let him enter their lines, blowing the most assuasive tunes upon the mildest of trumpets! Let him, while gentle smiles illumine his countenance, say tenderly to the Confederate armies, "You have done wrong! Lay down your arms, and you shall not be touched!" We can imagine his reception. Even while he blandly speaks, bowie-knives flash, revolvers are aimed at his sacred person, and an extemporized halter dangles aloft. Jefferson Davis and staff march from head-quarters to behold his execution, and Richardson of Illinois is soon no more a member of Congress, and the caucus is reduced to Thirty-four. If he pleases to make this excursion upon his own responsibility, let him depart as soon as convenient. Our opinion is, that he will not be back again in his seat, at any rate during the present session.

It must, we think, be taken for granted, by this time, that the Secession leaders are in earnest. They ask for no favors; they propose no treaties; they announce their intention of fighting out this quarrel. Are we never to take them at their word? Are we never to use the weapons which God and nature have put into our hands? It is not customary to approach a mad dog, holding an olive-branch in one hand and a leg of fat mutton in the other. The prejudice of the world is rather in favor of more active measures, whatever may be the opinion of the dog. And this is all we have to say at present of the Council of Thirty-five.

July 5, 1862.

DAVIS A DESPOT.

The Southern Confederacy has met with a dreadfully damaging blow in the hey-day of its existence. It lapsed into a bloody treason to save itself from intolerable tyranny; and the poor fish, if we may credit *The Charleston Mercury*, has only tumbled from a comparatively comfortable frying-pan into a most uncomfortable fire. It is the old story of Æsop over again; for some of the most notable frogs in the puddle are beginning to croak that King Jefferson I. is no better than a Domitian or a Nero. Our authority is the aforesaid *Mercury*, which ought certainly to be considered a good witness in the case. Its first grievance is that the Confederate Congress, in clear violation of the Confederate Constitution, has furnished King Jefferson Davis with a palace ready furnished, at an expense of Seven Thousand Dollars —a most shameful imitation of the rascally doings at Washington under the old detestable rule. It further complains, that all the doings of the Congress which should restore the Revolters to supreme political freedom, are kept profound secrets from the Southern people—debates, decisions, and all! It is only known that the Emperor—we beg pardon—the President Davis " vetoed more bills of the Provisional Congress than all the Presidents of the United States from George Washington to Andrew Jackson included." He is, therefore, very properly styled " a Despot." So the Southern Confederacy, in its enthusiastic pursuit of liberty, has secured, by the confession of *The*

Mercury, a Congress which merely registers the Edicts of a Tyrant! Pray, was this worth the crime of which the Rebels have been guilty, and the sufferings to which they have been subjected? Poor little fishes! why don't you come back to the old frying-pan?

Then there is another trouble, which is, that as soon as the Confederacy has provided even the semblance of a Navy, it is straightway blown up and annihilated, and all through the inexcusable negligence of a blockhead—Secretary Mallory—who may reasonably be supposed to act under the orders of Davis the Despot.

Upon this point *The Richmond Examiner* dwells with a deep pathos. From other quarters come most portentous growls; so that, although the Southern people are not now just in a position to depose King Davis, and to tar and feather his Cabinet, they would unquestionably do both, if it were not for the army. We do not mean to say that they would come penitently back at once to the Union which they have so insanely déserted. They would probably upset Davis only to set up King Somebody Else the First, but the inevitable anarchy would make their reduction to sanity comparatively easy. We may see something of this kind before the war is over. Davis is n't safe from the tar-pot yet, poor man! He should have thought, before he raised this busy devil of revolt, what means and appliances would be at his disposal should it be necessary to lay it. It is a ticklish experiment, as all history proves, to over-

throw an existing Government "for light and transient causes." Unless the injuries of a people are
substantial—unless they exist otherwise than in the
ambitious views of political schemers—it is the most
dangerous thing in the world to stimulate popular
passions, and to seduce communities from their allegiance to the laws and to fixed Constitutions. The
engineers usually get the first hoist from their own
petards. What became of the men who excited the
first French Revolution? Does Davis ever think of
their fate with prudent apprehension? And how
long can he be sure of his army? Its number is
stated in Rebel newspapers at 300,000 men; but how
many of these are Slaveholders? How many of these
have a stake in the contest? How many, not being
Slaveholders, have a direct interest in stopping the
war? Everybody knows that, in raising the Rebel
forces, there has been a continual resort to terrorism
and coercion; and how long can these go on without
a counter-revolution? Look at the case calmly and
philosophically. Suppose that a Southern soldier
owns no negroes, and does not hope to own any;
what has he to gain from the independence of the
Confederacy—what of office, of emolument, of personal consideration? Nothing whatever! If the new
Government were firmly established to-morrow, it
would leave him the same Poor White Man that he
was before. He would be cut off, as before, from the
rewards of industry, and even from the opportunity
of respectable labor. We understand, in a measure,
why the Man-Owners are fighting—it is for caste,

aristocracy, political power—but why are the Poor Whites fighting? It puzzles our comprehension, and it will soon begin to puzzle theirs. When it does, then let Jefferson Davis look out for himself. If his army be small, as *The Richmond Examiner* complains, Mr. Davis may heartily wish it much smaller. Poor whites, trained to the use of arms, may prove a most uncomfortable population.

But just at present it is n't from these that this usurper has the most to fear. He is the President of an Oligarchy unaccustomed to personal restraint. He has been raised to a bad prominence in these affairs by men who are themselves the petty tyrants of the plantations; who, in all their intercourse with those about them, have substantially possessed a power over life and limb as great as that of the Russian nobility over their serfs in the days of Peter the Great. Now, the plantation is not by any means a good school in which to acquire a habit of personal obedience, at least on the part of the master. What does a Slaveowner, upon an isolated plantation in Arkansas, care for the authority of a parcel of talking fellows in Richmond? He may fight for Jefferson Davis, if he pleases, but then it is no violent presumption that he may please to fight against Jefferson, and in favor of another man. South Carolina, according to her own favorite political theories, is a member of the Southern Confederacy only during the time of her sovereign will and pleasure. She comes in under protest, and when she sees fit she has, upon her own absurd principles, as good a right to bolt from the government of Davis as from that of Lincoln. Why should n't she? Here is one of her principal newspapers denouncing Davis as a Despot! By what worse name did this *Mercury* ever speak of President Lincoln? If this *Mercury* be right, it is already time for South Carolina to bolt again! Will she do it? How do we know? How can any man foretell what she will do? And should she declare once more her independence, by what authority will Jefferson Davis proceed to coerce her to her duty? He has made waste paper of all precedents. He has abolished all law in his dominions. He holds office not by the will of a majority of the States which he professes to govern, but by the will of South Carolina alone. If she sustains him now, it is only because he permits her to reserve the right to deal at him the deadliest of blows at any moment when it may gratify her whim or suit her convenience. He may be sure that she has well learned the lesson which he has assisted to teach her.

Thus it is that men involve themselves in palpable absurdities, when for light and transient causes they attempt the overthrow of long-established governments. Thus it is that men incur a thousand perils, when they permit their passions to hurry them into treason. We do not, in all history, remember a revolution undertaken for the gratification of personal ambition which has been permanently successful; and we do not believe that the Slaveholders' Rebellion is destined to furnish an exception to the rule. We see something like safety for its projectors in their defeat; but in their success we see nothing for themselves, and the States which they have misled, but ultimate ruin, and the final extinguishment of every vestige of the ancient liberty of their white population.

August 27, 1862.

ALL MEANS TO CRUSH!

IF one of our Northern newspapers—rebel at heart and half rebel in speech—should propose, here in New York, a loan to the Confederacy of the Traitors, is it not fair to suppose that the office of that journal would receive an early visit from the law-officers of the United States? And yet, morally considered, this offence is one of daily occurrence. When *The Herald* or other sheet of like sable tint vehemently urges that property in Negroes is something that should be sacredly safe from confiscation and from military meddling, we say that such protest is equivalent to a proposition to lend a certain amount of money to Davis's Secretary of the Treasury. We beg leave to quote, upon this point, the excellent authority of a Venetian Jew:

> " You take my house when you do take the prop
> That doth sustain my house; you take my life,
> When you do take the means whereby I live."

Immediately after the delivery of this indisputably correct observation, Shylock, we are told, left the

Court-House upon the plea that he felt very unwell—and no doubt he told the truth. There is a method which God, in the interests of His Eternal Justice, has put into our hands of making the Rebels a great deal sicker than Shylock was ; and we hum and haw and split a whole head of hairs, and leave the Rebel to the use of " the means whereby he lives." Wise—is it not ?

Look at the money which the Confederacy now owes, and which it has given paper promises to pay! There are $45,000,000 due to its soldiers ; $50,000,000 to banks; $65,000,000 for property seized ; $45,000,-000 for State aid to be reimbursed ; $100,000,000 of Treasury notes; and War Loans to the amount of $65,000,000. What is the property which this indebtedness represents? We answer emphatically—Black Men! And what would these certificates of indebtedness be worth if the Black Men ceased to be property? We answer with the same emphasis—Nothing! If the Government of the United States could, by some stroke of policy, make this rag-cash so utterly rotten that the hungriest Rebel would not touch it even with gloves on, would n't it be worth while to do it? Well, you can do it! This paper represents a debt. The debt must be paid by taxation. The property to be taxed is mostly in negroes. Of course, the most befuddled Secessionist must see the truth of the formula — No "Niggers," no Taxes ; No Taxes, no Pay !

The Confederate notes will be excellent for shaving paper ; but where is the bearded bankrupt to find soap? The United States Government has it in its power to utterly beggar the paper-shop at Richmond in a week. That swindling concern has no capital but slaves, because without slaves the Rebel planter, if we may credit his own testimony, will find his land worth nothing, and his four-legged stock very little except to eat. Take away his slaves and he cannot pay his taxes, and if he cannot pay his taxes, the Confederacy will burst like a soap-bubble! But when you prepare to subject him to this highly salutary discipline, ye gods! what howling! Take cows, bulls, sheep, oxen, lands, barns, crops—take anything but Blacks! There has been a great deal of foolish talk in this world from the time of its creation, but we do not believe that the world ever listened to such consummate folly before. It's like giving up to a highwayman his horse and his weapons, and taking from him, by way of forfeiture, his under-waistcoat! You meet a Rebel in the field, and you shoot him, or he shoots you. That's all fair, and we understand it. But suppose, having his life in your power, he proposed to you to buy his life at the cost of his negroes. "Oh!" you must answer, "the public interest demands that I have nothing to do with your blacks! Keep them in the name of the Constitution!"—and so you pop at him, and down he goes, leaving the blacks to his executors! What a charmingly sensible piece of Unionism! Or suppose a Rebel prisoner in Fort Lafayette, dreaming of a halter, and waking up to write to the President: "Dear Sir, Take my life, but pray do not take my 'niggers.'" How extremely probable! What the Rebels want, doubtless, is their lives and their negroes both—together with their cash and their plantations and their pretty little Confederacy—but if they are not entitled to all, they are not entitled to either.

The rule of all war is not only to hit hard, but to hit where you can hit hardest. Now, when the Confederates at the South, and their allies and accomplices at the North, set up such an agonizing yell, if the emancipation of slaves is but mentioned, we see at once upon what particular part of the back of this Confederate steed the raw is established, and we call for a vigorous application of the lash in precisely that direction. We do not approve of sparing the beast, merely because basting him will please the Abolitionists. We are not afraid of pleasing them too well —they are not so easily satisfied.

More than anything else, we want a restoration of our territory of which we have been plundered, and of our peace which has been wickedly disturbed! Give us back our great, prosperous and happy American Union! Give back to these wives and mothers the dear ones who are now risking their lives in this struggle! Give back to the honest mechanic the labor of which this Crime of Crimes has defrauded him! Give back to us the respect which we once inspired abroad! Restore the supremacy of the Laws! If our National integrity and individual prosperity cannot be recovered without Emancipation — then Emancipate! This is a War for the Enforcement of the Laws—Enforce them all!

August, 28, 1862.

NORTHERN INDEPENDENCE.

WE must conquer this Rebellion or it will conquer us. This is a fact of which we are reminded—and there is need that we should be—by the boasts of fugitive Secessionists in Canada, who, it is reported, "openly declare that the Union shall not be broken, but that if the North is beaten, it shall be subjected to the rule of Jefferson Davis, who will be next President of the United States." "There is nothing sacred," said Napoleon, "after a conquest." The theory of this war is plain enough. The Northern people well understand that they are contending for the Constitution and the Laws; but it may be questioned if more than a small minority of thinkers have permitted themselves to look—for they cannot do so without shuddering—into that seething hell of anarchy and confusion and ceaseless apprehension which would be our fate in the event of a Confederate triumph. Large as this continent is, it may be safely assumed that it is not large enough for two distinct nationalities, with natural limits ill defined, with military ambition upon one side of the line, and with a tantalizing opulence upon the other, and with reminiscences of success taunting continually a stern, sad memory of defeat; while a common language, instead of promoting peaceful alliances, would become merely a more convenient medium of debate and defiance. If we never knew it before, we know now, that Slavery is aggressive. It is unnecessary to say that it is more so than any other marked and dis-

tinctive form of social life would be. It is only
necessary to understand that, being of an absolutely
peculiar character, and at war with the general
moral conclusions of the age, Slavery, as it now exists
in the American States, is in that position of desperate and dogged defiance, in which it will dare all
things in self-defence. For reasons which we need
not recapitulate, a component part of that defence
must be its extension. It can no more exist within
confined limits than a rat can live under an exhausted receiver. It is clear, therefore, that in the event
of a military triumph of the system, the spirit of
territorial aggrandizement, which has heretofore
sought for new man-markets upon the frontier of the
Southwest, would begin to exert itself in a Northern
direction. Of the inability of the Slave Power to
conquer such States as Illinois, Ohio, or Indiana, we
might be tolerably certain, so long as a Northern
Union should remain; but the grave and alarming
question is, how long, after the establishment of a
Southern Confederacy, the Northern Union would
continue to exist. Itself a fragment, into how many
smaller fragments might it not, even within a quarter
of a century, be precipitated? Disunion is of bad example, and might prove contagious; while the Slave
States, united in a bad brotherhood, and by the ties
of a common iniquity, might not find it difficult to
cope with and to subjugate individual States, themselves exposed to the assaults of each other, and weakened by intestine disorder.

That it is no part of Slaveholding chivalry to spare

13

a State, either because it is weak or inoffensive, let the fate of Mexico attest! But inoffensive the Northern States, even with the best intentions, could not possibly be. The recognition of the Confederacy, however absolute and complete, would not for a day silence the Anti-Slavery discussions of the North. It is certain that they will never cease until Slavery is abolished. No laws, however rigid, no considerations of international comity, would be sufficient to restrain the voices of men who as much believe that Slavery is horrible in God's sight as they believe that there is a God at all. This of itself would be sufficient to keep up a perpetual irritation at the South, and to afford a continual pretext for an aggressive war. But the question of Fugitive Slaves, and of their rendition, would be a crowning difficulty, and one which, it seems to us, would be absolutely incapable of a peaceful solution. If we know anything of the temper of the Northern people, we can hardly believe that they will be ready to do that of their free-will which they have been so unwilling to do upon compulsion. Treaties might be made, but treaties would be perpetually broken. Laws, founded upon such compacts, might be passed, but who would obey and who would enforce them? Meanwhile, the Government of the North would be constantly involved in difficulties with its own recalcitrant citizens; and, the question of Slavery still coloring our politics, the people would be pretty sure to keep out of office "Northern men with Southern principles." War must inevitably follow. Peace, by infinite nursing and coddling, would be only the exception; and War—beggaring, blasting, and weary War—would be the rule. Into the probable history of this people, so agitated and assaulted, it would not be pleasant too closely to inquire. If the Slave States, stimulated only by imaginary injuries, have shown themselves ready to shoot from a condition of ill-temper into that of sanguinary hostilities, what will be the popular feeling of the North when it is found that all these lives have been given in vain, and that all our treasure has been expended only with the prodigality of the fool?

If the question, then, of the Union was an open one before, it is so no longer. We cannot afford to concede—we cannot afford to be conquered. There is a deadly duel between Freedom and Slavery, and one or the other must fall. The issue is but a matter of time. Freedom in the end must conquer. But over what dreary years of suffering and struggle, of paralyzed industry and social commotion, of private agony and of public bankruptcy, must that struggle, if we now temporize, extend! If there be in this great metropolis any man who, in his devotion to the pursuit of gold, thinks that we should give up all, and retire from this contest, we bid him look well to his money bags, when the arrogant and hot-headed Confederacy shall have triumphed and commenced its political career. If there be here any man who wearies of the noise and confusion of this conflict, we bid him beware of lending his influence to the adoption of any measure which may merely postpone the

final adjustment of this quarrel, and leave us, meanwhile, certainly for more than one generation, the
sport of political chances. If there be any philanthropist who shrinks, as well he may, from the butchery of battle, we warn him that the longest war, however bloody, is better for humanity than the smooth-
est of hollow truces. Do not let us be deceived!
There is no safety for this republic but in its integrity; there is no peace for it but in its indivisi-
bility; there is no economy in ending one war only
that we may begin another; there is no happiness
for us, there is none for our children, save in the complete victory of our Government. Five years of war
would be better—yes, fifty years of war would be
better than a century of imaginary peace and continual collisions. The time to acknowledge the Confederacy, if at all, was when Anderson pulled down
the flag of Fort Sumter. That time has gone by
forever!

September 12, 1862.

THE CONSTITUTION—NOT CONQUEST.

It is extremely unfortunate that an old gentleman
like Lord Brougham, who, in the course of nature,
cannot talk much longer in this world, should show
such an inclination to talk about things which he
does not understand. There may have been a time,
before his present period of senility, when he may

have comprehended the real political character of the American Union; but if so, that time has certainly gone by; and his Lordship babbled the other day at Scarborough in a way which would have been thought ridiculous in the most callous of Tories. He came, indeed, at last to the sensible conclusion that England and France have no right to interfere in American affairs; but in arriving at this point, he uttered the following extraordinary language: "We find one part of the States fighting for separation and independence, and the other part struggling for conquest." The first clause of this proposition is undoubtedly true. The rebels, unquestionably, are fighting for "independence," but it by no means follows, that they are entitled to it. We shall show, before we conclude, that they are not; but here we would merely suggest, that if Ireland should at present break into open revolt, why then Ireland would be fighting for "independence." Would the charming features of Lord Brougham beam benevolently upon such an enterprise? Would he be found in his place in Parliament making soft speeches in behalf of a Provisional Government established in Dublin, and voting against all bills for putting down an Irish insurrection? And yet Ireland is no more an integral part of the British Empire than South Carolina is an integral part of the American Union. Nay, if we look at the matter, and institute a somewhat closer comparison, we find that the connection of Ireland with the English throne, originating in one of those "conquests" which Lord Brougham so much deprecates, and since sustained by cruelties which no honest writer can extenuate, does afford a ground for rebellion; while the " Confederate States" in their present revolt are without the shadow of an excuse. It is not enough to say that jealousies existed. It is not enough to say that fierce discussions had arisen between the North and the South. There can be no apology for this insurrection, except in actual, unmistakable and tangible wrongs endured; and even these would be insufficient morally and politically, unless it could also be shown that the sufferers had exhausted all possible means of redress, either by legislative or judicial processes. We wish that Englishmen when they undertake to criticise American affairs, would, if only now and then, abandon their safe and convenient generalizations, and dwell a little upon the facts. We have repeatedly called attention to the pregnant circumstance that the rebels have, to this hour, never presented to the world the smallest manifest of their injuries. In the chancery of civilized nations, they have never filed the most meagre bill of particulars. There has been good cause for this; the world would have listened but coldly to the record of splenetic dissatisfaction, of eccentric prejudices, and of selfish discontent—of ambition ungratified, of hatred balked by the majesty of the law, and of an unreasoning violence which chafed at the smallest restraint. It is because the rebel States have really and morally no cause to sustain and no injuries to redress that they have been so reticent of rational speech, and so voluble in the utterance of old catchwords, moldy slogans and stale commonplaces. It is odd that a man of Lord Brougham's reputation should be deceived by them. It is strange that he, who is considered to be quite a universal scholar, should know a bit of law, a little chemistry, a morsel of philosophy, something of political economy, more or less of metaphysics, and should know absolutely nothing of the American Constitution—so little, indeed, as to be unaware of the fact that it is the fundamental law of the land, and that in no possible sense can a war in its defense be called a war of "conquest." Tipstaves who catch rogues are not "conquerors." The constable who carries a pickpocket to Bridewell is not a "conqueror." The thief who breaks jail certainly asserts his "independence," and is in pursuit of his "liberty." But we do not believe his aspirations would appear to be remarkably sublime, even to Lord Brougham's catholic mind, if the thief had been in custody for picking his Lordship's pocket, or stealing his Lordship's plate.

There seems to be a notion prevalent in English society, that the American Union was originally a limited co-partnership, from which any member has a right for any whimsical reason to withdraw, upon its own mere motion, and without the slightest regard for the wishes or interests of its associates. But the least reference to the history of the formation of the Union will utterly explode this feeble hypothesis. The question was argued, and it was settled before the present Southern belligerent expounders were

begotten.   The men who established the Union may
be reasonably supposed to have understood what they
were about—to have known what they desired to
effect, and to have been capable of effecting it.   The
identical question of the right of a State to withdraw
from the compact, was debated and decided at the
very time when the compact was adopted.   We quote
only Alexander Hamilton, who said : " A Law, by
the very meaning of the term, includes supremacy.
It is a rule which those to whom it is prescribed are
bound to preserve.   This results from every political
association.   If individuals enter into a state of society, the laws of that society must be the supreme
regulator of their conduct.   If a number of political
societies enter into a larger political society, the laws
which the latter may enact, pursuant to the powers
intrusted to it by the Constitution, must necessarily
be supreme over those societies, and the individuals
of whom they are composed.   *It would otherwise be
a mere treaty, dependent on the good faith of the parties, and not a Government ; which is only another
word for political power and supremacy.*"

We have nothing of our own to add to this lucid
exposition of the nature of the Union from the pen
of one of the most celebrated of its founders.   It is
not a co-partnership.   It does not exist by virtue of a
Treaty, but by virtue of a Law.   By what authority,
then, does Lord Brougham, or any other lord, pretend that the United States are waging war for
" conquest ?"   To assert this, is to be guilty of a
gross perversion of the record and of language.   The

Supremacy of the General Government is the Supremacy of Law. An attempt to overthrow that Supremacy is a felony; and fine words about "Independence" do not change the nature of the crime. Let Lord Brougham understand this, or make no more speeches upon American affairs.

September 24, 1862.

TRAIN'S TROUBLES.

ONE of the most painful delusions of the day is that of Mr. George Francis Train, who imagines that the restoration of the American Union depends upon his eloquence. He is n't the first man who has mistaken volubility for argument. A mountebank may prattle in a fair from morn till dewy eve, but it is only to fools that he sells his corn-plasters and cough-drops. He may no doubt be overheard by many wise men, but that does not make his medicines infallible as he would have you believe; nor does the fact that Mr. Train writes for the newspapers prove that he is a statesman, for men who are forever writing to the newspapers are always in danger of bringing up in a mad-house. If Mr. Train could only for a moment comprehend how infinitely silly his productions appear to sensible men, he would we think be mortified into something like reason, and would write no more letters like this absurd one now before us, which is addressed to Charles Sumner and others, and which begins fiercely:—"Conspirators!"

13*

As a general rule we suspect that a man who writes confirmed slip-slop, and is never easy unless he is gyrating absurdly through all the gymnastics of rhetoric is hardly a safe person to call to the rescue of an empire. It may be prudently assumed that a Senator of the United States is in no need of Mr. George Francis Train's instruction, and is quite above his reprehension—and for that matter, of his comprehension also. Mr. Train's only retort must be : " Well, neither does the Honorable Senator comprehend me !" —and for Mr. Train, the reply would be uncommonly just and sensible.

Mr. Train charges the gentleman to whom he addresses this lurid letter with " a damnable conspiracy against three races of men"—against the Irish, "by placing an inferior race alongside of them in the cornfield," and against the Negroes who will all be murdered by their masters, according to Mr. G. F. T., unless the Abolitionists cease their provocations. But one of Mr. Train's vaticinations fortunately knocks the other in the head. If the Negroes are all to be murdered by their desperate masters, may not the fastidious George spare himself all painful apprehensions of anybody being compelled to work alongside the Black in any corn-field or other field in this hemisphere. Massacred Negroes do n't dig, to the best of our knowledge, Mr. Train !

There is a race of men—it is that to which Mr. Train belongs—who make a living, not by hoeing and digging, but by gabbling about the infinite superiority of being white—by denouncing those who cannot see the exquisite equity of Human Servitude —by lecturing on Politics, as other men lecture on Mesmerism and Table-Tipping—who convert their country's agony into a raree-show and go about entertaining people with the public misfortunes—who achieve notoriety by rehashing stale platitudes and rejuvenating venerable libels—who were unknown yesterday, and are only notorious to-day, and will be forgotten to-morrow — and to this race Negro Emancipation will prove fatal, for it will ruin their business, which is that of frightening honest folk and manufacturing bugbears.

Mr. George Francis Train must not think that we mean to be disrespectful.   On the contrary, when we put him in this race, we are paying him the greatest compliment of all he ever received in his life, if we except those which he has paid to himself.   We are ranking him with Doctors of Divinity and Members of Congress and Ethnologists and Politicians of the most venerable variety, who, when Emancipation has finished them, will hail him as a brother in misfortune and will go hand in hand with him to oblivion !

It may be a satisfaction to the Cabinet to know that Mr. Train, in this very letter, announces his generous intention of standing by it to the end.   He professes the most unbounded affection for Mr. Seward ; but if that gentleman be as shrewd as he has the reputation of being, he will hasten to beseech Mr. Train to write him no more letters.   It is n't every Administration that can stand Mr. Train's admiration.   And so much for George Francis !

October, 2, 1862.

THE SLAVEHOLDING UTOPIA.

It is related that when the Utopia of Sir Thomas More was first published, "the learned Budæus and others took it for a genuine history; and considered it as highly expedient that missionaries should be sent thither, in order to convert so wise a nation to Christianity." Should the political dreamers of the South, by any stroke of fortune, be left to their abominable devices, and thus be enabled to try before the world an experiment of promoting the genuine prosperity of the few by reducing the many to the lowest pitch of moral and physical squalor, it is possible that missionaries might be sent from the North to South Carolina, as they are now sent to Central Africa; and that some new Livingston might win the noblest of laurels, at the risk of his life, by carrying Christian civilization to Alabama or Mississippi. For it is very certain that whatever perfection the South might attain in the art of civil government, it must still want the very elements of religion.

Indeed, if we understand at all this little extract from *The Richmond Whig,* which is now before us, it is the avowed purpose of a portion, at least, of the Rebels, to be rid, in the very beginning of the new Empire, of all musty notions of the equality of even white men before their Creator, which is the essence of Christian brotherhood.

The Whig complains that, in the tempest and torrent of the Rebellion, men are plotting for the establishment of something like a monarchy, and for an aristocracy founded upon wealth. *The Whig*, in an exceedingly bilious way, reprehends these schemes against Democracy and Human White Equality, because it fears, as we fancy, that in the good time coming Editors will hardly be made Royal Dukes, and Printers hardly Baronets. The titles to this new nobility will be found in bills of the sale of Slaves; we may have Count Cuffee, or Sir Benjamin Barracoon, Prince Cotton-Pod, or the Marquis of Fine-Cut; but although these great people may condescend to take *The Whig*, and although a few of them may very punctually pay their yearly bills, and be highly gratified by reading his effusions, it will be hard for the Editor, in the new arrangement, to achieve so much as the simple Squirehood. He does well to protest in advance against a scheme which will just as much fix him in a lower social status as it will fix the Black. His vision is already, to a certain extent, purged; and he will see clearly by and by, that the aristocrat cares nothing for color, and would just as soon, if the law permitted, enslave a white as a black man.

We have not the satisfaction of knowing with just how colorless a cuticle Providence has endowed this ready writer; but if he be whiter than many a poor fellow who, maugre his aristocratic grandfathers, has been sold for a price, then our Editor must have what we venture to call a corpse-colored countenance. No; it is not the tint of the epidermis that my Lord of the Lash will care for when he has brought the Middle

Ages back to Virginia; for then he will throw over-
board the Book of Genesis, and all the other Books,
and if he can catch and sell the Editor of *The Whig*,
he will catch and sell him—and so we tell that unhappy and apprehensive gentleman.

Slavery is Power—it is Might fancying itself right
—it is Laziness loving to eat, but disdaining to work
—it is Covetousness of other men's houses, and wives,
and men-servants, and maid-servants, and oxen, and
asses, and all else that is other men's. A pretty time
the Poor White Men will have of it in the new King-
dom! It will be charming to live in it as a prince,
but will it be charming to live in it as a printer or a
peasant? How nicely the yoke of military and aristocratic tyranny will fit the necks of wretched Caucasians, bright-colored but niggerless! Who knows
but we may see revived there the feudal times—
maiden-right, wardship, baronial robberies, the seizure of white children for the market, military service,
and all the hardships of that villanage which men
have fondly deemed forever abolished by advancing
Christianity!

It may be thought by those who have given an
insufficient attention to the subject, that we are speaking somewhat extravagantly; but if we are deceived,
then the best thinkers in the world, since the pro-
mulgation of Christianity, have been deceived also.
This we are aware is not the place for voluminous or
elaborate citation; but we venture to refer to a
writer so well known, and so little likely to be carried away by his emotions, as Dr. Paley, who says,

" Christianity has triumphed over Slavery established in the Roman Empire, and I trust will one day prevail against the worse Slavery of the West Indies." So, too, Dr. Priestly : " Christianity has bettered the state of the world in a civil and political respect, giving men a just idea of their mutual relations, and thereby gradually abolishing Slavery with the servile ideas which introduced it, and also many cruel and barbarous customs." So, too, Dr. Robertson : " It is not the authority of any single, detached precept in the Gospel, but the spirit and genius of the Christian religion, more powerful than any particular command, which will abolish Slavery throughout the world." So, too, Fortescue, hard and dry old lawyer as he was : " God Almighty has declared himself the God of Liberty." But we must not venture to multiply authorities, and in spite of temptation we abstain, simply referring the curious reader to Bodin's " Six Books of a Commonweale," (Lib. I., Cap. 5,) in which he will find the whole case of Christianity against Slavery summed up with masterly erudition.

To return to our original subject, we say that as Slavery is hostile to Christianity, it follows that it is hostile to Democracy. The Constitution guaranties to every white man, at least, in the Rebel States, a Republican form of government, which can never be maintained with social institutions based upon the worst practices of an outworn Heathenism. It is not only for territorial power; it is not only in defence of social order and the majesty of law, that we are contending, but for the conservation of civilization and the security of personal rights; it is that we may not, in our progress toward a higher greatness and more equitable social forms, be neighbored by a nation lapsing into the rudeness and barbarism of the Middle Ages.

"America!" sang Goethe, long ago—

> "America! thou hast it better
> Than our ancient hemisphere!
> Thine is no frowning castle,
> No basalt as here!
> Good luck wait on thy glorious Spring,
> And when in time thy poets sing,
> May some good genius guard them all
> From baron, robber-knight, and ghost traditional."

October 6, 1862.

TWELVE LITTLE DIRTY QUESTIONS.

WE should very much like to know what in the opinion of the Rev. Dr. Hawks constitutes a large and clean question. In the Protestant Episcopal Convention last Monday, Dr. Hawks, arguing that the Church must treat its rebellious children with "lenity, courtesy and affection," used the following language: "We must not lug in all the little dirty questions of the day which will be buried with their agitation." One might retort upon Dr. Hawks that the questions which have disturbed the diocese for some years past, have been many of them small, and one of them, at least, exceedingly dirty—to say nothing of piquant scandals in the neighboring diocese of Pennsylvania.

To the Protestant Episcopal Church is unquestionably due the reverence of some of us and the respect of others; but Heaven knows there is nothing in its history, nothing in its present position which justifies this sublime scorn of political affairs which Dr. Hawks professes. In England, from the days of Henry VIII. to the days of Victoria, the Church has been quite as much a political as a religious body —its Bishops have been courtiers, and sometimes generals—it has been a political institution in Scotland and in Ireland—the reigning monarch has been its legal head—among its clergy have figured the keenest and most unscrupulous politicians, while for the last twenty-five years, though Laud has been in his coffin for more than two centuries, this Church which never meddles with little questions, has been well-nigh sundered upon points of architecture, of upholstery, of tailoring, of genuflexions and of decorations; while in America we have had petty reproductions of the same differences, with the disgusting spectacle of a Right Reverend Father in God, riding, all booted and spurred, at the head of his rebel regiments. After this, to find Dr. Hawks so delicately squeamish and so doubtful about the authority of the Church in public affairs, must excite commiseration both for his stomach and his understanding.

Shall the United State of America be deprived of an immense territory acquired at a cost of blood and treasure absolutely incomputable? This is Dr. Hawks's Little Dirty Question, No. One.

Shall the Constitution of the United States be

overthrown by the perjuries of its sworn defenders? This is Dr. Hawks's Little Dirty Question, No. Two.

Shall the Loyal States see the rolls of their citizens decimated, the flower of their youth slain in battle, the homes only a little while ago the happiest in the world made desolate, the honest accumulations of industry scattered, the enterprises of benevolence arrested—and all without hope of indemnity or of security? This is Dr. Hawks's Little Dirty Question, No. Three.

Shall the wildest and wickedest perjury, the most Satanic defiance of the Majesty of Heaven, the clearest and least defensible of crimes flourish and bloom in the establishment of a great empire, and out of the dissolution of society secure the prosperous fortunes of the turbulent and the ambitious? This is Dr. Hawks's Little Dirty Question, No. Four.

Shall the great experiment of political self-government utterly fail, while we, crouching and crawling through the vicissitudes of anarchy, find refuge at last in blind obedience to the edicts of an autocrat? This is Dr. Hawks's Little Dirty Question, No. Five.

Shall a system of labor be perpetuated which, without regard to its abstract equity, without consideration of its injustice to the employed, has so demoralized the employer, that treason, robbery and murder seem to him to be Christian virtues? This is Dr. Hawks's Little Dirty Question, No. Six.

Shall a system of labor be perpetuated which so utterly degrades the spiritual nature of the enslaved, as to expose it in its very yearning for sacred culture to a fanaticism analogous to idolatry? This is Dr. Hawks's Little Dirty Question, No. Seven.

Shall a system of labor be perpetuated the very essence of which is a denial of the fundamental principle of Christian ethics—that the laborer is worthy of his hire? This is Dr. Hawks's Little Dirty Question, No. Eight.

Shall these acts be considered by the Church mere peccadilloes, when perpetrated by its Southern slaveholding members, which in its Northern communicants it would at once visit with its censure and even its excommunication? This is Dr. Hawks's Little Dirty Question, No. Nine.

Shall a Church which every Sunday prays the Good Lord to deliver us "from all sedition, privy conspiracy and rebellion," and "to give to all nations unity, peace and concord," still hold communion with a Church which is full of sedition, privy conspiracy and rebellion against the unity, peace and concord of the land? This is Dr. Hawks's Little Dirty Question, No. Ten.

Shall a Church which every Sunday prays for "the President of the United States, and all others in authority"—not merely as fellow-men, but because they are "in authority"—shall the Church withhold its censure of those of its members, who in contempt of authority are waging a felonious war against law and order? This is Dr. Hawks's Little Dirty Question, No. Eleven.

Whether, finally, these communicants of the Church in the rebel States who have been so disregardful of its discipline, and so false to its teachings as to avowedly violate all laws Divine and human, are entitled to anything more than Christian pity, are at all entitled in their double tort to Christian Fellowship, is a Little Dirty Question well worth the consideration of every Christian Patriot; and is Dr. Hawks's No. Twelve.

October 11, 1862.

DEMOCRACY IN LONDON.

THIS is an age of new loves and unwonted affections. That must have been a curious concatenation of events which has brought our Democratic Party into such high favor in Printing - House Square. When it was young and wickedly vigorous, the queer old women who create public opinion in England always denounced it as dangerous and disreputable; and it is only now when its vices have brought it to a premature dotage, with no virility to improve its fortuitous conquests, that they have suddenly grown in love with its stammering speech and shattered corporation. Our readers must pardon the peculiarity of the figure, for the sake of that emasculation which can only thus be indicated.

The London Times suffers itself to be cheated by majorities as fortune-hunters allow wealth to hide decay and infirmity; and fancies that if the Democratic Party was once more dominant in Congress, our feuds would be in a fair way of adjustment.

This is an eminent instance of forgetfulness and forgiveness. Democracy has proved its political skill
and pure singleness of purpose, by uttering bitter
slanders and bitterer truths whenever its policy has
clashed with that of England; by taking the lead
in every debate in which that country has been severely handled, by formal and perpetual denuncia-
tions of monarchies and aristocracies; by avowing
itself from its Presidents down to its bob-tail at the
polls, always and upon principle unrelentingly the
enemy of the British Empire. Nor has the favor
been unrepaid. Whigs and Tories in the Imperial
Parliament, if they have united in nothing else, have
agreed that American Democracy was but another
name for license and the synonym for anarchy.

Can any one doubt, when *The Times* thus suddenly shifts its key-note, and affects to be in love
with what it considers to be the popular party in
America, that it cares for nothing but a change in
the Administration, and patronizes our opponents
because they would be least likely, if in office, to ne-
gotiate a lasting and honorable peace? It is strange
that even the most distant observers should so soon
forget that four years of a Democratic Administration, with little or no check upon a policy which had
for its sole object the conservation and consolida-
tion of Slavery and its minutest interests, failed to
propitiate those conspirators who mean to mount
upon Southern passions and prejudices into a permanent oligarchy. It is strange that a fact so modern in history as the assassination of the Democratic

Party by its Southern members should be forgotten. Are these members likely to consider as valuable now what they then thought valueless? Are they likely now to heed in the heat of insurrection, voices to which, in the calmness and solemnity of high counsel, they turned an utterly deaf ear? We do not question the willingness of Northern Democrats to do whatever service the feudal lords of the South may prescribe, as the tenure of the old tugs at the Treasury teats.

But however willing the Seymour party may be to be bought, the rebels are not yet desperate enough to buy them. What, indeed, could a new Administration of the bad Buchanan variety offer, which could tempt these traitors back to loyalty? When with hasty passion they repudiated all Constitutional obligations, they gave up a legislative and judicial power far greater than that of the North, but still not great enough to satisfy their most unreasonable appetite. It was not enough for them to be potent in practice, but they insisted on being considered omnipotent in theory. We caught and surrendered their fugitives; we gave them in spite of prescription a fairer chance in the new Territories than we reserved for ourselves; and we hesitate not to say, that at the moment of rebellion, if we except the pressure upon it by the progressive moral sense of the world, slaveholding never was safer, never more profitable in States where it was by law established. Within the limits of the Constitution, upon the most liberal construction, slaveholders could ask for nothing more than they already possessed. It was not because they were dissatisfied with existing securities that they revolted ; but because they could no longer bear the moral dissent of the conscientious and enlightened North. Nor of the North alone. By the violence of their demonstration and by the inconveniences to which it inevitably subjected the commercial world, they sought to set aside that indignant verdict which was everywhere making up against them. They instituted an experiment, not only upon the morality, through material interests, of the Free States, but upon the integrity of Great Britain. They revolted not against the Federal Government, but against the Christianity of the Nineteenth Century. Strong in their monopoly of a single agricultural staple, they boasted of their power to change the religious convictions of great empires by sordid influences and pecuniary temptations.

The Northern States of America were not to be deluded into so much as a quasi endorsement of cruelty and barbarism even by old associations and cherished traditions, and still less by gross and direct appeals to the pocket. But the man-owners were more fortunate abroad, where we should have supposed the speculation would have been more desperate. It is at this juncture that England invokes the aid of her old enemies, the American Democracy, and tempts them to an utter abnegation of honor and honesty. It is now in a spirit of pure selfishness that she hints to them that by bated breath and whispered humbleness, by unlimited concessions and a thorough-paced flunkeyism, they may secure their own power and advance her prosperity. The leading journal of Europe, as some have called it, is not ashamed to stimulate what remains of the dough-faces to lower cringing and ingenuities of humiliation. It would use as the wheedled instrument of its selfish purposes, the very party which yesterday it affected to despise, and unquestionably detested. We do not think that political scheming has ever made a baser or more ludicrous descent than this, even when under the influence of commercial appetites.

November 19, 1862.

LAUGHTER IN NEW HAMPSHIRE.

THE late Democratic State Convention in New Hampshire, considering the fearfully funereal business upon which it met, was decidedly in luck. Remembering that it is, so to speak, a deposed dynasty, we may congratulate the New Hampshire Democracy upon the possession of a certain funny physician, named Bachelder, who introduced his method of cure—a kind of Gigglepathy—to the Convention, and made jokes for the members about the "inevitable nigger," which were received, we are told, with roars of merriment. Taking into account how small will be their temptations to laughter after the election, perhaps it was merely prudent for the delegates to exercise their diaphragms before that event; for if he laughs who wins, the victims of predestinate defeat must secure their quantum of the amusement before their solemn fate is determined, if they would have it at all. "To-morrow we may be dying,"—very justly thought these Democrats—"let us be merry while we can."

Of the pure philosophic school of Democrats, the drearier their destiny, the heartier their guffaws became, under the persuading influences of the droll Doctor, who is, we take it, like one of the old-fashioned quacks who, in other days, were wont to dispense mercury and merriment from a stage at country fairs. We give the Doctor this publicity because we cannot sufficiently admire his pluck in being jolly under circumstances which would have daunted Mark Tapley himself. We must add that we give him credit, too, for an exceeding ingenuity at discovering new materials for laughter in the "nigger;" for we really thought that Buckley and the rest of the lampblack boys had exhausted the fountain of sable farce.

If any of our readers are laboring under that green-and-yellow complaint called melancholy, we cordially recommend them to send fifty cents, and a few locks of their hair, to the New Hampshire Paracelsus. He is "death on gloom," as other accomplished quacks have been "death on fits." He is a walking, grinning, giggling, cacchinating, tittering, smiling proof of the excellence of his own theory, and the infallibility of his own practice. Here is the country in the condition of the most cruel anxiety; we are bereaved, we are drafted, we are impoverished; in hundreds of homes there is weeping for the dead, and

14

terrible suspense, and fear of the next news, and sickening anxiety until it shall come; but in spite of all this weary woe, the irrepressible Doctor Bachelder mounts the stage with his budget of quips and quirks, and soon has the grave Democracy of New Hampshire in a roar worthy of any peepshow or penny theatre. The man who could do this should not content himself with peddling pills in the rural districts. He has a right to aspire to metropolitan fame. With a little chalk upon his cheeks, and red ochre on the tip of his nose, he would be invaluable in a traveling circus. We cordially recommend him to our friend Barnum as quite a monster of merriment. With the two dwarfs to make jokes, and the Doctor to laugh at them, we believe it would be necessary to enlarge the cash-box of the museum.

If we are ourselves exhibiting a little ill-timed pleasantry, we must plead the contagion of example. It is impossible to write of this Medical Momus in a serious way. Perhaps if we were to take a few lessons of him in the Art of Laughing—will he be good enough to send us a card of his terms for twelve lessons?—we, too, might see Slavery in a ludicrous light. Who knows but the Doctor might found a new Pro-Slavery sect? Some say that the institution is patriarchal, others affirm it to be ethnological. Others, still, find authority for it in the curse of Canaan. Now, might not Bachelder take the ground that, whereas, "there is a time to laugh," so God gave us Slavery to laugh at—Slavery with its shames and crimes, its cruelties and inconsistencies. When

Sambo writhes under the lash, what can be droller? When his wife is cowhided, is there not entertainment in every scream? It is such a joke to part mother and child! It is such a perfection of comedy —this exhibition of human will, utterly depraved, and of human weakness, utterly down-trodden! Roar away, Dr. Bachelder! Roar until your breath fails, and your sides shake! Why should n't you laugh? Are there not laughing hyenas?

We believe that the jovial Bachelders of the day should be encouraged to new efforts in laughing at the Blacks, because it really begins to be doubtful whether, after all, the Blacks will not too soon have the laugh against us. We can imagine one of these ebony butts, of ordinary intelligence and a sardonic turn of mind, chuckling in a way that would afford a new study for the Ethiopian Serenaders, at the particularly hot water in which his light-colored superiors are floundering. While he has nothing to lose, and can hardly sink to a lower deep of misery, he has the retributive compensation of observing our wars and our wastes, our bereavements and our bankruptcies, our failures and our fears. The man must be purblind, at least, who does not see that, in all these distractions, the celebrated curse has been mysteriously transferred from the shoulders of Canaan to our own. The New Hampshire doctor does well to laugh while it is possible. He cannot tell whose chance it will be next!

November 28, 1862.

SLAVEHOLDING VIRTUES.

SOUTHERN statists have asserted negro-owning to be the nurse of public virtues, just as Southern theologians have found in it an abiding stimulus of personal piety. In the Free States it has been claimed by these polished Patriarchs that we have secured Liberty only at the expense of good manners or good morals. New York is a sink of iniquity. Philadelphia is the mother of mobs. Boston is the centre of free-thinking and general licentiousness. Yankee treasurers are always defaulters. Yankee merchants are always absconding. Yankee women are strangers to virtue, and Yankee men to honesty. We are not duellists; we are not street-assassins; we do not carry pistols in our pockets and bowie-knives at our backs; we do not lynch, summarily, those with whom we may happen to disagree; but every Northern mob and Northern murder is paraded in the Southern newspapers, as a proof of that social dissolution, which is always here impending. The Southern idea of a thorough Yankee is like Sir John Vanbrugh's idea of a Puritan,—"a fellow with flat, plod shoes, greasy hair and a dirty face—a friend to nobody, loving nothing but his altar and himself; a debauchee in piety and as quarrelsome in his religion as other people are in their drink." But our principal wickedness is our love of money. We do any thing for dollars. We think more of a shilling than of our own souls. "*Virtus post nummos,*" is written upon our heart of hearts.

The cosmopolitan moralist who admires honesty wherever it may exist will be painfully agitated to learn, that living in the actual centre of sweet and persuasive slaveholding influences, the respectable E. Hunter Taliaferro, first doorkeeper of the Confederate Senate of Virginia, by which we understand the front doorkeeper, has drawn forged warrants upon the State Treasury, to the melancholy tune of fourteen thousand dollars, and what is worse, has bagged the money, or those rags which are supposed to represent the money. The Richmond papers which report this backsliding of the wretched Taliaferro do not say that he has any Yankee blood in his felonious heart, but we suppose it will be eventually discovered that he has a great aunt living somewhere in New England, who is a church-member and an Abolitionist. Nothing less can account for his profound iniquity. He must certainly be of the old Puritan stock. Who but one purely of that strain could rob impecunious, starving, ragged Virginia? Surely it can not be one of her own children who has thus pilfered from an insolvent old mother, who has seen better days. Why, 't would be like filching coppers from the dead eyes of one's grandam. O Hunter Taliaferro! What a bad example you have set to the ingenuous youth of Virginia!

So, too, we lament to record that in New Orleans, Gen. Butler has not found that pure Arcadian simplicity of character which should have been engendered and cherished by auction-blocks and barracoons. It turns out that in this city of primeval in-

nocence, there are Secessionists upon whom all classes
have united in conferring the gentle name of
"Thugs." We suppose that most of our readers
know what a Thug is. He is a gentleman of Eastern origin who finds his principal pleasure in playing such scurvy tricks upon travelers as murder and
robbery. What does he do in the West when he
should serve his lord and master, the devil, in the
East? Why is he not operating in New England?
We do n't know. We only know that he is said to
be fearfully lively in New Orleans just now. Particularly is mentioned a certain "Red Bill" (or William
Rufus, we suppose,) who for many years in this Crescent City has performed a crescendo of crime, murdering, whenever and whomsoever he pleased, with
artistic enthusiasm, and finally closing his career
of glorious guilt by flinging a loyal person into the
river to be drowned.

Hitherto William the Red has pursued enthusias-
tically his brilliant career with no let or hindrance.
How many people he has drowned, how many bushels of brains he has scattered, how many hearts the
ball from his friendly pistol has perforated, into
whose bowels his bowie-knife has found a sudden and
unwelcome entrance, we shall know when we read
his Last Dying Speech and Confession; for, we are
happy to say that Gen. Butler, appreciating the merits of this sanguinary chevalier, and believing that
his career should be poetically rounded, had concluded at the last advices to hang him, and doubtless, before this, has hanged him, to the uncommon satisfac-

tion of the spectators. But what astonishes us is, that this rose-colored gentleman owned black-colored property, and should, therefore, by all established rules, have been also a person of the most altitudinous virtue. Instead of roaming about with a barker in one hand and an acute, persuading bowie-knife in the other, instead of giving himself up to the somewhat coarse dissipation of throwing inoffensive people into the river; the Rosy William should have remained at home, seated in his own tabernacle, perusing the Holy Scriptures, or under the shade of his own fig-tree he should have read and expounded them to his henchmen and handmaidens, making plain to their simple understandings, the profound commentaries of Doctor Lord or of Doctor Fuller.

But he does not appear to have been at all the sort of person to whom St. Paul would have been in a hurry to send back an absconding church-member. It is stated that his death will give great delight to his personal friends, as well as a calmer satisfaction to his enemies; and as we have every reason to believe, from Gen. Butler's well-known celerity in such matters, that William is now no more, we conclude our notice of him by expressing our mild regret that he ever existed at all.

The slaveholding theory is indeed charming. We have a benevolent old master, wearing his life out in the service of his own serfs and racking his amiable brains for inventions of kindness and caretaking. We have a society so perfectly ordered, and so utterly under the sway of even-handed justice, that wrongs are not only unknown, but impossible. We have an aristocracy of Roman dignity, and a peasantry perfectly happy and measurelessly contented. We have the State always serene and the Church forever in blossom. Such is the theory—but when we come to the practice—ah! that is quite another matter!

December, 11, 1862.

ROLAND FOR OLIVER.

No ONE will pretend that, for the purpose of philosophical discussion, personal recrimination is of any value. "You are another," proves nothing but bad temper, and a worse cause. From this point of view Gen. Butler's retorts upon his transatlantic censors seem to be simply amusing. They remind us, as we read, of Satan, with a savor of his normal brimstone exuding from every pore, creeping, tail and all, into some empty pulpit, and exhorting the congregation to abandon its sins. When lechers preach continence, when misers advocate liberality, when bullies set up for Chesterfields, when prize-fighters put on Quaker coats, when liars tender their corporal oath, it is the way of the world, a very wicked and uncharitable world, no doubt, to snicker and to sneer. It cannot be helped. It is only a simple resort to our natural defence against presumption and hypocrisy. It is no palliation, indeed, of our own wrongdoing, but it is a fair assertion of our right to be rebuked by honest lips, and to be smitten by clean hands.

By recrimination the woman taken in adultery escaped not only a cruel but a legal death ; and the consciousness that we are none of us without sin, saves society from perpetual collisions and an eternal wrangle. But when Gen. Butler, placed as he was in a most difficult and delicate position, found it necessary to resort to certain punishments, some of them extreme indeed, but most of them of a mild and municipal character—punishments which fifty years ago were as familiar to Europe as the bulletins of Napoleon— then every scribbler for the London newspapers felt it to be his duty to elevate his whine, and to represent the General as a blood-thirsty ogre, only deterred from dining upon Rebels by the extreme leanness of their corporcity. There was never a sillier slander.

Imagine a commander in military possession of a captured town, who allows his soldiers to be insulted, his authority to be questioned, his Government to be derided in the newspapers; who invites his own assassination by his fear of hanging professional bravos, and who runs a daily risk of ignominious expulsion, because he cannot make up his gentle mind to abandon the *suaviter* for a time, and resort, in his emergency, to the *fortiter !* Of course, under such circumstances, if he does his duty, he will be denounced by those whom it would be criminal to conciliate. It 's the rogue trussed up and haltered, with his ill opinion of the law, over again ! Particularly would the satisfaction under such circumstances be lively, in a city like New Orleans—a city in which, in the most peaceful times, the civil and judicial authorities have

14*

been notoriously corrupt and inefficient—a city in which mobs have always abounded, and human life has ever been unsafe—a city which has been a constant reservoir of Slaveholding rascality, and the refuge of lawlessness and violence. To the ruffianhood of New Orleans, the vigor, the promptness, the precision and the inexorability of Gen. Butler must have been, of necessity, astonishing and uncomfortable.

But, upon a review of his proceedings, this much-berated Major-General, so far from finding anything to regret, appears to regard the moderation of his course with no little complacency; and the *sang-froid* with which he reminds his English assailants of the little he had done, and the deal which, following established precedents, he might have done, is really entertaining. He has dealt lightly enough, he thinks, with men who, fifty times over, have forfeited their lives. He has n't smoked them to death, as the soldiers of Claverhouse did the Covenanters; he has n't roasted them as the French did the Algerines; he has n't scalped them, and tomahawked wives and mothers, as the Indians under British colors did at Wyoming; he has n't "looted" private property after the fashion of the English in China; he has n't blown his prisoners from his guns, as Bull did at Delhi; he has resorted to extreme penalties only when the law demanded them, and the commonest punishment which he has inflicted has been banishment to an island, where, only a little while ago, his own soldiers were quartered.

It seems to us, after the fullest consideration, that

a retort like this is perfectly fair. Gen. Butler may well urge in his own defence that England, with all her immense resources, has never found the work of arresting a rebellion a mere holiday task. He might have gone further, if he had seen fit to do so. He might have pointed to the atrocities of the English soldiery in Ireland—to that chapter of history which can never be recited without awaking the indignation of mankind—to cabins burned, to men and women indiscriminately murdered, to tortures mercilessly inflicted—to that whole catalogue of crimes which Lord Cornwallis, then the Lord-Lieutenant of Ireland, in vain endeavored to arrest, by the most pathetic remonstrance addressed to the English ministers in London.

It would have been no inequitable rejoinder, to have said something of the British Themis, advancing into the hovels of Ireland with a halter in one hand and a bag of guineas in the other, buying men's lives as drovers purchase cattle, and attended by a train of nine-times perjured sycophants, spies, and informers! Something, too, might have been said of Capt. Hodson's summary execution, with his own hand, of the two sons and the grandson of the King of Delhi —an act, the propriety and necessity of which we do not mean to question—but still an act of boldness and severity, in comparison with which anything done by Gen. Butler during his government of New Orleans, has been the milk of mercy itself! But if the perils of the Rebellion in India were such as to drive an excellent and amiable officer to the extreme of severity—if Capt. Hodson himself shot his prisoners, while it is n't pretended that Gen. Butler played Jack Ketch upon any occasion—why are we to be denounced for simply securing the safety of a city fairly captured by our forces? We are not fighting for entertainment. We are not engaged in mere pastime.

Unless, indeed, we are in grim earnest in this contest; unless we are determined, before we throw by the sword, to re-establish the Federal authority wherever it has been assailed; unless we mean war with all its incidents and consequents, we are verily guilty of blood carelessly and causelessly spilt, and must answer to God for incalculable suffering. But in view of the great and patriotic work before us, the little matters at New Orleans, which have furnished the London journals with themes for whole symphonies of sarcasm and wrath, dwindle into insignificance. General Butler has acted precisely as any English or French General would have acted; or perhaps it would be fairer to say, that he has displayed a moderation which, in an English or French officer, we should have looked for in vain. Without any particular admiration for his character, we feel that to say this is only to do him simple justice.

January 12, 1863.

HISTORICAL SCARECROWS.

The cheapest and, at the same time, the readiest of all subterfuges, when logic is lacking, is the Historical Bugaboo. Its employment is quite independent of sense or of scholarship. A single event, no matter how ancient, may be turned into a fresh fight upon twenty widely different occasions, and be pertinaciously, and often effectively obtruded, without the least regard to the indisputable fact, that the world is considerably older than it was on the day of its creation. The failure of past republics is made proof prophetic of the instability of all popular governments. Commonwealths must go to ruin eighteen centuries after Christ, because Commonwealths went to ruin ten centuries before Christ. History is only written to prove that "Nought is everything, and everything is nought."

Is it proposed, in countries principally Protestant, to emancipate the Catholics? Remember St. Bartholomew! Is it argued that governments derive their just powers from the consent of the governed? Think of the red rivers of the French Revolution! Do we ask for justice to the American Slave? Men with hearts as hard as their bigotry, or that of St. Dominic himself, parade the butcheries of St. Domingo! The fact of the massacres is sufficient. What caused them—who was in the right, and who was in fault—whether the Blacks did anything to be praised instead of blamed—these are minor considerations, unworthy of the attention of men who know absolutely nothing of that sad history, and who could not for their lives, upon a cross examination, tell us whether Toussaint was a black or a white man, what he did while living, or where, or under what circumstances, he died. It is enough to "scream" St. Domingo! and every abolitionist is considered to be effectually graveled. It is in this idiotic way that History is abused. *The Express* do n't know much, but it can whine "St. Domingo!" *The Herald* never makes a pretence of argument, but it can bawl "St. Domingo!" Women can whimper it — platform prophets can howl it—cross and crusted conservatives can adduce it victoriously—and persons vibrating between duty and dollars, finding that a defence of Slavery upon the Judaic basis involves abstinence from sausages, can abandon Palestine for the West Indies without interfering with their breakfasts.

It is of but little use to ask these people to hear the whole story. Why should they listen, if, by being tolerably well informed, they are to be diddled out of a good chronic cry? Why tell them that, after the decree of the French Convention of 1784 had confirmed the emancipation of the colony, the most respectable authorities declare that the freedmen were peaceable and industrious, working upon their own plantations and for their old masters? That of course is n't a fact of any importance. Why tell these historical gentlemen, who know everything, that nine-tenths of the atrocities committed by the Blacks were incited by the Whites and Mulattoes? That is of no consequence. Why show that, under

Toussaint, the colony flourished, the Whites living happily upon their plantations, the estates well and cheerfully cultivated by the Blacks, until the expedition of Le Clerc, sent forward by that wily Italian, to whom the very name of Liberty was detestable, arrived for the single purpose of restoring Slavery? What followed—the tearing of the Negroes by bloodhounds—the wholesale massacre of the Blacks—the infinite cruelties inflicted by the planters—is not so well known as the final expulsion of the French, and the horrors by which it was attended. That the Blacks took an ample revenge is not denied. That they were always humane is not asserted. But it is, nevertheless, equally true, that if ever cruelties were provoked it was when the needless and unjustifiable interference of Bonaparte aroused passions which, in men of a different complexion, would have been considered worthy only of the warmest praise.

Such is the case of St.-Domingo. Admitting all that the advocates of Human Bondage say of it, it proves nothing against Emancipation, and everything against Re-enslavement. To any rash deductions from its darker features, we are at liberty to oppose all the other experiences of modern times. Not to enter into more details, we fearlessly appeal to the great experiment in the British West Indies. We are aware of the commercial objections which have been made to that measure—the complaint of meagre crops and of reduced incomes—the ruin which it is asserted has overtaken the landed proprietors. But we are not now considering a question of pounds sterling, or of the diminished value of sugar-estates. We are investigating the chances of social safety and order under the new relations which Emancipation establishes. According to the doctrine of the Negrophobist, the West India Blacks should have cut every Englishman's throat—and the worst that Thomas Carlyle, in his diabolical hatred of the African, can say is, that while he can get pumpkins for nothing, the Freedman will not dig potatoes! This the sternest moralist will admit is something less than the murders, rapes, and arsons which should have followed that memorable First of August, and which we are invited to believe will follow our own memorable First of January.

For ourselves, if we are to be guided in our present duties by the precedents of the past, we prefer to select our own examples, and to draw our own conclusions. If the latest English newspapers come to us freighted with sarcastic sneers at the Emancipation of the American Slave, we can read them with equanimity, when we remember that Mr. Dundas, in 1792, proposed, in Parliament, the Emancipation of the British Blacks—that Mr. Burke proposed a bill for the same great purpose—that Mr. Pitt avowed that the abolition of the Slave Trade must be followed by the abolition of Slavery—that Sir Samuel Romilly, in pronouncing the doom of a barbarous commerce, anticipated the time " when the West Indies should no more be cultivated, as now, by wretched Slaves, but by happy and contented laborers,"— —that the careless but kind-hearted Sheridan declared, that the abolition of the Slave-Trade was "the proper preamble to the entire abolition of Slavery,"—that Lord Grenville, then Prime Minister, moved Emancipation in the House of Lords—and, finally, that old Dr. Johnson used to drink, as a favorite toast, "a speedy insurrection of the Slaves of Jamaica, and success to them!"

These were the views of enlightened English statesmen and thinkers nearly a century ago. These opinions, familiar as they are to our own educated classes, have done much to create and strengthen that hostility to Slavery which the great organ of the British shopkeepers now stigmatizes as fanaticism and folly. Let it rave! Let its passion for pounds sterling get the better of its moral principles! The world moves, and a century hence men will read its leading articles as they now read the Tory diatribes of Sir Roger L'Estrange.

January 13, 1863.

THE OTHER WAY.

"*In medio tutissimus ibis*,"—"down the middle," as they say in the dancing-schools—is a charming maxim when there is any middle to go down. But when some nice representative of the conservative species, who has adjusted his neat legs for a pleasant pirouette through unencumbered spaces of pleasantness and ease, finds his path incontinently blocked up, and discovers that there is no way through which he may glide to measureless content, it is very ridiculous in him to persist in figuring fussily about, no matter how melodious may be the fiddles which call upon him to demonstrate the perfection of his *glissando*.

Gentlemen who manufacture leading-articles for the London newspapers are much outraged by Mr. Lincoln's Emancipation Proclamation. Gentlemen nearer home have also their perturbations. To free the slaves is to be rash and radical, and to follow all precedents and to confiscate that property which is most valuable and upon which we can most readily put the just finger of the law, is to encourage the whole catalogue of crimes, and to awaken under the breast-bone of Jefferson Davis, passions which our best blood only can cool. The philosophic mind astutely contemplating these difficulties, and not discovering very clearly that middle course which should be pursued, but which will doubtless charmingly develop itself when two and two make five, seeks for a solution in the other extreme, and wonders if we should please our English critics better by avowing ourselves converts in soul and spirit to the doctrine of the divine right of Man-Owning. Better this than splitting hairs eternally! Better this than to be forever leering with one eye at Self-Interest, and with the other at Duty! Better accept in the full proportions of its gigantic diabolism, the Evangel of Brute Force, than to be always dyspeptically sighing at our troubles and shrinking like children from our medicine!

These modern apologists of treason want a few lessons in manly and muscular wickedness. Now they go bobbing about like the old Duke of Newcastle at a levee, shedding tears, hysterically laughing, asking what they shall do to be saved, following nobody's advice, cursing the Abolitionists heartily, cursing the Rebels just enough to be in the fashion, swearing that something must be done, pitying the North, commiserating the South and fancying that somehow—God only knows how!—if they were in Congress or the President's Cabinet, or at the head of the Army, they would smooth down every hair of this rebellious cat, and coax North and South, in the purple light of love, to fall amorously into each other's arms! Why will not these people see that comfort, convenience, necessity, consistency, all require them to say to the Rebels:

"Gentle Patriarchs! Legitimate descendants of Abraham, Isaac and Jacob! Most worthy and most injured Man-Owners! Salt of the Earth! You wish to own Niggers—Black, Yellow and White Niggers —without hindrance. A very reasonable wish! Believe us it shall be gratified. Not only shall you own them, but, to assist you in owning them, we will eat our own Bibles and Constitutions; we will fight your battles; we will pay your taxes; we will catch the fugacious for you without fee or reward; we will import Sambo for you in our brave ships; and whoever within our borders shall say one word against the equity, or the policy, of your unlimited charter, that man, by due process of law, we will hang, draw and quarter."

Now this it seems to us, is the precise opposite of

the Emancipation Proclamation which has proved so acrid to the tender interiors of some Englishmen and of some Northern Democrats. The Rebel asks you to admit that his Slave system is beautiful. Well, then, let us admit it! To be sure we involve ourselves in dreadful responsibilities by doing so—we pile a mountain of corpses upon the Northern conscience— we admit the utter fatuity of the Northern mind— we own an error more monstrous than any people ever before committed—we spit upon the loveliness of civilization, and advertise ourselves atheists, hopeless of human progress, acquiescent in the misery of man, confessing him incapable of advancement, and the sheerest plaything of his own idiotic dreams!

But·let the baubles go! Let us throw away our rattles—pity, love, charity, humanity—the baubles of our childhood, and, grimly advancing to confront our bitter destiny, and crying piteously, "Good devil!" seal our Manichæan faith in the blood of the helpless and the despairing! Why should we not? The shuttles of Lancashire will again fly merrily— the great Juggernaut of Printing-House Square will grin approbation at us, with his gaping, bloody mouth—the bulky bales will again fill our ships— the Patriarchs will again adorn and fortify our Legislative halls—dear, delightful internal, not to say infernal, commerce will be resumed—churches will flourish and missions will multiply—of ploughshares and pruning-hooks there will be no end in the land! Talk about conscience! We assert without fear of contradiction from any good Conservative of the

Seymour-Brooks-Wood-en order, that no nation can afford to maintain a conscience. Conscience neither sows nor reaps, nor gathers into barns, nor lays up treasure on earth, nor spins nor owns ships. What do they care for conscience in Downing Street? Where would Louis Napoleon have been now, if instead of keeping two or three mistresses, he had been fool enough to keep a conscience? Tormented still by his tailor in a London garret! Of all ridiculous things in this ridiculous old world, thrice the most ridiculous is conscience. It belongs to ecclesiastical establishments—it is something to talk about—it is a handy thing to have in the house—it is an article for which you may have use upon an emergency—but, as for a homely, good, every-day conscience, why you might as well keep an elephant to do odd jobs in the scullery. Bold Britons find conscience a capital thing when they wish to form a Society for Propagating the Gospel in Foreign Parts—but egad! when you come to Conscience *vs.* Cotton, John Bull is for the Defendant!

Our little plan we trust will make everything easy. It is simply to give the Rebel Slaveholders all they ask—Slaves, the Presidency, the Congress, the Army, the Navy, the Treasury, the Control of Trade, the Direction of the American Church. Will they kindly consent to take us in hand? Will they intimate to our new government what we must do first? Do we kiss their hands or their feet? Or do we knock our forehead three times upon the ground in token of submission? Must Mr. Lincoln stand at a

church-door in a sheet, with a candle in his hand?
Give us the etiquette of our formal surrender that we
may be preparing for the final ceremony.

January 14, 1865.

SAULSBURY'S SENTIMENTS.

MR. SCANDAL in the play declares that Astrology is a
most valuable science, because, according Albertus
Magnus, "it teaches to consider the causation of
causes in the causes of things." We suspect that
Mr. Senator Saulsbury must devote his leisure hours
to occult learning; for last Thursday his givings-out
were extremely weighty and oracular; and if he
could but have kept his temper, which we are sorry
to say he lost in the most unphilosophical manner,
his utterances would have been prodigiously solemn.
Every gentleman in this free and enlightened country
is at liberty to reason badly, should he chance to have
a propensity for bad reasoning; but when a Senator
comes back from the Christmas holidays in a condition of complete obfuscation, we are apt to think that
the wassail-bowl has been too much for his everyday
intellectuals.

In descanting upon the "causes of things," Mr.
Saulsbury thus enlightens the universe: "The raid
of John Brown, the Liberty Bills, or the election of
Abraham Lincoln, were not the causes of this war,
but the assertion of the right to abolish Slavery and
the evidence of such a purpose." As a specimen of

assertion perfectly naked and therefore unusually
cool, we do not believe that this can be excelled. It
is indeed curious. This Union Senator Saulsbury,
who is n't a Rebel, who has n't been sworn into the
Confederacy, who still abides after a certain fashion,
and in profession at least, by the Constitution, feels
it to be his duty to go mousing about for a plausible
palliation of public crime, and discovers nothing for
his purpose better than what we are obliged to brand
as a bit of outrageous falsehood.

Why the Senator is deeper in the secrets of Rebellion than the Rebels themselves. He knows better
than they do, why they bolted and why they are
fighting and bleeding and dying. For if ever men
gave a clear reason for pursuing a particular course,
the Seceders have assigned " the election of Abraham
Lincoln" as an all-sufficient defence of their folly and
sin. They waited for the result of the Presidential
canvass, and because it was not to their mind, they
betook themselves to the heroic remedy of treason.
It is not pretended—no man in his senses will pretend, that if Breckenridge had been elected, even
South Carolina would have refused to acquiesce.
The truth is, that Mr. Senator Saulsbury does not
see, in his volunteer defense of the Rebels, that in
ingeniously making out a case for them, he proves
too much either for their patriotism, or their honesty
or their sincerity. It is cruel to take John Brown
out of their mouths. It is unfriendly to deprive
them of their pet grievances—the Liberty Bills. It
is ungenerous to deny that the election of Lincoln

generated Secession. Take away these causes, and why the Rebellion at all? Saulsbury says it was "because of the assertion of the right to abolish Slavery." Saulsbury may say so, but the Seceders don't say so, and never have said so. The right to abolish slavery!—who has ever claimed it? and when?. and where? It will not do to bring one mere guess to bolster up another mere guess, for guesses are not evidences in Courts of Justice, nor should Mr. Saulsbury offer them as such in the Senate of the United States.

No newspaper that supported Mr. Lincoln—no public man who canvassed for him—no Republican, who as a Republican voted for him—expressed the least intention of abolishing Slavery as legally established. You may search files, you may hunt up speeches, you may unearth long-buried electioneering documents, but you cannot find there, nor in the official Resolutions and Addresses of the Republican party, any expression of any unconstitutional desire or intention—you cannot find it, for the simple reason that it is not there! There were indeed a few Immediate and Unconditional Abolitionists at the North, but as every intelligent Seceder knows, they were not Republicans, and they did not vote for Abraham Lincoln for the all-sufficient reason that they never voted at all. As a mere matter of fact, we believe that if the Seceding States had quietly acquiesced in Mr. Lincoln's election, they would have immeasurably strengthened their favorite institution. It is now only in peril because their outrageous conduct has driven the President to do what, when he assumed office, he had no intention of doing at all. We suppose that we understand the reason of Senator Saulsbury's diatribe. Now that it is necessary to hunt up ammunition against the Administration, it is found convenient to say, that Slavery must not be interfered with, because the Rebels are in arms to prevent such interference and the result of it must be hopelessness of conciliation. The Proclamation, Saulsbury tells us, is "brutum fulmen"—it is nothing, and will amount to nothing—it is ludicrously inefficient and absurdly impotent—and yet— for here Saulsbury hoists himself over the other horn of his dilemma—and yet, this "brutum fulmen," this ludicrous, inefficient, absurd and impotent thing, is to have the most extraordinary effects—it is to intensify the Rebel wrath and confirm the Rebel hate—is to make re-union simply impossible. A very remarkable effect for such a ridiculous document! Are the Rebels such asses that they allow themselves to be thrown into convulsions of rage by a little bit of printed paper with no more virtue in it than there is in an old almanac? Why should they be so angry at a policy which is not to free a single "nigger," and which has its beginning and end in the President's library?

If we get at the condition of the Rebel mind with any accuracy from a careful perusal of Jefferson Davis's speeches, it is certain that, for the present, it has no leaning towards compromises and does n't pant to be conciliated. It hears of the victories of

15

its Northern Democratic friends with infinite non-chalance. It does n't vouchsafe a "Thank you!" to any of its volunteer Knights in the loyal States. It laughs at Saulsbury and with great justice, since it is not given to any mortal to sit upon two stools at the same time. No human being can gaze with profound respect upon a Union Senator with Secession principles. The late Democratic victories which cost so much money, and hard swearing, and sinfully persuasive speeches, and general and unblushing self-stultification, are regarded by the rebels with a really cruel contempt. Gov. Seymour may be ready to fall weeping upon the neck of Jefferson Davis, but Davis is sensitive about the neck and begs leave to decline the proffered embraces. After all conceivable negotiations and tender diplomacy, we come back again to dry knocks at last, and one of the driest of these, if we may credit Saulsbury, is the Emancipation Proclamation.

January 14, 1863.

JEFFERSON THE GENTLEMAN.

There is one point upon which our rebellious citizens mean that we shall be well informed. They claim, like ladies' maids and gentlemen's own gentlemen, a monopoly of good breeding; and they prove their polish by continually advertising it. Their news-papers, presided over by the Chesterfields of ink and and shears, are forever saying:

"We are refined and chivalrous, and honorable, and knightly, and dignified, and urbane, and accomplished, and elegant, and fascinating and high-toned; while the Yankees are coarse and degraded, and mean, and false, and vulgar, and rustic, and ignorant."

Indeed, these models of humanity lack nothing but modesty, which has heretofore, absurdly we suppose, been deemed an element of the perfect gentleman. There are those who might think that refinement to be a little dubious which its claimants are obliged to vindicate so often in the public prints. The best bred men have heretofore been content to let the world find out their merits, without obtruding them, with such an outcry, upon the general attention; but we cannot condemn the Rebel Bayards in this particular, since the world has been so culpably slow in acknowledging their superiority.

The arrival of one living English Marquis and a genuine English Colonel in Richmond, has afforded *The Whig* of that sweet city a charming opportunity of showing that it knows a gentleman when it sees one, and of making quite a little triumph of its sagacity. It rejoices that the Marquis of Hartington has visited Richmond, "for he will have an opportunity of contrasting the dignified manners of Southern gentlemen with the coarse vulgarity of the Executive Head of the Northern States." We hope the Marquis was not disappointed. We remember that Bull-Run Russell paid his respects to a certain Southern Governor, and was astonished to find him with his mouth full of tobacco, his heels upon the table, and his general appearance, rather than else, the reverse of dignified. Still, that was in the Provinces, so to speak, and not in refined Richmond. But what did they do with poor Letcher, the unpresentable, during the visit of the Marquis? Did they keep him hushed up in a garret, under lock and key, with the restraining solace of pipe and bottle? We ask the question, because a great many Secession papers have been troubled about Letcher, and have printed leading articles to prove his vulgarity. We trust that they didn't let him go loose during the sojourn of these great English visitors.

Well, we don't envy the elegance of our Southern friends; we rather admire it. It comes of having such a perfect model of propriety at the helm of their affairs as Jefferson Davis is. It is not customary, we believe, for the head of one belligerent power to call the presiding genius of another belligerent power a baboon, as this Davis called Mr. Lincoln in a speech at Mobile. The kings of England have thought terrible things of the kings of France, but they have never styled them monkeys, nor made allusion to wooden shoes and frog soup in their speeches to Parliament. It was Swift, and not the Prime Minister, who had so much to say of Louis Baboon. But the President of the "Confederacy" forestalls the penny-a-liners, and cheats the pamphleteers out of their perquisites; which proves that, if not a gentleman, he is that mysterious next-thing-to-it, sometimes denominated QUITE A GENTLEMAN.

January 16, 1863.

THE CONTAGION OF SECESSION.

WE are beginning to feel the effects of woful example. The diabolical spirit of Rebellion not only encounters us in the field, but it has entered our legislative chambers, and under the malign promptings of the Democratic party, bent upon rule or ruin, it is tampering with the popular loyalty. One year ago men only murmured treason; but success has opened their mouths and filled their hearts with abominable political devices. We are beginning to see that about the worst battle lost to the Union cause, thus far, is that of the New York State election. Nobody believes Horatio Seymour to be friendly to the Administration, or to feel any honest sympathy with its embarrassments—yet he is elected Governor. The mob in Albany has given us a bitter foretaste of possible anarchy.

From the West we hear of schemes designed by the desperate and disaffected—conspiracies tending to fresh ruptures, and the final overthrow of the Republic. Wicked men, even at the North, are beginning openly and shamelessly to dally with disunion, and propose, since dislocation has come into fashion, to multiply the fragments of our institutions. All this is terrible. We can better afford to lose fifty fights than thus to weaken the morality of our cause. We can better afford to submit to invasion, than thus to make disintegration familiar to our constituencies. We can better afford to let the Slaveholding soldiers bivouac in the capitol, than to be betrayed into negotiations which are full of danger, or to dally with compromises which, with their adoption, must precipitate us into unmitigated anarchy.

Already we begin to hear of Western Confederacies, of New England Confederacies, of Middle States transmogrified into Middle Confederacies. Already we have hints of new and tempting combinations, aiming at safe and convenient boundaries, and the monopoly of internal navigation. Already the coming Congress casts its dark shadow before; and busy as the devil always has been in Washington, a time is coming when he will redouble his activity in that uneasy seat of an endangered Government. Hitherto the restoration of the Union has been, with the mass of the people, a matter of sentiment; but a time is at hand, which will not be in the least poetical, and when we must confront public danger hardened into the most vulgar concrete.

Gentlemen who desire to be elected to Congress, not as patriots, but simply and nakedly as Anti-Republicans, or Anti-Government men, cannot be supposed to care much for the perpetuity of our institutions. They expect to fatten upon our national troubles. They are ghouls who will care little how cold the corpse may be, if, sooner or later, they may fairly get their teeth into it. They live, plot, plan, spout, intrigue, bargain, and scheme, solely for personal aggrandizement. Their loyalty is limited by their own lives, and no thought of the weal or woe of posterity enters into their calculations. If, with the recognition of the Confederacy, these moral traitors could be banished, and with them their whole brood of venal voters—if we could send them to rest in the black bosoms of their Confederate friends—if the honor, worth, religion, intelligence, and wealth of the North could have but a fair chance of exercising their legitimate influence, we might consider with greater coolness the success of the Southern treason. But these men, after the accomplished dismemberment, would remain—would still be with us, though not of us—would be then as they are now, and as they always have been, the ready agents of Slavery, and the paid pimps of the Slaveholding interest.

Establish a State upon the basis of Man-owning upon this continent, and the minds of Wood, Brooks, Seymour, and all that *genus* will gravitate towards it with all the force of a bad nature. Given these men in power, and the Northern Republic would be the bought, if not the born, thrall of the Davis Dynasty, ready in Cabinet and Congress to do its dirty and demoniac work—ready to catch its runaways—ready to wink at the revival of the African Slave trade—ready to join an alliance against the moral sense of mankind — ready to promote the Secession of the West from the East—ready for war upon New England—ready to make our poor shadow of a Government at Washington as much the tool of the Southern Confederacy as ever the Cabinet of Charles II. was the tool of the French monarch. Political chafferers in the sacred name of Democracy would sell themselves first, and next their neighbors. There would be for us no permanence, no prosperity, no private happiness, and no public greatness.

It may be said that we exaggerate the danger. We do not think so. For the political power of the Confederacy would be in the hands of a few men, who have been educated to detest the Union, and who would be ill satisfied with that partial success which left even a respectable fragment of the old Republic yet entire. Once fairly separated, they would begin to feel wants, the existence of which they do not now admit, and they would be only too ready to avail themselves of those commercial abilities which they have heretofore affected to despise. The great serpent of Slavery would reverse its trail, and look with longing eyes towards a North left at its mercy by the dissensions and disaffection of its own children. Our social freedom would be a perpetual aggravation of the bad temper and jealousy which are the inseparable adjuncts of Slaveholding. If we were prosperous, our prosperity would be a continual rebuke of that sin which has been called "the sum of all villainies;" and if we were hopelessly weakened by the dismemberment, our cities and our farms would be the cheap prey of every mad partisan who chose to promote a raid.

Nor should we be without a hatred of Slavery, intensified by the woes of which it had been the fruitful mother; and any effort to check or to silence the expression of that sentiment would but complicate the public dilemma. We should still have Pro-Slavery governors, Pro-Slavery senators, Pro-Slavery presidents, and Pro-Slavery representatives; and the very existence of a determined and uncompromising

opposition would drive them into disgraceful diplo-
macies and intrigues, not to be thought of without
horror! If we speak sharply, we beg the reader to
believe that we speak sincerely. We have not, nor
will we pretend to have, any confidence in the public
virtue of that hungry place-hunter who prates of the
wrongs of the South, and of the sins of the North—
who has fine words for the Richmond *régime*, and
foul words for his own constitutional rulers—who
would restore the Union by muzzling discussion, and
by a declaration of the sanctity of Involuntary Servitude, with all the solemnities of an act of public faith
—who feels it to be a duty to apologize for his own
loyalty and for the treason of the public enemy—
who is half this and half that, and not wholly, body,
soul and spirit, the honest and unquestioning devotee
of the Constitution and the Laws—who wastes that
indignation upon the foes of Slavery which he should
naturally bestow upon its friends—who is utterly
without pity for the poor and defenceless, as he is
ignorant of that simple law which makes the prosperity of the employer dependent upon his justice—
who is, in short, a creature of shams and subterfuges,
and participates in public affairs without one en-
nobling sentiment, or one benevolent aspiration.
Why should this poor hybrid, half monarchist and
half Democrat, pretend to any reverence for human
rights, or be at all coy about selling others, since he
is so ready to sell himself? Let us see to it, that the
triumph of the Secessionists does not open for him a
market.

January 23, 1863.   15*

DAVIS TO MANKIND.

APPEALS to posterity are very cheap, because whatever may be posterity's decision, it can not disturb the repose of appellants who are snugly slumbering in their coffins. Appeals to mankind, excellent as they are, for rounding a speech, or for filling up the moral hiatus of a pronunciamento, are seldom more than specimens of pretty rhetoric. Mr. Davis being in a lofty passion at the Emancipation Edict, appeals to the civilized world, and " to the instincts of that common humanity which a beneficent Creator has implanted in the breasts of our fellow-men of all countries, to pass judgment on a measure by which several millions of human beings of an inferior race— peaceful and contented laborers in their sphere—are doomed to extermination, while at the same time they are encouraged to a general assassination of their masters."

It is astonishing to mark how exceedingly fraternal this Confederate Champion has become in his serene mind—in what an affectionate manner he opens his arms and begs to be embraced, and with what tenderness he preaches to this great globe of " the instincts of our common humanity." This might be justly regarded as a rouser of the humanity, common and uncommon, of our Common Humanity, did we not know, that the selfishness of man, and particularly of man enthroned, is usually quite too much for his self-abnegation. Humanity, as Squire Davis ought to know, is most warmly interested in frying its own fish. Humanity in far-off regions toward which the Confederate ruler is so amorously looking, across the broad Atlantic, is not without its own complications and embarrassments, its questions of bread and butter and bullion, its privileged classes to be coddled, and its pauper classes to be crushed, its dying oligarchies and awakening masses, its certain demands and its uncertain supplies.

Humanity, as such, does not care to be appealed to, and it particularly dislikes, in all diplomatic conferences, anything like a whine. Davis should know better than to suppose that he can gain any consideration abroad by a studied display of the Confederate ulcers. Foreign cabinets will not assist him any the sooner because he protests, though never so pathetically, that he is in instant danger of having his throat cut, his crops destroyed and his house burned over his ill-fated head. Of this indeed, the Confederate Sachem has a shrewd suspicion. He is therefore like Orator Puff, and has two tones to his voice—the "B alt." of appeal and the "G below" of defiance. If he whines, we must do him the justice to say that he also roars. The Confederacy wants everything, and it wants nothing. The "nigger" loves Davis dearly and will slaughter him upon the first opportunity. The Slave, who is so "peaceful and contented" to-day, is to be transformed into a homicidal devil to-morrow, through the mysterious influence of a bit of printed paper, six inches long by two broad, which to save his life, he cannot read! The careful hands which smooth Mr. Davis's virtuous sheets in the

evening, will be at his wind-pipe before he can rise
to his morning prayers.   In short Mr. Davis is very
much alarmed and not in the least frightened—in
great peril, but never so safe before in his life—
highly suspicious of Sambo, in whose fidelity he has
the highest confidence!   No doubt he is in a dreadful quandary—but why should he advertise it to
mankind ?

A man in a situation so highly uncomfortable may
properly be pardoned though his logic limps a little.
If the Black be a compendium of the Seven Cardinal
Virtues, · tender, affectionate, peaceful, and contented—what is there in the Proclamation by which
he is " doomed to extermination ?"   Who is to be the
exterminator ?   The master beloved !   Who is to be
exterminated ?   The affectionate, peaceful and contented slave !   Surely this is a most inscrutable concatenation.   The world may not be prepared, as J.
D. supposes, to abandon its humane instincts, but
still less will it be prepared to abandon its common
sense or to bestow its admiration upon a statesman
who gravely informs it, with tears gushing in rivulets
from his swollen eyes, that in order to maintain the
State he anticipates the necessity of putting to the
sword, of "exterminating," "several millions of
peaceful and contented human beings," in order to
prevent this peace and content from developing itself
in " a general assassination of their masters."   With
all due respect to his Excellency's intellectuals, we
must say that he seems to have a weak preference for
the circular style of reasoning.

In another way this titular President makes quite as deplorable a show of fatuitous sagacity. He takes it for granted that mankind does not know what Human Slavery is. He supposes that man just now emerging from the darkness of social degradation, has lost all recollection of the pangs inflicted by his oppressors; that those who are only now casting off the manacles of the Middle Ages, are to be cozened into the belief that involuntary servitude is the most blessed of human conditions. Davis should remember that he is asking the statesmen of Europe to acknowledge as excellent in America, a social policy which they are fast abandoning at home; and that the enfranchised of the old lands comprehend well enough what Slavery must be in the United States. Human nature will have something to do with that common humanity, to which Davis officially tenders the assurance of his most respectful consideration.

There is no man in Europe who is so ignorant as not to know that Slavery means unrequited toil, unrestrained cruelty, the despair of man and the degradation of woman. Whips speak a universal language as they fall upon the bare and blistering back; all ears understand that their hiss is hellish, and that the mystic characters which they write upon the cracking and furrowed skin do not hide any new gospel of ineffable tenderness. Common humanity has a common cuticle and refuses to comprehend the delights of flagellation. Common humanity instinctively shrinks from a forced concubinage, from the sunderings of marital ties, from the paternity which sells its own children, from a system of labor which is pitiless in its demands and worse than niggardly in its rewards. Common humanity is not so utterly besotted as to find virtue in unrestrained violence and beauty in systematic brutality. Common humanity has its instincts, and of these Davis should have said as little as possible. What had he to do with humanity at all? Why should he take the trouble of reminding mankind that there are, even in this hardhearted world, such things as sacred pity and eternal justice? Why transfer his assaults from the pockets of commerce to the heart of the human race? Why talk of anything save cash and cotton? Why not be contented with a good merchantable Message addressed not to the Man of Feeling, but to the Man of Trade—a Message bristling with figures to prove the profitableness of Man-Owning, and stiff with the fascinating statistics of well-requited wickedness?

The Confederacy should understand that it can have no recognition except upon contemptuous conditions, no good will which it does not buy, and no hearts which it does not bribe. Men will trade with it, and so they will trade with Hottentots. In respect of its Slaveholding, mankind will loath this new and hybrid republic; but in respect of its cotton crop, it is supposed by the Richmond sages that mankind will be good-natured. We shall see. Mankind may prefer a certainty of cotton supply. Mankind may not fancy the dubious product of unrequited and discontented labor. Mankind, or that portion of it which is devoted to the weaving of cotton cloth, may have prejudices in favor of a well-assured and steady production.

January 24, 1863.

UNION FOR THE UNION.

WHO could have thought that Northern Doughfaces had so much life in them?—that they would survive the bombardment of Fort Sumter?—that they would at last turn upon the Constitution, which they had professed to adore, and be ready to surrender the Union which they had pretended to reverence? Brooks & Co. are like Garrison, without Garrison's virtues and good conscience. We thought the Senate chamber purged of plantation insolence, and the well-weaponed Saulsbury starts up to convince us of our mistake—Saulsbury the Disunionist.

We can imagine some rebellious Abraham—the Patriarch of Slavery, as Voltaire was the Patriarch of Infidelity—we see him reading his Northern newspaper, and grinning gloriously over his grog, as he peruses the Pro-Slavery journal! Nobody will mark more keenly than the Confederate observer, the opposition to the Administration which has been gathered by the concretion of all the dusty particles of a commercial self-interest. Why shouldn't he be chippery? He has newspapers printed for him without cost to his own flaccid purse—he has Union Governors plotting pretty things for his advantage—he has

Northern clergymen tearing out the heart of both Testaments to offer it upon the altar of Involuntary Servitude—he has hordes of white slaves who do his voting, his mobbing, his fighting, and his philoso-phizing in the Free States, so called—he wins here, over the graves of our murdered soldiers, political victories which strengthen him more than fortresses or captured fields—why should he not be in the best possible humor?

Nor can we think the merriment confined to the Master. Why should n't the Slave have his private jollity also? He has been told over and over again, that he was incapable of self-government; and why? Why, but because he was black! Because the wrong pigment colored his cuticle! But we Northern men, we White men, we Caucasians of the pure red and white —excepting, as will sometimes happen, when we are yellow by reason of excessive bile—cannot we govern ourselves? 'Tis a mysterious matter. Our hair is straight, and yet we are in difficulties! Our noses are prettily Grecian, or sublimely Roman—and yet we take care of ourselves but ill! We have no blub-ber lips to demonstrate our political incapacity—and yet, what, in spite of sacred suffrage, have we come to? We have shins of the most orthodox configura-tion—but what good do they do us? Sambo may well think, what with our botherations, factions, anarchies, Congressional squabbles, petty discussions, free and fraternal fights, Democratic victories, and other pal-pable swindles, that, after all, a white skin will not do everything for its possessor?

Delays are proverbially dangerous; but delay in crushing the Rebellion, according to all human experience, is peculiarly so. Sedition is like a great snow-ball—*crescit eundo.* Three or four victories would have made the Forty Thieves respectable members of society. In war, the virtuous, honest, amiable and admired party is that which wins the greatest battles; and in this wicked world, while we still submit to the ordeal of arms, it will be thought, until we become better Christians, that Providence is on the side of the best bayonets. The Confederates have an advantage over us which only decided defeat can take away from them—they have actually held out against us for many more months than anybody, when the war began, anticipated. The world accepts the fact, and troubles its head little enough about the "why" and "wherefore." We may manufacture small excuses for our present consolation, but they will be of no value to anybody but the owners. It is only the plain practical fact which, in public affairs, stamps itself upon policy and opinion. The cabinets of the world will not stop to inquire which side, in this war, has the majority of cardinal virtues, or which is the patriotic party; why should they? When was it resolved by nations, that right should be dominant in all negotiations? Why, if ever a people had plain, pure, abstract, naked justice upon their side, we are that people. There is n't a morality, however trite, or however rare, that does not attach to our cause. We have with us truth, justice, honor; but, alas! these do not prevent us from cutting a very shabby figure in Paris or London when the news is against us. The Rebels have lied, stolen, perjured themselves, and have tens of thousands of murders to answer for, but bustling men of the Bourse, and the Bulls and Bears of the London Stock Exchange, have had dealings with desperate scamps before, and have made no end of money out of them. It is enough for the nonce, that the rogues are up and the honest men down in the world.

Union is strength. The remark is a simple one, nor is it brilliantly novel; but we venture to make it once more. That the Rebels are united, we do not venture to say; but they are strong in an oligarchy, the members of which are always ready, in times of public danger, to postpone personal differences. They are in earnest. If a man within their jurisdiction votes against them, they imprison him. If he is pertinacious, they hang him. If a woman exhibits signs of dissatisfaction, it is n't her sex that can save her from outrage. What they want they take—men, money, munitions, supplies — wherever they find them. Whoever is bold enough to imply, even by silence, his dissatisfaction, does so at his personal peril. For him the tar-pot seethes and the rope is already twisted. The masses submit to tyrannies which the mob of Paris would not endure for a day; and the Slave Power, when it ruled the Union, exercised a sway less imperious than it has now assumed.

No one, however hearty may be his detestation of despotism, can deny that it is sometimes terribly effective. Tyrants are successful and strong, because they do their bad work well, and punish words and thoughts as lighter-handed rulers punish deeds. Against the usurpations of a handful of Slaveholders, who are simply formidable for their energetic audacity, we have to oppose a Democracy which is restive under the slightest restraint, and will not bear the least check upon public opinion.

But, if properly employed, this secures to us corresponding advantages. This was sufficiently evident upon the breaking out of the war, when there was a race of giving and a competition of munificence—when designing men had not begun to calculate the advantages of a dishonorable peace—when, by common consent, political differences were put in abeyance. Let us recall the spirit of those proud and memorable days, and that, too, speedily! There is no time to be wasted. "Now, or never!" should be written upon every loyal banner! We want Union, Energy, and Action, and we want them Now. Shall we have them?"

February 3, 1863.

THE NECESSITY OF SERVILITY.

ONE of our Major-Generals recently remarked that "no nation can be great which does not have a servile class." There is a fine fragrance of the camp about this neat bit of solemn loquacity. It could have come only from one who believes that the whole duty of man consists either in drilling or in being drilled. The philosophical warrior who emitted, should certainly have enlarged, this observation. He should have said, "No nation can be great without wars of aggression and conquest—without a rapacious aristocracy and down-trodden, popular mass—without an enormous public debt and proportionate taxation—without an Autocrat at the head of affairs."

After this, Pro-Slavery reasoning would have been as easy as any other style of falsehood. Rome was great—Rome submitted to a Dictator—therefore all nations desiring to be great, must establish a Dictatorship, raising to that dignity some successful soldier. Greece was great—but then all her slaves were white—therefore no nation can be great without white slaves. Imperial France was great, but it was by theft—therefore no nation can be great without stealing territory. That is why Prussian Frederick is called Great—because he stole Silesia. Alexander frequently was carried to bed much intoxicated—therefore he was styled the Great—"Drinker," we suppose, being understood. Jonathan Wild was dubbed the Great by Fielding—why remind our readers that the novelist meant "The Great Thief?" It is, we repeat, a pity that our General, who believes Greatness and Rascality to be convertible terms, did not expatiate a little upon his discovery. For our own part we have thought, fondly, we suppose, that the kind of greatness to which he alludes, and which can only be secured by systematic cruelty and the oppression of man had, in this nineteenth century, gone pretty much out of fashion.

Some of the clearest thinkers of the present age, if we have read aright, have supposed—was it after all, nothing but supposition?—that we had passed, or at least were rapidly passing, from feudalism to freedom, that Christianity was beginning to consummate its victory over heathenism; that the century had brought with it clearer views of social science; that honest rulers, if they must be great, now endeavor to be so, without ignoring natural right. The world has had ages of human slavery and they have been ages of sanguinary and unsatisfactory experience—have all these speculators been mistaken who have foretold better things in store for this "groaning globe?" Must we ape the vices of the past before we can copy its achievements? Must we ignore all the advantages which discovery and invention have brought to us, and seek for national greatness only in the resuscitation of bygone realities? Would we, if we could, make the United States, but a poor copy of Assyria, Greece, Rome, Carthage?

> "O agony—that centuries should reap
> No mellower harvest."

Greatness!—why there is n't a greater potentate in all Africa, than the King of Dahomey! In the midst of his butcheries, wading ankle deep in human blood, building his pyramid of human skulls, he is feared by surrounding tribes, and positively adored by his own! Nations calling themselves civilized, can be great in the same way—that is, if they please

to relapse into savagery, there is a backward path for
them, as there is for individuals—and so they may
discard refined apparel for nose-rings, war-paint and
nakedness—they may pull down what reporters call
"palatial residences" and live in wigwams without
chimneys and without windows—they may be content with subsisting upon the uncertain supplies of
the chase.

Brigham Young has nine wives or ninety, we
forget which; and very much is he censured for an
impropriety which, some will think, must carry with
it its own punishment.   But this may with perfect
truth be said for the Polygamous Prince of Utah—
that he has the ancients upon his side.   In comparison with Solomon, President Young is a model of
moderation, and in plurality of ribs, he is unquestionably far below Darius, Xerxes, or the Grand
Turk.   Was n't Persia a great nation?   All polygamy, sir?   Was n't Mahomet a great conqueror?
Look at his ten wives, sir! to say nothing of his
mistresses, sir!   Pray, if our Pro-Slavery sages may
argue in their way from the past, in support of their
favorite wickedness, why should n't poor Mr. Young
be allowed a similar logic?   It does not seem to
occur to the philosophical doughfaces that there may
be danger in their passion for other histories of for-
getting our own.

Admitting that all great nations have heretofore
been cursed by a servile class, it is certainly as true
that our Revolutionary Fathers aimed at the establishment of a Republic which should rival antique

greatness without recourse to antique crimes. They
did not profess to aim at a revival of Grecian or
Roman characteristics. They knew, for they were men
of culture, quite as well as the sciolists of the present
know, that Involuntary Servitude existed in Greece
and Rome; but it would be difficult and probably
impossible to find in any act of their hands, or in any
word of their mouths, the evidence that they sought
for national greatness through the enslavement of
their fellow-creatures. The whole current of testimony runs in the other direction.

The feeling of the founders of the Republic made
no distinction between black and white. The
debates in the Congress, the known opinions of Jefferson, of Franklin, and of other leading spirits of
the Revolution, and the weight of tradition, all prove
this to a certainty. They did not pretend to establish institutions which should merely equal those
of the past. Their honorable and humane ambition
was to present to the world an ameliorating discovery
in political science—that of the equality of all men. If
they had been absolutely faithful, in spite of temptation, to the great idea which animated their career;
if they had valiantly stood by the truth in practice,
as they did by the truth in theory, from what sorrows and crimes and bitter experiences would they
not have saved their children? It is for us to finish
the work of the Fathers! It is for us to accept their
teachings and to transmute them into the fine gold
of a truly Christian polity! As we are wiser than
the men of the Middle Ages, let us prove that ten

centuries of hard experience have not been thrown away upon the race!

February 4, 1863.

WHAT SHALL WE DO WITH THEM?

NOTHING could be more ridiculous and insignificant than many of the reports which have been forwarded to the North, respecting the character and demeanor of the emancipated Slaves. It has been our misfortune, in too many cases, to find this information miserably deficient in liberality, intelligence, and sympathy. A corporal trusts his shirts with a sable laundress, who receives three of these garments and returns two, and those perhaps aggravatingly bereft of buttons, whereupon this indignant brave writes home to the village newspaper, that the contrabands, to an individual, are all thieves. A sturdy black, despairing of remunerative meal or money, declines to dig, at least assiduously, and we are treated to the deep deduction, sometimes by electric telegraph, that, without the lash, all negroes are lazy.

Some venerable Sambo, in confidence, imparts to a gaping letter-writer the fact, that he wishes to go back to his master, and we have leading columns occupied by delighted editors, who conclude from this wonderful premise that all other Sambos wish to go back to their masters also. Hard upon this follows another conclusion, namely, that upon being immediately restored to the bosom of Abraham, this curious descendant of accursed Canaan, unless properly flogged, will experience an inexplicable revulsion of feeling, will murder his master and fire his master's house. It appears to us astonishing, that the Civil War, which is not only such a sombre but such a serious business, and which demands of the best mind of the nation such careful and practical judgment, should have led to no wiser reflection. We have had all this before. For a quarter of a century we have been compelled to listen to the same bold assertion and to the same inconsequential reasoning—the same dogged denial of the fitness of the slave for freedom, and of the policy of doing him common justice. The pertinacious assumption of his incapacity for social liberty has been the stock-in-trade of the Man-Owner and of his sufficiently servile apologist, until Heaven is sick and earth weary of hollow words and ingenious subterfuges.

For our own part, as we have been found among those who believe Emancipation to be not only right, but safe, we beg leave to say, that we have never supposed that the liberation of so many human beings, heretofore irresponsible, would be without some embarrassments. It is Freedom that fits men for Freedom, be the man black, white, or yellow, just as the athlete grows sturdy by the exercise of his profession. The crime of Slavery has been, that it has found, in the incapacity of its victims, an argument for the continuation of its emasculating influences, and has continually pointed to the ruin it has wrought, as an apology for postponing reparation. In elevating

16

masses of men, there must be, as in every other human enterprise, a beginning; and it has been just this costly step which we have been afraid to take.

Emancipation has been opposed particularly by dough-faces, not because it would diminish crops or endanger human life and public order, but because it was felt that its inevitable effect would be to raise the Black to something like social equality with the White. The fear has been, not that the Freedman would be idle, but that he would be industrious; not that he would become still more degraded, but that he might become tolerably enlightened; not that he would prove unworthy of the experiment and of the confidence impliedly reposed in him, but that he would, by his development of good character, give the lie to his libellers. Men who have spent their lives and their best intellectual energies in proving the inferiority of the African race, cannot be expected to regard a practical refutation of their notions with equanimity. The Freedman can do them no greater disservice than to exhibit the good qualities of which they asserted he was incapable. It is petty vanity which refuses to give emancipated man a chance. Nobody in his senses has supposed that the Black race would emerge instantly from a degradation continued for two centuries. Nobody has expected to find the Freedman altogether beautiful in all parts of his character—a model of possible excellence, a miracle of virtue, a wonder of wit, a paragon of prudence, and a marvel of industry.

In him who was yesterday a slave, we should expect to find the vices of a slave—the traces of that falsehood which heretofore has been his sole protection against cruelty—of that thievishness which may have saved him from the pangs of hunger and guarded him from the inclemency of the elements—of that insubordination of the animal passions which his superiors in society have encouraged for their own profit and by their own example—of that unthrift which has been strengthened by a whole life of jealous guardianship and of restraint in its pettiest forms. We might as well expect to find in new-born babes the fullest muscular development, as in the captive just unchained all the excellencies of human nature.

Emancipation will not remove the scars which Slavery has inflicted. There is many a brow from which the brand can never be erased, and many a feature distorted by involuntary servitude which can never recover its rounded and comely proportions. So much the greater is our crime! So much the deeper should be our shame! So much sooner should we, with all the courage of a genuine repentance, dock this entail of human misery, and at least turn the faces of future generations toward kindlier opportunities and less discouraging vicissitudes!

The character of the African as it now is, or as it is supposed to be, proves nothing for or against his future well-doing. It is easy to say of a man whose lungs are full of carbonic acid gas, that he can never breathe atmospheric air again; but most medical men would favor the opening of the windows. It is n't only the African who succumbs to an unnatural position, and through systematic disuse loses his moral and many of his physical faculties. Very white men have exhibited no greater capacity for resisting the degrading influences of bondage. Mr. Dupuis, who was long the British Vice-Consul at Mogadore, tells us that the Europeans and Americans who were rescued from enslavement in the desert, were found to have their spirits completely broken by their masters. When they came into Mogadore, he says, "They appeared degraded, and below the negro slave—every spring of hope or exertion was destroyed in their minds—they were abject, servile, and brutified."

This is said by a white observer of white men just emancipated—we believe that no Pro-Slavery scribbler has said anything worse of the liberated black man. The gist of the matter is just this: if we should take Gov. Seymour, for instance—we take him as at present the leading white man of New York—if we should put him upon a year-long course of short rations and sharp floggings, and heavy task-work, the presumption is that he would not come out from his disciplinary probation that choice combination of excellent qualities, that epitome of grace and greatness, that abridgment of all that is pleasant in man, that ornament and safeguard of the community, which the majority now thankfully acknowledge him to be.

If a Tammany brawler, in some unfortunate hour, should be compelled to change his beloved bar-room for a barracoon, to go from gluttony to starvation, and, instead of flogging others, to submit himself to the lash, he would deem it unfair if his friends, upon his return, should think the fine gold of his nature grown dim. He would ask time for a due course of recuperative cocktails, and the reviving influences of a few fights, before final judgment against him as a man shamefully destitute of an immoral character. We ask for the black man only time and opportunity, and he will have them whatever may be the mind of the public. Maugre the disgust of the delicate, the mortification of the skin-proud, the wrath of the selfish, the profane protests of the ungodly, and the carefully-selected texts of the overgodly, the freedman must have his chance upon this continent, or worse will come of it. Those who think that our safety lies in beastializing more and more completely four millions of the inhabitants of this country, if it were possible to reduce their barbarous theory to practice, would but earn the execrations of their children. But, thank God, it is not possible. Providence is sometimes kind enough to put special restraints upon human folly, and the people of the United States, having reduced the theory of Slaveholding to an absurdity, will hardly cling to it at the cost of bloodshed and bankruptcy.

February 5, 1863.

POCKET MORALITY—WAR FOR TRADE.

In the year, 1787, Benjamin Franklin wrote to an English gentle man as follows : "I read with pleasure the account you give of the flourishing state of your commerce and manufactures, and of the plenty you have of resources to carry the nation through all its difficulties. You have one of the finest countries in the world ; and if you can be cured of the folly of making war for trade, in which war more has been expended than the profits of any trade can compensate, you may make it one of the happiest." This advice, we suppose, would be quite thrown away upon a newspaper irrevocably wedded to the system here so pointedly condemned.

The London Times accepts the well-known aphorism of Franklin with a qualification—it thinks there never was a good war if it was unprofitable, and never a bad peace if it added to the British wealth. Such a publication should be treated with all possible candor. If its principle be to have no principle, and if it would quite as severely scorn to affect a virtue as to possess one, let it at least aspire to the praise of a sublime consistency. If it must serve mammon, let us be thankful that it does not pretend to serve God ! If it must ignore consistency, it should have the credit of a frank advertisement of its renunciation. What it thinks *upon* the first of January it thinks *for* the first of January, and by no means for the second. Its avowed business is not ·to speak the truth, but to " bull " this stock and to

"bear" that. This being understood, why should
we be angry with it? All that can be said of it is,
that it follows its instincts, and that its instincts are
commercial. It does a wholesale business in a retail
way. Who blames it? Who blames the Calmucks
for eating raw horse-meat? Who blames the cannibal of Sumatra for eating cooked man-meat?—not
because he likes it—for he is very careful to tell the
traveler that he does not like it—he only devours it
as a religious duty—only that he may propitiate the
god of war by masticating, swallowing and digest-
ing the slain. He does not quarrel with the flavor
of the tid-bits, from the deglutition of which he anticipates such immense advantages. It is in the
same bold and devoted way that this *Times* newspaper swallows Slavery on Monday, rejects it on
Tuesday, and swallows it again on Wednesday, rel-
ishing the morsels well or ill, according to the fluc-
tuations of the cotton market. Yesterday it pronounced human slavery to be a Divine Institution,
and quoted St. Paul out of its borrowed Bible; to-
day it declares that it "would unfeignedly rejoice"
if the Emancipation Proclamation could only be
effectual! What will it say to-morrow? Exactly
what it may think the interests of trade demand.

"Joey B. is sharp, sir! devilish sharp!"

It would ill become us, members as we are of a
great commercial community, to speak disrespect-
fully of mercantile prudence and sagacity. We
yield to no one in our most respectful estimate of
the ameliorating influences of trade in promoting

the comfort and even the higher morality of man. We know enough of monetary operations to understand that they can only be successfully promoted by forethought, caution and deliberate prudence. We are ready to make all proper allowances for the instinct of self-preservation when it is shrinking from insolvency. We believe money to be a good thing, and that it is a good thing to have money. We believe that society has no member more worthy of its respect than the high-minded merchant, who, without casting discredit upon trade by unscrupulous rapacity, increases our sources of happiness, brings capital to the assistance of civilization, and supplies that material aid without which the progress of mankind would cease.

But all our respect for the honorable and enlightened trader, cannot conceal from us those moral perils which environ him. Indeed, in every scheme of religion they are admitted ; and the most solemn warning against absolute devotion to money-getting came from the Founder of our Faith, and has since his time been repeated in countless bodies of divinity, and uttered from ten thousand pulpits. Money can do much and buy much, but there are some things which it cannot do and others which it cannot purchase. We may admit it to be the sinews of war, but is it the heart or the muscles ? In England, we think, very unfortunately, the tendency has been toward a worship of wealth simply as such, and a contempt, not, perhaps, for personal, but certainly for national poverty. "He's so very poor," says one person to another in an English comedy, "that you would take him for an inhabitant of Italy." This is the perfection of purse-proud complacency. De Tocqueville observes, that "in the eyes of England her enemies must be rogues and her friends great men." It is this association of arrogance and acquisitiveness which has given to England a bad public reputation. "When she seems," says De Tocqueville, "to care for foreign nations, she cares only for herself." A man who acquires a character like this will find money powerless to purchase public respect; he may be feared, but he will also be detested; nor do we believe that there is one rule for nations and another for individuals.

Finally, in the spirit of Franklin's observation that the rapacity of England has usually cost more than it came to, we beg leave to suggest that an unjust and selfish policy is equally short-sighted. Have British economists been able to determine that the establishment of the Confederacy would promote the manufacturing interests of their country? Have they in their calculations recognized the intense prejudice against England which exists in the Slaveholding States? Have they estimated the chances of a certain production of the coveted staple, if the present system of slave-cultivation is to be continued? Have they considered the difficulties which they may encounter in maintaining amiable relations with the unreasonable and impetuous oligarchy which now controls, and, in the event of their independence, will continue to control, the revolted States?

16*

These, it seems to us, are questions which even selfishness can afford to consider.

February 6, 1863.

WAITING FOR A PARTNER.

AN eminent journal, printed in a neighboring city, the managers of which care more for their own crotchets than for the country, has promulgated a patent labor-saving method of saving the Union, to which we extend the benefit of this advertisement.

Imprimis, Gen. Geo. B. McClellan, at present upon a tour of exhibition in the principal cities, is to be restored to all his honors, dignities and commands.

We object to this, though not very strenuously, because Gen. McClellan having received a great many houses and horses, the donations of tender-hearted friends, we think that he should be permitted to stay at home to reside in the first and to drive the second. Otherwise the intentions of the charitable bestowers of roof-trees and free rides may be entirely - defeated. At any rate, if the General is to go back, we think that he should reconvey to the donors the houses and horses and shawls, as having been given by mistake.

Secondly, Gen. McClellan is to be furnished with "a fresh body of troops."

We object to this, because from what we know of Gen. McClellan, we believe that he would prefer

veterans to raw recruits. We believe that he is considered to be perfectly immense in drill, but we
cannot in conscience ask him to repeat those gigantic
labors from which he is resting amid the enchant-
ments of numerous donation parties.

Thirdly, Gen. McClellan, with his "free body of
troops," is to "maintain the forms of Government
until the opportunity occurs to elect another Administration."

We object to this, because it is n't complimentary
to Gen. McClellan, who seems to be the best entitled
to compliments of any man in the United States. It
does n't look very friendly for his professed friends
to propose him for a mere *locum tenens*, a post, a peg,
a stalking horse. And it is certainly alarming to
consider that we can now do no more than merely
"maintain the forms of Government." Pray what is
the enemy to be doing all those fine months? Maintaining the forms of *his* government, we suppose,
by assaulting, worrying, surprising, harassing and
hunting the "fresh body of troops" which, meanwhile,
will display a masterly inactivity, except when compelled to "mizzle."

Fourthly, Nothing is to be done until we have "a
new Administration."

Of the Democratic stripe of course! And what,
pray, is to be done then? Is the fighting to be
resumed? Then why not fight now? Or is the new
Administration to be of the diplomatic, assuaging,
persuading, intriguing, compromising, palavering,
protocoling and rose-water variety? More bargains,

propositions, conferences, communions, conventions, speechmaking, enacting, and Heaven knows what beside? And is Gen. McClellan expected to shine in these grand palavers? Is that the reason why, with his war-paint off, this chieftain has been perambulating the country! Practising the Art of Speaking—eh? Are epaulettes and buttons to yield to the peace-of-the-toga? Was it for such reason that the General was presented with two coach horses instead of one charger?—with a carriage instead of a saddle?

We are sorry that the gentlemen who propose this notable plan of restoring the Union, should forget that its success would prove their Secession cronies to be liars of the first magnitude. Davis *et al.* are certainly committed fairly enough upon the record against a reference—they have said distinctly enough, a thousand times in all manner of State papers and newspapers, that come back they would not and could not, unless compelled to come back by force of arms. And yet by this scheme we are to proffer them new chances of returning to loyalty—for the scheme can only mean that, or letting them go in peace.

The talk about "fresh troops" is literally insulting to the gallant fellows now in the field; is only a blind. For who supposes that a National Administration of the Horatio Seymour tint would fight? Who would expect them to display any extraordinary vigor in the field or to maintain the Constitution there with any tenacity? Nobody in his right mind. A Democratic Administration—we say it without fear of contradiction—would be a Peace-at-any-price

Administration. Nothing better than semi-treason would be expected of it; nothing better than haggling, patching and most disreputable bargaining. "Erring Sisters, depart in peace!" would be its legend. If the people choose to trust Brooks, Seymour, the Woods and men of like kidney with the adjustment of national differences, why the people are omnipotent and can do that in haste which they will bitterly rue at leisure. If the army be in the least demoralized and the progress of the war at all suspended, the fault lies at the door of the Democratic party. If it has done so much mischief out of office, of what will it not be capable in power? Wise and honest men, true lovers of the Union, would look with fear, trembling, distrust and disgust upon any postponement of the assertion, sharp, vigorous and offensive, of the sanctity of the laws, until after the coming election. We think that to save the whole country from the anarchy which now distracts so great a part of it, we need prompt, muscular and decisive action, military and naval; and that any attempt to carry the question of Peace or War into a Presidential election, might result in schemes of demagogy and in scenes of bloodshed frightful to anticipate.

We say nothing of any delays occasioned by military necessity; but we do say that any other is abominably cruel. The Emancipation Policy which, after all, is what these schemers hate, rests upon the plighted faith of this Government, and any attempt to evade it, will be followed by national miseries which will be all the harder to bear because they will be so richly deserved.

February 12, 1863.

AT HOME AND ABROAD.

THE style of *The London Times*, in its observations upon the President's Proclamation, is simply one of fussy impertinence. It is certain that, in private life, any vulgarian assuming similar airs, would be either laughed at or kicked out of the company. Men would not endure, probably, to be told, by a dogmatic and testy companion, that they lied, that they were hypocrites, that they were devising fraud, that they were attempting a disreputable swindle. Unless we are willing to believe each other occasionally, there must be an end of human intercourse of the friendly description. And what is true of private comity, is true of the comity of nations. State-papers for all the usual purposes of diplomacy, must be taken to mean just what they profess to mean. The lackeys of legation, the footmen, cooks and scullions of his Excellency, the Embassador, the gentry of the backstairs, the old women who sweep the offices and light the fires, are always deepest in state-secrets, and always pronest to put their faith in nobody. The valet intrigues while his master opens his heart with his snuff-box.

When *The London Times*, with owlish gravity and

innumerable shrugs, professes to doubt the entire sincerity of the President's Proclamation, its uncivilized incredulity makes the suspicions of lackeys, footmen, cooks, scullions and char-women respectable and dignified by comparison. Whether it be worth while to maintain a character for uncommon perspicacity at the expense of a character for common veracity, the stock-jobbing managers of the newspaper in question must determine.

The charge against the President is, that he is not in earnest, and against his policy, that it is not sincere. The newspaper to which we have referred, speaks of Mr. Lincoln as issuing his Proclamation, "with his tongue in his cheek." This is a rare bit of rhetorical refinement. If any of our transatlantic friends think that its truth is equal to its beauty, we beg leave to assure them, that here, even the enemies of the President view the Proclamation in an entirely different light. They believe, if *The Times* does n't. The Pro-Slavery newspapers howl with a sad sincerity. The Northern politicians, in the interest of the Rebellion, do not affect to consider the Proclamation a joke. The editors of Davis's Republic swell, as they refer to the document, with an unusual venom. From Davis himself it has evoked a proclamation more than commonly bloodthirsty. And it may be asserted generally, that whatever objections may be made to the Proclamation, they have found all their point and force in the assumption that so far from being mere flummery and subterfuge, it means precisely what it says. Nobody here, however en-

raged by its contents, has hit upon the notable expedient of regarding it as a mere morsel of party
management. The London critics have the advantage of their negro-hating friends in America in that
particular. The members of Congress from the Border States, whose love of Slavery is stronger than
their love of the Union, are exceedingly loud in their
lamentations. The politicians of the pot-houses read
the Proclamation, and as they do so, curse the negro
with a renewed vehemence; while the intelligent
masses of the Northern people accept it with a
good faith, which we say, without any disrespect to
the President or distrust of his fidelity, will compel
good faith in return. It matters not, for the purposes of this argument, what may have been the concealed intentions of the Government in making the
Proclamation; it will be construed with straightfor-
ward literalism by men enough, at any rate, to be
troublesome, whether they may be in the majority or
not. Indeed, English gentlemen who have supposed
that the American people, with all their faults of
character, are so thick-witted as to be the easy victims of official pranks, do not themselves show any
great powers of intelligent observation. It is not the
habit of our men in office to make experiments upon
popular credulity. And in the present case, neither
those who dislike the Proclamation, nor those who
support it have for a moment doubted its sincerity.
It has been discussed upon its own merits, and nobody here has been sharp enough to see the tongue
in the President's cheek. The people of the United

States have suffered, and are still suffering too much to affect any levity or nonchalance in this business.

February 20, 1863.

MR. DAVIS PROPOSES TO FAST.

MR. Davis's continual resort to religion indicates something of the straits of a condemned malefactor, who, when he hears the carpenter at work upon the gallows, concludes to send for the chaplain. The Confederate President has issued another Proclamation for a public fast in his dominions, which, considering the condition of the flesh-pots in those demesnes, strikes us as just a little supererogatory. We have no fear that any of the Rebels will eat too much. There is yet another point upon which his friends should warn Mr. Davis. There is danger in his recent and rather awkward piety : for Fast-Days are a puritanical institution—they have Fast-Days in wicked, praying, hypocritical, religious and revolutionary New England—to tell the honest truth, the first Fast ever kept upon this continent by a Protestant congregation, was kept in Plymouth, by Praise-God-Barebones and other scurvy Pilgrim Fathers, whom it is the fashion in all Rebel newspapers and speeches to berate as incendiary and godless scoundrels. We bid Mr. Davis to take heed of too much austerity. At the same time we will do his subjects the justice to say that not only by man but by beast will his injunctions be obeyed. The Armenian Christians make their horses fast with them; and should Mr. Davis be pleased, in default of any other, to declare the Armenian to be the State Religion, it will be a great saving of oats in a rather than else attenuated commissary department.

We regret to say that Mr. Davis, being a novice in these matters, has made the singular mistake of appointing a Fast, when he should have appointed a Thanksgiving. In his Proclamation, which is quite a compendium of practical piety, he solemnly sets forth that, whereas the affairs of the Confederacy are in a pretty prosperous condition—everything going on well—nothing but victories, bloody and decided—the Confederacy evidently under the peculiar care of its Creator—therefore, I, Jefferson Davis, do declare a day of Humiliation and Fasting! This is an anti-climax at which, but for the solemnity of the subject, we should be tempted to titter. But we are glad to learn that, upon one day of the year at least, the Confederates propose to be as humble as—Uriah Heep! Mr. Davis says that "in the midst of trials," the Rebels "gathered together with thanksgiving;" and now in their prosperity, they propose to fast! There has been nothing like this since Sheridan cried at Cumberland's comedies and laughed at his tragedies. We sadly fear that Mr. Jefferson Davis's theological education has been neglected.

As there may be some religious patriarchs in like condition, and who may have doubts of their ability to fast, in a genteel, orthodox and acceptable manner, we advise them, before the 27th of March, which is the day appointed, to take a few lessons of their "nig-gers." Many of these are great adepts, through sad and involuntary experience, in the ascetic art of fast-ing; many of them are living monuments of the ability of man to exist upon next to nothing; and most of them have quite as much religion, to say the least of it, as their masters. Let Mr. Davis and his friends apply at the quarter-houses of the "men-ser-vants and maid-servants," as brother Davis calls them, for all necessary information.

There are scrupulous persons who might object to the prayers of Rebels, as, to a certain extent, blas-phemous. But we do not. Let them pray. The cannibals of Sumatra pray. The greasy and mud-smeared savages of Central Africa pray. There is said to be no heathen without a religion—all the other heathens pray,—and pray why should not the Confederates ?

March 11, 1863.

MR. B. WOOD'S UTOPIA.

Ben Wood's speech that was not spoken, has, of course, been printed by him, just as the play-wrights of the last century, when managers were inexorable, exclaimed : "Zounds, I'll print it." It is in this way that Brother Ben, when not permitted to bore the House, with malice prepense, attempts to bore the nation. We have read, at least a part of the docu-ment—that part in which the tender Benjamin assures us that " were he certain that, in a military sense, this war would prove successful, nevertheless he would oppose it, for with the resisting power of the South would vanish every hope of their existence as equal and contented members of one household."

There is a fine paternal aroma about this remark, which reminds one of that title which has been conferred, by the general consent of mankind, upon Benjamin, by reason of his relation to Fernando, and which has suggested to the world, not Cain and Abel, but rather, with an entire reverse of the Scripture story, two most amicable and complying Cains. This will account for Benjamin's pathetic allusion to " equal and contented members of one household." Brother Wood's proposition seems to be, that we should lay down our arms and disperse. With the disappearance of our armies he anticipates several tons of hot coals heaped upon the head of Jefferson Davis, who will, upon the receipt of the intelligence, burst into tears, repent of all his sins, receive a new heart and take an express train for Washington, that he may throw himself at the feet of President Lincoln, who will " take him up tenderly," kiss him upon each cheek, and having assured him of his entire forgiveness, will call for two cocktails of reconciliation and two cigars of peace.

Pleasing picture ! Fine figment of the brain of Benjamin Wood! Shall we mortals ever see you realized, exquisitely embraced and enchantingly reduced to a dead certainty ? There may be chances of it. So there may be chances of drawing $100,000 in one of Frater Ben's truly lucky lotteries. But the chances in one case are about as good as the chances in the other. At any rate we had better not disband the Army, until Ben has been dispatched to Richmond, there to wave the olive-branch in our behalf. When we hear the result of his apostolic mission, it will be time enough to consider the question of disbanding.

Benjamin is far different from the rest of us, being, we suppose, of a finer philosophical spirit. When we are fortunate enough to pick up a victory, the fraternal Wood mourns. By a parity of reason, when we are so unfortunate as to encounter defeat and disaster, we suppose that he rejoices exceedingly. We have fondly thought that the success of the Federal arms would bring back peace and prosperity, but our prophetic member, his visual orbs being beautifully purged, is convinced that nothing more ruinous could happen to us than the most refulgent triumphs. He dreads in the recesses of his soul, " the destruction of the resisting powers of the South." We may take Charleston. That would be "a resisting power." Everybody else in these parts would be glad, but Benjamin is sorry. There is one chance the less of " a contented household." Vicksburg may be reduced. More misery! Really, under such circumstances, one would, as a matter of curiosity, like to have Benjamin's estimate of the moral, political, and religious effect of the Battle of Bull Run! With his views he should consider it a blessing to this community. Thinking as he does, he should go down every night upon his blessed knees and pray that we may be routed, horse, foot and batteries, by sea and land. He is opposed to success upon principle—that is, to *our* success—and the inevitable sequitur is that he desires the success of the Confederate Army. Otherwise a plain man does not well see why he should be so timorous of "the destruction of the resisting powers of the South."

But let us try the logical Wood's philosophy by the rule of contraries. It is very clear to our mind, that the dissolution of our armies would not be followed by a flood of millennial glories. The next thing to disbanding is a defeat. We will suppose that the Davis forces have smitten—hip and thigh— the Federal forces, and that, after the mortifying agonies of capitulation, we have arrived at the delicate delights of negotiation. The surrender would be morally equivalent to Ben's proposed withdrawal of our army—and yet does he suppose that the Southern diplomatists would at once commiserate our wretched condition, and themselves first propose a return? Would the happy and contented household then and there be with due ceremony organized? Member Wood may believe, but we do n't.

By "the destruction of the resisting powers of the South," this astute and benevolent gentleman can only mean, as he evidently does, the destruction of Rebels—and if they were every one of them destroyed, by the sword, the axe, the gallows or ratsbane, the chances of Wood's Happy Family would be considerably multiplied. The object of the Government, if we understand it, is to enforce the legal and most righteous jurisdiction of the Constitution over certain territories of great extent and value. If we conquer, the Moguls of the Rebellion will, if they can, levant to European, Mexican, or South American parts; and those who cannot get away, must be dealt with according to law. This will finish the matter neatly, and it will be finished quite as neatly, though not quite so pleasantly, if we are worsted.

But Mr. Ben Wood's peace would settle nothing. Instead of the Felicitous Family of his dulcet dreams—rats, mice, rabbits, and terriers in one cage—we should only go back to ancient riots and quondam rows. The voice of the bully would again be heard in the Capitol—the old system of bluster would be resumed—the Slaveholder would come back infinitely more insolent and more awfully outrageous—in conjunction with the rejuvenated Democracy of the North, the Man-Owners would begin the game of nominating and electing dough-face or slaveholding Presidents—and after another period of labor dire and weary woe, we should, ere long, find ourselves again compelled to fight, even if a Slaveholding or Doughface President should not sell us out completely to the Man-Owners. This is not the kind of Happy Family to which we look forward with unutterable yearnings. So we think upon the whole, that it will be just as well not to act upon Ben's brilliant suggestions.

March 13, 1863.

MR. BUXTON SCARED.

FOWELL BUXTON's philanthropy, we are compelled to believe, is of that description which is limited by the price of beer and the rent of ale-houses. It is of the hereditary description, and, like most hereditary virtues, it has suffered a diminution by transmission. The present Buxton would never have divided the House of Commons, with only a meagre minority to back him. His father did this, and divers other bold things, of which even the tradition seems to have prematurely faded out in the family. The present Buxton is reported to have written to *The London Times* a letter, in which he reiterates his detestation of Slavery, but says he "cannot endorse President Lincoln's Emancipation scheme, as it contemplates an insurrection of the negroes and untold misery."

Of this we have to observe, in the first place, that it is a criminal carelessness of language for any man to say that the Proclamation *contemplates* insurrection. It is an indefensible and impudent and sheerly gratuitous slander to utter this of Mr. Lincoln, or of any other officer of the Government; it is a fair specimen of the loose speech which Englishmen, since the commencement of our civil war, have permitted themselves to use when descanting upon American topics; and the reply to it in the present case is, that the Proclamation is better calculated to prevent insurrection than to provoke it. There can be no doubt of the fact that the masters are very much at the mercy of the Blacks ; but the Negro, by nature, has no particular penchant for bloodshed, and has never been guilty of any atrocities, except when goaded to them by intolerable cruelties. Should he, in any section of the " Confederate States," have been contemplating, or planning an insurrection, he is far more likely to await the approach of the Union armies, the presence of which would necessarily repress all lawless violence on his part, than to rush madly into a massacre by which he can gain nothing and may lose everything. Thus considered, nothing could be more merciful to the Slaveholders and to their defenceless families, than the Proclamation.

From this point of view, Buxton's " untold misery " is easily calculated. It is certainly strange, that a history with which he should be familiar has taught this man nothing. He must know that during the violent debates in the House of Commons, it was confidently predicted, in terms of extreme pathos, by gentlemen in the interest of planters, that the first of August would be a bloody day in the British West Indies—a new and more terrible Bartholomew. The minacious bathos of Mr. Peter Borthwick cannot have faded from the memory of a Buxton. The dreadful day came which was to inaugurate " untold misery," and it found the poor blacks, not rushing to deeds of blood, nor busy in the avengement of long-continued and exasperating wrongs, but humbly bending the knee in their little chapels, to thank God for the great salvation which had been vouchsafed to them. If Buxton knew anything of the American

17

Blacks, he would anticipate no worse evil from their enfranchisement. They are vastly more likely to assume the care of their imbecile and impoverished masters, than to cut their throats.

But whether from Emancipation come evil or come good, peace or the sword, it is inevitable. The Ruler of the Universe, weary of our wicked and interminable delays, appears in righteous indignation to have taken the work out of our trembling and ignoble hands; or rather, He has, by the force of events, compelled us, even for the sake of self, to do justice to the outraged and oppressed. The first gun which was fired at Charleston announced to the world the demise of American Slavery. Already the diplomatic representatives of the Rebels are seeking to propitiate the Anti-Slavery sentiment of Europe, by promises of emancipation — by admissions that Slavery is neither profitable nor desirable in any way — by a loose talk of manumission when it shall be safe. Should their independence ever be acknowledged by the political powers of the world they will be reminded of these words; and in any event, the chances of an insurrection infinitely more sanguinary than any which can possibly occur as the remote result of the Proclamation will be multiplied, when the moral power and the physical force of the Union shall no longer deter the Black from making a decided though desperate stand for his freedom.

We deprecate as much as any timid Englishman an insurrection of the slaves. But while with Fowell Buxton we contemplate the " untold misery " which such an event would occasion, we cannot banish from our thoughts the " untold misery " to which an inoffensive race has been subjected by the cupid-ty of man. A general massacre of all the whites in the Slaveholding States, would hardly present so terrible an aggregate of suffering as that which the American slaves are expected to encounter with Christian patience, and in a moment to forgive and forget. God preserve us from a lawless insurrection! God preserve us from crimes and breaches of good faith which will make such an insurrection inevitable!

March 18, 1863.

CHARLESTON COZY.

If we may credit the epistle-monger in Charleston, who writes with a kind of rosy rapture to *The London Times,* that city, so far from partaking of the pains and poverty of the Confederacy, is a scene of sybaritical pleasures and Corinthian joys. Though half the town has been burned, the moiety is an Earthly Paradise, in the midst of which stands that eminent caravansary ycleped "the Mills House," at the bar of which, we suppose, fluid happiness is still dispensed, albeit at gigantic prices per draught. Interminable walls, countless breastworks, ditches of unknown depth, batteries of Gibraltarian impregnability, forts whose frown alone would repel a Grand Army, hornworks, ravelines, counterscarps and escarps, glacis, and the god of War knows what else—all these have been combined after a fashion which would have filled the heart of Marshal Saxe with envy, and not less have delighted the benevolent soul of Uncle Toby.

Within these strong defences, which have been entirely built, as we are told, by the hands of the busy "niggers," the originators of the Rebellion and dry nurses of Treason do most peacefully repose and laugh to scorn the Federal fleet and the Federal foot. They have nothing to do but smoke, drink, swear, sleep and be happy. After Macbeth had hung out his banner, there was a cry upon the outer wall, which made him feel quite ill and led him to a long conversation with the Doctor.

It is quite different with the chiefs of Charleston and their families whether *blanc*, black or yellow. They have all the titillations of a siege without the torments. Not yet have they been driven to devour their boots, as the French were in Genoa. On the contrary they have what the landladies of minor boarding-houses call "enough, and that that's good." "Fraser & Co. have ta'en order for it." Fraser & Co. are merchants who would rather give away than sell. Fraser & Co. run the blockade regularly three times a week. Fraser & Co. supply all manner of comfort for back and belly. Those benevolent Dough-faces, therefore, who have permitted the saline tears to bestain their linen cheeks at the thought of all the misery which their Charleston friends were encountering, can dam the sluices of their grief or weep for some less-favored Man-Owners. Charleston is, if we

may believe this correspondent, far better off than
she was when in a death-grapple with the pestilence,
or after a desolating conflagration, she cried aloud to
the rascally Yankees for aid in meat or in money,
and uttered no unheeded appeal. We forbear, out of
motives of delicacy, from making more than a bare
allusion to the money which has been raised in
Northern parts for Missionary purposes, to be expended in South Carolina, because the religious result
has been so preposterous that we are inclined to spare
the feelings of the amiable donors. Meantime the
content being so measureless in Charleston, we wonder if the Palmettoes ever think of the quite opposite
condition of their friends and fellow-sinners in Virginia—that unfortunate State, the once-fair territories
of which have been scathed and blighted by the
actual presence of war—its towns besieged and bom-
barded—its profitable commerce (in tobacco and
oysters) almost destroyed—its capital city, ragged
and writhing Richmond, full of the various distresses
incident to belligerent humanity—its importance
diminished by a political division which will never
be reconsidered—its historical glories so faded, that
future ages will hardly believe that it gave birth to
Washington—Virginia that was politically so great
and so honored, turned into a tilting-ground upon
which South Carolina compels her humble and complying sisters in secession to fight her quarrel with
Massachusetts!

We get no boast from Richmond of the happy
condition of affairs in that city. There is no Fraser

& Co. there, to supply gratuitous dry-goods and groceries to the naked and hungry. With what flowings of unspeakable bile must a Virginian, who has had no breakfast and who cherishes not the wildest hope of a dinner, who is out at the elbows, out of money and out of temper, read, should it come in his way, the letter in *The Times*, and reflect that while he suffers in purse, person, and estate, the Charleston Rebel eats well, sleeps well, dresses well and calmly reads the bulletins of the campaign in Virginia?

We believe we assert no more than she would claim, although in different terms, when we declare that this rebellion originated in the mean selfishness of South Carolina—in the arrogance and passion of her public men—in the recklessness of a little knot of pestilent politicians in Charleston and the adjacent demesnes—in the teachings of such apostles as Calhoun and Butler. The Virginia abstraction was comparatively harmless until the action of South Carolina gave to it a practical and malignant activity. That State has found the fire and the chestnuts—the others must burn their fingers in the roasting. Do they suppose that the culinary process would be over and the digital blisters permanently abated, if the Confederacy were once fairly put upon its legs? O credulous Confederates! Have you yet to learn that South Carolina can confederate with nobody? that her temper is too waspish to afford the least hope of jocund conjugal relations? that she has lived so long in a state of quarrel, that it has become her normal condition? that she feels or affects a contempt for all mankind outside her own little territory? The restoration of the Union will save you from much else, but over and above all, it will save you from her!—from her pettish pride and absurd humors, from her calculating frigidity which all her fire never tempers, and her indomitable selfishness which she dignifies as patriotism.

March 18, 1863.

THE TWIN ABOMINATIONS.

MOST men would think polygamy to be an offence carrying with it its own punishment. If the tendency of even monogamous simplicity be to tiffs and breakfast-table debates, what must be the magnificent wrath of a patriarch who can arraign a score of wives upon an indictment of cold tea and half-baked rolls; but who is still compelled to withdraw his charges by the rattling musketry of twenty nimble tongues? Brigham of Utah is represented to be a stout creature, with quite an oriental talent for administering the affairs of his scraglio; and we will do him the justice to say that, to our knowledge at least, he has never sacked any insubordinate spouse in his Salt Lake Bosphorus.

But the mild and truly affectionate government of the United States is quite right in taking it for granted, that Young, who is getting to be a little old, will be relieved by taking from him ninety-nine per cent. of his uxorious embarrassment. To our utter astonishment the Mormon objects to this proceeding—is unwilling to part with one single individual rib of his whole magnificent collection, and must be mildly persuaded, for his own good, through the potent logic of an indictment. 'T is a curious world. Here at the East, hundreds of wretches are clamoring to the courts to rid them of one spouse, and there at the West, Brigham, and other much-married saints, are struggling for assorted lots, numbering from a dozen to a gross, of the same article. Thus it is that human nature is most inconsistently asinine. Thus it is that the barbarous Mormon Bible, which is notoriously a pack of lies, has taught to its admirers a patience which, in too many instances, the highest revelation has failed to inculcate in its professors. Wonderful is habit, and the world is really indebted to the Sultan of Salt Lake for a new proof of its potency. Mithridates breakfasting upon belladonna and lunching upon arsenic was a fool to him.

We shall await the result of this curious experiment in social ethics with considerable interest; for if the government can put down a plurality of wives in Utah, who will doubt its ability to put down the Rebellion? In both cases we confess that we entertain a lively hope of the most favorable results. In both cases we have a right to anticipate the triumph of that imperious civilization which makes no terms either with legalized brothels or barracoons. There is a restraining power somewhere, which forbids man to go backwards, and effectually prevents the reconstruction of barbarous institutions. The Anglo-Saxon race is as likely to discard its coat and breeches, and, oblivious of gunpowder, to betake itself in its own painted skin to the spearing of game, as to sustain a society having for its base either Polygamy or Slavery.

It is one of the divinest things in the economy of this divinely-created world, that there is no resurrection for a convicted and executed and buried falsehood. There is no consolation for us in this chaos of conflicting moral elements, except in a steady faith that, Whatsoever things are unjust bear but a limited life. It is not in vain that so many of the incorporated blunders of mankind have already tottered and tumbled into a tomb from which there can be no resurrection. It is not in vain that our eyes, placed in the frontal regions, must look forward. That was no hard command which directed us to forget the things behind and to press forward.

Polygamy claims the same divine sanction to which Slavery makes a pretence. It is a Patriarchal Institution. It bottoms itself upon Abraham, Isaac and Jacob. It sticks closely by the historical letter of the Old Testament, and that, too, upon points which the Jews themselves have, in deference to the difference of ages, wisely abandoned in practice, if not in religious theory. No Israelite, however opulent, astonishes the world by a magnificent and multitudinous concubinage. Rothschild, in such a display, might rival the traditional glories of Solomon. But the Synagogue has discarded an institution inconsist-

17* .

ent with the social phenomena of the age to the bastardized Christianity of Brigham Young; while the Christian Slaveholder, contemptuously overleaping the gap which divides the Old and New Dispensations, claims, as an extenuation of his crime, the authority and example of Moses and the Prophets.

Polygamy is an offence against reason, decency, policy, and the enlightenment of the times; but in the system of Human Slavery the most indecent and revolting features of Polygamy are included. Each of these systems tends to the gratification of unhallowed lusts, to the pollution of woman, to the degradation of the marital relation, to the desecration of home, to a loose and promiscuous association of the sexes; but these odious peculiarities of Slavery are mixed with others which are so much more revolting, and which appeal so much more directly to human sympathy, that we forget the lesser wrong (if there can in such case be any comparison) in our indignation at the greater. Brigham's polygamous institution is bad enough at the best; but it is free from that taint of remorseless and calculating selfishness which makes Southern Slavery an almost unmitigated evil.

Nobody can calculate how many children call Brigham Young by the endearing title of father; but we must say this for him, that however numerous they may be, he has brought none of them to the auction-block. He keeps no market for the sale of his own flesh and blood. He does not advertise the bone of his bone. He makes no merchandise of his little boys and girls. And finally, it may be stated for the satisfaction of gentlemen disposed to dabble in ethnics, that all the youthful Youngs are indubitably white, and present to the world a bleached Caucasian aspect. For the soul of us we cannot help regarding Mawworm preaching from his tub as a far more agreeable character than Inkle selling his Yarico for filthy dollars.

There are sundry good Samaritans of the Copperhead variety who cannot speak of the wrongs which the Man-Owners have suffered without bursting into a flood of tears. Slavery is established by positive law, and it is cruelly unjust to meddle with it so much as by a mere mention of its iniquity. Well, concubinage is established by the positive law of Utah, backed by the authority of the Mormon Bible. Will the husbands, of one wife, here and elsewhere, convene to sympathize with the husband of many wives?— We shall see.

March 19, 1863.

VICTORY AND VICTUALS.

Up through the agonized œsophagus of the Confederacy comes the piteous prayer for prog. The most ardent rebel must eat—so must his rib and his responsibilities, both of the sable and the Caucasian tint—so must the gallant steed which bears him to the battle. Jeremy, in Congreve's "Love for Love" pathetically protests his utter inability to breakfast upon a certain chapter of Epictetus, although his

more philosophical master declares it to be "a feast
for an emperor." The insurgents are just discovering
that a hungry man cannot satiate his physical appetites by the perusal of the speeches of Mr. Calhoun
and the Resolutions of '98.

The reading and marking and inward digestion of
crazy political theories go but a little way toward
producing chyme and chyle. The duodenum is n't
a patriotic organ; and the bravest armies can never
successfully fight a famine. Napoleon's principle
was to make war support war; but here the case is
different, for what pleasure can a Rebel take in a raid
on his own hen-house, especially when no feathered
creature is roosting therein? The chief luxury of the
Roman soldier was a daily mouthful of vinegar, but
the bibatory needs of a full-blooded Seceding Chevalier are by no means so simple.

Like Mrs. Gamp, he not only likes to have the
bottle on the shelf, but he rather than else prefers to
find something in it stiff and strong when he draws
the cork. A parched and empty warrior may be
just the creature to attack the enemy's commissariat
train; but when it comes to long and steady cam-
paigning, or the great exertion of a pitched battle,
nothing can compensate for the want of regular
rations. And if soldiers find short commons debili-
tating, notwithstanding their presumptive devotion
to the cause, what must have been the intolerable
agony of civilians, especially in the city of New
Orleans, where until lately, the sale of fluid rapture
was invariably suppressed by the provost guard at

half past nine o'clock, p. m. ?   The considerate and
benevolent Banks, we notice, has mitigated this dry
hardship.   Thirst may now be quenched by the citizens of that region up to midnight—as for the soldier,
the gates of mercy are shut upon him, or rather for
him the generous decanters are inexorably stopped.
Disloyalty and drink go together in those parts—
there are no cocktails (except in their caps) for the
defenders of the Constitution.

But it is in Richmond that famine is the fiercest—
a fact from which we draw the happiest augury.   For
Mosheim, in his Ecclesiastical History, tells us that
fasting was introduced into the religious polity "from
a notion that the demons directed their stratagems
principally against those who pampered themselves
with delicious fare, and were less troublesome to the
lean and hungry."   Now if this be so, what a sorry
time these demons, who may in some sort be considered as spiritual tape-worms, must be having just
now in rationless Richmond !   'T is felt there, we are
sorry for the craft to say, most excruciatingly in the
printing-offices, and consequently the howls which
issue from these nurseries of Secession civilization
are truly tremendous.   The Editors find that fire-
eating is a mere figment of the imagination—no man
can grow fat upon theoretical, ignited carbon—the
bravest of the brave may make others eat his sword,
but he cannot himself lunch upon it without fatal
consequences.

The Richmond Examiner dolefully declares that
while citizens, editors, private soldiers, and other

humble creatures are undergoing semi-starvation, and submitting to what we should suppose, from the passionate earnestness of the appeal, must be something like the pangs of Ugolino, the resources of the city are employed " to pamper idle pride and official indolence." The officers of the Rebel Army it is asserted, keep, at great charge, an unconscionable stud of chargers, of a voracity almost as great, we should think, as that of the marés of Diomedes; and draw rations of oats, and other fodder, for those superfluous beasts, which are used only in the peaceful business of airing the Richmond ladies upon pleasant evenings. This, the editor, who evidently wishes himself one of Capt. Gulliver's renowned and cultivated steeds, comments upon with much bile. But he forgets the law of self-preservation. How does he know that these Lothario-like officers are not feeding the horses that the horses may hereafter feed them ? It may come to that and worse in Richmond yet. Indeed, our troubled brother, in our opinion, should look upon this stable luxury with a philosophical leniency ; for in default of fat horses, how can he be sure that these epaulctted epicures may not betake themselves to the eating even of lean Editors ? *Fiat justitia, ruat cœlum,* roars this excited *Examiner,* which being interpreted, signifies—Give me my bit of bread and butter, though the bits of blood belonging to the officers get never an individual oat. Well, poor man ! we think that he is right. By what legal authority is the wearer of many buttons permitted to set up as a Dives, while this poor Editor plays the unsatisfactory part of Lazarus, with no chance whatever of finding solace in Abraham's bosom ? Why should Letcher be allowed, in respect to strong waters, to create a kind of Sahara wherever he goes, while an intellectual creature, like *The Examiner*, is unable to find a drop, examine he the closets never so closely ?

There are those who by the folly of the Rebel faction have been utterly ruined; there are others who, of an ample fortune, have little enough left to keep the souls and bodies of their household together. These the hungry oligarchs propose to subject to a third or, for ought we know, to a thirtieth skinning. Private property is to be seized wherever found, for the use of the Rebel Army, and to be most magnanimously paid for in Rebel paper-money not worth one cent on the dollar. But if it stood proudly at par, no hungry Virginian could eat it, with or without pepper and salt; nor can he buy anything with it when there is nothing to sell. Unhappy, hungry Virginian!

March 25, 1863.

SUS. PER COLL.

The Charleston Mercury, with that charming suavity which characterizes Man-stealing civilization, calls loudly upon the magnates of the insurrection summarily to hang all those Union officers who may be captured while in command of Black Regiments.

There is a spice here of the old ferocity which whilom tar-feathered Northern travelers, and ravaged the portmanteaus of Yankee school-mistresses. It is a curious philosophical fact, that the Slaveholder always connects energy and murder. He has no idea of any effectual action without homicide. He takes it for granted in reconstructing his scheme of public ethics, or of police regulation, that there is no virtue except in violence, and that the readiest way to convince a man of his error is to put him to death.

The fires of the Inquisition have long since been quenched; thumb-screws and iron-boots have long rusted in the museums of antiquaries; the cannibal has ceased to satiate his revenge by first grilling and then gobbling his adversary; and only the Chinese, of all nations the most averse to change, unite with Confederates in continuing to practice the revolting barbarities of war. But this is not wonderful, for Slavery is legalized, continued, and consecrated violence, depending for its very existence upon the ferocity of the few and the fears of the many. The discipline of the plantation naturally falls to a low level of coarse cruelty; and the imbruted Slave has his revenge in a brutified Master. The patriarch neither attempts nor cares for any other ratiocination than that which he finds in the hiss of the scourge, the bark of the pistol, and the clash of the bowie-knife.

In some departments of human economy, contact with beings less sanguinary than himself may, to a limited extent, have meliorated his manners; but in all points of character which touch his relations to his Slaves, he is hardly more human than the blood-hounds which yelp in his kennel. He is the Nero, the Caligula, the Domitian of a few acres, responsible to no earthly tribunal for the excesses into which his animal rage may betray him. His experience has taught him, in his own little hell upon earth, the efficacy of unlimited swearing and truculent threats; and because he can scare a score or two of helpless, trembling, cowering creatures into dumb obedience, he fancies that the universe is to be intimidated in the same way. Moreover, he has so often bullied the North into an unmanly acquiescence, no matter how absurdly outrageous might be his demands, that he imagines the force of swaggering yet unexpended; and so he erects his scare-crow gallows, announces his intention of hanging his prisoners of war, and fully believes that he can thus intimidate us into a conduct of the war which will be agreeable to his feelings, and accommodated to his peculiar necessi-ties. He would thus nullify the acts of a Congress which he has deserted, and still control a govern-ment which he has disowned.

Under these circumstances it may be profitable for the insurgents to consider that there are still several large cordage factories at work in the Northern States, turning out, among other ropes, those which will well enough suit the purpose of the executioner. Should any white commander of a Black Regiment in the service of the United States be hanged, ac-cording to the threat of the Charleston newspaper above quoted, our impression is that ropes will be

immediately resorted to in these parts; and whatever
may be the skill of the Confederate Ketch, we have
confidence in our ability to produce an artist of equal
accomplishments.   We do not believe that our Rebel
prisoners bear a charmed life.   Beastly as they are,
they were born of woman, and have vertebræ and
wind-pipes, and the muscles adjacent thereto formed
quite after the fashion of our own; and should the
uncivilized threat of the Charleston paper be carried
into execution, sundry chevaliers may also be carried
up to execution, to the great grief of their surviving
compatriots in Secessia.   This game of murdering
prisoners would be highly entertaining, if it were like
Solitaire at cards; but when both sides betake themselves to the amusement, our impression is that it will
be speedily abandoned.

The subterfuge of the South, that we are inciting
the Blacks to insurrection, with all its traditional
horrors, is the sheerest and falsest nonsense.   By all
the laws of war, we have a perfect right to employ
the Slaves against their Masters—Caius Marius did
it, and he was esteemed a tolerable soldier in his day;
and Napoleon, at St. Helena, regretted he did not do
it in Russia; the English did it during our Revolutionary War; but we have never read that Washington
threatened to hang English prisoners upon that account.   The general who should refuse the services
of half, or more than half, of the population of a
country which he was endeavoring to subjugate,
would not deserve a court-martial merely, because he
would deserve to be shot without one.

It is all very well for this Charleston editor, in the
security of his sanctum, to howl for hempen ven-
geance; but Davis, who sorely needs the good opinion of the world, which may not prove very apt at
discriminating between White and Black Regiments,
will hardly consent to place his new Republic in a
position of unnecessary ignominy. The natural scorn
with which he must inevitably be regarded by all
good Christians is, in all conscience, enough for even
a Slaveholder's stomach.

March 28, 1863.

THE END.

INDEX.

		PAGE
Adams, Rev. Nehemiah		58, 248
Average of Mankind		183
Army, Patriotism of		189
Abolition and Secession		192
Americans in England		251
Buchanan, James		6, 7, 29, 82, 128, 129
Benton, Thomas, his estimate of John Y. Mason		16
Bird, Rev. Milton		80
Bancroft, George		106
Bickley, K. G. C.		111
Bliss, Seth		136
Brooks, Preston		182
Beaufort, the Bacchanal of		197
Bodin on Slavery		303
Butler, General		317, 318, 320, 322
Burke, Edmund, an Emancipationist		328
Bachelder, Dr., a Funny Physician		312
Buxton, Fowell		384
Choate, Rufus		43, 58, 84
" " Scrambles of his Biographers		102
Cumberland Presbyterian Church		68
Cumberland Presbyterian Newspaper		79
Columbia (S. C.), Bell-Ringing in		125
Commons, House of, on Gregory's Motion		163
Colleges, Southern		172
Cotton, Moral Influence of		201
Congress, The Confederate		222, 238
Clergymen, Second-Hand		224
Carlyle, Thomas		323
Davis, Jefferson		42, 274, 279, 282, 283, 288, 330, 338, 346
Diarist, A Southern		124
Dargan, Chancellor		160
Dahomey, the Original of the Confederacy		175

(404)

De Bow on Confederate Manufactures.................................... 230
Debt, The Confederate... 285

Everett, Edward.......... .... 45, 181

Fielder, Herbert, his Pamphlet................................... 46
Fillmore, Millard 116
Floyd, John B 162
Fortescue on Slavery 308
Free States, Southern Opinion of.. 316
Freedmen, Probable Vices of... 362
Franklin on British Policy...........• 366
Fast Day, Mr. Davis's... 377

Gregory, M. P.. 163
Greenville, Lord, on Emancipation..................................... 329
Goethe on the Future of America........................... 303
Greatness, Historical.. 356

Hamilton, Alexander, on the Union...................................... 207
Hawks, Dr., his Twelve Questions....................................... 305
Independence, Declaration of... 139
Independence, Southern Association for................................. 265
Ireland, The Case of... 294

Johnson, Reverdy.................................... 42
Johnson, Dr., his Favorite Toast....................................... 329

Lord, President 3, 319
Lawrence, Abbot... 23
Ludovico, Father 54
Lincoln, Abraham.. 181, 384
Letcher, Governor.......... 340

Mason, John Y.. 13, 24
Mitchel, John... .... 20, 50
Matthews, of Virginia, on Education.................................... 92
Montgomery, The Muddle at... 131
Morse, Samuel and Sidney................................. 136
Meredith, J. W., his Private Battery................................... 141
McMahon, T. W., his Pamphlet... 214
Monroe, Mayor, of New Orleans.. 234
Malcolm, Dr., on Slavery... 248
Maryland, The Union Party in..................... 260
Mallory, Secretary 280
McClellan, General, as a Pacificator 370
Mercury, The Charleston.. 399

Netherlands, Deacon.. 17
North, Southern Notions of the... 144

Olivieri, The Abbé, on Negro Education................................. 56

Pierce, Franklin... 29
Pollard, Mr., his "Mammy"... 63
Palfrey, General, in Boston.. 73
Perham, Josiah, his Invitation... 97
Parker, E. G., his Life of Choate.. 103
Patents Granted in the South... 134
Polk, Bishop... 172
Parties, Extemporizing... 242
Platform Novelties in Boston... 247
Paley, Dr., on Slavery... 303
Pitt, William, an Abolitionist... 329

Rogersville, the Great Flogging in... 16
Roundheads and Cavaliers... 151
Russell, William H... 158, 187
Repudiation of Northern Debts.. 162
Red Bill, a New Orleans Patriarch.. 318
Romilly, Sir Samuel.. 328
Robertson, Dr., on Slavery... 303

Screws, Benjamin, Negro Broker.. 8, 38
Society for Promoting National Unity....................................... 186
Stevens, Alexander H... 148
Secession, The Ordinance of.. 178
Slidell, Miss.. 204
Secessionists, The Dissensions of.. 219
St. Domingo, The Argument from... 326
Saulsbury, Senator.. 334, 351

Tyler, John, his Diagnosis... 128
Times, The London.................................... 158, 177, 309, 366, 374
Toombs, General, his Trials.. 269
Thirty-Five, The Council of.. 278
Taliaferro, Mr., his Defalcation... 316
Thugs in New Orleans... 318

University, a Southern Wanted.. 61
Utopia, A Slaveholding... 300

Van Buren, John.. 44
Virginia, Democracy in... 185

Wise, Henry A... 2, 95, 135, 155
Walker, William, his Letter to General Cass............................. 33, 85
Winslow, Hubbard... 186
Williams, Commander.. 206
Winthrop, Robert C... 248
Wood, Benjamin.. 379, 383

Yeadon, Richard.. 8
Young, Brigham.. 358, 392

MODERN · WOMEN

AND

What is Said of Them:

A Reprint of a Series of Articles in the *Saturday Review*, with an Introduction by Mrs. CALHOUN.

CONTENTS.

THE GIRL OF THE PERIOD.

FOOLISH VIRGINS.

LITTLE WOMEN.

PINCHBECK.

FEMININE AFFECTATIONS.

IDEAL WOMEN.

WOMAN AND THE WORLD.

UNEQUAL MARRIAGES.

HUSBAND HUNTING.

PERILS OF "PAYING ATTENTION."

WOMEN'S HEROINES.

INTERFERENCE.

PLAIN GIRLS

A WORD FOR FEMALE VANITY.

THE ABUSE OF MATCH-MAKING.

FEMININE INFLUENCE.

PIGEONS.

PRETTY PREACHERS

AMBITIOUS WIVES.

PLATONIC WOMAN.

MAN AND HIS MASTER.

THE GOOSE AND THE GANDER.

ENGAGEMENTS.

WOMAN IN ORDERS.

WOMAN AND HER CRITICS.

MISTRESS AND MAID, OR DRESS AND UNDRESS.

ÆSTHETIC WOMAN.

WHAT IS WOMAN'S WORK?

PAPAL WOMAN.

MODERN MOTHERS

PRIESTHOOD OF WOMAN.

THE FUTURE OF WOMAN.

LA FEMME PASSÉE.

THE FADING FLOWER.

SPOILT WOMEN.

COSTUME AND ITS MORALS.

In one Volume, 12mo, handsomely printed and bound in cloth, beveled boards.

PRICE TWO DOLLARS.